Paper Hearts

Center Point
Large Print

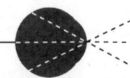

**This Large Print Book carries the
Seal of Approval of N.A.V.H.**

Paper Hearts

Courtney Walsh

CENTER POINT LARGE PRINT
THORNDIKE, MAINE

This Center Point Large Print edition is published
in the year 2016 by arrangement with
Tyndale House Publishers, Inc.

Scripture quotations are taken from the *Holy Bible*,
New Living Translation, copyright © 1996, 2004,
2007, 2013 by Tyndale House Foundation.
Used by permission of Tyndale House Publishers, Inc.,
Carol Stream, Illinois 60188. All rights reserved.

Paper Hearts is a work of fiction. Where real people,
events, establishments, organizations, or locales appear,
they are used fictitiously. All other elements of the novel
are drawn from the author's imagination.

The text of this Large Print edition is unabridged.
In other aspects, this book may vary
from the original edition.
Printed in the United States of America on permanent paper.
Set in 16-point Times New Roman type.

ISBN: 978-1-62899-829-0

Library of Congress Cataloging-in-Publication Data

Names: Walsh, Courtney, 1975– author.
Title: Paper hearts / Courtney Walsh.
Description: Center Point Large Print edition. | Thorndike, Maine :
Center Point Large Print, 2016. | ©2014
Identifiers: LCCN 2015042181 | ISBN 9781628998290
  (hardcover : alk. paper)
Subjects: LCSH: Large type books. | GSAFD: Love stories. |
Christian fiction.
Classification: LCC PS3623.A4455 P37 2016 | DDC 813/.6—dc23
LC record available at http://lccn.loc.gov/2015042181

For all of our Studio kids.
May your dreams be big enough
to scare you . . . because the good stuff
is on the other side of fear.

Chapter 1

"I can't believe she did this to me again." Abigail Pressman stared at the computer screen in disbelief. Her own photo stared back, her pasted-on smile frozen in time.

"I can't believe you still own a pair of overalls." Mallory leaned down over her shoulder, eyes wide at Abigail's most recent public humiliation. "Not flattering."

"Understatement." Abigail covered her face with her hands.

The four other dating websites were bad enough, but one exclusively for farmers? Abigail sighed. "I'll never recover from this one."

Elizabeth "Teensy" Pressman had two goals in life: first, to marry off all her children; and second, to have lots of grandbabies. It seemed the woman would stop at nothing until both were accomplished.

"I think she means well," Mallory said, her wince audible.

Abigail groaned. Last month it had been a setup at her mother's bridge club with Eunice Middleton's forty-five-year-old son, Jasper, who lived two hours away in Denver.

Which left Abigail wondering, shouldn't a

woman with a name like Eunice know better than to name her child Jasper? Of course, who was she to talk with a mother who went by "Teensy"? The nickname she had picked up as the youngest and smallest of eight children had never gone away. Jasper, it turned out, wasn't interested in Abigail any more than she was interested in him. Jasper had already found the love of his life, a tattoo artist who called herself Tipsy. In addition to being happily unmarried, he was also a wretched coward who couldn't tell his mom about his live-in girlfriend.

Abigail peered at her own photo on the laptop screen on the counter in front of her. "She has officially lost her mind."

"Do you think it costs money to sign up for these websites? She's got to have a fortune in it. What is this, number four?"

"Five. Don't forget the Young Loves Park Professionals site, which is local and even more embarrassing than FarmersOnly."

Mallory shrugged. "City folks just don't get it."

Abigail grimaced. "Is that their slogan?"

Her store manager pointed at the screen. "Yep. See, the logo's right here beside your straw hat and braids."

Abigail only stared.

"The cow's a nice touch."

Teensy had clearly dug this one out of the archives. Abigail in the cow pasture next door to

8

her parents' house during a church picnic, her dark hair pulled into two braids. There happened to be a cow in the background, which, she supposed, enabled her mom to pass her off as a farm girl.

"We have to explore every avenue, Abigail," her mother would say. "You're not getting any younger, and Loves Park is only so big."

"I'm wearing flannel in this picture, Mom," Abigail would say in protest.

"But your teeth look so white."

Again Abigail entertained the thought that she should move somewhere else, but not for the reasons her mother suggested. She had always dreamed of living in the city—or at least in a more sizable town. Loves Park, a small community known for its celebration of all things romantic, had targeted Abigail—single and almost thirty— like a cheetah eyeing a limping wildebeest.

As if she needed to be reminded of her inability to find the right guy and settle down. As if romance were the only thing she should want out of life. How barbaric to assume that. Yet here she was, living and working in Loves Park—a town that wouldn't let her forget even for a moment who she was.

Maybe a fresh start was what she needed. Denver wasn't too far a drive, yet it felt a whole world away from here.

But as quickly as the idea entered her mind, reality bumped it out of the way. Her father had entrusted The Book Nook to her upon his death. It was the only thing that had ever connected the two of them when he was alive: a shop full of books. Perhaps it was a silly legacy. It certainly hadn't made her wealthy and it wouldn't change the world. But it was all she had left of him, and she wasn't about to let it go. Besides, she had a plan to expand her little shop—a plan that had once felt like a whisper on the wind but that might actually come to pass.

Two months before, her landlady, Harriet, who ran a mercantile in the other half of the building, told Abigail she'd decided to retire and shut down the mercantile. Abigail received the news with the appropriate amount of sadness, amazed at her own ability to act forlorn when, in truth, she fought to contain her joy. Of course she'd miss the shop next door—Harriet was a kind woman, and her two sons were always bringing home the most unique items from their worldwide travels. But it meant that finally—*finally*—she could expand her own store. She could already see the expansion in her mind. She'd visualized it every time she walked into the mercantile.

Abigail had already decided how to transform one of the mercantile's walls into a gallery of her favorite local artists. She knew exactly where she would display vintage treasures and handmade jewelry. And in her spare time, she'd already refinished a number of flea-market furniture discoveries that customers were sure to love. Abigail was sure The Book Nook could be much more than a tidy, cozy shop packed with wall-to-wall books. Adding the café with local gourmet coffee last year was a nice touch, but her dream was more venti than tall.

Plus, she'd finally be owner, not tenant, and something about that made Abigail grow a bit inside. Wyatt Nelson, premier Realtor of Loves Park, had given his word she'd be the first to know of any interest in the property, but his offer was about to expire. "The sign is going up in ten days," he'd recently told her in his I'm-a-very-busy-man voice.

She made a mental note to pester Harvey at the bank and find out what on earth was taking him so long. Once that sign went up, stiff competition would follow. Loves Park, nestled up in the Rocky Mountains, was prime real estate. The picturesque backdrop and nearby national parks brought thousands of tourists to their little town each year. Add to that the never-ending celebration of romance, and much to Abigail's dismay, Loves Park became a prime location for weddings, honeymoons, and those looking to rekindle what they once had. Despite how she felt about the endless supply of couples, it all contributed to the fact that Abigail's building, right in the heart of Old Town, was one of the most desirable within city limits.

"So what do you want me to do about this profile?" Mallory asked, pulling the laptop to her.

Abigail shot her a look. "Delete it. Please?"

"Working on it."

Out of the corner of her eye, Abigail saw someone walk past the side window. She turned toward it. "Is that Aaron?"

Mallory barely glanced up, fingers tapping on the keyboard. "Is it twenty after?"

"I think it's just now seven."

"Then he's not here." Mallory punched a few more keys and leaned back, triumphant.

"Do something about that, will you?" Abigail hoisted her bags over her shoulder and started for the office.

"Like, fire him?" Mallory shut the laptop and stashed it underneath the counter.

"He's too cute to fire. Just give him a warning or whatever." Abigail let the office door swing closed behind her, not wanting to hear Mallory's dry retort—something like, "Because that worked so well the last time." Who needed the reminder that she was a soft boss?

Abigail sank into her desk chair, the quiet solace of her office washing over her. *Another dating site? Really, Mom?*

In that moment, the embarrassment of being the black sheep of Loves Park's romantic tradition washed over her like cold water from a bucket. Why had God seen fit to give everyone but Abigail their Mr. Right, despite her years of praying, despite knowing she'd make someone a perfect wife? At least she hoped she would. Correction. She *had* hoped she would. She wasn't sure about much anymore. No sense pining away for something—someone—that might not exist.

Being twenty-nine and single might be difficult for any woman in *any* town, but Abigail had to believe that she had it just a little bit worse than most. Not only was she Teensy's pet project, she was living in a town named by her great-great-grandparents as a celebration of their cherished love story. And that town had one obsession: romance.

Double whammy.

A loud knock startled her. Mallory didn't wait for her to answer, instead pushing the door open and poking her head in. "Why are you sitting here in the dark?"

Abigail stared at her. Had she forgotten to turn the light on?

"Sorry, my hands were full," she said, wondering if that counted as a lie. "What's up?"

"Nothing."

"You left the front unattended to come back here for nothing?" Abigail stood, smoothing her peasant top and the blazer she'd thrown on at the last minute in an attempt to make herself more professional than bohemian, the familiar struggle that plagued her every time she got ready for work. Always striving to be taken seriously as a business professional when her natural tendencies were far more casual.

"No, Aaron just got here." Then Mallory stared at her with that familiar grimace.

"What now? A want ad in the *Loves Park Daily News*?" Before long, her mother would have a spot on channel five about her daughter's inability to find a husband in a town with *love* in the name. Worse, around here it just might play as a valid story.

"No, it's not that," Mallory said. "I think there's something you should see."

Mallory's tone rattled her, and Abigail fought the hollow worry that settled in her gut. She waited a moment before following her manager to the front of the store. The sun illuminated the large space, casting warmth and light across the rows and rows of bookshelves, some along the wall, others neatly positioned throughout the store. Abigail reached the coffee counter and stopped, following Mallory's gaze through the glass.

While their view was partially obstructed from this angle, it was clear something was going on next door. Harriet had moved out a few weeks prior, so that wasn't it.

Abigail dared a few cautious steps toward the oversize front window, the pit in her stomach warning her of impending doom.

Wyatt Nelson stood outside. Next to him was a

man wearing jeans and a North Face jacket. She couldn't make out the stranger's face, but she saw sales pitch all over Wyatt's.

"What is he doing?" Abigail crossed her arms over her chest, begging herself to calm down.

Just then, Gerald and Anita Jensen strolled in from off the street.

"Looks like you've got a new neighbor," Gerald said, grinning at Abigail.

Anita walked right up to Abigail and squeezed her arm. "A *handsome* neighbor too." She smiled. "And no wedding ring. I checked. You should get out there and be charming." A wink in Abigail's direction and the older couple headed to the coffee counter. She barely heard them place their coffee and muffin order with Aaron.

"He promised I had ten more days," Abigail said, her voice barely audible.

"Why don't you go say something?" Mallory asked, still staring at the two men on the street. "Maybe it's not what it looks like."

Abigail sent Mal a sad look. They both knew it was exactly what it looked like.

Wyatt was going to try to sell her building without honoring his word. Typical of him.

"Why does that guy have to look at our building?" Mallory's shoulders dropped. "Aren't there a dozen more on the market right now?"

Abigail hadn't been paying attention to the other downtown storefronts. Her brick building on the

15

corner provided the perfect bookend for a block of equally unique shops, all independently—and locally—owned. The Book Nook had been her only focus for six years, and now her vision of expanding into art-filled walls and renovated furniture was blurred.

Abigail hated to admit it to herself, but the shop was more than a way to pay the bills and honor her father's memory. It was a diversion whenever her naked left hand bothered her—though that only happened every now and then. Some days she even convinced herself it was enough. Who needs a man when you have shelves of beautiful books and dreams of growth and success?

Her heart raced as she stared at Wyatt and the stranger from the safety of her front window. While she couldn't hear what the slimeballs were saying, she had the distinct impression from their pointing that they were now discussing *her* half of the building.

No way was she going to let this . . . this . . . *man* move into her building, steal her dreams, and force her out.

She drew in a deep breath. She didn't even know North Face, and already she considered him a horrible person.

"What are you going to do?" Mallory asked.

"I don't know, but I'm not going to let them get away with this."

She didn't believe those words. Not yet. With a

little bit of courage, perhaps she could find a way.

Sadly, last time she checked, courage wasn't something she could find on the Internet, which meant somehow Abigail Pressman had to come by it naturally.

But some things just didn't come naturally to her.

Chapter 2

Standing there, watching the two men pointing and talking, Abigail realized she had a choice. She could remain inside and watch someone else buy her dream right out from under her, or she could do something about it. Fight for it. Maybe casually strike up a conversation and let North Face know about how the basement flooded in the spring. Or . . . *I know you're interested, sir, but have you seen the lack of parking? The bad wiring and the old furnace?* Could she? Could she scare him away from her building, her dream? Her imagination, as it often did, betrayed her with an onslaught of what-ifs.

What if he had a plan for his own retail store? What if he was a vintage treasure hunter? What if he bought the whole building and forced her out? Her stomach turned at the thought.

No. Stop being ridiculous, she told herself. The town would revolt. The Book Nook was the heart of Old Town Loves Park.

People told her so all the time.

After ten minutes of peering, pretend cleaning, lurking, sulking, and wondering what these two men could possibly have to discuss for so long, Abigail had nearly worked up the courage to head outside. She could feel Mallory and Aaron watching her as they took orders, made lattes, and answered questions in hushed tones about "why Abigail is still cleaning the same spot in the front of the store."

So I'm close enough to keep an eye on Wyatt and the new guy, but far enough away that they can't see me. That's why. Duh.

Before she talked herself out of it, Abigail pushed herself toward the front door, nearly barreling into a customer as she did.

"Heavens, child, slow down," Sharon Harmon said, catching her breath.

"So sorry. I just need to get outside." And apparently knock down a few regular patrons along the way.

Sharon peered at her over the top of her glasses. "He's awfully handsome. Like one of those television actors. Better claim him before someone else does."

Abigail frowned. "Who?"

"The man buying your building." She patted

18

Abigail's shoulder. "Girls your age can't be too choosy, you know."

Abigail let out a groan as she pushed the door open and found herself face-to-face with both Wyatt and the other man, who was, unfortunately, "awfully handsome." For once couldn't she get a break?

Abigail reminded herself that she was an adult, and while she'd always had a hard time talking to members of the opposite sex, she'd gotten increasingly better with age.

At least she hoped she had.

She certainly hadn't gotten less nervous.

Especially around handsome men. Like him.

I'll bet he's *not on a dating site for farmers.*

This whole fifteen-second conversation with herself happened in her mind—but in reality she was just standing there, staring, without saying anything.

Wyatt and the other man awkwardly glanced at each other. "Ah . . . ahem. Abigail! We were just talking about you," Wyatt said, towering over her. Where'd he find clothes big enough, anyway? Legs that long surely needed to be special ordered.

She bet the tag read, *Smarmy. Wash in cold with like personalities.*

"Is that right? I thought you'd be talking *to* me, considering our deal."

The man standing beside Wyatt shifted and stared at something across the street. *Nice profile.*

Good cheekbones. Abigail chided herself for letting her thoughts get away from her. *He's the enemy.*

It was so hard having handsome enemies.

"We're just talking here, Abs," Wyatt said, all slickness.

"Been talking for an awfully long time." She wished he were shorter. Eye contact would go a long way right about now. "And my name is Abigail."

How many times had she corrected him? Did he shorten her name just to annoy her?

Wyatt chuckled. A legitimate chuckle encased in condescension. "Maybe we could talk later, *Abigail.*" Extra emphasis. Very effective.

"Now's as good a time as any." She looked at the handsome stranger, shorter than Wyatt but still taller than her. Probably some natural grocer or something equally as granola. Probably planning to open a hemp store or sell essential oils.

Abigail shook the meanness away. It wasn't the stranger's fault Wyatt Nelson was still a jerk. Besides, she liked essential oils.

In a flash, Abigail was sixteen again, standing on the front porch with a gawky, clumsy Wyatt Nelson. His clammy hands holding hers, the tension of his wanting to kiss her good night thick between them. That she'd ever allowed herself to date him—for four full months, even!— still embarrassed her.

Did he remember those moments with as much discomfort as she did? He'd known her in her most awkward phase, and it still humiliated her. Sometimes she still felt like that nerdy sixteen-year-old girl, consumed with all the things she wasn't—outgoing, pretty, popular.

Abigail forced the mocking thoughts aside. She'd grown into her looks. She had plenty of friends. She wasn't a kid anymore.

"I'm sorry. Maybe I should wait inside," the man said.

Polite too. Great.

"Tell ya what, Jake," Wyatt said. "Head on in to Abby's store and take a look around for yourself. We'll be there in just a minute."

Abigail's jaw tensed at Wyatt's suggestion. Who did he think he was, sending the enemy in to scope out her base camp?

The man—Jake—started toward The Book Nook, then stopped. "It's actually Jacob," he said, a polite smile warming his face. He glanced at Abigail, and for a split second she thought she saw a twinkle in his hazel eyes. Before Wyatt could respond, the man—Jacob—vanished inside.

She supposed he thought they were buddies now since they'd both corrected Wyatt on his inability to call anyone by their proper names. Ha. He had another think coming if that's what he believed. He'd have to do a lot more than flash those warm eyes her way to win her over.

Pretty good start, though.

"Why'd you have to do that, Abby?" Wyatt practically whined now, reminding her of the boy she'd grown up with, the teenager she'd dated, and the man she avoided in the supermarket.

She attempted to level her gaze, but glaring into Wyatt's chest certainly didn't have the effect she was going for.

"You promised me ten more days."

"Then I talked to Harvey."

Abigail frowned. "Why would you do that?"

"He's your banker. I'm the Realtor. We talk."

In place of an answer, she folded her arms over her chest. She couldn't form a coherent thought for the panic that had just set in, and crossing her arms just might stop her heart from leaping through her rib cage.

Wyatt ran a hand over his clean-shaven chin. "They're not giving you the loan. You can't expand —at least not right now."

Abigail lost her breath and had to physically force her legs to stay underneath her to keep herself from falling. "Why would he tell you and not me?"

Wyatt shrugged.

"So, what? I'm getting a new landlord?" She attempted to swallow around the dryness in her throat.

Another shrug. "Sounds like this guy might need the entire space." He reached out and put a clammy

22

hand on her shoulder. "Sorry, Abs. I know it's a blow to your ego, but could you please not ruin this for me? I need the sale."

Her jaw went slack as she dipped out of his grasp.

Before she could respond, Wyatt's phone buzzed in his jacket pocket. "Excuse me, Abs. I've got to take this."

Tears burned her eyes. *My name is Abigail.*

Oh, why bother? Wyatt had never been good at listening to anyone but himself. He answered the phone and stepped away from her, their conversation apparently over. She could fill in the blanks on the rest. He'd found out from Harvey—probably during their weekly poker game—that the bank wasn't lending her the money, and then this Jacob person showed up, interested in the whole property.

Jacob must have the money.

There must be money in hemp.

Abigail sighed and pushed through the door of The Book Nook. Mallory stood behind the counter, taking Jacob's order, that look of dread on her face.

How did Abigail tell her employees that instead of expanding, they might be closing up shop? And if she lost The Book Nook, what on earth would she do with herself?

Sure, life as a single business owner might not have been her original plan, but she'd adjusted.

She couldn't imagine losing this place now. If she lost the store, everyone would know she'd failed. Not only failed at finding a husband and settling down, but at the one thing that had been going seemingly well for her.

The memory of her father's quiet gaze entered her mind. All the hours they'd sat in that store talking about books. The one thing they had in common. Some days they'd sit and read together, neither one saying a word.

Funny how silence healed old wounds.

Abigail's gaze narrowed as she watched Jacob move toward the other end of the counter. What had the rich intruder ordered? Whatever it was, she'd give it to him free if he'd just go away and leave her building alone.

Behind the counter again, Abigail avoided the man's eyes, though she was hopelessly aware he was not avoiding hers. When Mallory capped the lid on his drink, Abigail swiped it from her and walked it to the end of the counter, intent on making her position known.

If only she could figure out what that position was before reaching him.

He watched her approach, stealing the few precious seconds she had to try to construct a good argument. When she set the drink down in front of him, he smiled. Not a toothy smile, just friendly upturned lips. Still, it was nice, and it crinkled his eyes at the corners. And it made her more nervous than she wanted to be.

"Thanks."

She gave one stern nod, which made her feel like a librarian or her mother when she was trying to make a point.

"You're Abigail?"

Another nod.

"I'm Jacob Willoughby."

Willoughby. How appropriate. The backstabber of *Sense and Sensibility*.

"I heard." She told herself not to be nice to the enemy, no matter how good his manners were, but it wasn't in her nature to be mean. Still, her shop was at stake. Her livelihood. Her dreams.

"This is a nice place you've got here." He took a drink. "And the coffee's good."

Abigail glanced at the side of the cup where Mallory had written *BC*—black coffee. "I think so."

"Guess we might be neighbors."

Her mouth went dry. What he meant was *Guess I might be your new landlord. I might kick you out and rob you of your life's work. I might take your dreams, ball them up, and stomp all over them like a playground bully staking his claim.*

Here's some hemp to tie up your moving boxes.

She told herself to behave. "How well have you inspected the old mercantile?"

He met her gaze. "Well enough, I think."

Abigail looked away. "Harriet used to complain about the old pipes all the time."

"Is that right?" Another drink underneath raised eyebrows.

"And the toilets overflow almost weekly."

"I'm pretty handy. I think I can take care of that." Amusement skittered across his face. The man wasn't buying any of it. How much had Wyatt told him about her?

"I don't think you'd be a good fit here."

Jacob's eyes widened. "You just met me."

"I can tell. I have a sixth sense about these things." Abigail had no idea what she was talking about. She had no sense at all when it came to men, thus the wretched dating history. "Your store might do better out by the new mall on the other side of town."

"Well, I do have another space to look at this morning, so we'll see." He regarded her for a long moment. "At any rate, thanks for the hospitality." He held his cup up as if to toast her. "And the coffee."

"Of course." Abigail watched as Jacob turned, surveyed the space with a bit too much interest, and walked out the front door to where Wyatt stood, still on the phone. Moments later the two men got into Wyatt's Mercedes and drove away— hopefully to find another space, far, far away from The Book Nook.

"He sure was handsome," Mallory said, her sigh

reminiscent of a 1940s cartoon character. Abigail resisted the urge to see if she'd popped her foot up too.

But Mallory was right. He *was* handsome, unfairly so. She found herself thinking about the color of his hair. Brownish, like a mocha with extra cream. What would that color be called?

"Abigail?"

She glanced at her manager. "Handsome or not, that man is not our friend. And if he thinks he can just waltz into town and steal this building from me, he's about to get a shock."

"So it's a staged protest, then?"

Abigail pulled her phone out of her pocket, not in the mood for snark. "No. I'm going to start by investigating everything Wyatt Nelson told me. He must be wrong. There has to be a way for me to get that loan."

When the receptionist at the bank answered, Abigail took a deep breath, almost afraid to find out the truth. But she had to know where she stood if she had any chance of winning this fight. "Hey, Marilyn, it's Abigail. I need to talk to Harvey."

Chapter 3

"Don't let Abigail Pressman spook you," Wyatt said, making the turn onto Dover Parkway. "She's a spinster in the making, clinging to the only thing she has."

A glance at Wyatt's left hand told Jacob the Realtor was as unattached as Abigail. He supposed being a single man was somehow different from being a single woman.

At least for men like Wyatt Nelson.

Jacob wouldn't have used the word *spinster* to describe the woman he'd just met. She seemed passionate and maybe a little bit spunky with her wavy, dark hair that was only slightly out of control.

Cute. He'd say she was cute. Guilt nipped at the heels of his mind. It was perfectly fine for him to think of Abigail as cute, but it still felt like a betrayal.

So sorry, Gwen.

"She had this crazy idea that she could expand that place. It's a bookstore, for pete's sake. Nobody buys books in a bookstore anymore." Wyatt's voice dripped with superiority. He had everything figured out.

Jacob finished off the last of his coffee. "Maybe

she's looking to diversify her business to make up for that."

Wyatt shrugged. "All I'm saying is, owning that building would be a good move for you. It'd take some renovation, obviously, and if you wanted to grow, you could always choose not to renew Abigail's lease. Or you could probably just kick her out."

Jacob would rather drill screws into his fingertips than ride around in a confined space with a sketchy salesman like Wyatt Nelson. But as new in town as Jacob was, he needed the advice of a Realtor.

The new outdoor mall on Dover Parkway was beautiful, and a space here on the outskirts of town might be a better fit for his plans, though Jacob had done his research on this space the same way he had with Wyatt Nelson. Word on the street was, the contractors had changed halfway through the Dover Parkway Mall project, which sat just off the interstate fifteen miles between Loves Park and the next closest town. When the new contractor took over, he didn't hold to the same high standards as the first one, which meant the back half of the mall was shoddily constructed.

Would Wyatt tell him any of that?

They parked in a space in front of an empty storefront right next to a hair salon—one of those high-end kinds that overcharged and tried to dip your hands in wax while you waited.

Gwen had raved about those wax treatments. Said they relaxed her as soon as she pulled her hands out. For a brief moment he saw her face in his mind's eye; then he shook the thought—and the pain—away. He couldn't let himself walk down memory lane. Not here.

Inside, the building was standard. Wyatt brought him to an open space just like every other one in the mall. Nothing special. Nothing interesting. It smelled of new construction: part sawdust, part fresh paint, part no character.

"Think of it as a blank canvas," Wyatt said, shoes clicking on the tile. "Great location, really. Your practice might do better out here, if I'm honest. Downtown is all quaint shops and antiques. Old ladies and tourists. Locals might respond better if you set up shop away from Old Town."

Wyatt's opinions changed with each location, selling whatever space they were in at the time. Jacob knew he was on his own with this one. He'd never required someone else's opinion to make up his mind.

He walked the perimeter, checked the bathrooms and the storage space. Music from the salon next door blasted through the paper-thin walls, practically making his decision for him.

When Kelly, Gwen's old college roommate, called him with this crazy idea, he'd almost hung up on her. But something inside told him to hear her out. He knew he needed a change, so he figured it'd be stupid not to accept Kelly's offer to help with the business side of setting up a new medical practice in a new town. Sure, he hadn't talked to Kelly in years—she'd always been more Gwen's friend than his—but people came out of the woodwork after the settlement became public.

Everyone wanted something from him. Unfortunately Kelly caught him in a weak moment—one of those that had him wishing for a fresh start, away from everything that reminded him of all he'd lost. Besides, he couldn't go back to that hospital.

Too many whispers. Too many ghosts.

Before he knew what he'd done, he'd sold his house in Denver, packed a U-Haul, and moved to Loves Park.

He told himself he'd do things differently this time. His practice. His terms. And if he could help it, he'd never step foot in a hospital again. His thoughts floated back to Abigail Pressman. Abby. No, *Abigail*. He wouldn't make Wyatt's mistake.

How would she take the news if he settled on the Old Town location? According to Wyatt, she'd wanted to buy the building for years, but when her landlady was finally ready to retire and sell, she found herself low on funds. Bookstores weren't viable businesses these days, it seemed, even though her Book Nook seemed to offer more than just a good read. The local gourmet coffee was a nice touch. Still, he could see why she'd want to expand to make the store even more attractive. He wondered what her plans were for the old mercantile.

They probably didn't include a medical practice or a new landlord, but Jacob had already been looking for weeks, and he didn't want to waste any more time. The sooner he could get the practice open, the better. His mind played tricks on him when it wasn't occupied.

If Kelly had her way, the new practice would consume an entire city block. Jacob would make it clear to her that he didn't want a big business, but that didn't mean the mercantile space on its own would be large enough. The Book Nook and the old store combined were about the perfect size for what he had in mind. But . . . could he somehow make it work without taking over Abigail's space?

He'd figure it out later. He'd have to. He reminded himself that he couldn't make life decisions based on the personal woes of a girl he'd just met anyway.

His phone buzzed, pulling him from his thoughts. A number he didn't recognize lit the screen.

"This is Jacob."

"Dr. Willoughby," a woman's voice said. "This is Loves Park Elementary. It's your daughter."

"Is she okay?"

"Stomach bug. You need to come get her."

"Can I talk to her quick?"

A rustle, then Junie's small voice. "Daddy?"

"Hey, sweetie. Your tummy hurts?"

He could tell that she was holding back tears. "Yeah." A slight pause. "Can you come get me?"

"Don't like the nurse, huh?"

"She smells like ham," Junie whispered. He pictured his little girl glancing around to make sure no one had heard her.

Man, he loved her sense of humor. Like her mom, that one. His daughter hadn't been sick since Gwen—how would he handle a sick child on his own?

"I'm on my way." He ended the call, telling himself that he'd be fine. He took care of sick people for a living.

Again, not so persuasive.

As he and Wyatt drove back toward the real estate office, where Jacob had left his truck, Wyatt rambled on about the various properties they'd seen that day and the day before, seeming to recite a mental checklist of pros and cons.

Jacob tuned him out.

On their way through Old Town, Jacob paid more attention to his surroundings than he had on the way out to the new mall. Oversize hearts decorated the old-fashioned streetlamps all along the main road. He'd barely noticed them before.

33

The hearts were all red with messages hand-painted in white.

Love you forever, Beth Ann. Love, Rick

Marry me, Samantha. Love, Scott

Jerry loves Geri. True love always.

Jacob was familiar with the legend of Loves Park—how its founders had an epic love story and the result was a town that celebrated romance. He knew all about the town's traditions. Knew that people—people like Gwen—got caught up in the wistfulness of sending envelopes to this town just to have them stamped with a heart and the Loves Park postmark.

He'd even let his wife talk him into a vacation to the little town. Because of her, he had enjoyed it, despite the fact that the whole thing bordered on ridiculous.

Truth was, he'd have done anything for Gwen. Even buy one of those hand-painted lamppost decorations. Even send his own anniversary card through the Loves Park postmaster for that stamp that said he'd gone the extra romantic mile.

But until he actually moved here, Jacob hadn't understood the magnitude of the town's romantic obsession. He never realized it was a yearlong affair.

Perhaps he should've done a bit more research on his new hometown.

He'd already had three older women ask if he was open to dating their daughter/niece/granddaughter—and that was just this past weekend.

He started to ask but then thought better of getting Wyatt's take. Even though Jacob hadn't been in this town for long, he knew he didn't want its seemingly quaint traditions to become another slick sales gimmick.

He also didn't want to give Wyatt any more reasons to speak. Not that the man was asking permission.

Once they reached his parked truck, Jacob said a quick good-bye and drove toward the grade school. Junie had been anxious on the phone, hadn't she? Too anxious. It made him nervous and, honestly, a bit angry. He hated how helpless he felt. Dads should be fixers, Dr. Dads doubly so, but so far, nothing about Junie's life had gone the way it was supposed to, and he couldn't do a thing to change it.

The receptionist buzzed him in and led him back to the nurse's office, more a closet than a room. Inside, Junie lay in a fetal position on a makeshift cot with a small pillow under her head. Sweat glistened on her forehead and cheeks.

"She's got a fever and she's thrown up twice," said the nurse, whose name Jacob realized he didn't know. "I'm sorry to call you down here."

Jacob shook his head. "Don't be. I'll take her home now."

"I'm glad she's in such capable hands," the woman said with a smile. "You get better now, Junie. We want to see you back here as soon as possible."

Jacob leaned down, right in Junie's face, and whispered, *"Ham,"* with a wink. Junie stifled a sickly laugh as he scooped her up into his so-called capable hands and left the office, wondering why caring for his own child suddenly felt so foreign to him.

"I want Mommy," Junie whispered as he tucked her into the backseat of the truck.

Me too, baby girl, Jacob thought. *Me too.*

Chapter 4

The Valentine Volunteers—or the Loves Park Meat Market Matchmaking Guild, as Abigail called them—arrived at their usual time and took up the entire back corner of The Book Nook. Normally, Abigail would be thrilled to see them come in with their stacks of envelopes to stamp with the Loves Park seal because they always ordered drinks and sandwiches and ran up quite a bill, but today the whole thing overwhelmed her.

After spending the entire day haggling with Harvey, Abigail didn't think she could stomach it.

Especially since nothing about her meeting with the banker had gone in her favor. "The business plan isn't quite there yet, Abigail," Harvey had told her. "The numbers are too risky for us at this time. Let's see what Wyatt can do to find you a new landlord and hope for the best."

Abigail's face heated at the memory of the conversation.

Gigi Monroe approached the counter and spotted Abigail before she could take cover.

"Abigail!" Gigi exclaimed at top volume. All the better to embarrass Abigail. The woman banged her hand on the counter. "Well, it's decided!"

Abigail didn't even want to know, and yet she heard the words "What's decided?" come out of her own mouth.

Gigi's eyes narrowed underneath penciled-on brows, her lips drawn into a tight, knowing smile —a smile that seemed to accuse Abigail of knowing what the woman was talking about.

After a long pause, Abigail realized Gigi had no intention of answering her question.

"Do you want your usual?"

"Don't change the subject, missy," Gigi said, pointing a perfectly manicured nail.

"There's a subject?"

"There's a subject, all right. A *good* one. You must've been waiting for the results."

Abigail's heart dropped, her mind spinning back to the farmers' dating website. "What are you talking about?"

"The Valentine Volunteers."

Abigail tossed a glance in the direction of the other women in the corner—five total, including Gigi, ranging in age from twenty-seven to eighty-one. These women sorted through the 160,000-plus pieces of mail that came through Loves Park every year, stamping them with the seal of the Sweetheart City.

Everyone in town knew, however, that their real mission involved targeting the single (read: lonely) members of the community and finding them suitable companions. Surely they hadn't set their sights on Abigail. Surely she was far too busy for their wacky antics. Surely not today.

The way this day had gone so far, though?

Thankfully, only the truly desperate received the attention of the Valentine Volunteers. And Abigail was hardly desperate. She was an independent woman. She'd grown quite accustomed to the single life. On the outside, in fact, one might think she preferred it that way.

Right?

Gigi seemed to mistake Abigail's horrified silence for anticipation, and a grin crept across the old woman's face. "We voted just yesterday."

"On what?"

By now the others had perked up, unsuccessfully pretending not to be listening.

"Our newest addition, of course."

"Oh? I didn't realize it was like a club." She of all people should've known how they worked. After all, with the exception of Abigail's own mother, the Pressman women had a long history of being a part of the Volunteers. Teensy herself would probably be running the group by now if her pride hadn't gotten in the way.

Gigi chuckled. "Not a club, Abigail, an honor. And we want you."

"Me?" It was worse than she thought. They weren't just targeting her—they were bringing her into the fold. That must mean they saw her case as being especially difficult.

Newlywed Tess Jenkins rushed over. "You're a well-connected, well-liked local business owner." Tess, a good three years younger than Abigail, had been the Volunteers' target two years prior and had joined the group only weeks after her engagement. Because she was indebted to these women for her happiness. Or something.

Abigail couldn't help but notice the diamond sparkling on Tess's left hand. Her whirlwind wedding had been the talk of the town. To celebrate, Abigail stayed home watching YouTube videos on how to knit a scarf.

She dubbed it her "Ben & Jerry's day." And she never did finish the scarf.

A girl was allowed a moment of weakness now and then, right? And there was no way the Valentine Volunteers—or anyone else—could have found out about that lapse.

Abigail shook off the memories and focused on filling a carafe of coffee. "Right, I'm a business owner, which is why I don't have time to volunteer for stamping envelopes."

Gigi scoffed. "Is that all you think we do?"

Abigail frowned. "Isn't it?"

"You should know better, Miss Pressman. All that time you spent underneath my dining room table when your grandmother was one of us. Didn't she teach you anything?" The old woman scrunched her forehead in a disapproving scowl, wagged her finger, and took a few steps to inspect the pastry display, leaving Abigail face-to-face with the newly minted Mrs. Jenkins.

Abigail hadn't forgotten those hours underneath Gigi's table, listening to the women conspire about one person or another. Her grandmother had promised it wasn't meddling, that they simply had a knack for mending broken hearts.

That's what she'd said, anyway.

From Abigail's perspective, those women worked hard to pump everyone in town—herself included—full of unrealistic ideas about love and romance, starting with retelling her great-great-grandparents' love story at every Sweetheart Festival.

John and Elsie Pressman, the founders of Loves Park, adventurers who defied all the odds to leave their homes and colonize a town in the middle of nowhere. No friends. No family. Only their love to see them through. A love so deep and so meaningful they'd devoted themselves to it wholly—so much so that they named the town in its honor.

Abigail had believed the stories too but quickly learned the hard way that what those women were peddling wasn't real.

Love—the kind she read about in books—didn't seem to exist. She'd lived long enough and had her heart broken enough times to doubt, and now Abigail wondered if there was any sense in hoping for it anymore.

She glanced up and found Gigi in front of her again, staring at her, and she dug down deep to locate her focus and resolve once more.

No thank you, Gigi Monroe. You can peddle that sack of love-filled lies somewhere else.

"This is quite an honor, Abigail. These women haven't added a member for two years. I was the last addition." Tess's eyes were wide like a child's.

"I do appreciate the offer, Tess, but I have a lot going on right now." Abigail's thoughts spun back to her conversation with Harvey. No loan. Not enough equity. No collateral. No chance of expanding. Sadness lingered at her edges.

Gigi huffed and walked back to her table.

"I think you've offended her." Tess wore a shame-on-you expression, and it occurred to Abigail that she couldn't afford to offend Gigi or anyone else for that matter. She needed all the business she could get.

"I'll talk to Gigi, but I don't think I have time to volunteer right now."

"We'll start you off with something easy. Stamping the letters. You don't even have to come to our meetings. At least not all of them." Tess clearly had her mind made up. "You'll be great at it, and in a pinch, you can take them home and do them there."

Abigail pushed the carafe of freshly brewed Loves Park blend across the counter and arranged four ceramic Book Nook mugs on a tray with cream and sugar. "I really am so honored, Tess, but I wasn't making it up when I said I probably wouldn't have time."

"You care about your community, don't you, Abigail?" Tess said, picking up the carafe.

"Of course I do." Abigail followed her to the table with the mugs.

"Your community needs you." Tess filled the mugs one by one, passing them around the table to the other women.

Ursula Pembrooke, who looked every second of her seventy-five years, liked hers prepared half and half—half coffee and half cream with two heaping spoonfuls of sugar.

Doris Taylor, the group's oldest—and flightiest —member, took hers black.

Evelyn Brandt, only a few years older than Abigail, brought her own coconut-milk creamer from home.

Gigi, the most maternal of the ladies, added a dab of cream, half a sugar.

And Tess drank a chai tea latte instead, which Abigail would prepare for her as soon as she returned to the counter.

Abigail knew plenty about these women. She knew their game, their drinks. She knew they loved to meddle and they wouldn't stay out of her business. Why, then, was she still standing here with them as if their conversation wasn't over?

Doris took the first sip of coffee, leaving a bright-pink lipstick ring on the mug. Abigail would have to scrub to get that off. "Gigi's right, Abigail. We do much more than just stamp the letters." She must have better hearing than Abigail gave her credit for.

"Though that's important," Evelyn said. "People from all over send their wedding invitations and Valentine's Day cards here for the Loves Park seal."

As if Abigail didn't know all about this. And the limited-edition Valentine's Day Card, specially designed each year by a local artist. And the Miss Sweetheart Valentine. And the Valentine's Day

Festival and the Sweetheart Festival. And the love letters sent straight to the postmaster, not unlike the notes a child might send to Santa Claus. The list went on and on.

"You'd think you, a first daughter of Loves Park, would want to give back to your community." Gigi had affected an innocent tone, but her barbs weren't covered in sugar.

"That's right," Tess said as if she'd just remembered. "Surely your great-great-grandparents' traditions must mean something to you."

Abigail recognized the wistful expression that swept across her face.

"I love the part where Sir John Pressman rode his horse for days to find his beloved bride, captured by warriors."

"Tess, he wasn't a knight."

"He should've been. How dreamy."

Abigail stifled a groan. Before anyone could retell her great-great-grandparents' love story *again,* Abigail adjusted her apron and took a step away. "I'll think about it, ladies, okay?"

Gigi harrumphed.

Abigail sighed. "I will. Honest. I'm very honored you've thought of me. I . . . just have a lot going on with my business."

"We know," Ursula said. "We heard."

Abigail stopped fussing with her apron and glanced up. "You heard what?"

"About you not getting the loan to buy the

building." Ursula shrugged as if she'd just made the most obvious statement ever.

"Who told you that?" Her heart raced.

"Oh, it's all over town," Doris said, waving her off. "I don't know why you'd want to expand anyway. This is the perfect size for a bookstore. It's so cozy in here."

Abigail looked away, her vintage dreams flittering through her mind. Why did she think a little boutique was a good idea anyway? It was silly and frivolous. Doris was right. She had the perfect-size shop right now.

Except she'd somehow gotten it in her head that The Book Nook wasn't enough. How could it be when the thought of selling refinished furniture and other treasures interested her so much more? And she couldn't deny the fact that many people had started buying books online. Sure, she did okay, but if she wanted to hold on to this dream, she needed to grow her business— offer something for both the tourists *and* the locals.

She'd been in business for seven years, and she was practically a baby when she started. It was time to prove she wasn't a kid anymore. She was a savvy businesswoman with a valuable idea and something to offer this town.

She had to believe she had something else to contribute. Something wholly her own.

Abigail pulled herself back to the present. How

could the rumors already have started around town? Who thought it was appropriate to discuss her private business matters anyway?

"Miss Pressman, did you know that in addition to stamping all of those envelopes, last month we also organized a meal train for Joyce Richmond?" Gigi's high-and-mighty tone told Abigail not to respond.

"We also arrange for housekeeping for new mothers and the elderly," Doris added.

"And we found volunteers to paint the nursery at Loves Park Community Church," Tess said.

Ursula dabbed at the corners of her thin lips with a napkin. "We're about more than postmarks, young lady."

Abigail knew where this was headed.

Before these women were through with her, they'd have her not only volunteering but leading the charge, and she wasn't about to let that happen.

The group existed because of this town's infatuation with the very thing that most often annoyed her. Did they really think she would ever agree to be a part of their crazy schemes?

They must know how she felt about their mission.

Still, she couldn't ignore the fact that despite her hesitation, these women offered her something she needed right now. Allies. The kind with community influence.

As one of the Valentine Volunteers, she at least had a fighting chance when it came to saving her shop. Without them . . . Well, could she risk finding out what business would look like without them?

Besides, no matter how nosy they could be, these women were doing good work for their little town. And serving other people might do Abigail some good in taking her mind off her own worries.

Abigail tucked a piece of hair behind her ear and held up her hands in surrender. "Fine. Fine. What do you want me to do?"

Gigi clapped her hands together, salmon-colored fingertips tapping as she did. "Well, darling," she said, "you can start with these." She reached into her roomy tote bag and pulled out a tall stack of envelopes, along with a stamp and an ink pad, and set them on the table. "Welcome to the club."

Chapter 5

"That was easier than I thought it would be," Gigi said. "Teensy made her daughter sound a lot more difficult than she seems."

Ursula set her mug down on the table. "Teensy Pressman? Exaggerating? What else is new?"

True. Gigi hadn't considered that their old friend

might've painted her daughter in a more desperate light than necessary.

"It's shameful, Gigi," Teensy had said after barging in on last week's meeting at Gigi's home. "She's halfway to life as an old maid."

"Don't be dramatic, Teensy," Gigi replied, setting a saucer of cookies in front of Abigail's mother. "What do you expect us to do about your daughter? She seems perfectly happy staying single."

Teensy nearly spit her tea across the table. "She most certainly is not happy, Gigi Monroe. She has convinced herself that she doesn't need a man, but you and I both know better."

"Do I?" Gigi had been quite happy with her Al for many years, but since he'd passed away, she'd figured out how to find happiness in the days she had left. Perhaps young Miss Pressman had learned this lesson early.

"I know none of you are satisfied unless you're meddling in someone's love life," Teensy said. "And I'm begging you to meddle in my daughter's."

Teensy, the one Pressman who'd opted out of the Valentine Volunteers, unable to put aside her shame after her own marriage failed, seemed intent on doing her own share of meddling. The woman might have walked away from their group when her husband left her, but she certainly hadn't stopped giving her opinions.

Now it seemed her obsession had settled on her daughter's love life.

Poor Abigail.

After Teensy had left, Gigi and the other girls discussed her request. Despite the fact that the Volunteers often met at The Book Nook, when they thought about it, they realized they didn't really know the store's owner very well. She kept to herself, which didn't give them much to go on. How could they appropriately match her without all the facts?

It was Doris who had the idea to invite her to join the Volunteers—an idea that was as brilliant as it was ludicrous. The one thing they did know was that Abigail seemed not to share this town's obsession with anything related to love and marriage.

Who could blame her, really? It couldn't have been easy growing up under the shadow of "the most inspiring love story this side of the Rockies," as the Loves Park website boasted—and that didn't even take into account the girl's plight of having Teensy for a mother.

In the end, asking Abigail to join them was the best way to get close to her. How else could they chip away at the wall the girl had built around herself? According to her mother, she had hardly any friends, let alone prospects for romance.

But now she was one of them.

"We're going to have trouble with this one,

Gigi," Doris said in that high-pitched voice of hers. "Even you have to admit that."

Gigi spotted Abigail across the bookstore in what appeared to be an in-depth conversation with one of her employees. "Yes," Gigi said. "We are."

What happened to you, Abigail Pressman? Once upon a time, you were so full of hope, so enthralled with love . . . and now the sparkle that used to fill your eyes is gone.

The image of Abigail as a very young girl flashed through her mind. Her grandmother had made a point of bringing Abigail to their meetings—to spend time with her, sure, but Gigi always suspected it was more than that. Abigail's parents hadn't exactly had a good marriage, though Teensy was intent on keeping up appearances even after her husband walked out. Abigail was smart, though, and she'd seen too much. Her grandmother must've been trying to protect her from the jaded sadness that, in the end, was exactly what seemed to have happened to her.

With her tie to the town's founders, Abigail should be the first one to celebrate the Loves Park festivals, and yet even on Valentine's Day, The Book Nook had not a single heart in the windows.

Gigi had to wonder if all those conversations Abigail had overheard as a child had contributed to the sadness that seemed to hover around the girl now. Was it their fault she seemed so

desperate to fill her life with anything and everything that wasn't a romantic relationship?

Yes, Abigail Pressman might prove to be their
most difficult case yet. Hard to match—and more
stubborn than most—because Gigi suspected that
their new target had no idea she even wanted to
fall in love at all.

And in her experience, those were the ones
who needed the Volunteers the most.

Chapter 6

Two days after she was press-ganged into the
ranks of the Valentine Volunteers, Abigail sat in
her office looking over the figures in her ledger.
Dismal. *Those numbers should really be a
different color,* she thought absently. On paper,
she shouldn't have a single cent to her name.
Thankfully she had some reserves, but if she
didn't turn things around soon, it might not
matter. Of course, if her new landlord evicted her,
red numbers would be the least of her worries.

Sure, expanding would've meant more overhead, but she could have broadened her appeal,
maintained the local bookstore business while
reaching out to the healthy tourist contingent
Loves Park brought in each year. One-of-a-kind
artwork, distressed furniture, handmade jewelry—

tourists would eat that up. Not to mention the fact that selling higher-priced items like these would automatically help her bottom line. She'd already estimated that she could triple her business in the first year. Why didn't Harvey see that? Why didn't anyone else believe in her ideas?

Okay, maybe that wasn't fair. It's not like she'd broadcast these ambitions. She'd always been more of an I-can-do-it-myself kind of girl.

She rubbed her temples, unsuccessfully willing the dull ache away.

The stack of envelopes stared back at her. A pile of wedding invitations perfectly addressed in what they now referred to as "modern calligraphy" awaited the precious Loves Park stamp, and after Christmas, everything would ramp up for Valentine's Day.

"Things are always busiest come January," Doris had told her after the group had dispersed. "Gigi has big plans for your artistic eye."

Abigail hadn't asked the older woman to explain, though now she wondered if that was a mistake.

She pulled the stack of envelopes toward her, but before she could stamp the first one, she was startled by a loud banging—so startled, in fact, that she knocked over her coffee and spilled it across the desk, drenching the envelopes entrusted to her care.

"No!" Abigail grabbed the envelopes, coffee

dripping down her wrist and into her sleeve as the banging continued. "No! No! No!"

Mallory rushed through Abigail's office door. "What happened?" One look at the dripping envelopes and her eyes widened. "Uh-oh."

"What is that banging?"

"It's next door." Mallory wiped up the spilled coffee, then handed Abigail a dry towel for the envelopes.

The mercantile. There was no way that Jakc-Jacob person could've already bought the building. However, she wouldn't put it past Wyatt to begin construction before the final paperwork was finished.

Abigail did her best to dry the dripping invitations and steady her pulse at the same time. The crisp white envelopes were now stained brown and she couldn't do a thing about it. The pounding seemed to be getting louder and more frequent, annihilating her already-shot nerves.

Abigail stood dumbfounded for too many long seconds before finally reaching the conclusion that she had the right to say something. She was running a business and leasing the space, after all. Did they think the banging wouldn't disturb her customers? Did they consider her at all? She was here first!

"That's it. I'm going over there."

Mallory took a step back and Abigail thrust the envelopes into her hands. She stormed through the front of her shop and out onto the sidewalk, marching next door only to find the front entrance locked. She peered into the dark building but saw no one, so she trudged around the building and into the alley behind The Book Nook. A beat-up truck sat in Harriet's old parking place. Next to it, Wyatt's slick Mercedes.

The back door was locked too, but Abigail knew where the spare key was—in a slim plastic box wedged between two loose bricks. She opened the door, stuck the key in her pocket, and followed the banging.

The mercantile had been a community staple for years. As she took in the thick moldings and original wood floors, sadness pinged her heart all over again. Maybe she could call up the historical registry and see if the building fit the criteria. Could she cash in a favor and have remodeling requests denied? Did she know anyone who owed her a favor?

Her mind stayed blank.

Light filtered in through the windows all along the sidewall. The mercantile always did have the perfect morning sun.

Marring the tranquil scene was a man in plastic goggles, back turned to Abigail, hammering a hole in the wall that separated their two spaces. To add insult to injury, Wyatt was standing next to him, looking on.

"What do you think you're doing?" Abigail's

tone came off firm and forceful, not at all like she felt.

The man in the goggles—Jacob, of course—stopped his hammer midswing, but it was Wyatt who spoke.

"Hey," he said, his face drawn tight like a new pair of shoelaces.

Hey? They were pounding a hole through the wall and all he could say was hey?

"You have a new landlord." Wyatt's smile dripped with superiority. He'd won. She'd lost. A tired tale.

Abigail felt the horror spread across her face. How was it that she'd been planning for years to buy this building and a perfect stranger swooped in and stole it from under her nose in less than a day? She thought of her notebooks full of sketches of the new space. She'd added to them every time she visited Harriet.

"Just like that?" She begged herself not to cry. Sometimes her anger wore tears.

Wyatt shrugged. "Play nice, Abs."

Jacob pushed the goggles to the top of his head and looked away. "I thought you said she was okay with this."

Wyatt's arrogant expression pulled at her as if to expose the nerves of a fresh wound. "I said she *would be* okay with this."

Abigail narrowed her eyes, not sure which one of them made her angrier.

"We got a tip on some leaky pipes," Jacob said, tossing a glance her way.

Was he trying to be funny?

"So you're just going to tear out the wall?" Abigail crossed her arms over her chest as if that could protect her from this deluge of horrible news.

"The inspector said it would be fine." Jacob seemed unwilling to make eye contact with her. Was it possible that, unlike Wyatt, this man took no pleasure in throwing her dreams out the window like a child chucking a bottle out of a moving vehicle?

"Harriet must've forgotten there's a business next door," Abigail muttered under her breath.

"I think Harriet is looking out for Harriet, Abby," Wyatt said. "You could learn a thing or two from her. She's a shrewd businesswoman. Got this guy to agree to paying cash. Sealed the deal with her son this morning." He jabbed Jacob in the shoulder while Abigail tried to pick her jaw up off the ground.

He paid cash?

Why hadn't she thought about contacting Harriet's son? She'd mistakenly assumed he was off on one of his business trips, but with Harriet out of the country, apparently he was in charge.

And now he'd sold the building right out from under her. For cash.

"This time next week, you two will officially be in a relationship." Wyatt grinned. Jacob's eyes found Abigail's for the briefest moment, but he quickly averted them. She hated herself for glancing at his left hand. Sure enough, no ring, just as Anita had said.

That realization brought an onslaught of questions—ones she wouldn't let herself entertain for one more minute.

Wyatt laughed. "The landlord-tenant relationship can be a trying one. You two should get to know each other, come to some sort of mutual understanding." He turned to Jacob. "Or you could always kick her out." He cackled, doing that thing Wyatt always did: laughing at his own jokes no matter how unfunny they were.

Would he ever grow up?

Abigail shifted. "I've never heard of a building being sold this fast. Isn't there red tape?" *Her* business seemed to be wrapped in red tape.

"I'm handling it." Wyatt checked his phone. "Speaking of which, I gotta run. You okay here for an hour or two?" He glanced at Jacob, then at Abigail, then back to Jacob.

"I'll be fine." Jacob shook Wyatt's hand just as the Realtor's phone chirped.

"Wyatt Nelson." He exited out the back, leaving Abigail face-to-face with her new landlord.

She took a few steps away from him. He didn't look particularly comfortable being alone in the room with her either.

He watched her, unsure. It seemed she'd put him

on the defensive. Well, good. He should be defensive. Who was he to come to town, buy up her building, and knock down her dreams brick by brick?

"So." She searched for a starting point, found nothing.

"So."

She grasped. "What are your plans for the place?" Abigail thought her question almost sounded cordial. She felt anything but. Angry and bitter about summed it up.

"I'm starting a new practice."

"Lawyer?"

"Doctor."

Figures. Abigail caught herself. No sense being angry with the man for his career choice. Being a doctor was a perfectly noble profession—and one that afforded you a bank account with enough cash to buy entire buildings.

She swallowed her jealousy. Why couldn't she have been good at math and science instead of art and literature?

"So you're going to turn the mercantile into a sterile, boring clinic? Seems like such a waste." As she often did, Abigail admired the wide-planked floors under her feet. They could stand to be refinished, but she decided their condition was part of their charm. She couldn't imagine some flecked tile floor in this space. Especially not next door to her little shop.

"Actually, I'm going to keep as much of the original interior as I can. Part of the reason I like this building is because it doesn't look like a hospital." Jacob ran a hand over a thick wooden post at the center of the space.

"That's an odd thing for a doctor to say," Abigail replied. "Shouldn't you love hospitals?"

He regarded her for a long moment. "I don't know anyone who loves hospitals."

Something in the way he said it gave her pause.

The back door opened before she could say anything else, and in walked a stunning blonde woman dressed in a black power suit, wearing heels that *click-click-click*ed on the beautiful wooden floors.

"Is it a done deal?" She grinned at Jacob, her hair bouncing as she clicked.

He tossed a sideways glance at Abigail, who suddenly felt out of place in her tunic top and leggings. Was there a rock she could hide under?

"Almost," he said.

"What did I tell you about this place?" the woman said, looking around. "It's great. The location is the perfect spot for our practice."

Our practice?

She turned then and, moving like a bulldozer toward Jacob, pulled him into a hug. "It's been too long, Doc."

Doc?

He patted her back twice, the way men do when

they hug each other, and then pulled out of her grip. The woman reminded Abigail of a predatory animal. Like a lioness or a cheetah.

"Kelly, this is Abigail. She runs the bookstore next door." Jacob motioned toward Abigail, who suddenly felt very self-conscious, like a high school freshman wanting to hang out with the popular girls.

"Kelly is my business manager," Jacob said.

The woman let out a laugh. "That's funny. You make it sound so formal." She let her hand rest on his shoulder for a long moment before she turned to Abigail and gave her a once-over. "Good to meet you." Back to Jacob. "Have you looked at the plans?"

"Let's discuss it later."

Now Abigail felt like the third wheel at the prom. Her stomach dropped, her hands tingled, and her breath caught in her throat. What plans? What were their plans for the building?

"She's going to find out sooner or later," Kelly said.

Jacob remained silent.

Kelly shifted. "We're sorry about your shop."

"What about my shop?" Abigail's pulse started racing.

"Once those papers are signed and this is all a done deal, we're going to be working fast and furious to get the practice open." She glanced at Jacob. "This doctor's healing hands have been dormant too long. They really are magical, aren't they?"

Abigail couldn't be sure, but now her heart might've stopped beating. "What does that have to do with my shop?"

Kelly laughed. "Well, we need your space."

Abigail decided not to like this woman. *This can't be happening.* She steeled her jaw. "Oh."

"Let's not get ahead of ourselves," Jacob said to Kelly, a bit of warning in his voice. He seemed almost apologetic when he turned to Abigail again. "We're still considering our options."

Kelly didn't take the hint. "I have a business plan, benchmarks to grow our practice. Within the next year, maybe two, I'll need more space. It only makes sense to renovate in stages. Start here, then—" she shrugged, glancing at the wall as if to indicate Abigail's side of the building—"tackle the other side."

"A year?"

"Maybe two," Kelly repeated, eyes dancing.

Abigail looked at Jacob, though he didn't seem to be the captain of this ship. "Just like that?"

"I'll give you plenty of time to find another space. I'll even help you move," he said.

Well, that's big of you.

Tears sprang to her eyes. Hot tears that needed her full attention, but she refused to let the barracuda see any sign of weakness. And Jacob? How could he just go along with this woman?

Didn't he know this store was Abigail's whole life? "I can't just find another space."

"Wyatt seems to know some good ones. I'm sure he could—" Jacob started.

"You have no idea what you're talking about," Abigail blurted, louder than she'd intended. "This isn't just a building to me." Her father would have been so disappointed at this turn of events. She stared at the dumbfounded look on his face and got too flustered to continue.

Kelly raised her eyebrows, startled.

"Oh, never mind." Abigail started for the door.

"Wait a minute." He took a few steps sideways, blocking her. "I didn't mean to upset you."

"You're taking my store," she snapped. "What did you think I was going to do, throw you a welcome-to-the-neighborhood party?"

He looked away, giving her an opening to push past him, straight outside and back to the safety of her office. She locked the door, fell into a heap on her chair, and cried, her dreams spilling across the desk like a careless cup of coffee on someone else's wedding invitations.

Chapter 7

Abigail had gone and had taken all the air out of the room with her. Jacob turned to Kelly. "Was that really necessary?"

She sighed. "Come on, Jacob. This is the way business works. Don't tell me you feel sorry for her."

He did, in fact, and why shouldn't he? When he'd agreed to Kelly's proposal, she hadn't made any mention of putting out the locals.

"I've done my research on Abigail Pressman," Kelly said. "She isn't going to be a problem. She doesn't even have a business degree." She laughed. "It's a good thing you've got me. I know what I'm doing here."

He'd forgotten how intense this side of her could be, though he knew she'd been a type A roommate who always told his wife what to do. But Kelly knew business, and when she suggested the partnership, Jacob took it as a sign. He'd been asking for a clean slate, hadn't he? He never meant to start over like this, though. Maybe he'd made a mistake after all.

"Her store is part of this community—you can't just go ticking her off like that." Besides, he wasn't completely sure he hadn't settled on this space so he had the excuse to be around Abigail. If he kicked her out, he might as well set up shop at the mall. No, that wasn't true. He'd chosen the space because it was right in the center of town. And because nothing about it reminded him of a hospital.

Kelly raised a brow. "Oh, Jacob, you like her." Her words crawled under his skin.

Jacob scoffed. "Wanting to treat people with decency doesn't mean I 'like' them."

"Well, not everything in business is easy, Doc." She took a few steps closer to him. In her heels, she was nearly as tall as he was and capable of staring him down, eye to eye. "This isn't personal —it's business. And not everyone is going to like you."

"I didn't move here to make enemies." He had enough of those back home.

Kelly's tilted head and isn't-that-cute? expression made him feel like a puppy or a small child.

"Jacob," she said, "I know you're used to saving everyone, but you might have to accept the fact that you've got to think about yourself sometimes."

Jacob took a step back, putting much-needed distance between them.

"You can rip the Band-Aid off slowly and let her hang around, prolonging the inevitable, or you can tear it off quickly. It'll sting for a minute, but she'll be fine."

Kelly was right. It was why he'd hired her in the first place—because she understood all the things he didn't want to think about.

"Are we good?" she asked.

Jacob nodded.

"Good. Then let's get started." She pulled out a tape measure and handed it to him. "You said yourself we don't have a minute to waste. I hope you're ready for a wild ride. We'll have you up and running in no time."

Two hours later, Jacob pulled into the driveway of the home he'd bought on the outskirts of town. His dream house, really. Surrounded by mountains with a good-size backyard and not a neighbor in sight. It was exactly what he'd wanted, and yet something about it felt so hollow.

He parked in the circle drive behind Rosemary's minivan. The nanny had been a blessing over the past few weeks while he hunted properties and worked on the business plan with Kelly every time she drove in from Denver. Now that they'd found the space and he saw the amount of work ahead of them, he knew Rosemary would be even more helpful.

The upcoming remodel would be a welcome distraction. Keep his mind occupied. Keep his hands busy. That was the way to move beyond the past. The only way.

Inside, he hung up his coat and inhaled.

"Dr. Jacob." Rosemary stood at the stove, stirring a large pot of sauce. Probably homemade. His mouth watered as the tangy smell of garlic wafted to his nostrils.

"Evening, Rosemary," Jacob said, flipping through the mail on the counter. "Smells delicious."

She smiled, but seconds later her face fell.

"What is it?"

"I've really loved getting to know you, Dr. Jacob." Rosemary covered the pot and set the wooden spoon on the spoon rest.

Uh-oh. In the month he and Junie had been in town, he'd already had their first nanny quit after a week. Tabitha had cared much more about painting her nails than taking care of Junie or the house, though, so in the long run that had been for the best. But Rosemary? She'd been like a gift from God.

But then God had a way of taking back the things he gave, didn't he?

"Don't say it, Rosemary." Jacob propped himself on one of the barstools, that familiar feeling of dread in his gut.

"And I love Junie. You know I do." Rosemary's eyes turned glassy.

Please don't start crying.

"But my husband thinks I need to be home more. He likes dinner on the table right at five thirty. And he thinks our son is missing me." She wiped a tear. "He got in trouble at school last week, and Paul—that's my husband—he thinks it's because I haven't been home to keep an eye on him."

It wasn't Jacob's place to have an opinion about Rosemary's personal life. Instead he just nodded, hugged the plump woman, and thanked her once again for dinner, though he had a feeling it wouldn't taste as good now that he knew it was her farewell meal.

She hugged Junie before she left and told Jacob she'd watch for them at church on Sunday.

He wanted to say, "Don't bother," but something stopped him.

Now what? He'd promised Kelly they could start full-time renovations next week, and he had no one to shuttle Junie to and from school, much less take care of her until he got home. What about the nights that went long? He'd have several if he wanted to open by summer. That was the goal, after all. Jacob would just have to find someone else to help with Junie. What other choice did he have?

He dished up the spaghetti and meatballs that Rosemary had prepared, covered it all with sauce, added the garlic bread, and called Junie to the table for dinner. When she didn't come, he headed down the hall toward her bedroom.

"Junie?"

No response. Her room, with its bare walls and plain wood floors, looked nothing like a little girl's room should. Gwen had known how to take a space and make it feel like home. Come to think of it, anywhere Gwen was had felt like home to him.

He couldn't give that to Junie. He didn't know how.

And he couldn't stand it.

Again the anger rose up inside him, then the guilt. He hated that he was mad at Gwen, but he hated even more that he hadn't been able to do anything for her. And he'd tried and he'd prayed, and he'd believed for a miracle.

But none came.

Junie's empty bed gave him pause. Her light was on, but she wasn't in her room. "Junie?" Was she feeling sick again?

As he turned to check the bathroom, he heard rustling from the walk-in closet.

He opened the door and saw her feet sticking out from under the hanging clothes. "Hey, Mouse."

She pulled her feet in.

He sat down inside the closet, resting his back against the wall. "Kind of nice in here, huh?"

Nothing.

"It's quiet and private. I can see why you'd want to hide out here, but your dinner's getting cold."

No response.

Carefully, Jacob parted the clothes, revealing his little girl and her tearstained face. He frowned, and that parental heart tug yanked him sideways. "What's wrong, Junie?"

"Miss Rosemary is gone." Junie hugged her legs and rested her chin on her knees. "Just like Mommy."

The words sat in the air between them, weighty and unfair.

"Not like Mommy, Junie," he said. "We can find time to go see Miss Rosemary."

She scrunched her lips together. "Why do they all leave me, Daddy? Did I do something wrong?"

He reached over and pulled her onto his lap, wishing he could extract every ounce of pain she felt, fighting the anger that always bubbled below his surface. "Junie, you didn't do anything wrong."

"Then why do they all leave?" She let the weight of her head fall onto his shoulder, and he wished he could stay there forever, just the two of them hiding away from the rest of the world.

"I don't know, Junie. It's not fair." He hugged her. "But I can promise you something." He leaned in closer, his mouth on the back of her head. "I'm not going anywhere."

Without a word, she turned and buried her head in his chest, clinging to him in a way she hadn't since the day they buried Gwen.

He held her and let her cry, willing away the sorrow that hung over them like a black fog, too thick and close to the ground. Zero visibility.

Moving hadn't taken away the pain; it just packed itself right up in their U-Haul and came along with them.

He couldn't change anything for his daughter the same way he couldn't change anything for Gwen. Some healer he turned out to be.

If only he'd been there for her—seen the signs, done something, anything. This whole mess they were in was his fault, and that was something he'd never live down.

"I miss Mommy."

The words were soft, whispered in the air of the only place that felt safe to either one of them.

"That goes double for me, Junie Moon," Jacob whispered back.

Chapter 8

How Abigail ended up on Gigi Monroe's doorstep after work, she really had no idea. She'd peeled herself off her desk chair in a daze, which was how she'd finished out the day until it was finally time to leave for the night. Her intention had been to go home, take a hot bath, put on pajamas, eat a bowl of cereal, and fall asleep.

Abigail acknowledged that this plan was based on the misguided notion that, when she woke up, she'd find that someone else had figured out what she should do next. Clearly she was embracing blissful ignorance as to the amount of work it would take to arrive at a good next step.

And unfortunately, she'd lost the right to pawn her problems off on someone else when she stopped living under her parents' roof. Not that Teensy had ever had much insight when it came to her business anyway.

"The store is a fine way to pass the time until you can find someone to marry you, Abigail," her mother had told her only last month. "But you're so busy all the time. It's starting to look like more of a hindrance to you getting a life. And goodness knows you don't need any more hindrances in that department. Plain girls can't afford to be too busy."

Abigail had chosen not to ask her to elaborate, tucking away the adjective *plain* as yet another insult doled out with expert precision by the woman who was supposed to love her unconditionally.

In spite of all this, the cereal-and-sleep plan seemed like the most promising option. Until she realized she couldn't stop thinking about the ruined wedding invitations. She had to come clean—the guilt was too much for her to bear. She knew the women were meeting tonight, though they'd made it clear it was just business and she didn't need to attend. She glanced at the stack of coffee-stained envelopes protruding from her purse. What choice did she have? It wasn't like she could fix this mistake.

Memories she'd pushed aside had come tumbling back at her as she drove to Gigi's house—all those Volunteers meetings Grandma dragged her to, and for what? All they'd done was set her up for disappointment. It turned out those letters people sent professing their undying love for each other were only snapshots of the relationships they represented. Written in moments of nostalgia by people who were pining for what they'd lost or never had. That version of love was about as true as Shakespeare's.

Fiction.

When Gigi answered the door, her eyes went wide. "Oh, hello, Abigail," she said loudly and over her shoulder as if speaking to the others in the next room.

Abigail felt her whole face frown.

"So good of you to join us, dear. We didn't want to overwhelm you right off the bat with all of our meetings, or else we would have asked you to come to this one." Gigi peeled Abigail's jacket off as she ushered her into the house, which smelled of peppermint and sugar cookies. "We didn't expect you tonight, but we're glad you're here."

Abigail forced a polite smile, but her mind screamed at her to dump the ruined invites on the floor and run for the hills.

As she and Gigi entered the living room, Ursula stuffed some papers into a manila folder and shoved it into her bag, and Abigail caught a glimpse of Tess hurrying into the kitchen. She returned seconds later.

Awkward glances crisscrossed around her, and Abigail had the distinct impression she'd interrupted something.

Her "I don't have to stay" was met with a chorus of "Don't be silly!" and "We love having you here!" and before she knew it, Abigail had been plopped down on the sofa in the circle of women, a mug of hot cocoa in one hand and two very crispy cookies in the other.

Now five pairs of eyes were fixed on her. Abigail set her mug down. "There's something I need to tell you ladies."

"We know, dear," Doris said, smiling.

Abigail frowned. *No, you don't.*

"Your mother told us."

"Teensy?" How would her mother know about the coffee disaster?

"Doris!" Ursula's warning shot silenced the other woman.

"Don't listen to Doris, dear," Gigi said. "She gets confused a lot these days."

"I do not!" Doris set her own mug down. "I'm perfectly lucid 96 percent of the time."

Ursula leaned closer to Abigail. "Take a sip of her cocoa and see how lucid she is."

Abigail put her hands up in surrender. "I can't do this."

"Can't do what, Abigail?" Tess moved to the

edge of her armchair on the opposite side of the circle, the weight of her stare heavy on Abigail.

"I agreed to volunteer with you ladies because I couldn't afford for you to boycott my shop, but none of that really matters anymore since I'll be out of business in about a year anyway." Abigail reached into her purse and pulled out the invitations. "Besides, I ruined these." She stood, dropping the stack of envelopes on the coffee table at the center of the circle.

Tess gasped, picking up one of the coffee-stained invitations and turning it over in her hand. "Abigail, if you were upset, you didn't have to take it out on this poor bride."

Abigail sighed. "I didn't do it on purpose."

"Accidents happen. That's no reason to quit." Evelyn sank a little deeper into her chair.

Easy for her to say. She married a rich politician. She was probably only part of this group because she was bored.

Doris crossed her arms over her ample bosom. "No, but ruining someone's wedding invitations might be. She's obviously not cut out for this." Doris harrumphed, sitting back in her seat.

"Doris!" Ursula barked.

"No, she's right." Abigail dropped in a heap onto the sofa, the heaviness of the day settling squarely onto her shoulders. "I'm not cut out for this any more than I'm cut out for running a business."

"Tell us what's wrong, dear," Gigi said, crossing the room and creating space for herself on the sofa where there was none. "Maybe we can help."

Abigail was horrified when her attempt to swallow the lump in her throat failed. Tears sprang to her eyes as Gigi patted her knee with her fragile hand. On her other side, Tess sat up and, like the others, focused all of her attention on Abigail.

The outcast. The one who didn't belong. That feeling was too familiar, and she'd worked hard to get rid of it. How did it keep returning, uninvited?

She'd created a place where she fit perfectly. Without The Book Nook, who was Abigail Pressman?

"Why don't you tell us your troubles, dear?" Gigi said in a gentle, motherly voice.

"We'd like to help you if we can," Evelyn added.

Despite every effort to withhold her feelings, Abigail listened to her own voice as it betrayed her, pouring out the events of the day: from the spilled coffee fiasco to finding Dr. Jacob Willoughby pounding holes in the wall next door to that horrible Kelly woman dropping the bomb that Abigail had only another year or two with her store.

Somehow she felt like the mourning process had already begun.

"I've been trying to scrounge together the

money to buy the place for years, just waiting for the right moment," Abigail said, wiping the tears from her cheeks. "And every time I made a little bit of progress, my car would break down or the price of coffee would go up." She covered her face with her hands. "He waltzes in there with his businesswoman girlfriend and pays cash for the place. I really thought this was going to be the year everything changed."

She felt a kind hand on her back but imagined confused glances being exchanged over her head.

"This may still be the year everything changes," Tess said, too much optimism in her voice. "Just not the way you expected."

Somehow Abigail didn't find that very comforting.

"Tess is right, dear," Gigi said. "You just have to readjust your sails."

"I don't see another course," she said. "Expanding was going to save my business. That *was* me readjusting my sails."

Across the room, Ursula scoffed.

Abigail looked at the woman through her tears. She didn't know Ursula Pembrooke very well. Of the five Valentine Volunteers, Ursula was the most eclectic. The one who didn't seem to mind being the talk of the town. Flamboyant and bold, Frank Pembrooke's widow knew how to keep Loves Park on its toes.

"Businesswomen don't cry like little girls."

Ursula popped a cookie in her mouth. "Is the doctor's girlfriend crying like a little girl?"

"Ursula!" Evelyn's voice warned, but Ursula clearly wasn't used to taking orders.

"You're not cut out for business if you're going to give up the second it gets hard."

Abigail sniffed. "All due respect, Mrs. Pembrooke, but it's been hard for quite a while."

"Hogwash." Ursula downed her cocoa. "Why are you all staring at me?"

"Ignore her, Abigail," Gigi said, resuming her motherly back rub.

"Don't ignore me. I am the only one here who knows anything about business."

It was hard to believe with her eccentric manners, but Abigail knew that Ursula Pembrooke had learned all there was to know about business from her husband. In his day, Frank had made a fortune restoring Old Town Loves Park. He'd been shrewd and callous, but brilliant—and he'd withheld his knowledge from everyone but Ursula.

"Frankie always said when it comes to business, you fight or you die," she said, wiping her lips with a napkin. "He never said, 'Curl up in a ball and cry your eyes out.'"

Abigail again thought of Kelly. She was the kind of woman Ursula was talking about. And Abigail could say with complete certainty she was nothing like her. She shrugged. "I already lost the fight. What else can I do?"

Ursula set her plate on the coffee table with a clank and scooted forward in her armchair. "You can start by quitting the pity party. No one ever made it in business by feeling sorry for themselves, young lady." She stood. "Get up."

Abigail glanced at Gigi, whose horrified expression told her this wasn't customary behavior among the Volunteers. "Ursula, I don't know if she's in the right frame of mind for this."

"You're too soft, Gigi. Be quiet." Ursula pulled Abigail away from the rest of them, into the open part of the living room. "Now, the way I see it, you can roll over and let this stranger push you out of your own store, or you can *fight.*"

"With what?"

"Figure it out." Ursula tucked a lone gray flyaway behind her ear and narrowed her eyes at Abigail. "How can you force the man out of his own building? Indian burial ground? Asbestos?"

"Ursula!" Gigi gasped. "Abigail, don't listen to her. She's off her bean."

Abigail shrank under the weight of Ursula's gaze. "I'm not cut out for this, Mrs. Pembrooke." Besides, neither of those things applied to her building.

"Nonsense. You just have to stop thinking like a polite little girl."

Abigail frowned. "I am polite."

"Exactly. But this is business." She stared

at Abigail, who only stared back. "Fight or die."

Abigail started to glance toward the others for support when Ursula grabbed her by the chin and forced her eyes to focus. "Say it."

"Say what?"

"Fight or die."

Out of the corner of her eye, she saw the others stand up. For a split second she felt like Rocky Balboa getting a prematch pep talk from Mick. Ursula clearly took her job as trainer quite seriously.

"Well?"

Abigail met the old woman's gaze and complied. "Fight or die?"

Ursula practically melted into a puddle of disappointment. "No wonder you're in this situation." She turned away, though she did nothing to hide her disgust.

Abigail frowned. "What's that supposed to mean?"

"There are a million things you could've done to prevent this from happening, but you didn't think outside the box." She tapped her temple with one crinkled hand. "You'll never make it if you think like everyone else."

Abigail's mouth went dry at the disapproval. She'd been here before. A long-suppressed memory washed over her, and just like that she was standing in front of Jeremy, tuning out the words she'd dreaded for two years.

"I'm just not ready for marriage, Abigail," he'd told her.

Teensy had cried when Abigail told her the news.

"Did he find someone else?" she'd asked.

Abigail shook her head.

"So it wasn't that he was in love with someone else? He just wasn't in love with you." Teensy's words still needled her to this day.

As if the shock of her broken heart weren't enough, Abigail had disappointed her mother— again. At some point she'd convinced herself she'd never live up to Teensy's standards and she'd stopped trying.

Sort of.

Now, with Ursula staring at her, that same disappointed look on her face, she realized maybe there was a part of her that would always want to make her mother proud.

"I'm sorry, Ursula. I just don't see that I have any options."

"You know what else Frankie told me?" Ursula stared at her as if waiting for a response.

Abigail slowly shook her head.

"No one really knows what they're doing. But as long as they're doing something, they're getting somewhere. And that's a whole lot better than sitting around."

Abigail fought the urge to dart out of the room. She hadn't been sitting around—these weren't self-inflicted troubles.

"Get out of the box," Ursula said. "Who do you know that might be able to help you?"

Abigail scanned her mental database, running through names of customers and city officials. Despite the fact that her great-great-grandparents had founded the town, she didn't really have any more pull than anyone else. She'd settled into her place as part of Loves Park's middle class quite nicely. She didn't need much in her simple life—even if what she wanted was a different story. When she came up empty, she shrugged.

Ursula practically shrieked. "Me! You should've come to me the second Harriet decided to retire." Ursula folded her arms over her chest, covering the long, beaded necklaces she wore around her neck.

Abigail frowned, resisting the urge to point out that other than taking her coffee order, this was the first real conversation she'd ever had with the woman. "What good would that have done?"

"I'm rich! Don't you know that with enough money, you can buy anything?" She flung her hands up over her head.

Abigail knew her expression matched the way she felt—confused.

"Don't look at me like that," Ursula said.

Abigail turned away.

"Look at me."

"I'm sorry I'm—"

"You're a little girl. And it's time to be a woman."

Abigail chose silence.

"Ursula, maybe—" Evelyn began.

But the old woman's hiss of a shush ended Evelyn's thought before she could finish.

"So ask me."

Another quick glance at the others, none of whom offered even a hint that they knew what she should do.

"Ask you . . . ?"

Ursula let out an annoyed sigh. "Ask me to buy the building."

"I don't think you understand, Mrs. Pembrooke. The doctor bought the building."

"I don't think *you* understand, Miss Pressman. I will buy it back."

In her mind, Abigail replayed the events that had brought her here tonight in the first place. If only she hadn't spilled that coffee and felt the need to confess at this meeting, she'd be safe in her house, sanding and painting that beautiful armoire she'd picked up last weekend at the flea market. Instead she was here, serving as a human punching bag for someone she now realized was one of the toughest women in Loves Park.

Gigi finally came to her aid. "Forgive me, Ursula, but how does that help dear Abigail?"

"She can buy it from me." Ursula turned to Abigail. "I would've cosigned your loan applica-tion, but you never bothered to ask." She walked away, grabbed another cookie, and shoved the whole thing in her mouth.

Gigi met Abigail's gaze with raised brows. "That could work, right?"

"You haven't talked to this man or his—" she searched for the word—"his Kelly. Oh, he seems kind and charming, with his ridiculous good looks and those cheekbones, but I'm not buying it. Not for a second." Abigail turned to find them all staring at her with accusing eyes.

"Good looks?" Doris's eyes widened.

"Cheekbones?" Tess practically exhaled the word.

Abigail faced Ursula, who'd returned to the armchair and now sat like a queen on a throne. "He won't sell it to you," she informed the older woman.

"How good-looking?" Gigi's brows were still raised.

Ursula shook her head. "Fight or die, Miss Pressman. Fight or die."

Chapter 9

Gigi opened the door for Abigail, who looked even more horrified than when she'd come in. Returning to the living room after saying good-bye to the young woman, Gigi shook her head at Ursula, who nibbled a crunchy cookie Tess had brought. Gigi made a mental note not to allow Tess to supply refreshments for these meetings anymore.

"You can come out, Teensy," she called toward the bedroom.

Teensy Pressman emerged, wearing a pair of black dress slacks and a sparkly sweater. Her hairdo always reminded Gigi of a newscaster's, and her makeup looked professionally done. No wonder it bothered her so much that her daughter hadn't married yet—appearances were everything in Teensy's world.

In fact, when her husband left her, Teensy made a point of going to the grocery store in her Sunday clothes just to prove to everyone she was fine. Gigi knew better, of course. They all knew better. Teensy's light went off that day, and she hadn't been the same since.

Her husband's desertion had made a lifetime of difference to Teensy and, it would seem, to at least one of her children.

"I thought she'd never leave," Abigail's mother said.

"It's a good thing you drove over with Doris, or she would've seen your car," Tess said, crunching one of her tooth-breaking cookies.

Teensy took Abigail's spot on the sofa and clapped her hands in front of her. "This is wonderful news, don't you think?"

They all stared at Teensy, confusion on every face.

"Don't you see? She'll finally be rid of that dreadful business. It'll force her to start evaluating other aspects of her life." Teensy reached toward the tray of cookies and caught Gigi's eye. The slight shake of her head was enough to communicate that it wasn't a good idea, and Teensy retreated.

Tess frowned and started to speak, but Gigi jumped in before she could say anything. "I don't think you understand how much that business means to her, Teensy."

Teensy waved her perfectly manicured red fingers in the air. "She doesn't know what she wants. She's just a child."

Ursula leaned forward in her chair. Gigi knew that look. It was the put-her-in-her-place look, and it wouldn't go over well. These two women had butted heads before, and Gigi still hadn't decided which one was more stubborn.

"You have no idea what you're talking about, Teensy," Ursula said. "She is not a child, and that store is all she has."

Teensy turned to Ursula. "Exactly my point. She needs to branch out and see what else is out there. She needs to get married. Start a family. It's what she's always wanted."

Doris's head began moving back and forth, as if the woman were having a conversation in her head. "I don't think that's true, Teensy. I think she wants her store to succeed."

Teensy's lips drew into a tight line. "I didn't ask you all to evaluate my daughter. I asked you to find her a husband. I came to you because I mistakenly thought you were the best." She gave Gigi a pointed look. "But maybe you've lost your touch."

"Teensy, evaluating Abigail is part of the process," Gigi said. "Girls?"

Ursula pulled the manila folder from her purse and Tess retrieved the large bulletin board from the other room. They'd barely stashed the evidence away when Abigail arrived.

"Your daughter will be one of our toughest cases yet," Gigi said.

"Is she that unlovable?" Teensy opened the folder.

"Not at all. Just that wounded." Gigi reached across the table, opened the folder, and flipped to a photo of Abigail and her former boyfriend— a Loves Park native named Jeremy who had dumped her and married Lynn St. James after dating her for only two months. To add insult to injury, the young couple wasted no time starting a family and had since produced three blond babies.

Teensy turned another photo over and gasped. "Where'd you get this?" She picked up the faded square photo of Abigail and her father.

"Oh, I found that in the church archives," Doris said. "We evaluate every aspect of a subject's life, Teensy."

"This isn't relevant." She tore the photo in half. "*He* isn't relevant."

A notable stillness passed through the room. Gigi knew Teensy still held a grudge, but she hadn't realized how big it was.

"You want to know why your daughter is still single, don't you?" Ursula's usually gruff voice sounded almost kind.

Teensy's eyes filled with tears. "*He* is not the reason Abigail hasn't found a husband."

"No, Teensy," Gigi replied quietly. "You are."

Teensy's face flashed anger. "Gigi Monroe, how dare you?"

Gigi had a long history with Abigail's mother. She knew the woman was difficult the day Teensy quit the Volunteers. It was only a week after her husband walked out, and she'd given a ludicrous excuse about having too many other commitments.

And now her anger had turned her into an obsessed mother who'd practically driven her daughter away from the one thing Teensy most wanted for her.

"I'm not trying to be unkind," Gigi said. "But maybe it's time to move on."

Teensy's jaw locked in defiance. "We're not talking about me, Gigi."

Gigi could see it was pointless to try to convince the other woman that she needed to let go of a grudge that was so many years old. "You did hire us. Stop signing her up for those terrible dating sites and let us do our job."

Flustered, Teensy picked up her purse and hugged it to her chest. "I did not come here to be insulted."

"We're not insulting you, Teensy, just asking you to give us space to do what we do," Gigi said. "For Abigail."

Teensy pressed her lips together and fidgeted for several long seconds. Finally she stood. "Fine. I'll leave you. But I'm telling you one last time—" she directed this at Ursula—"saving the store is not your priority. Saving my daughter is."

Evelyn—saint that she was—volunteered to drive Teensy home. Once they'd gone, the others sat in silence for a few long moments before resuming their conversation about Abigail Pressman, great-great-granddaughter of Loves Park's founders and the least likely to get married.

"This poor girl," Gigi said, examining Abigail's photo.

"Let's discuss what she has going for her," Doris said. "I always like when we compare and contrast. Makes me feel like a judge on one of those competition reality shows."

Ursula rolled her eyes. "You're no Heidi Klum, Doris."

Doris scowled.

Gigi stuck Abigail's photo on the bulletin board

and took a step back. "She's quite pretty, in a sweet way."

"She does have wonderful hair," Tess said. "And she's a little quirky but always looks very put together."

"She has a good heart," Doris said. "And she knows every single one of her customers by name."

"She's weak," Ursula said.

"We're doing the pros, Ursula. Say something nice." Doris sipped her drink and stared at the other woman, waiting.

Ursula said nothing.

"She's quite smart," Tess offered, a fact no one could argue. "But she doesn't think she wants to get married."

"Because she wants to be a successful businesswoman." Ursula's tone was like an audible eye roll.

Gigi squared off with her old friend. "Ursula, she *is* a successful businesswoman. Not everyone does business like they're part of the Mafia."

Ursula stared at her. "I resent that, Gigi."

"You know what I mean. Just because she's different doesn't mean she's not successful. This girl has a lot going for her, but I don't know anyone offhand who would be a good match for her."

Gigi had combed through their files of eligible bachelors and come up empty.

"She said the doctor was handsome," Ursula said.

Doris gasped. "The evil doctor who is trying to take over her building?"

"He's not evil," Tess said. "And he is quite handsome. I saw him the other day."

"I don't think he is right for Abigail," Gigi said matter-of-factly.

Ursula frowned. "Let's find out."

Gigi turned to her. She'd known Ursula since they were kids, and she knew there was little she could do to sway the old bat once her mind was made up. But in this case, for Abigail's sake, she had to try. "That is a very bad idea."

"He's handsome. Successful. And if he is a good match, he'll never kick her out of that building. Isn't that the goal here?" Ursula leaned back in the chair with a pleased look on her face.

"I thought the goal was to find her a husband," Tess said, wide-eyed.

"Exactly."

Ursula shrugged. "Two birds."

"Didn't Abigail say he has a girlfriend?" Evelyn asked.

"A businesswoman girlfriend who didn't sound very nice." Tess pulled her legs underneath her and cozied up in the chair.

"What's your point?" Ursula tossed another cookie in her mouth. "Girlfriends are not wives. Let me snoop around. I'll make an offer on the building. I should've bought it a long time ago anyway. Prime real estate. It's like a gold mine."

"And when he refuses your offer?"

The old woman smirked. "He won't refuse it. Everyone has a price, girls. Besides, it'll be just the excuse I need to find out some things about this doctor. Once he's not her landlord anymore, you'll see he's the perfect match."

Gigi sighed. "I'm not going to convince you this is a terrible idea, am I?"

Ursula stared her response.

"We need to be careful with Abigail. She's fragile."

"She does seem rather breakable, doesn't she?" Doris had taken on a maternal tone. "Perhaps trying to match her with her worst enemy isn't a good idea, Ursula."

"I do have a nephew," Ursula said, though her statement seemed to be less a response to Doris and more a side note in whatever conversation she was having with herself.

"We all have nephews," Gigi said. "But are any of them a good fit for Abigail?" She pulled the younger woman's photo off the bulletin board. "This isn't the kind of girl we can just throw out in the field. Her next date has to be the right date, or she'll bolt." Abigail had no reason to want to fall in love at all. Between her parents' failed marriage—something her mother clearly hadn't gotten over—and her own heartbreak with

Jeremy, it was no wonder the girl was still single.

"No." Ursula stood in front of Abigail's photo, studying it like she was planning a hit. "My nephew Duncan will be just what Abigail needs."

Chapter 10

The day Jacob closed on the building, he immediately ramped up his work on the interior. He started on the bathrooms, which desperately needed updating, and was thankful for the distraction of faulty pipes and old toilets.

He dragged a full garbage can out to the back alley, surprised to find Abigail closing the lid of the Dumpster. His wave was met with an icy stare. She quickly disappeared inside the back door of The Book Nook.

He deserved that.

After the way Kelly had dropped that bomb on her, he deserved worse. How he could simply stand by while the shark ate the helpless minnow, he had no idea. Not his finest hour.

But that didn't change the fact that he needed to get his practice off the ground. He had every right to open a medical office in Old Town Loves Park. In fact, he was convinced people would be grateful one day.

Today was not that day, however.

He shut the door behind him and moved toward the center of his empty building, plans for his renovation spread out across the counter.

As he stood in the center of the space, Jacob wondered if his relationship with his tenant could be salvaged. He glanced down at the plans. He had to admit the possibilities excited him. He hadn't been this excited about anything in a long time, and while he hadn't quite gotten over his ambivalence toward practicing medicine, throwing himself into this project might prove to be exactly what he needed.

Besides, what other option did he have? He had a little girl to consider. And maybe *he* didn't deserve to be happy, but she certainly did.

Jacob could appreciate Abigail's predicament, and he knew it was unlikely he'd ever earn her forgiveness. But his life with Junie was what mattered now.

Outside, a group of five women lingered on the sidewalk in front of The Book Nook. They stood for a few long moments, talking about who knew what. Then, in unison, all turned toward his building.

Jacob wasn't a good lip-reader, and he certainly wouldn't pretend he had any idea what women talked about among themselves. But if he had to guess, in this case he'd say it had something to do with him—and none of them looked happy.

Four of the ladies went inside Abigail's store,

but one of them, a tall elderly woman with a scowl on her weathered face and at least five necklaces hanging down past her scarf, headed straight for his front door. Surely she couldn't see that he was inside, could she?

She pressed her face to the window, then pounded on the frosted glass.

Who did this lady think she was?

Filled with dread, Jacob opened the front door. "Ma'am?"

The woman squinted at him. "Aren't you going to invite me in?"

"I wasn't going to, no."

She leaned in a bit closer—too close—until Jacob took a step back and let her pass. He shut the door behind her, but not before he thought about running down the street.

"Do you know who I am?" The woman moved to face him, still staring at him through narrow eyes.

"I'm sorry, ma'am. I don't."

"Hm." One sharp nod and the woman turned away, lips pursed with disapproval. "My husband is the reason you're standing here today."

Jacob leaned against the large wooden counter. "Oh? And have I ever met him?"

The woman picked up the end of her nappy gray scarf and tossed it over her shoulder. "Don't get smart with me, Doctor."

"I wouldn't dream of it." He ran a hand over his

whiskered chin as the woman took a step nearer.

"What are your plans for this place?" she asked.

"I guess you'll have to wait and see."

"I don't take well to a smart aleck, and I can see you've got smart aleck written all over you."

"No offense, but I don't take well to strangers barging into my building and asking me a bunch of questions before they've even told me their name."

"Ursula Pembrooke."

"Ursula."

"You can call me Mrs. Pembrooke."

Jacob thought better of responding.

"What possessed you to buy this building anyway? It's old with leaky pipes and a bad heating system." The old woman dropped her oversize purse on the counter and started rummaging through it. When he didn't respond, she peered at him from underneath a raised brow. "Well?"

"I thought it was a good investment. It's got that small-town charm everyone loves so much."

"Right, because charm is what I look for when I'm sick."

"Is there anything else I can do for you, Mrs. Pembrooke?"

After a few long seconds, the woman broke her stare. "How much?"

"Excuse me?"

She'd pulled out her checkbook and a pen and

now stared at him. "I know what you paid for it. What will you sell it for?"

Jacob's pulse quickened at the *click-click-click* of her pen. He frowned. "I'm not going to sell it for anything, ma'am. I'm going to renovate it and open up a new medical practice."

"Doc, you're new in town, so it's not likely you know how things work around here. There's the locals and there's the tourists. Which are you?"

"I'm not sure I follow."

"You're neither. You aren't local and you aren't just passing through. And this town doesn't take well to strangers, if you get my drift."

As much as he appreciated the Loves Park history lesson, *he* didn't take well to being threatened. "I'm not sure what you're after."

"I'm offering to take this building off your hands. Name your price."

All at once, his attempt at rebuilding a broken life felt like a huge mistake. Kelly had convinced him this was the perfect location to start over. Only two hours from Denver, which was where he and Junie had lived, Loves Park wasn't too far away. And she'd done her research and claimed he'd have a built-in clientele before he even opened. He didn't realize the town's ridiculous infatuation with love—something a grieving widower would just as soon forget—would get under his skin the way it was starting to.

What difference did that make, though? Jacob

couldn't uproot Junie again, not so soon after moving here, not after everything they'd been through. He had to make this work. He couldn't sell to Ursula Pembrooke even if he wanted to.

"I'm sorry, Mrs. Pembrooke," Jacob said. "I'm not selling it."

"You'd be crazy not to sell. You can take the money you make on this building and find another one."

"What's so special about this building?"

The old woman scoffed. "That's my business."

Now he regarded her more closely. "Did someone put you up to this?" His thoughts turned to a feisty brunette.

"Don't be ridiculous. I never do anything out of the goodness of my heart."

Now that he believed.

"How much?"

Jacob shook his head.

"Everyone has a price."

"Not everything is about money, ma'am."

She scoffed again, then met his eyes. "Oh, you're serious?"

Junie's face flashed through his mind. He could never put a price on a normal life for her. He owed her that. And he'd already worked too hard to find this place—he couldn't just let it go.

Ursula Pembrooke waved her checkbook in his face. "Last chance, Doc. This offer expires in ten seconds."

"Don't need the full ten," Jacob said. "You can put it away."

She glared at him. "Is this about your girlfriend?"

He crossed his arms over his chest. "What girlfriend?"

"The mean one with the slick black suit. You're doing this for her, right?"

They thought Kelly was his girlfriend? "If our business is done now, Mrs. Pembrooke . . ." He moved toward the door. "Thanks for stopping by." He opened the door and waited until she finally shoved her checkbook back into her bag.

"You're making a huge mistake," she said as she left.

He watched her trudge over to The Book Nook, where he imagined she'd meet with the woman who put her up to this in the first place.

Abigail Pressman might have seemed sweet as sugar on the surface, but Jacob had the distinct impression there was a fiery side to her that would do anything to get him out of this building—even solicit the help of crazy rich women.

He didn't know whether to be angry or impressed, but he did know that he likely had a battle in front of him. And he wouldn't stop until he'd made a new life for himself and his daughter.

Even if it meant that Abigail Pressman and her little bookstore were collateral damage.

Chapter 11

Abigail still hadn't painted the armoire waiting in her workshop.

She'd left Gigi's house the night of the meeting with a new stack of envelopes—those that didn't necessarily need a response.

"You can't mess anything up with these," Tess said, handing her the box. "Be as clumsy as you want."

Abigail stared at the hodgepodge of envelopes in the box, none of them opened. "What are these?"

"Sometimes people get confused," Doris said. "It happens to the best of us."

"We get all kinds of letters," Ursula said, ignoring Doris. "Like kids writing letters to Santa, only they're usually really depressing and whiny." She sized up Abigail from behind her reading glasses. "You'll probably love them."

Judging by Ursula's tone, that wasn't a compliment.

"What do you want me to do with them?" Abigail riffled through the envelopes. The handwritten addresses on the fronts had gotten them delivered to the Valentine Volunteers, though she couldn't quite understand how. Most were addressed to the Loves Park postmaster. Many of them had no return addresses.

"Read them. See if anyone is in immediate danger. Report back." Gigi had moved them all into the kitchen, where they now stood around her island.

Ursula continued to scarf down cookies while they stood there sorting through Abigail's new assignment.

"That's it?"

"Sometimes we're the only people who ever know how the authors of these letters are really feeling," Gigi said.

"We could prevent a suicide. Or—" Doris's eyes widened—"a murder."

"Have you ever prevented a suicide or a murder by reading these letters?" Abigail asked, flipping through a couple of nondescript envelopes.

Doris pressed her lips together. "There's a first time for everything."

"We respond to the ones with return addresses," Gigi explained. "Those people would only put their addresses if they wanted a response."

"So you want me to write back to these people?" Abigail would rather stamp gold-embossed wedding invitations, which said something about how much she dreaded this task since she'd prefer to have twenty-eight cavities at the same time than stamp gold-embossed wedding invitaions.

"You can do it, dear. You own a bookstore." Gigi smiled as if what she'd just said made sense. "Besides, it's in your blood."

And there it was again. Her legacy of romance —the one she'd been trying to escape for most of her adult life. Ever since Jeremy. Or if she was honest, since her early teens when her father ran off, leaving his family on their own and The Book Nook in the hands of a manager.

Abigail had stuffed the box in her bag and dragged it around with her ever since, but she'd yet to open it up.

Tonight, she told herself. Furniture painting and loads of depressing love letters.

What could be better?

Abigail stood behind the counter, purposefully ignoring the Valentine Volunteers, most of whom had overtaken the big table in the back as usual. Whatever "business" they had to tend to, they certainly did take it seriously. They chattered away, with the exception of Evelyn, who appeared to be lost in her own world.

Sometimes Abigail wondered what went on in Evelyn Brandt's head. She always seemed pre-occupied, as though she had a pile of other thoughts on her mind. Though Evelyn had given up painting years ago, Abigail wondered if she still saw visions of objects coming together on canvas.

There had to be a reason for the absent look in her eyes.

The door swung open and Ursula stormed in, the last to arrive. She took one look at Abigail and practically growled, "That man is a real piece of work."

Abigail moved out from behind the counter and followed Ursula to the big table. Ursula dropped her huge bag on the table and turned to Abigail. "You've got your work cut out for you with that one."

"What are you talking about?" What had Ursula done? Abigail's heart felt like it was being gripped in a vise.

"The doctor. I went to see him. Made him an offer."

"An offer for what?"

"The building, you ninny." Ursula practically spat the words into Abigail's face.

"I take it he didn't go for it."

"Turned me down flat. Stupid man. He doesn't know who he's messing with."

Abigail joined the others in staring at Ursula, who must be unaccustomed to not getting her way. She decided it wasn't the best time to remind the old woman to fight or die.

"I appreciate you trying to help me, Ursula."

"I didn't do it for you." She plunked herself down on one of the seats. "I'm so bored my eyes are crossing. That man hasn't seen the last of Ursula Pembrooke."

Abigail sat down. "I think we should just let it go."

Ursula leaned in, that same disgusted expression on her face. "Fight or die, Pressman."

She heard Doris let out a quiet "Oh, my."

"What else can be done?" Abigail asked. "He bought the building fair and square. With cash."

Ursula's bushy eyebrows drew together in one pronounced line. "Is that right? Well, Mr. Buy-It-in-Cash has met his match. Frankie taught me well. I'll find a way to get us this building fair and square. And if that doesn't work, I'll find a way to get it not so fair and square."

"Abigail, maybe you should go. I want to be sure you have plausible deniability." Gigi shot Ursula a look, but the other woman seemed unfazed.

Abigail stood. "I appreciate it, but I'll be fine. They said I had at least another year. Plenty of time to figure out a plan B."

Even as she said the words, Abigail's stomach turned. She supposed she could start looking for a new space. Or close the shop altogether, regardless of the hours she'd poured into it.

How this stranger could waltz in and destroy her livelihood without a second thought, she'd never understand. She'd never met anyone so heartless.

As these thoughts entered her mind, she caught a glimpse of Dr. Jacob Willoughby out back, hauling garbage. He'd obviously wasted no time making that space his own. She'd already run into him at the Dumpster once. She'd have to get Aaron to take the garbage out from now on.

Panic shot through her mind, spinning her stomach in a loop-the-loop. How long until he brought up Abigail's rental agreement? Was her lease even valid anymore? She had the distinct impression Jacob's girlfriend wanted her out sooner rather than later. He could put her out tomorrow if he wanted to. At least, Abigail assumed he could. She needed a lawyer. But how could she afford that?

She returned to the counter, where Mallory stood shaking her head.

"What?"

"I hope you aren't listening to those women," she said. "That good-looking doctor is a man. Make him like you and he won't evict you. Better yet, make him fall in love with you and he'll *give* you the building."

Her manager winked and walked away, but her words lingered. She'd said it like it was the simplest idea in the world. *"Make him like you."* But Abigail had never been very good at making anyone like her—especially not men.

No, she was better at hiding in the background.

"In order to make him like me, I'd have to spend time with him," Abigail said, following Mallory to the other side of the store.

Mallory shot her a look. "Duh."

"Not gonna happen." Abigail walked away. As she passed by the table of Valentine Volunteers, she overheard one of them say, "What if we *accidentally* broke things on this side of the building? Leaky pipes. Bad plumbing. The cost of repairs could sink the good doctor."

Abigail made a beeline for her office. Too many opinions had her head spinning. Ursula was right about one thing, though. She couldn't keep feeling sorry for herself. She had to do something to save the business her father had given to her care.

But what?

She sat in the quiet office for several long moments, relishing the silence and wishing for more of it. Life was too loud right now. Made it nearly impossible to daydream, let alone make any actual plans. And when it came to hearing God—forget about it.

The noise had a way of drowning out the still, small voice Abigail used to know how to hear.

Fight or die.

What did that even mean? Abigail wasn't the type to wage war on other human beings. It wasn't in her nature. Maybe her mother was right—this business was just a way to pass the time until she found a husband.

But with no prospects and another birthday just around the corner, she had to make the most of what she had. She had to fight.

The witch's theme from *The Wizard of Oz* rang out from her phone. Abigail groaned and shut the door. When Abigail's brother, Justin, set her phone to play this ringtone whenever Teensy called, their mother was not amused. Justin would do anything for a laugh. That was just his way. He'd be content with his current lifestyle—living on a beach and renting surfboards to tourists— regardless of whether it paid the bills.

Oh, to be that relaxed.

It tormented their mother to have a son as smart and handsome as Justin who seemed to have no goals or aspirations. Justin always told her he'd grow up "later."

But here he was, twenty-seven years old, and "later" still hadn't come.

The ringtone persisted. The memory of her brother's musical prank might have made Abigail laugh if it didn't mean her mother was waiting to talk to her right now. She gritted her teeth and took the call.

"Hi, Mom."

"Can you pick up some rolls on your way to dinner?"

"Dinner?" If horror had a sound, Abigail's voice had just found it.

"You forgot." A statement. Not a question.

"I didn't—" Abigail braced herself for Teensy's martyr persona, her mind trying to locate the precise moment she'd agreed to have dinner with her mother.

"Of course you forgot. You're so busy being a

business owner." The way she hung on the words twisted something in Abigail's stomach. "Your sister is coming. She has news."

"What kind of news?" Abigail propped her elbows on the desk, her thoughts turning to Betsy. The youngest of the three Pressman kids, Betsy had settled in Boulder after college, though *settled* might not have been the best word to describe her little sister. Everything about Betsy was laid-back and carefree—like a gypsy, and most certainly not like Abigail.

How had she become the lone responsible one of the family? Or maybe a better question would be *why* she had become the lone responsible one. Didn't Justin or Betsy feel the pressure to do something great with their lives? To be more than their parents were?

Or was that feeling relegated to Abigail?

But if Betsy was in town, Abigail supposed she had to go to dinner. It had been a while since they'd seen each other.

"She said it was a surprise," Teensy replied. "Hopefully she's not starting a business too. See you at six."

Her mother hung up before Abigail could protest. Or think of a reason to say no. Or pack her bags and drive far away.

Ugh.

What news could Betsy possibly have to share? Last time Abigail talked to her sister, she was considering some marine biology expedition in Florida. It's what she'd done since graduating college—flit from thing to thing like a bumblebee in a box of daisies. Why their mother had no problem with that, Abigail would never know, but she had to admit Betsy had a lot more vision than appearances indicated. It was unfair, though—if Teensy was disappointed in her business owner daughter, how could she not have a heart attack over her swimming-with-sharks daughter?

Abigail pulled up to her mother's house, dinner rolls in hand, and took a breath before going inside.

"God, I need your help if I'm going to get out of here alive," she said under her breath, feeling a whole lot like Daniel must've right before they threw him in the lions' den.

These family dinners never went according to Teensy's plan. And, boy, did she always have a plan. She had a knack for setting herself up for disappointment.

Abigail let herself in the side door of her mother's home and inhaled the smell of pot roast. At least she'd be well fed.

Teensy's house was cozy. Small since it was just her, but homey in spite of, well, Teensy. Abigail hadn't spent much time there, as her mother had moved in after Abigail had her own place. It was as if she'd been waiting since the day Daddy left to get out of the home they shared, and finally, after her children were grown, she had permission to make the change. She'd been so heartbroken by his betrayal and embarrassed given the family's love legacy. A part of her had never recovered.

Maybe Abigail and her mother did have something in common after all.

At least in her mom's new house, she didn't have images of her father. So many moments she'd rather forget, like the night he packed a small suitcase and walked out the door.

Her mom had collapsed in a heap in the entryway then, sobs overtaking her body while Abigail, who was barely thirteen, took her siblings into her room, guarding them from the vision of their mother falling apart.

After Betsy and Justin had gone to bed, Abigail peeked in on her mother and saw, for the first time, how a broken heart could steal someone's spirit. It was as if the life had been drained from her mother's face. Like someone reached inside her and tore her soul clean away.

Despite her father's shortcomings, though, Abigail knew he had been a good dad to them while they were all together. Sometimes she missed him so much, she awoke in the middle of the night with an aching pain down in the recesses of her soul.

Everyone said time would heal that. So far it hadn't. Even now, all these years later, the memory of that night—the night everything changed—made her fingers tingle. The Pressman family spent years not knowing why their father didn't want them anymore. And even though he visited his children now and then, it was never the same. His choice changed everything. Did he know what he'd put them through?

She still regretted never asking him that question.

She said another prayer, silent this time, as she did whenever her father came to mind. *I forgive him,* she prayed, though the words felt anything but true. How could she love someone so much and be so angry with him at the same time?

She stood in the kitchen and inhaled deeply, listening to the chatter from the other room—Teensy, Betsy, and a man whose voice she didn't recognize. Justin had texted her from Belize or some other tiny, sunny country just yesterday, so it wasn't him. She fought the jealousy that crept in when she thought about her brother and the haphazard backpacking trip he was taking with three old college buddies who also didn't realize they were on the back half of their twenties.

She edged toward the living room. When she stepped on a creaky floorboard, she cringed, knowing what would come next.

Teensy flew into the kitchen. If there'd been a baseball bat handy, the woman might've clocked Abigail on the head.

Teensy gasped. "Abigail! What are you doing sneaking around like a burglar?"

"I wasn't sneaking, Mother. I was just . . . preparing myself."

Teensy frowned. "For what?"

"Never mind. Is Betsy here?" She'd barely gotten the words out when her sister squealed her way into the room. A vision in a white sundress with a dainty cardigan, Betsy still looked like a college sorority girl even though she'd graduated college three years prior. Full blonde curls cascaded down her back, and her big brown eyes were bright and sparkly, like the eyes of a person who had no idea every one of her dreams wouldn't come true.

Abigail had always been the more realistic of the two. She shoved aside her pessimism as her sister pulled her into a hug. Abigail reminded herself not to tense up at her touch. *She's your sister.*

Her younger, bubblier, always-had-to-be-the-center-of-attention sister.

Okay, that wasn't fair. But Abigail's shyness certainly stood out when she was in Betsy's shadow. People always gravitated to the youngest Pressman.

They said Betsy was warm and inviting. Abigail—difficult to know. She supposed it was true, but could she help it if she preferred not to rush into relationships that could eventually disappoint her?

"Oh, Abigail, you look like you need a spa day," Betsy said, stepping back and studying her.

"I think so too," their mother said. "I have a cream for those dark circles under your eyes."

Betsy's laugh could only be described as buoyant as she abruptly changed the subject. "I have a surprise."

Teensy let out a squeak, and within seconds, the two of them had practically swallowed Abigail, leaning close, voices lowered as if secrets were the order of the day.

"There's someone I want you to meet," Betsy said as their mother linked her arm through Abigail's, two Pressmans ganging up on a third.

"She's met someone," Teensy hissed.

Abigail's tongue went numb. "Oh, really?"

Betsy had always had boyfriends—boys loved having Betsy on their arm—but she'd never been serious about any of them and she'd rarely brought them home. It was the only thing she and Abigail had in common these days, their unified front against their mother.

I don't need a man to be happy.

Before she could get control of her spiraling thoughts, a man appeared in the kitchen doorway. A man who looked like a walking cliché—six feet tall, dark, and handsome.

Betsy flashed her left hand in Abigail's face. "We're engaged!"

Shrill gasps and sighs filled the kitchen,

reminding Abigail of everything she'd hated about junior high school. At that age, girls became giddy over boys, and in this town, it seemed to continue well into adulthood. No wonder Abigail was still single. She'd never been that way.

"Abigail," Betsy said, taking her hand, "this is Romano." Abigail couldn't be sure, but she thought Betsy might've slipped into an Italian accent as she said his name. Betsy led her over to the doorway, in front of the hulking giant who took up the space of two normal-size people. "He's Italian."

Teensy's face resembled something straight out of a classic romance movie. Abigail tried not to look disgusted.

"We met through my friend Joy. She thought we'd hit it off." Betsy giggled. "She was right."

Romano took Abigail's hand, drew it to his lips, and kissed it, all while maintaining unnerving eye contact with her. "So nice to meet you," he murmured.

Betsy leaned in. "Swoony, right?"

"Bets," Abigail said, pulling her hand away and wiping it on her jeans. "Can I talk to you in the other room?"

Her sister and the Italian exchanged some sort of knowing glance, the kind of silent communication Abigail would never understand—at least never again. She shook off thoughts of Jeremy.

She pulled Betsy into the den, the room farthest

away from the kitchen, and closed the door. "What has gotten into you?"

Betsy's smile faded. "What do you mean?"

"Who *are* you out there? You're practically drooling. Over a guy. You're like one of those sappy girls we used to make fun of."

Betsy whisked across the room and sat on the ugly floral armchair their mother refused to throw away. "Abigail, I'm in love. I can't explain it. I guess we were wrong all those years when we were making fun of those sappy girls." She shrugged. "We just hadn't experienced it yet."

A glazed-over look washed across Betsy's face. Abigail recognized the expression. Hopeless romantic. Head in the clouds. Begging for devastation. "What about Florida?"

"I don't have time for that now. We've still got the whole wedding to plan. Oh, that reminds me. We're getting married on Valentine's Day. Will you be my maid of honor?"

"Valentine's Day? Betsy! Why the rush? How long have you known this guy? And what about all the big dreams you have?"

"Now I have big dreams with Romano. He's a soccer player. I'm going to travel with his team. See the world."

Abigail could not believe what she was hearing. Her sister was about to make the biggest mistake of her life, and she couldn't even see it because she'd convinced herself this was love. Had she learned nothing from Abigail's own heartbreak?

Betsy frowned. "Why do you have that look on your face?"

"What look?" How could she tell Betsy what she really thought without destroying their relationship? She didn't pretend very well.

"That disapproving-big-sister look." Betsy stood. "I know what you're thinking, and I don't want to hear the cynicism right now, Abigail. Someday, when you meet the right person, you'll understand. You'll turn into one of those girls you've always despised. That's the power of love." She took Abigail's hand. "They're not all like him, you know."

Abigail ignored this last statement. "None of that will ever happen." *And I resent your Disney princess tone of voice.*

Betsy steeled her jaw. "You're going to end up alone if you keep this up, Abigail."

Abigail did a little steeling of her own jaw and squared off with her sister. "What is that supposed to mean?"

"You are so closed off. You refuse to put yourself out there. You think that you—all by yourself—are more than enough, and you're not."

The words burrowed their way into Abigail's heart, but she quickly recovered. "Don't act like you've got everything all figured out in the love and romance department, Betsy. Not everyone has to rush into marriage to be happy. In fact, lots of people do it and end up divorced a year later."

"You think we're going to end up divorced?"

Abigail groaned. "That's not what I meant and you know it."

"What I know is that you are too scared to admit that you want someone to love you—and if you keep that up, no one ever will." Betsy walked out of the den, through the living room, and into the arms of her too-good-looking soon-to-be-husband.

Hot tears stung Abigail's eyes.

Not because what Betsy had said hurt her feelings but because Abigail feared her sister's words might actually be true.

Abigail was on the fast track to solitude, but she didn't see another way to keep from dealing with more disappointment or another broken heart. Betsy simply hadn't been at this long enough to know that the risk of being let down was very high. And the only way to protect yourself from that kind of pain was not to let anyone get too close.

Quietly, she let herself out the side door, more aware than ever just how important her business really was.

Chapter 12

"You're not seriously considering this." Kelly walked in the front door of his house and tucked her phone into her purse.

Jacob had been sitting on this offer from Ursula Pembrooke for days, but he couldn't shake the idea that he'd made a mistake in choosing the Old Town building.

"Shouldn't we think about it?" He took her coat and hung it on one of the hooks by the front door.

"No. After all that hunting, you found the perfect space. It's unique and unexpected. Why on earth are you letting this Pembrooke woman get to you?" She dropped her purse on his kitchen counter and fished a Diet Coke from his fridge. She cracked it open, took a drink, then eyed him. "Oh."

"Oh, what?"

"It's not Ursula Pembrooke who's gotten to you, is it?" She set the cold can on the counter with a clang.

"I don't know what you're talking about." Jacob pulled out one of the barstools at the island and sat down. "Can we discuss the renovations?"

"It's the book girl."

Jacob scoffed. "You're being ridiculous, Kelly."

"No, I'm not. That girl has gotten under your

skin, and you can't bear the thought of putting her out." Kelly moved around the island and faced him. "Jacob, you have to toughen up if you're going to do this."

"I'm plenty tough, thanks." But Kelly knew him too well. He didn't like the idea of kicking Abigail out—of being the one to swoop in and steal the business she worked so hard for right out from under her.

He'd been so convinced that throwing himself into this project, opening a new practice, was the best idea, but every time he caught Abigail glaring in the general direction of his side of the building, he questioned his resolve.

Kelly stood right in front of him now. "Jacob, I get it. You're a nice guy. You don't want to be the reason she has to file bankruptcy."

Oh, man. He hadn't even thought of that.

"Why don't you let me handle these decisions?" She put her hands on his shoulders and turned him toward her. "That way your kind bedside manner stays intact, but we still end up with what we need for the practice to get off the ground."

He stiffened at her nearness, but before he could pull away, she took a step back, dropping her hands from his shoulders. "Gwen always said you were the good guy."

His pulse quickened at the mention of his wife's name. "I hate to tell you this, Kelly, but where I come from, that's not something to be ashamed of."

A smirk played at the corners of her mouth. "Of course not. I'm just not sure it makes you a natural businessperson."

"I disagree. I appreciate your expertise, but if this is going to be my practice, we've got to run it my way. I'm not interested in hurting people."

Kelly put a hand on her hip. "You know what else Gwen said?" She locked onto his eyes.

Jacob leveled his gaze.

"That you always had to be the hero."

"Well, we both know how that turned out, don't we?" Jacob didn't want to think about Gwen or his failed attempts to be the hero.

"You're too hard on yourself, Doc," Kelly said. "All I know is that you don't have to be book girl's hero. For the time being, you're her land-lord. Nothing more." She took a step back, still studying him.

He shifted. She was right. He only needed to be one person's hero: Junie's. He glanced at Kelly. "Why are you staring at me?"

She shrugged. "Maybe I just like what I see." A smile played at her mouth and she tossed her hair over her shoulder.

"Kelly, I appreciate everything you're doing to help me here, but—"

She waved him off. "Oh, Jacob, don't be so serious. I just like to admire things that look good. That's all." She took another drink of her Diet Coke. "Besides, Gwen was like a sister to me."

He didn't like talking about Gwen. He didn't like her talking about Gwen.

"I miss her too, you know."

He looked at Kelly and for a fleeting moment remembered how Gwen's death had devastated her. Sometimes he forgot he wasn't the only one hurting over the loss.

She turned away. "Promise me something." Kelly reached down and started shuffling through her purse. "No more talk about selling this building. This is the best plan—let's run with it."

He stood, suddenly feeling claustrophobic. "It was a serious offer. I thought we should at least consider it. It has nothing to do with Abigail."

Kelly rolled her eyes. "Even the way you say her name."

"That's her name, Kelly. How do you want me to say it?" He didn't have time to be psycho-analyzed.

Kelly reached across the island and stilled him with her touch, covering his hand with her own. "You're doing this for Junie, right?"

Yes. Junie. That's why he was doing this. He nodded.

"That's all that matters." Kelly sounded so matter-of-fact. "I mean, really, who's more important? Book girl or your daughter?"

Obviously that was a rhetorical question.

He didn't answer.

Instead he flipped open one of the folders Kelly

had set on the counter. "Should we look at these contractor bids?"

Kelly flashed him a smile as if to give her approval. Not that he needed or wanted it. "I've made some notes about each of these options."

Jacob spent the rest of the night listening to Kelly explain the pros and cons of each and every inch of their plans, but he found his mind wandering as it often did when Gwen's name came up. Here he was, knee-deep in a fresh start, yet still imagining what Gwen would say about this new adventure.

"You get to set your own hours? Maybe now you can spend more time at home. You deserve that, Jacob."

Gwen had always been disappointed by the long hours he had to work. She understood and never nagged, but he'd left her and Junie alone for too many nights. And too many mornings, she'd woken up to find his side of the bed empty.

He'd been so absent, even when he was present.

Not this time. Junie might've lost her mother, but she wasn't going to lose her father too. He had to make up for the way he'd failed her. This time he'd do things the way he should've done them when Gwen was still alive.

As if that could make up for his part in her death.

"Daddy?"

Junie's voice snapped him back to reality. He'd

121

scheduled the meeting for after her bedtime on purpose, but looking at her now, he felt like he hadn't really seen her in days. The rides to and from school were hurried, and his daughter rarely spoke.

"Hey, Mouse," he said, moving toward her. "What are you doing up?"

She stared at the floor.

"Another bad dream?" He kept his voice soft, almost a whisper.

She nodded.

"I'll take you back." He scooped her up, wishing his arms were strong enough to protect her from the demons that haunted them both. *God, I can get through this, but Junie? Can you show a little mercy?*

Once he'd tucked her back in bed, he sat in silence for a moment.

"Daddy? Will you pray for me?"

His stomach sank at the simple, honest request of a frightened child. He didn't feel like praying. God could've prevented all this pain in the first place, but he hadn't.

Why should they be on speaking terms now?

"Please?"

Jacob swallowed in spite of his dry mouth. "Sure, Mouse." He watched as she closed her eyes and folded her hands, placing them just below her chin.

Why was it so hard to find the words for a

simple prayer? Had it really been that long?

"Lord," he said, closing his eyes, "thank you for my daughter. She is so funny and smart and kind, and I am so glad I get to be her dad." He opened his eyes and saw Junie peering at him through one open eye. She quickly closed it as if she'd been caught.

God, I love this girl. Take this pain away from her. Please.

"Keep going, Daddy," she whispered.

"I pray that all the scary thoughts and dreams go away so she can rest. Send your angels to watch over her tonight, Lord, and bring her peaceful sleep. In Jesus' name . . ."

"Amen." Junie smiled. "I can sleep now, Daddy. Thanks."

He kissed her forehead and closed the door, stepping into the dimly lit hallway. Sadness wrapped itself around his heart and squeezed.

It shamed him that it took a request from his little girl for him to offer up any kind of prayer.

Rustling in the other room drew his attention, and he forced himself to regain his composure. He returned to the kitchen, where Kelly was packing up the files she'd strewn over the counter.

"Leaving?" He sat across from her.

"You seem preoccupied," she said.

"Sorry." He pulled one of the folders from the pile. What had they been discussing? He flipped open. Contractors. "I like these guys. They aren't the cheapest, but they aren't the most expensive either, and I asked around. They have a good reputation."

Kelly frowned. "Well, it's your call," she said. "But I'd probably go with this one." She slid another folder toward him across the island, letting her hand linger on it until he reached out and took the file.

Jacob hadn't dated anyone since Gwen died, but he wasn't an idiot. He'd begun to wonder if this whole thing was just a way for Kelly to spend time with him.

Didn't it matter to her that he was Gwen's husband? She said it did, but her actions told a different story.

The thought met resistance as soon as it entered his mind. What was he thinking? He was nobody's husband. He could date Kelly—or anyone else—and it would be perfectly acceptable. Acceptable to others, that is.

"I'll look them over," Jacob said, though he'd already decided on the first option.

She smiled. "You always seem so stressed-out, Doc."

Something else Gwen had told her?

"You need a good massage."

Jacob stood. "No, just a good night's sleep."

She gave him a once-over and shrugged. "About that."

Uh-oh.

"Can I just crash on your couch? I thought the drive wouldn't get to me, but two hours is a lot when it's this late." Before he could respond, she'd already made up her mind. "You won't even know I'm here, and I get up before the sun, so I'll be out of your hair nice and early—before Junie even wakes up."

Two hours was a long way at this time of night. He shrugged assent, and she leaned forward and kissed his cheek "Thanks, Doc."

She disappeared into the bathroom, leaving Jacob wondering where the extra blankets were, but knowing Kelly, she'd figured that out too.

As he lay in bed, he already regretted the idea and even wondered if he should lock his bedroom door.

Don't flatter yourself, Jacob.

But Kelly was the kind of forward he didn't much care for. And while he didn't have any problem telling her what he thought, he saw no reason for a confrontation—especially since he needed her help.

Still, what if Junie woke up again and found a woman on the couch? Worse, what if Kelly took too long in the morning and Junie started asking questions? The last thing he wanted was to give his daughter any reason to question his integrity.

His thoughts quickly turned to Abigail and her henchwoman, Ursula Pembrooke. The plan they'd hatched had failed, and while Jacob felt bad about that, Kelly was right. He had a little girl to think about and a new life to build.

He hoped one day Abigail would understand.

Chapter 13

After she left her mom's house, Abigail finally sanded and primed the armoire in her workshop, which didn't do as much to relieve her stress as she'd hoped. Weariness washed over her, though her mind was wide-awake.

Over and over, she replayed her conversation with her sister, wishing she could turn back the clock and be properly happy that Betsy had found someone worth loving. It wasn't Abigail's place to judge her sister's choices. It's not like she'd had any success in this area.

But she had to admit, Betsy's lack of discernment wasn't the main thing troubling her. Abigail allowed her sister's words to claw at her like a kitten with a ball of yarn. Both Betsy and their mother seemed intent on believing Abigail wasn't really happy. And that she'd never be happy until she found a man, got married, and had a bunch of kids.

A faint image of a happy family flittered through her thoughts. It happened sometimes that she'd see herself in her own mind's eye, laughing with a child on her lap and a faceless husband's arms wrapped around them both.

Fantasy.

Angry, she shoved the image aside. No. Betsy was wrong. Abigail could manage on her own. She had been doing it for years.

And yet, lately, the store had caused her nothing but worry. She *had* to figure out a way to convince that doctor and his dragon lady girlfriend that kicking her out was a terrible mistake.

Unsure of her next step, she did what she always did when her brain had reached its capacity for complicated thoughts. She pulled out her journal to make a list of her concerns, but as she flipped through the pages, she discovered all the other lists she'd made in moments like these. She even found a floor plan of what she'd hoped her expanded store would look like, complete with furniture and signage all sketched to scale.

It was good to see all those frivolous art classes had paid off. At least she had a very clear picture of what the business could have been.

Brainstorming about her business—and experimenting with various furniture restoration techniques she'd use for her future inventory—consumed much of her free time, and she'd come up with countless ways to promote The Book Nook once the whole building was hers. It would be like a grand reopening.

Live music. Concerts by local musicians.
Free coffee and snacks.
Kids' story time with crafts based on the books.
Exhibitions by Loves Park artists.

She'd had these ideas for months, but until now she'd only imagined implementing them once she owned the whole building. But maybe they could play a defensive role as well. After all, if she could prove to her irritating new landlord that she had a valuable business, one the town supported, he wouldn't kick her out—would he?

If he did, then he'd be shooting himself in the foot.

Abigail already had the hometown advantage—maybe she just needed to tap into that a little more. She needed to stay focused and determine how to get more people in the door. And then, how to get them to really fall in love with The Book Nook.

Abigail rolled her eyes at the thought. Like she could get anyone to fall in love.

Discouragement wound its way through her. She could always tackle plan C: find a new building.

Her heart dropped. The Book Nook had been in her family for so many years. All those mornings she'd helped Daddy put books away—the store was *their* place. When her father left, she swore she'd never return to the little shop, no matter how much she yearned for the quiet solitude it provided.

It took a long time, but eventually, after her dad was gone, she learned to appreciate it for what it was—the one place where she still felt like she belonged.

The day he left, she assumed he'd also sold the business. She didn't know until eight years ago, when his will was read, that he'd been saving it for her. He'd hired an old friend to manage the place for him, but The Book Nook still belonged to him. And he'd left it to her in his will.

He didn't own the building, but he'd negotiated the terms with Harriet.

And Abigail had come to love it.

How could she not adore the thick crown molding and the built-in bookshelves? The wide-planked wood floors and the way it now smelled of coffee and books? She'd grown to appreciate the buzz of energy every day when locals conducted business meetings, artists searched for inspiration, and friends met and chatted right here in her shop.

Daddy would be so proud of her. He'd been a lousy husband to Teensy, but he'd always been Abigail's biggest fan.

An image of her father flashed through her mind. If she concentrated long enough, she could see every line on his face when he smiled at her.

He never had explained why he left. Or why

leaving Teensy meant walking out altogether.

Had he missed their Saturday mornings as much as she did?

She supposed so. Otherwise he would've sold the shop and called it good. Instead he gave the business to her. And she couldn't bear the thought of losing it.

Abigail stopped and reread her list. The shop was already cute—all she needed to do was play it up. She'd resisted that for so many years. But if she had to tap into what Loves Park loved, so be it. Even if what Loves Park loved was what Abigail loathed.

She read over her list again. She obviously knew how this town worked. She knew what they would get behind—what they would fight for.

And though people did, in fact, need the occasional trip to the doctor, the fact remained that most people came to Loves Park for the charm and sentimentality.

Abigail smiled to herself, finally feeling like she had some sense of direction.

She'd remind Loves Park why they adored The Book Nook. She'd make it irresistible, and Dr. Jacob Willoughby would be so enthralled with it himself, he'd decide forcing her out was the biggest mistake he could make.

Never mind that she still needed to see if he'd even honor her rental agreement with Harriet. She should be paying more, and she knew it, but

Harriet had a soft spot for single young women trying to make it. Not soft enough to wait to sell until Abigail could pay for the building, mind you, but still soft. Besides, her father had gotten the rental agreement in writing—and he'd watched out for his daughter. As if he somehow knew that one day, everything could change.

Abigail had a sneaking suspicion the doctor and his "partner" had no soft spot and no inkling of how to honor someone else's agreement.

Even Daddy couldn't have foreseen that.

Her homework from the Valentine Volunteers stared at her from the other side of the room. She pulled the box with the castoff letters onto the bed and removed the lid—not that she wanted to read about unrequited love, but maybe drowning herself in someone else's sorrows was the way to forget her own.

She riffled through the stack of envelopes until she found a pink one with frilly handwriting on the front. It was addressed to "Cupid."

Abigail rolled her eyes. She knew the kinds of letters she was in for. *The guy I love doesn't love me back. Is there anything I can do?* Somehow she'd turned into the Dear Abby of Loves Park. The very thought of it warranted another eye roll.

Who was she to give romantic advice? If anything, she should be the one writing in.

She sighed and opened the letter. Sure enough, she found exactly what she expected.

Dear Cupid,

Finally, after years of being alone, I've fallen head over heels in love. There's just one problem. The man is my sister's husband.

Abigail flicked the letter to the other side of the bed. It drifted to the floor.

Next.

Dear Whoever-You-Are,

My name is Justus Mulligan and I'm in federal prison. I'm looking for someone to spend quality time with.

Flick. Next.

Dear Loves Park Cupid,

I've lived in this Sweetheart City my whole life. I know this isn't the real purpose of these letters, but sadly I have no wedding invitations to send you because I have no fiancé. No boyfriend. No prospects. It's kind of depressing watching everyone else grow up and find the perfect person when I've never even come close.

Abigail could've written this one herself.

I'm pretty fun-loving. I mean, people like me, but mostly guys think of me as their friend. I'm a great shoulder to cry on. This Valentine's

Day, for once, I just want to have someone special in my life. Friends are great and everything, but I'm almost thirty. Well, I'm three years away from thirty. That's too old to be alone.

Abigail turned thirty this year. What did that make her?

Hopeless.

I guess I just wanted to put it out there. A prayer, maybe, that finally this year might be my year. The year someone looks at me as more than just a friend.

Abigail went back and reread the letter. The prayer.

She'd been plenty angry with God over the years when relationships didn't work out. When she first realized the whole town's idea of romance was a fairy tale. When her parents split up. When Jeremy left. When she put herself out there and suffered for it. But had she ever even prayed that she'd find someone to share her life with?

Had she prayed when she started dating Jeremy in the first place?

Had she ever trusted God with this worry?

She'd been so caught up in her self-pity that she'd failed to ask God to intervene—yet she'd blamed him when he didn't.

Somehow she always assumed it was up to her to figure out this part of her life, but maybe she'd given herself too much credit.

Maybe, for once, she should stop trying to handle everything on her own and actually let God have some control in her life.

Did she even know how to do that? Really?

She shoved the letters back in the box and closed the lid.

Enough love for one night. Enough love for a lifetime. She was perfectly happy with her life the way it was. Well, she had been happy—before the doctor came to town. She'd focus on making sure everything went back to normal. That was the goal.

Save her store. Get her life back. And try to figure out what love meant for her anyway.

Chapter 14

After a restless—worthless—night of sleep, Jacob awoke Saturday morning hoping Kelly had kept her word and left before Junie got up, but when he stepped into the kitchen and saw her purse still sitting on the counter, he knew that was just wishful thinking.

A pot of fresh coffee welcomed him. He poured a cup, wondering when his houseguest would be done in the bathroom and on the road back to Denver.

He was thankful he and Kelly didn't talk shop on the weekends. Sure, he had a building to renovate and boxes to unpack, but he'd promised Junie his weekends were hers. How could he politely get his business partner out the door?

Junie's bedroom door opened, and his little girl stumbled out into the hallway, hair messed up, sleepiness still on her face. Seconds later, Kelly joined them in the kitchen, looking like she was ready to go walk a runway somewhere.

A moment after that, the doorbell rang.

What was this? The perfect storm? Jacob stood paralyzed, not sure which to attend to first.

"I'll get that," Kelly said, smiling as she headed for the door. "You look cute in the morning." She rubbed his back as she walked past.

"Daddy?"

"Junie, hey." Jacob scrambled to set his coffee down and intercepted Kelly. "I've got the door."

"You sure? It's no problem." She turned and flashed him a smile. "I'm a little more presentable than you are."

"Yes, but you don't live here."

She shrugged. "Whatever you say. I'll get Junie some cereal."

"No, Kelly, you should go."

Her eyes widened and Jacob groaned. He didn't need this right now.

Ding-dong.

He pulled the door open, wishing he could go back to bed and start this whole day over again.

"Morning, sunshine!"

"Kate. What are you doing here?" His sister hadn't called. He didn't even know she had his new address.

"Aunt Kate!" Junie practically tackled her on the front porch.

Jacob hastily followed Junie outside in spite of the chilly morning, the screen door slamming behind him. He registered the huge purple bag over Kate's shoulder and the guitar at her feet. When did she learn to play guitar?

"Where've you been, Junie Moon, Junie Moon?" Kate squeezed the little girl tight.

Jacob looked away at the memory of Gwen's nickname for their daughter. From the day their daughter was born, his wife had called her Junie Moon.

"Because she has such a round, chubby face, like the man in the moon," Gwen had told him, cheeks red after delivering their baby. She'd even written Junie a sweet little children's book called *Where'd You Go, Junie Moon?* She'd had dreams of publishing that one day.

Jacob always thought they'd have a barrelful of children by now, but some things just didn't work out.

"Hey, Jacob," Kate said. "You look—" she gave him a once-over—"well, pretty awful."

"I just got up."

She pressed a button on her phone to check the time. "It's almost seven thirty. You're slacking in your old age."

"That's what I've been telling him, but he insists on working at a snail's pace." Kelly's voice met them from the kitchen. Jacob didn't turn around. He should've pulled both doors closed.

Kate's jaw dropped, and she stared at him.

"It's not what it looks like."

She pushed past him, Junie still clinging to her hand, and he had no choice but to follow them inside.

"I'm Kate Willoughby. Jacob's sister."

Kelly smiled, clearly enjoying the way it looked that she was standing in his kitchen at seven thirty in the morning on a Saturday. "I'm Kelly."

"She's my business manager," Jacob added, his palms sweating. "We were working late, and she crashed on the couch."

Kate shook Kelly's hand, then shot Jacob a disapproving look. "You sound guilty," she said under her breath. She turned all her attention to Junie then, leaving him feeling—like she said—guilty.

"Did you come to see me, Aunt Kate?" Junie asked. "I have a new doll."

"I did, Moon-Face, but I'm starving. I was

hoping you were going to take me to town for pancakes." Kate adjusted the yellow beanie floating on top of her messy, long blonde hair.

Jacob wondered if she'd just woken up that morning and decided to make the drive up the mountain from Denver. Oh, to be that spontaneous.

Except that her spontaneity often got her in trouble. Kate didn't always make the best decisions. Sometimes Jacob wondered if his little sister had a death wish or something. The bottom line was, if it was dangerous, Kate did it. Cave jumping. Hang gliding. Rock climbing.

After Gwen died, she promised she was done playing games that could put her life in jeopardy. If it weren't for that promise, he'd still be worried sick about her.

Junie squealed. "Can we, Daddy?"

Jacob hardly remembered what they'd been talking about.

"I love pancakes," Kelly said.

Kate shot her a look, and Jacob intervened before his sister could say anything. "Kelly, you should probably head out. You know I promised Junie no work on the weekends."

Kelly laughed. "That's a good one, Doc. You're opening a new practice."

"Right, but the work will still be there on Monday." He took a few steps toward the front door, opened it, and waited for her to finally get the hint.

"Fine." She picked up her bag and her purse. "Good to meet you, Kate."

No response.

Kelly shrugged and started for the door, stopping in front of him. "Thanks for letting me stay."

He chose not to interpret the message her eyes communicated.

"Talk Monday," he said, stepping back.

Unfazed, she lingered for too long before finally walking outside. He shut the door and turned to find Kate glaring at him.

"What was *that?*"

"I told you. Not what you think." He turned to Junie. "Now get dressed and we'll go out for pancakes."

Junie cheered. "Will you fix my hair, Aunt Kate?"

Kate held Jacob's gaze for another long, disapproving moment before following Junie into her room. "I'm thinking pigtails, Moon."

"I love pigtails! Daddy always does them lopsided."

Jacob rubbed his temples, willing away the dull ache that had already set in. He quickly showered, shaved, and dressed, silently praying Kate would drop the Kelly topic and focus on Junie—not him—during breakfast.

He emerged from his room, thankful Kate was fixing Junie's hair, though it did magnify his ineptitude at caring for the basic needs of his little girl. "You really need to get some groceries, Jacob," Kate said as she finished wrapping a hair band around the end of Junie's left braid. "Want me to hang around for a few days?"

"You don't have to take pity on me, Katie."

"I'm your sister. That's what we do, Jakey." She flashed a smile. "Besides, I kind of . . ." She looked away.

"What?"

Kate shook her head. "Never mind." She squeezed Junie. "Let's go, girl!"

"Kate."

"Seriously, it's nothing. Let's get going before my stomach eats itself."

There was no sense pushing her. Kate never did anything until she wanted to do it. She'd always been that way.

"You know you look like a vagabond."

"And you know no one says *vagabond* anymore." Kate popped a piece of gum in her mouth. "But I guess that's what happens when you become an old man."

He frowned, catching a glimpse of himself in the window as he locked the front door. He did, in fact, look older than his thirty-four years. Kate must've thought she hurt his feelings because she clapped a hand on his shoulder and said, "You'll get your mojo back."

On the walk to the truck, as Junie chattered away to Kate, he inhaled and forced himself to count to five. To slow down and look around. From a distance, he bet his new house looked like something in a painting. Shake shingles on all sides. Smoke spilling out of the chimney on cold nights. The back porch faced the lake, giving him the most magnificent view of Longs Peak.

A dream come true, living like this, surrounded by nature, no neighbors for miles. It might as well have been another country. Yesterday he spotted an elk grazing in his backyard.

He never saw anything like that in the city.

It was nice that there wasn't much in the way of medical competition here in Loves Park, of course, but that wasn't why they'd moved here. Some days he questioned whether or not he should open up a practice at all. After what he and Junie had been through, he might be happier if he became a white-water rafting guide.

Of course, he'd visited Loves Park once before. That was before Junie, before a lot of things.

He could practically hear Gwen's laughter echoing through the mountain air on mornings like this one. She had the most infectious laugh. He called it her reckless-abandon laugh because of the way she threw her head back and let loose. It was the best version of her, the best version of them. How he missed that.

Guilt tugged at his heart as he climbed into the driver's seat. *For better or worse.* They'd had their share of the latter in more recent years, hadn't they? He could've handled things so much differently. He glanced into the backseat at Junie, who had coaxed Kate into a loud rendition of "You Are My Sunshine." For her sake, he should've handled things differently.

"Whatcha thinking about, Mr. Stick-in-the-Mud?" Kate tucked both of her feet beneath her on the seat.

"Thinking about what a loudmouth you are," Jacob teased, pulling out of the driveway.

She stilled, attention focused on something out the window. "I am kind of obnoxious, aren't I?"

He frowned. "That's never bothered you before."

She laughed, but something about her seemed . . . off.

He hated to admit he didn't know what Kate had been doing the last year. Not really. Somewhere along the way, she'd stopped filling him in about her latest adventures. Or maybe he'd stopped asking.

At least she was in one piece—that was a decent start after countless trips to the emergency room over the years.

The horses. The skydiving. The rappelling. She'd had more than her fair share of injuries, but she'd promised she was done with dangerous hobbies. Whatever was bothering her, it had to be something else. Maybe guy trouble?

Shoot. Maybe he didn't want to know.

Jacob looked in the rearview mirror and found

Junie flipping through one of the books that seemed to have a permanent home back there. "Why are you really here, Kate?"

"I don't think you should be the one asking me questions, given what I walked in on this morning," Kate said. Always changing the subject.

"You didn't walk in on anything," he assured her, knowing full well what it looked like.

"Are you two . . . ?" Kate also glanced at Junie, then back to him with a wide-eyed expression that filled in the blanks.

Jacob sighed. "Of course not."

"Do you want to be?" Still the wide-eyed look.

"Kate."

She held up her hands in surrender. "All I'm saying is, you better be careful around her. She's obviously after you. And she doesn't have business on her mind."

"Pancakes!" Junie hollered from the backseat, pointing to her new favorite restaurant.

" 'Pamcakes'!" Kate corrected, reading the sign. " 'Sonny Pamcakes,' no less."

"They're yummy, Aunt Kate. I'm getting mine with chocolate chips. Can I, Dad?" Junie unbuckled as Jacob found a place to park on the street outside the restaurant.

He glanced at Kate, who appeared to have completely recovered from whatever it was that was bothering her—recovered enough to put all her focus back on him. He wouldn't let her off the hook that easily, but maybe he'd save the interrogation for later, when Junie wasn't around.

After breakfast, Kate wanted the grand tour of Old Town, and of course she asked to see his office.

"It's just an empty building right now."

"Yeah, but it's yours. Your fresh start." She grinned. "And I want to see it."

He knew what that meant. She'd find the space and break in if she had to, but she was going to see the building.

He hoped they could get in and out without anyone in The Book Nook spotting them. The last thing he needed was an encounter with one of those old ladies—or worse, with Abigail Pressman. He'd reviewed the details of her lease, and frankly he might as well give her the space for free with what Harriet had been charging her. He dreaded the conversation he knew he needed to have before Kelly discovered the numbers.

If he were smart, he'd kick her out sooner rather than later. He never wanted to be anybody's landlord in the first place—she just happened to come with the building.

Under other circumstances he might've thought of that as a nice gift.

Jacob examined his building from across the street. He did love the way it looked. He had great plans for it, and regardless of his conflict of conscience, he was anxious to practice medicine again. He needed to feel like he had a purpose. Even if he'd royally screwed things up with his own family.

Outside, Abigail's folding sign had been set up as usual, but today there were balloons on it and two of her employees stood nearby, handing out what appeared to be drink samples.

" 'The Book Nook,' " Kate said out loud, reading the name above Abigail's door. "How cute."

Jacob tried not to groan. "Yeah, cute."

"Can we go in, Daddy?" Junie tugged his hand as the three of them crossed the street. "I love books."

"And I love coffee." Kate took Junie's other hand and swung her over the curb and onto the sidewalk. "This looks like such a great store." Kate practically ran over to the girl handing out the tiny cups of what happened to be some cold coffee drink.

"You picked a good day to come in," the girl said with a smile. "We have all kinds of activities inside for your daughter."

Kate tugged one of Junie's braids. "My niece."

The employee checked her watch and knelt in front of Junie. "We're making bracelets in about five minutes. Head to the back of the store, to the children's section."

"Can we, Daddy?"

Jacob glanced toward the door, wishing he could see if Abigail Pressman—or those old-lady friends of hers—were sitting inside, watching him.

Somehow, when he was out, he always felt their eyes on him whether they were there or not.

Junie tugged on his sleeve. He couldn't say no to her. Not after everything she'd been through. He'd spend a lifetime trying to make amends. "One bracelet."

She let out a cheer and ran for the door, Kate following closely behind. "Hurry up, Jakey," Kate said, flashing a toothy grin. "You want to make a bracelet, don't you?"

"Been a lifelong dream," he said.

The inside of The Book Nook was indeed charming. The kind of store you'd only find in a town like Loves Park—part vintage-library feel, part coffee-shop personality. The words on the wall facing the door encouraged customers to *Sit. Read. Caffeinate.* And from the looks of it, Loves Park patrons were happy to oblige. The store was bustling with activity. The children's section at the back looked like a zoo, one he'd happily let Kate navigate.

He ducked into the nearest row, marked *Biographies,* and pretended to be engrossed in a book about a nun. What were the chances he could escape Abigail's detection?

"Did you need help finding—? Oh."

So much for that.

She stood at the end of the row, a stack of books

in her arms. "I assume you aren't here to buy a book."

He regarded her for a moment before answering. She really was pretty, though he got the distinct impression she had no idea. Pale skin. Big brown eyes. Light-pink lips. Untamed hair pulled into a loose braid. Chip on her shoulder. An interesting assortment of seemingly unrelated parts that fit together quite nicely.

Today she wore a loose sweater over jeans with boots and smelled of vanilla sugar.

"I might be in the market for some new reading material," he hedged.

She looked at the book he was holding. "You have a deep interest in Benedictine nuns, do you?" Her eyebrows accused.

He stuck the book back on the shelf where he found it. "Listen, this might not be the best time, but since we're both here . . . I was reviewing your lease."

"Oh?" The books she held shifted as she took a step back, the one on the top slipping onto the floor. It must've been just enough to disrupt the whole stack because within seconds there was a pile of books at his feet.

Her face flushed red and she blew a stray piece of hair out of her eyes. "I'm so sorry."

"Let me." He bent down and started stacking the books.

"I can't believe I did that." She kept her head

down as she stacked, and for a second Jacob just watched her. She must've sensed his attention on her because she stopped and looked at him, making him feel like an idiot—and worse, a creep.

He handed her his stack. "We can talk about the lease later." *What was I thinking?*

"That'd be good." She stood, newly stacked pile secure in her grip. "That'd be just great." She stared at him for a few long seconds before finally turning and walking away.

He caught a glimpse of her as she reached the counter, handing over the stack of books to a young guy who wore his ball cap low on his head, making his eyes hard to see.

She sent him off to restock the books and disappeared in the back, leaving Jacob standing in the aisle, the memory of her vanilla scent lingering in the air.

Chapter 15

Abigail rushed into her office and closed the door behind her. Why was her heart pounding? Why were her palms sweating? She caught a glimpse of herself in the small mirror she kept on the wall. *Why* was her face beet red?

She covered her cheeks with her hands. *Get ahold of yourself, Pressman.*

The knock on the door startled her, and when she turned, she knocked over her jar of pencils.

Seriously?

Mallory's face showed up in the doorway. "What's gotten into you?"

"Don't ask."

"The kids are ready to make bracelets."

Abigail sighed. With any luck, Dr. Jacob Willoughby would be long gone by the time she emerged from her hiding place.

What was he doing in her store anyway? Had he come to tell her she had a month to vacate the premises?

Her heart lurched at the idea. Her whole future was in his hands.

The thought shamed her. Everything she'd learned in Sunday school told her that wasn't true, regardless of how it seemed. God was in charge of her life. Not some man with a wad of building-buying cash.

God, you said you'd never leave me. The verse rippled through her mind. *But it sure does feel like you're on vacation.*

She followed Mallory out into the store, where two long tables had been set up with bracelet-making kits, all promoting a new children's craft book that had just arrived. Part of Abigail's grand plan to grow her business. She'd just dived in headfirst, determined to make The Book Nook the kind of place people would fight for.

It seemed to be working. They hadn't been this busy on a Saturday morning in months.

But one look at her captive audience told her this was not her lucky day in any other respect.

At the second table, seated next to a little girl and a beautiful young woman, was her landlord. Something else Abigail hadn't thought through. Standing up in front of a group of kids was one thing. Their parents? An entirely different story. And Dr. Willoughby? Worst. Idea. Ever.

She'd assumed the doctor was dating the blonde in the power suit, but it appeared that he had an actual family—a wife and daughter.

Either that or he liked to play the field. She glanced again at his left hand. Still no ring.

She supposed not everyone wore a wedding ring, though she couldn't imagine why not. She said a silent prayer of repentance for thinking someone else's husband was handsome in the first place.

Even if he was.

Abigail cleared her throat and met Mallory's eyes. Mal made a face that seemed to say, *"What are you waiting for?"*

"Hi, everyone." Her voice shook as she spoke. She wet her lips and tried to remember to breathe. She'd never been particularly good at public speaking. She'd have to take a look at the rest of her plans to expand the business. Having events in the store was a great idea—as long as someone else did the talking next time.

She scanned the crowd. Mostly parents and children she recognized. Only a few new faces, thankfully. She accidentally made eye contact with Jacob and was surprised when he gave her a polite smile.

Probably felt sorry for her.

Abigail had to show him she knew what she was doing. She couldn't let him think he could just push her over. And she had to make this the most exciting bracelet-making session of these kids' young lives. She'd show him. All of them.

She held Jacob's gaze, took another deep breath, and started speaking. This time her voice was strong and clear. She even impressed herself, the way she took charge of the room. After she gave her spiel about the book and talked the kids through the first few steps of making their brace-lets, Mallory handed out instruction sheets for the parents so they could work together at their tables. Within minutes, the bracelet making had begun.

Abigail watched as the young woman with Jacob took the instructions and grinned, smacking the doctor on the side of the arm. His face brightened just slightly. He looked equal parts miserable and amused.

The girl started to get frustrated with the threads, and he read the instructions aloud, his voice patient.

"Did you forget to take your meds today?" Mallory came up behind Abigail and stuck the extra instruction sheets in her hand.

"What are you talking about?"

"You're all over the place." Mallory stared at Abigail.

"I thought I did great." Abigail tucked the extra sheets of paper in a folder and scanned the crowd again.

"Yeah, after your near-incoherent start." Mallory leaned closer. "I know the doctor makes you nervous."

"What?" Abigail said a bit too loudly. "He does not."

"I don't blame you. He's hot."

"He is my landlord. And he's taken, obviously."

Mallory rolled her eyes. "Is Operation Make Him Love You in play? I can help, you know."

"Don't you dare." Abigail hoped Mallory could hear how serious she was.

"It's the only way to save this place, boss." She walked away.

Abigail already had a plan to save this place, faulty though it may be.

"I did it wrong, Daddy." The girl sitting next to Jacob sounded like she might cry. Jacob held up the half-made bracelet and compared it to the instruction sheet, his brow furrowed. The woman with them peered over his shoulder, but she seemed confused too.

Abigail almost felt sorry for the guy. *Almost.* She walked over and sat down next to the girl. "Do you need some help?"

The girl took the bracelet and handed it to Abigail. "I did it wrong."

"Let's see if I can fix it." Abigail studied the bracelet.

"My daddy isn't good at this," the girl said innocently.

Abigail laughed. "It just takes some practice. Maybe if you and your daddy buy the book and the bracelet-making kit, you'll both become experts."

The girl let out a gasp. "Can we, Daddy? Please? I want to be an expert."

Abigail could tell Jacob was staring at her, but she stifled her smile and kept her eyes on the girl's bracelet.

"I suppose we'll have to get our very own kit, Junie Moon."

Abigail glanced up in time to see him wink at the girl.

"Why don't you go pick one out? Then we should get going," he told his daughter.

"She's adorable," Abigail said after she walked away, pulling the blonde-haired woman with her.

"She gets that from my wife," he said.

Her face flushed as if he might know that in a misguided moment, she'd allowed herself to daydream about him a bit. Before she knew he was taken. She told herself it was Mallory's fault for suggesting she make him like her.

"Cute nickname too," Abigail said, finishing up the bracelet.

"Also from my wife."

She glanced up and saw the young woman he'd come in with standing a few feet behind Junie, who had located a display of dolls. There was something surprising about her. Abigail would've imagined Jacob with someone older—more professional or elegant. Someone like Kelly. This woman couldn't even have been thirty, and she looked . . . cool.

Like someone Abigail wished she could be friends with.

"Your wife is beautiful," she said, a little too wistfully.

Jacob followed her gaze to where his family stood, then laughed. "Oh no, that's not my wife. That's my sister, Kate. I should introduce you."

"Your sister?"

"She dropped in this morning and wanted to see the building. The people outside coaxed Junie in here."

Abigail grinned. "So it worked."

"What worked?"

"My drinks-on-the-street plan." She couldn't help feeling pleased with herself. "Got you in the door."

His face warmed into a soft smile. "I suppose so."

"So your wife—that's the woman I met the other day." Abigail attempted to sound nonchalant, but she wasn't sure if she succeeded.

He raised a hand as if to protest. "No. That's Kelly, my business manager. She's . . ." She imagined he was searching for something nice to say about Kelly and wasn't at all surprised when he came up empty.

His sister and his business partner.

Why did these revelations make Abigail's stomach jump up like cheerleaders at a play-off game? He still had a wife.

Remember that, Pressman.

Behind her, she heard a commotion near the front counter, and she turned just in time to see Ursula Pembrooke plodding toward her.

"Abigail!"

Jacob hopped up and took a step toward a nearby bookshelf. Was he trying to hide? If so, he was being far from subtle. Abigail let out a quiet groan in spite of the smile on her face.

"Good morning, Ursula."

"What in the world is going on back here? Where's our table?" Apparently Ursula didn't believe in inside voices.

"Saturday is community day at The Book Nook," Abigail said in a quiet voice, hoping the old lady would get the hint.

"Since when?" she practically growled.

"What can I do for you, Ursula?" Abigail

stepped away, though she knew Jacob was still well within earshot.

"You can start by putting my table back."

"I'll consider it."

The old lady hugged her furry purse tight to her chest. "I've been thinking about your problem."

Abigail's heart jumped into her throat. *Please shut up, Ursula.* "Let's talk business later."

The old lady waved her off, clearly unaware that Jacob was only a few feet away. "Not the doctor problem. The other problem."

"I have another problem?" Abigail started cleaning up the demonstration table, willing Ursula to move away from Jacob.

"The *relationship* problem." Ursula stared at her.

Heat rushed to Abigail's cheeks. "I have a relationship problem?" She practically squeaked out the words.

"Do you have a relationship?"

Abigail shook her head.

"Then you have a problem." Ursula began tossing books and bracelet kits off the demonstration table and onto the long plastic ones Abigail had crammed into a too-small space earlier that morning, oblivious to the fact that children and parents were still working at them. "My nephew Duncan is in town from Tampa."

"No way, Ursula." Abigail didn't even care who heard. She wasn't going to go along with this one.

"It's Gigi's neighbor Ty or my nephew Duncan. Take your pick."

Abigail gawked at her.

"Don't pretend you have better options, what with your first-daughter-of-Loves-Park status and your, ah . . ." Ursula took her hand and motioned to Abigail, moving it up, then down as if to include, well, all of her.

Abigail heard a tiny, vocalized breath escape from her throat.

Ursula plopped her purse on the table and rummaged through it. A sort of paralyzed state had come over Abigail. She was helpless to move.

"There just aren't a lot of eligible bachelors in this town, Miss Pressman, and you don't exactly put yourself out there. You should really consider some makeup once in a while. Paint it up a little."

"Ursula, please tell me the Volunteers aren't trying to find me a match."

Ursula stared at her for a long moment. "Of course not. I'm trying to match my nephew." She thrust a photograph in Abigail's direction. "Duncan. He's an accountant. With his quiet demeanor and his tendency to be really dry and boring, he might actually be a good fit for you."

Abigail stared at the photo of this stranger named Duncan, who wore tiny spectacles and a gray suit and had his hair slicked back with something that made it shiny. *"A good fit for you."*

Finally—after what felt like an hour—Abigail felt the life return to her body. Jacob still stood a few feet away, clearly pretending not to listen as the old woman repeatedly humiliated her.

"I figure if you get together now," Ursula said, "you might be engaged by Valentine's Day. Surely you don't want to spend another lonely Valentine's Day in Loves Park. Can't think of anything more depressing than that, especially with your sister's big announcement."

"I have work to do." Abigail handed the photo back to Ursula and walked away, tears stinging her eyes.

"Your *younger* sister," Ursula shouted after her.

Before she reached the counter, she nearly ran into the woman who'd arrived with Dr. Willoughby. His sister. Not his wife.

"I'm sorry," she said, not sure if she meant for almost knocking her over or just for being a disappointment.

Kate spun around, her face bright. "Not at all. This place is adorable. Are you the owner?"

Abigail forced a smile, which in her current state was about as easy as pushing toothpaste out of a squeezed-empty tube. She nodded.

"I love it. Too bad you don't have a stage. It'd be the perfect place for live music."

Abigail's embarrassment subsided as she followed Kate's gaze to the corner of the area where all the tables were set up.

"A little corner stage is all you would need. I could get my brother to build it for you. He's actually pretty handy even though he's a doctor." Kate flashed a smile. "You know, because doctors are usually so bookish."

Abigail raised a brow.

"Not that there's anything wrong with being bookish."

She smiled. "It's fine; I know what you mean. Are you a musician?"

Kate nodded. "Guitar. And this is just the kind of place I love to play. I've been told I have a real coffee-shop vibe. If you ever need anyone, I mean."

"How about next Friday?" Abigail had no idea what it would take to host a musician in her bookshop. She didn't even know if Kate was any good, but there she stood, inviting her to play, mostly out of some innate need to do everything she could to get people in the door. And bringing in live music was one of the things on her list.

No time like the present.

"I'm in," Kate said as Jacob joined them. "And Jacob will be over tomorrow to build your stage."

Judging by the look on his face, Jacob was about as happy about that as Abigail was.

Chapter 16

"What were you thinking, Kate?" Jacob loved his sister, but she had a knack for disrupting his life.

She followed him into the old mercantile, Junie close behind. "I don't know why you're so bent out of shape. It'll take you maybe half an hour to build a little stage in the corner *for your tenant*. Who happens to be adorable, by the way. She's the kind of girl you should be letting sleep on your couch."

He let out a sigh. "I don't want to outfit her space with a stage, and I certainly don't want her sleeping on my couch."

"Why not? It's a great idea. The stage, I mean. And I get to be the first musician to try it out." She grinned. Always grinning. Always seeing the bright side.

So different from him.

He rubbed his temples. "I have to kick her out, Kate."

She frowned. "What? Why?"

"For one thing, we're going to need the space. For another thing, the previous owner practically gave that space to her. You wouldn't believe what she's paying."

"So what? You can't extend a little goodwill?"

She dropped her knapsack of a purse on the floor to punctuate her sentence.

"I can't take on her bleeding business just because I feel sorry for her. I have my own business to get off the ground. Besides, as soon as Kelly reviews her lease, she'll . . ."

"So that's what this is about. You can't do something kind for a perfectly wonderful person —your neighbor—because you're afraid Kelly will think you're too nice." Kate's eyes narrowed.

"I know you don't really care for her, Katie, but the woman knows her stuff."

"The woman knows how to spin something to get what she wants—and, Jacob, I don't think it's just your money she's after."

He looked away. This wasn't exactly news to him. He could tell when a woman wanted to be more than friends.

He hoped he didn't have to address that anytime soon. He didn't want their business relationship to turn awkward.

Jacob glanced at Junie, who had sprawled out in the back corner with the book they'd just purchased. Of course she was his primary focus— no one would question that—but that didn't stop him from wishing there was something he could do to protect Abigail too.

The very thought of it made him cringe. He had to stop trying to protect everyone all the time. He wasn't put on this earth to be anyone's savior.

Hadn't Gwen taught him that?

"I don't like it any more than you do." He looked out the window to where a group of tourists had stopped in front of The Book Nook. They glanced in the windows, took samples from the girl in the hat, and went inside.

He had to hand it to Abigail Pressman. She knew how to get people in the door. It didn't escape him that she could be his greatest ally.

"Give her a chance at least," Kate said. "She's got a good thing going."

Jacob sighed. "I'll think about it."

And think about it he did. For the rest of the day and well into the night. He thought about it so much, he wanted to pack his house in his truck and move away. Maybe Kelly was right. He needed a thicker skin.

Maybe if he were smart, he'd turn the whole thing over to Kelly and let her decide what to do. But he couldn't do that. This was his business. His responsibility.

Jacob's cell phone buzzed in his pocket. His stomach wound into a tight knot when he saw Kelly's name on the screen.

"Jacob, were you downtown this morning?"

"Yeah, I brought Kate and Junie down there for breakfast and—"

"That bookstore was packed. I couldn't even find a place to sit," she said.

"That's great. A good sign for business, right?"

Jacob didn't want to get into a debate with Kelly right now. It was Saturday, for pete's sake.

"You know what she's doing, don't you?" Kelly's laugh lacked any sense of amusement.

He pressed the ridge at the top of his nose, willing the stress away. "I'd say she's doing a good job of getting people in the door."

Another laugh. She had to be mentally pacing—he could hear it in her tone. "She's the Loves Park sweetheart, and she is on a warpath to turn the whole town against us before we even open the doors."

"Kelly, I don't think—"

"No, Jacob, I know women like this. Quiet and mousy, the kind no one ever notices. They're the most dangerous because you never see them coming."

But he had noticed Abigail. More than once.

"What game do you think she's playing?" he asked, losing patience.

"The kind of game that makes us public enemy number one. Don't you get it? If we boot out the Loves Park darling, they'll hate us. It's sabotage."

"I'm not sure that's really her style."

"Don't let her innocent act fool you. She's dangerous."

He didn't argue with that. He'd spent so many minutes thinking about Abigail Pressman, he could see the danger.

"You have to kick her out now, before she does

any more damage. Give people time to forget it ever happened before we open," Kelly said, not seeming to realize that he didn't take orders from her. "I'm serious, Jacob. You go talk to her or I will."

She hung up before he could respond.

Sunday morning, Jacob awoke to the smell of coffee. A welcome aroma after tossing and turning the whole night, playing out scenarios that all involved Abigail Pressman. It didn't matter so much what Kelly or Kate told him to do about his tenant. The real trouble was that his own heart seemed to have betrayed him because, whenever there was a lull in his thoughts, his mind turned to the color of her eyes or the softness of her skin. He'd quickly shove the thoughts aside, reminding himself he had no time or interest for romance. This town wouldn't have the same bewitching pull on him as it did on everyone else.

Kelly was right about one thing—if they put Abigail out on the street after she campaigned for the affection of Loves Park for a year, the town would never support his practice.

Jacob pulled on a plain T-shirt and brushed his teeth. It was ridiculous to keep speculating. He and Abigail were both adults. He'd go talk to her. Maybe an agreement could be made.

In the kitchen, his sister flipped pancakes with the kind of flair that had Junie cheering—the kind of flair that was sure to end in culinary disaster.

"You're up early," he said.

"You should be up early," Kate said without pause in her flipping.

He didn't miss the accusation in her voice. His morning routine used to be quite different, especially on Sundays. Until his wife's death, every day he'd been up at dawn for a little coffee and Jesus. He'd spent hours in his old recliner praying—no, begging—that God would intervene for Gwen.

But God had stayed silent. Now Jacob returned the favor to the Almighty.

He ignored his sister and poured a cup of coffee, put on his sweatshirt, and went out on the back deck to take in the view. A dense fog hovered over the lake like steam, camouflaging the mountains in the distance. It almost restored his faith in his Creator.

Almost.

Kate joined him after a few minutes, but she didn't speak. Not right away. He got the impression that his little sister had her own questions for God. A part of her had always seemed restless, but there was something different about her now. Happiness didn't radiate from the depths of her anymore. All of that smiling felt more like a put-on.

What was she running from?

He glanced inside, where Junie sat with a

plate of pancakes, watching one of her cartoons.

"You picked a great place to start over," Kate said, inhaling the mountain air.

"We always talked about moving here. It's touristy but with that small-town charm you girls like so much."

Kate laughed. "I was surprised, given the whole love and romance thing."

"I promise I didn't factor that in."

It was mostly true. He and Gwen had only been here once, but the town had become part of the fabric of their relationship.

"I read an article online about this place. I guess they're pretty famous for their Valentine's Day celebration. And their Sweetheart Festival. And their Rose Ball." She let out a sigh. "Yeah, you'll fit right in."

He groaned. "I get the impression that being single here is practically like being a leper."

"How are you doing?" She looked at him. "Really."

He shrugged. "Okay."

"I half expected to see Gwen when I got here yesterday." She tossed her blonde hair back. "Sometimes I forget."

He wished he could forget. Wished for the day when he would wake up and the empty space on her side of the bed wouldn't be the first thing he thought of. Wished the pangs of guilt would subside. If only he'd been there for her. All that medical training and he'd still been helpless.

And he'd taken the coward's way out.

"Can I stay with you for a little while?"

Kate's question brought him back to the present. He welcomed the distraction. "I thought you had an apartment in Denver."

She shrugged. "It didn't work out."

"What's going on, Katie?"

Another shrug. "Let's just say you're not the only one who needs a fresh start."

He didn't like the way that sounded. He'd always been *that* brother. The one who threatened Kate's boyfriends. The one who carted her off the field with a broken leg when she was thrown from her horse at a riding competition. The one who x-rayed her head when her mountain bike flipped over. He'd spent years worrying about Kate, and still, he'd never seen the uncertainty behind her eyes the way he did now.

"You okay?"

His sister rarely showed any emotion except optimistic joy. It usually got on his nerves because it challenged the cynic in him. But now that it seemed to have disappeared, he missed it. Missed the version of her that didn't seem wounded. He couldn't stand the thought of anyone else he loved hurting.

That pain was too familiar.

"I'll be fine. Just need some time to clear my head." She pressed the bridge of her nose—hard

—and emerged with a smile. "Can I stay here? I can help with Junie."

He looked away. "What makes you think I need help?"

He felt—not saw—her look at him.

"Of course you can stay, Katie." Then he made her hold his gaze. "As long as you promise to tell me if you're ever not okay."

She touched his shoulder. "I'll never be *that* kind of not okay, Jacob. I promise."

An unspoken understanding passed between them.

He smiled, then took another sip from his mug. "You have to make coffee every morning."

"You like it?"

"It's really good." Another drink. "Better than when I make it."

"You won't be able to get it anymore if you kick Abigail out of The Book Nook. She told me it's her exclusive Loves Park blend." She bumped his arm with her own and let the silence hang between them. "You're in such a hurry to get your practice open."

He knew where she was going with this. After the lawsuit he didn't need the money—why did he need to work at all? Guilt plagued him every time he thought about that lawsuit. Suing his own hospital hadn't been his idea, but he'd been so filled with anger—and so desperate to blame anyone other than himself—that he went along with it.

He'd stashed most of the money in a fund for Junie. He didn't want it. No amount of money was worth that cost.

No. Not working wasn't an option.

Kate had to understand why he was anxious to get his new practice up and running. On second thought, maybe having Kate here wasn't a great idea. Did he really need someone analyzing him every morning before he'd even finished his first cup of coffee?

"Jacob?"

He responded with a silent glance.

"I found the paper hearts."

He sighed. "Going through my stuff?"

"They fell out of the desk when I was looking for my car keys."

"You're a terrible liar."

She gave him a crooked smile. "I think you should let Junie write some too."

He tossed a glance over his shoulder and spotted Junie, still sitting in her spot in front of the cartoon. He shook his head. "I shouldn't even have written those. It was just habit."

A habit he seemed unable to break.

She was quiet. "Will you put them up?"

Jacob swallowed, wishing their conversation hadn't taken this turn. Finally he shook his head. "Do me a favor and throw them away."

Kate didn't respond.

"Or I guess I can throw them away."

169

"No. I'll do it," she said, leveling her gaze. "But promise me you'll tell me if *you're* ever not okay."

He gave one quick nod, finished his coffee, and went back inside, not wanting his sister to know he'd passed that point a long time ago.

Chapter 17

Gigi hadn't been so personally involved in a case in a number of years. Not since the Volunteers worked to match her own daughter, Laine, who'd since married and moved away. Every time Gigi found herself alone, her thoughts turned to Abigail Pressman and Teensy's desperation to get the girl married off.

Maybe Teensy simply wanted to believe Abigail's love life wasn't a by-product of her own failed marriage.

Or maybe she didn't want her daughter to end up alone, which was likely the way Teensy felt most of the time. Gigi should've been a better friend to Abigail's mother. They'd practically grown up together, but Teensy had gotten so negative over the years.

Still, that wasn't a reason not to reach out to a grieving friend. No matter how difficult she was.

Gigi struggled to parallel park her Buick across the street from The Book Nook. Finally, after several readjustments, she turned the engine off, locked the doors, and got out of the car.

"It's like watching a teenager take her driving test." Ursula stood beside the car on the sidewalk, an incredulous expression on her face.

"I don't appreciate your tone, Ursula. I do just fine." Gigi joined her on the sidewalk and began walking toward the end of the block.

"We can cross here," Ursula said, unmoving.

"The crosswalk is this way," Gigi called over her shoulder.

Ursula groaned. "At some point you should be old enough to make the rules up yourself." After a few long strides, she caught up to Gigi.

"When that day comes," Gigi said, "you let me know. I have a few rules I'd like to rewrite myself. Like no white shoes after Labor Day."

Ursula's expression soured. "That's a rule?"

Gigi waved her off. "We should hurry. The others will be waiting for us, and we need to check on Abigail."

She pushed the button for the crosswalk and waited for the light.

"I've already got a plan in play." Ursula stepped into the street and started crossing, holding her hand up to the barely stopped traffic.

Gigi's pulse quickened. "What does that mean?"

Ursula didn't look at her as she continued across the street. "You're not the only one who can play this game, Gigi."

"It's not a game. It's a girl's life."

They reached the other side of the street, and Gigi put a hand on Ursula's arm. "Stop."

She did, but she wasn't happy about it.

"What do you mean you have a plan?"

"The Duncan plan."

Gigi gasped. "No. You are not setting Abigail up with your nephew."

"I resent that. He is a good man. He's just a little—"

"Creepy." Gigi finished the sentence for her. This wasn't the first time Duncan had come into the picture.

Ursula began walking again. "You have no faith in me, old friend. Trust me."

Gigi didn't like her tone. "Do you know Abigail at all?"

"Yes, which is why I know Duncan will be perfect."

"No. He is not a good match for her, Ursula."

The older woman let out a cackle. "Of course he's not. That's the point." She winked at Gigi, then joined the other Volunteers, who were waiting at the front door of The Book Nook.

Clearly when Ursula Pembrooke took matters into her own hands, she didn't see any need to include the rest of them in her plans. The thought of it left a ball of anxiety wedged somewhere below Gigi's rib cage. Of all of the Volunteers, Ursula was the one she trusted the least—and as much as Gigi hated to admit it, Ursula appeared to be the only one with a plan of action for Abigail Pressman.

Abigail stood inside The Book Nook watching in horror as the Valentine Volunteers plodded toward her, all moving in one unified clump. They had a look on their collective faces. The kind that told Abigail she'd be better off hiding under the counter.

"Abigail. Just the girl we've been looking for." Gigi smiled, clutching her patent-leather purse. "We wanted to see how everything was going."

Abigail forced a smile. "I'm still working my way through those letters, Gigi."

"Oh yes, dear. I didn't mean that," Gigi said. "I just meant in general. Life. The store. You know." She looked around as if she had more to say but decided to stop talking.

"Things are fine." Abigail began making their usual orders while Gigi stood directly in front of where she worked.

Tess moved chairs around the large table at the back of the store while Evelyn perused the art section of the bookstore. For a brief moment, Abigail allowed her gaze to linger on the slender woman who radiated artistry even in the way she dressed. Abigail was sure she remembered that the young senator's wife used to paint—might've had a show at the local gallery once.

Did she give all that up when she married a politician?

Evelyn glanced up from the book in her hands, and a warm smile crossed her face. Probably felt sorry for Abigail.

"I have something to say." Ursula shoved Gigi aside, hair a mess, a wild, multicolored scarf thrown around her neck in a seemingly haphazard fashion. Abigail couldn't be sure, but the scarf appeared to be unfinished. She could only imagine Ursula had started crocheting it and then lost interest. Somehow that didn't stop her from wearing the thing.

Abigail was beginning to think the woman didn't own a mirror.

When Abigail didn't respond, Ursula continued. "Duncan's here."

"What do you mean?" She wondered if her face looked as horrified as her words had sounded.

"I brought him here. To meet you." She raised her bushy eyebrows.

"No. I'm working!" Abigail's face flushed. She could feel it.

"Ursula, it's time to stop this now," Gigi said through clenched teeth. "Abigail, if Duncan isn't your type, what kind of man would you say is?"

"She doesn't have any idea if Duncan is her type or not. Go talk to him, Abigail." Ursula pointed—not subtly—to a man standing next to a stack of books on the other side of the store.

Abigail spun around and faced the old woman. "I am working," she repeated.

"You're the owner. You can do whatever you want. Speaking of which, there might be some leaky pipes in your back room."

Abigail frowned. "What are you talking about?"

"Might want to call your landlord." The old woman winked.

The bell over the door jangled, drawing all of their attention. Dr. Jacob Willoughby. Of course. He must've felt like he just entered the twilight zone.

"Speak of the ever-lovin' devil." Ursula stomped over to the man. Abigail couldn't help but feel sorry for him.

"Leaky pipes in the back, Jake," she barked.

He glanced at Abigail.

Ursula was relentless. "Landlord takes care of leaky pipes."

"I'll take it from here, ladies," Abigail said, wondering how many stars had to misalign for so many things to go wrong at the same time. "Why don't you all go sit down and I'll have Mallory bring your drinks?"

Ursula gave Jacob a once-over before finally joining the others at the big table.

"Is she always like that?" Jacob took a seat at the counter.

"Pretty much." She filled a mug with Loves Park blend and handed it to him. He looked at her, surprised. "Did you not want coffee?" she asked.

"No, it's great. Thanks." He took a drink. "Do you really need me to look at the pipes?"

Abigail frowned. "I didn't before, but I might now. It's possible Ursula took a wrench to them."

Jacob laughed. "I'll check it out, just to be sure."

She heard herself thank him, but her mind had begun spinning in an attempt to find something—anything—else to talk to him about. Why did he make her so nervous?

Jacob took another drink. "Junie really loves that book you sold us Saturday."

She had to smile. She'd manipulated that one for sure. "Is your house overflowing with bracelets yet?"

He pulled his sleeve up, revealing three bracelets on his wrist.

She laughed. Huh. Was this actually the beginning of a polite conversation?

It might've been, but as soon as she realized it, everything changed. Their polite conversation turned awkward. *She* turned awkward.

"I think I owe you a stage." There was a question in his voice.

She wiped down the counter. Twice. "Don't be silly. I didn't take your sister seriously when she said that." Though in the back of her mind, she'd hoped Kate was serious. Who else could she get to build her a stage on such short notice?

"It's fine. I don't mind."

"But you have, you know, a daughter at home. Not to mention your own space to renovate. I can figure out something."

"Before Friday?" He took another drink. "Because if I ruin Kate's big Loves Park debut, she'll never let me live it down."

Abigail laughed.

Ursula appeared at the counter out of nowhere. "Duncan. Front table. Reading the newspaper." She walked away, but not before giving Jacob her signature stink eye.

Abigail groaned. "Be thankful you're married."

Jacob took another drink. "I'm actually not."

She frowned, begging the awkwardness to stay far, far away. "I thought you said . . ."

"I'm not married . . . anymore." He looked away, thereby ending the conversation on that topic.

Abigail recognized heartache when she saw it. And she should know—she'd seen it on her own face for years. "I'm sorry. My parents divorced when I was a kid."

Jacob nodded but avoided her eyes. "This is really good coffee."

"Thanks." *Don't kick me out and I'll give you all the free coffee you can drink.*

"I've got supplies in the car. I can take measurements and build the foundation over in the mercantile. Then I'll bring it over here. It shouldn't take too long."

His kindness embarrassed her. "Okay, but lunch is on me." Hardly payment, but it would have to do.

He extended a hand in her direction. She shook it—the way she was supposed to—and tried not to think about his firm grip and the way his green eyes sort of danced when he smiled.

He's the enemy. He's trampling on your dreams. He's going to kick you out, and then what will you have? A fat lot of nothin', that's what.

He gave her a sideways smile, and only then did she realize she'd been holding his hand well past the acceptable length of time for a handshake. "Sorry." A nervous laugh escaped. How many times would she have to apologize to the man?

"I'll be back."

Abigail's heart pounded. *Not soon enough.* She shook herself. What was going on with her?

She felt Mallory move in next to her. "Good work, boss."

Abigail stuffed the bar rag in her apron and walked away.

The shelves needed tidying. Or at least she could pretend they did. Anything to keep up the pretense of work and avoid her own thoughts . . . as well as avoiding Duncan, who, she realized, was still creeping around here somewhere.

She collected books her customers had failed to return to the shelves and began the process of putting them away, forcing herself to stop watching the door for Jacob's return.

A few minutes later he walked back in. From a distance, a person might think he was a nice man. Not the dream killer she knew him to be.

She watched as he measured the corner where the little wedge of a stage would go. Just enough space for one, maybe two performers. Nothing fancy.

She'd lose a table or two, but it would be worth it.

Especially if it made Loves Park love her more.

It occurred to her that he didn't have to do this for her. It was actually kind of him. Maybe kindness would get the better of him and he'd let her keep her business right where it was. Nothing had to change—her life could just go on as usual. Or maybe he'd reconsider Ursula's offer. Sell the old lady the building and open a practice somewhere else.

She spent the better part of the morning steering clear of the Volunteers—and hiding from Ursula's reptilian nephew.

She finally finished tidying the shelves in the fiction section and had turned toward religion when, through the stacks, she saw a pair of beady eyes staring at her. She gasped. *Caught.*

"You scared me."

Duncan stared at her for an uncomfortable beat and finally slithered his way around the shelves.

"My aunt says you're the last single girl in town." His voice had a distinctly nasal quality about it.

"Well, that's hardly true." Abigail tossed a scoff over her shoulder and went back to shelving books. It felt true most days, though, didn't it?

Duncan took a step closer, just close enough to invade her personal space. "How about dinner? Tonight at Lovie's." His breath smelled like onions and it wasn't even noon.

"Oh, I'll have to check my schedule."

He handed her a business card. "I'll be there at seven. I'll take the liberty of ordering for us. Do you like fish?"

Abigail only stared.

"Very good. Seven it is." He walked away, leaving her slack-jawed.

I hate fish.

Suddenly the FarmersOnly website looked pretty good.

She glanced at the table of older women at the back. Ursula gave her a smirk, but Abigail only groaned.

Lunchtime came and went. Abigail pretended to wipe down the tables near the windows as she stole a glance outside, wondering if Jacob had plans to return from the mercantile anytime soon. Or if he expected her to bring his lunch over there.

She'd promised, hadn't she?

Of course, she had no idea what he liked.

She had Aaron box up a sandwich and their

homemade potato chips, then exited out the back. She chose to ignore the nerves dancing in her belly.

The man had the power to destroy her business, and that was what made her nervous. It had nothing to do with his perfectly straight white teeth or his well-built frame, though those things were just . . . lovely.

Abigail knocked, but there was no answer. She pushed on the door, which opened, and let herself in. Before she announced her presence, though, the sound of Jacob's voice stopped her.

"I'm sorry you see it that way, Cecily, but Gwen made her choice, and now I'm making mine." A pause. "Name-calling isn't going to change anything." Another pause. "Look. I'm settled here. If you want to see Junie, something can be arranged, but for now I think we need a little space."

He cleared his throat. Abigail felt trapped in the doorway. If she left now, he'd know she'd overheard him having what was obviously a very private conversation.

"It makes her sad to see you, Cecily. Reminds her of her mom. Just give her time." He sighed. "I won't keep her from you forever. Just until we're back on our feet."

Now Abigail knew she shouldn't be listening. She took a step back and, as was customary with her, ran into a broom, which toppled over. When she reached out to catch it, she dropped the boxed lunch with a thud and missed the broom, which clanked onto the wooden floor. The soda in her pocket fell to the ground and rolled across the floor, stopping right where Jacob stood.

He spun around, anger on his face.

She met his eyes, horrified.

"I'll have to call you back." He hung up and stared at her.

Abigail swept the hair away from her face. "Lunch?"

Chapter 18

Great. Just what he needed, to be the center of town gossip. How much of his conversation with his former mother-in-law had Abigail overheard?

Jacob wanted to throw the phone into the wall, as if smashing it would keep his past from haunting him.

He shouldn't have answered the phone in the first place. But Cecily had called from work—a number he didn't recognize. She had loads of advice about how he should be grieving. What did she know? Maybe if she'd been a better mother . . .

No. It wasn't Cecily's fault, what had happened to Gwen.

It was his.

That was the truth he had to live with. And that was the reason why people like Abigail Pressman needed to stay as far away from him as possible. He'd been a fool to even entertain his fleeting attraction to her. Remaining her adversary was the best thing he could do for her.

"You didn't have to bring me lunch." He tossed the phone onto the old mercantile countertop and returned to the stage he'd finished only moments before Cecily's call. Odds were, Abigail didn't have more than a year left in her space, and he'd just wasted valuable work time building a stage.

Kate owed him.

Abigail finished collecting the contents of what appeared to be a boxed lunch. A sandwich. Chips. Both individually wrapped, thankfully, or he'd have quite a mess to clean up.

A gentleman would help her.

The thought jabbed him, but before he could act on it, she stood. She still seemed off-balance.

And cute. She was cute.

Knock it off. That's the last thing you need right now.

She approached him, lunch box held out. "I said I would. I'm a man of my word." Under different circumstances, her half smile might've calmed him down.

"Besides, it's the least I can do." She set the box on the counter and retrieved the can of soda from the floor. "It'll probably explode if you're not careful." She slid it down the counter in his direction. "I think it got a pretty good shake-up when it fell."

"Thanks." His stomach growled. He was famished.

"You can try tapping on the top. They say that's supposed to keep it from exploding." She must be a nervous talker. A nervous talker who'd run out of things to say.

The awkward silence between them begged to be filled, but he didn't oblige. He wanted to punch something—or someone. Cecily Gregson knew how to get under his skin. Mostly because she wasn't wrong.

"How long are you going to stay mad at the world, Jacob?" she'd said. "Do you think that's good for you—or for Junie?"

He had a right to his anger. For as long as it took.

Abigail cut into his thoughts. "I hope you like turkey. I had Aaron put bacon on it." She looked away. "Bacon makes everything better." The words came out soft, a space filler.

"Thanks."

"I'm sorry I didn't knock louder."

He met her eyes. She looked genuinely sorry. Or maybe she pitied him. And men just *loved* to be pitied.

"The stage looks good." She walked toward his

handiwork and gave it a quiet inspection. "Thanks for doing that."

"I'll install it tonight after you close, if that's okay," Jacob said, his tone short.

"Sure."

Just go already.

As if she sensed his silent plea, she started for the door. "Thanks again."

"Don't mention it." *Don't mention any of it. Please?*

As she turned toward the door, it opened and Kelly appeared. She looked at Abigail, then at Jacob with an expression that made him feel like he'd done something wrong. "What's going on here?" she demanded.

Jacob watched Abigail shrink in Kelly's presence, illuminating the differences between the two women in vivid color.

He took a few steps toward Abigail. "Nothing to worry about, Kelly. Just getting to know our neighbor."

Kelly's eyes narrowed. "Our *tenant*."

He shot her a look.

Kelly turned to Abigail. She towered over her, and not just in stature. "We should discuss your lease."

Abigail stilled, her body tense as if she was afraid to face the subject.

"You had a pretty good thing going with Harriet," Kelly continued.

"Kelly," Jacob warned.

She ignored him.

Abigail lifted her chin. "Yes, Harriet was very generous with me. She was an old friend of my father's."

"I'm afraid we're not in the same position she was." Kelly stared at Abigail with her head tilted to one side, a look of condescension on her face.

What a lie. After the lawsuit, he was set for life. Two lives. Kelly knew money wasn't an issue for them. This was about power. Abigail's full store that weekend had ticked her off, and this was Kelly's way of putting herself back on top.

"We're going to have to raise your rent for this final year."

Abigail's face fell.

"My lawyer is drawing up the papers. I'll bring them by later this week."

"We'll discuss it later, Kelly," Jacob said, wishing Abigail had escaped before she arrived.

Finally Kelly looked at Jacob, but she didn't say anything.

Abigail met his gaze, her eyes pleading. He hated that his plans for a second chance would force her to find a second chance of her own.

She gave a wordless nod and slipped out the back door, leaving Jacob alone with his anger, guilt nipping at his heels.

Way to stick up for her, buddy.

Kelly shot him a look. "There is nothing to discuss later."

"This is not how we're going to deal with our neighbors."

Her eyes went wide and she feigned innocence. "*All* our neighbors or just book girl?"

Jacob set the box lunch on the counter, ignoring her question.

"If we raise her rent and she decides to go find another space, no one can say we kicked her out. She's gone and our reputation is intact. It's the best option, and I'm pretty sure you know it."

"We could've tried talking to her," Jacob said, irritated that he'd allowed her to bully Abigail like that.

She took a step closer to him. "You're so tense, Jacob. Are you going to admit you have a thing for this girl?"

"Don't be ridiculous. I have a thing for treating people with respect."

Kelly laughed. "She's playing you, you know. Getting you to feel bad for her so you won't raise her rent or kick her out. It's a classic female move." As she turned, her eyes fell on the stage. "What is that?"

He raked his hands through his hair and took a step away from her. "It's a stage."

"For what?"

"For The Book Nook." He relished it a bit too much.

Slowly she turned. "You're kidding, right? She's on a mission to turn her little store into a national treasure and you're helping her?"

"I'm helping my sister."

Kelly's hands went to her hips. "I know business is new to you, but we agreed that I wouldn't be a silent partner in all this. That you'd listen if I had something to say."

Boy, was that a mistake.

"You know how much Gwen meant to me, Jacob. I would never do anything to steer you wrong." She closed the distance between them. "You and Junie are my main priority. You're like family to me." Her hands found their way to his arms; her eyes locked onto his.

Too many uncomfortable seconds passed before Jacob pulled out of her grasp. "I don't see how building a stage is going to hurt anything." But the truth was he didn't want to entertain the idea that Kelly might be right. What if Abigail really was playing him?

Could her kindness be an act? A way to get her hooks into him? How would he ever know if it was?

Maybe it was better to let another woman handle her, even if he didn't agree with Kelly's tactics. He didn't need thoughts of a pretty girl filling his head, making him think—even for a moment—that he had any right to be happy ever again.

No, he'd had his chance, and he blew it.

And he'd live with that for the rest of his life.

Abigail could not believe that woman. Or that man, come to think of it. How could he just stand there and let her say those things? Raise her rent without so much as a conversation?

Because he wasn't the nice guy she'd thought he could be, that's why. Any supposedly kind gestures were just numbing her pain before he ruined her life.

She stripped off her jacket and threw it on her office chair, stormed into the store, and immediately started cleaning everything in sight, terrible thoughts filling her head.

She couldn't lose this place.

"Uh-oh." Mallory kept her distance.

"That Kelly woman is awful." Abigail's voice cracked as she said the words.

"What happened?"

She shook her head, trying to calculate what it would take to pay more rent and still keep the store open. She dropped the cleaning rag, sat down at the counter, and started jotting down numbers, but it only frustrated her. She didn't know exactly what kind of rent they'd be charging her, so how could she make any plans? If they made her pay what she should be paying, she might have to close down at the end of the month.

"Do you have any legal recourse? Does he have to honor your lease?"

Abigail let her head drop into her hands. "I don't think so. I think he can do whatever he wants."

"But your father and Harriet had an arrangement."

Harriet. Of course. She'd been out of the country, but maybe she was back now. Or maybe she still had access to her cell phone.

Abigail pulled out her phone, found Harriet's number, and pushed Send.

Abigail paced while the call tried to connect. Finally, after several unanswered rings, Harriet's voice came on the other end.

"This is Harriet. I'm out of the country for a few months having the time of my life. Leave me a message if you want to, but I probably won't get it. Doesn't mean I don't love you—just means it was time to get a life."

Abigail ended the call, silencing Harriet's loud, recorded laughter.

Mallory's face fell. "Maybe it's time we took matters into our own hands."

Abigail couldn't take another fight-or-die speech. At that moment, she might choose death.

"You want me to break pipes in the basement? Rack up some serious bills for your landlord?"

Abigail laughed. "I think Ursula beat you to that."

Mallory clapped a hand over Abigail's. "I think we need to show the doctor whose town this is."

"I don't follow."

"Abigail, if Loves Park knew there was even a threat of you having to move out, don't you think they'd revolt? We could easily make sure his practice is over before it even starts." Mallory swiped a crumb onto the floor. "What kind of rumor could we start about him?"

"No, I couldn't do that." She didn't want to destroy his life—she just wanted him to agree not to destroy hers.

"I hate to tell you this, but those two aren't giving a second thought to whether or not it's mean to raise your rent or kick you out. You need to refocus. What do you really want?"

She could see the vintage furniture—furniture she'd painted and distressed. She could see the hand-stamped jewelry for sale and the gallery of local artwork. She wanted The Book Nook to grow. To prove that she could make something of herself. Even without a man. She wanted to create something of value. *She* wanted to be valued.

"The only way to accomplish your goal is to get rid of the doctor. When we're done, he'll be begging Ursula to buy the building—and she'll let you buy it from her."

Abigail shook her head. "No. No sabotage necessary. I just need to make the people of Loves Park embrace the store."

Mallory's raised brows told her what a stupid thing that was to say.

"You know what I mean. They have to love this store. I just need something special to really capture their hearts."

Mallory sighed. "Good luck with that."

Back at home, Abigail treated herself to extra bubbles in her bath. She replayed the day's events, including the save the date she'd received in the mail that afternoon. The save the date for Betsy's wedding. She hadn't spoken to her sister since the big announcement. Just one more reason she emerged from her soak more depressed than when she went in.

Even the furniture waiting to be painted couldn't cheer her up.

She pulled on her favorite old sweatshirt, the one with the rips on the ends of the sleeves, and curled up in bed, the box of letters pulled close. While her relationship with the letters had started off rocky and suspicious, she'd actually begun to look forward to this time with them. Mostly anonymous, they gave her the chance to imagine entire stories for their authors.

And while she had no intention of changing her position on love and romance, she did have to admit to the occasional tearjerker.

One last night was from a seventy-two-year-old man named Monty. He sent the letter to the Loves Park postmaster because his wife, Sylvie, had died the year before, and the little town was her favorite place in all their travels.

Abigail cried when she read the way the man signed the letter.

I suppose it's silly to send a letter to you—I'll never even know who you are. But I guess I just wanted someone to know how very special my Sylvie was. Oh, if you could've seen her smile. It lit up the universe. Brighter than all the stars on the clearest Loves Park night.

I wish you'd known her. I pray it's not too many more days before I see her again.

Love,
Monty

Rereading the letter now, Abigail felt her eyes fill with fresh tears. Love like that just couldn't be real, could it? At least, not for most people. And yet Monty believed in it, even after all that time.

Abigail's mind spun back to her childhood, hearing her grandmother and the other Valentine Volunteers reading letters just like this one. But experience spoke louder than any love letter, and her experience told her not to be fooled.

She set the letter aside. She wouldn't be duped again, no matter how lovely it all sounded. No matter how much she wanted to believe that one day someone would love her like that, that someone might refuse to let her memory die.

A small manila envelope caught her eye. Hm. Larger than the others she'd read. Maybe there was chocolate inside.

Like she'd ever eat candy from a stranger.

Unless it was Ghirardelli. That she might have trouble resisting.

She pulled out a plain sheet of white paper, and as she did, a small stack of paper hearts fell out of the envelope, spreading over her quilt.

She sat up and read the handwritten note.

Dear Cupid,

It's our eighth year, and you've probably been waiting with bated breath for our paper hearts, haven't you? This year was full of ups and downs, all of which are reflected right here in our strands and strands of memories.

As you already know, we don't hold on to the past; we send it to you in hopes that maybe someone else will be inspired by our little tradition. In this envelope are stacks of hearts from last Valentine's Day all the way to this Valentine's Day. That's when we strung them up all around the house. We spent the whole day reading them to each other just like always, but now we're sending them off into the world for you.

Maybe you know someone who needs to

believe in love. I can tell you—it really does exist. And I'm enclosing proof in our paper hearts.

Happy Valentine's Day, until next year.

She picked up the hearts that had spilled out on her bed. Paper hearts of various sizes and colors, linked together with a white string. Some looked like they'd been carefully handwritten. Others were more haphazard as if scribbled in haste so as not to be forgotten.

The sentiments written in a masculine hand were sweet, mostly things like *You have the best laugh. Do that more often.* And *I prayed for you this morning.* And *That dress you wore tonight . . . wow.*

Others, in distinctively female handwriting, were equally touching. *Thank you for loving me. I know it's not easy.* And *Loved seeing you dressed up last night—took me back to the night we met.*

Abigail reread the introductory letter, trying to piece together how these hearts worked. She gathered that this couple spent a full year writing out sweet sentiments but keeping them from each other until the following Valentine's Day, when they strung them up around the house.

She imagined the couple—whoever they were—spending the day in bed, looking through all the kind words that boiled down to one thing: they loved each other.

Abigail flipped through more of the hearts, loving the playfulness in many of them, when she stumbled upon one with an entirely different tone:

A dark day. I want to protect you, but you won't let me. I'm sitting outside our room, praying that you feel how very much I love you. Come back to me. Please.

She imagined the difficulty in loving someone on their worst day and wondered how it would feel to have someone else love her, even at her worst. It had been so long since she'd been in a real relationship, she wasn't even sure someone would be able to handle her worst.

Abigail stared at the hearts, and a longing pushed its way through her.

"Ask for what you want."

The thought had popped into her mind uninvited, the memory of her father's words rushing back at her—long-forgotten words.

"You'll never know if you don't ask, Abigail," he'd said. "And that goes for God too." Daddy always taught her that God put certain desires in her heart so she'd ask for them. She'd never thought to ask her father if God had given him what he wanted most.

She'd never thought to ask him what it was he wanted most.

Sometimes it still hurt knowing it wasn't a family.

She glanced down at the letter and wondered why some people seemed to get it right the first time, and others, like her parents, got it so very wrong.

Before she knew what she was doing, a soft whisper escaped her lips. "I want *this,* Lord. I want to know the good and the bad. I want to love and be loved. Without reservation."

The admission bubbled there, underneath her surface.

What was she saying? She didn't want this! She didn't want to risk any of the heartache again. Ever. Her parents had risked it, and what had it gotten them? Sorrow and misery—the kind her mother still hadn't recovered from.

She herself had risked it. And loving Jeremy had just about killed her.

She could still remember the days she didn't want to get out of bed. Days she *didn't* get out of bed. His wedding day had been one of the darkest days of her life, only two months after he told her she was too serious for him. He swore he didn't meet his new wife until after he'd broken up with Abigail. She'd been so captivating that he ran right up to the altar and made it official, leaving Abigail to wonder what was wrong with her.

That kind of raw pain inside was not welcome here—and not searching for love was the only way to avoid it.

And yet, as she piled the hearts in a neat stack,

an unwelcome desire needled her. Had she just been fooling herself to think she didn't believe in the possibility of love? A part of her had always believed it was God's plan for her to be a wife and a mother. The old-fashioned kind. The kind who baked cookies and served on the PTA.

She'd spent hours trying to figure out where she'd misunderstood God. Was it possible he didn't want her to be happy at all?

Her thoughts turned to her own great-great-grandparents. She supposed their love story was the kind that people would string up hearts over. After her dad left, Grandma told her and Betsy and Justin the story every chance she got. Probably trying to counter the example left by their father.

Abigail had loved hearing the story then. Her great-great-grandparents were two kids, really, who abandoned the home they knew out East to go on an adventure together. They left not long after their marriage, forging their way across unfamiliar territory, often with only their love to keep them going. And they'd done it. The legend said John's writings told of his great love for Elsie, and he knew he wouldn't have had the courage to go on if it weren't for her. Elsie loved that man so much she'd given up everything she knew to build a life with him.

Once upon a time, Abigail had bought into the story and fully expected that one day she too would have a love story worth naming a town after.

She closed her eyes and swallowed the lump in her throat, then stuffed the stack of hearts back in the envelope and begged herself to forget she ever read them. Getting caught up in someone else's love story was no way to pass the time.

For now, at least, she'd keep these notes to herself. No sense bringing up something that seemed too personal to broadcast anyway.

And she'd do her very best to be content—to stop wishing for something she knew she'd never have.

Chapter 19

Abigail spent the next few days trying—and failing—to push the paper hearts out of her mind. Despite her efforts to stay away from them, she'd been drawn back repeatedly. Over and over, she'd pulled them out and pieced them together, her imagination heading off in directions her own heart did not appreciate.

She'd read them so many times she practically had them memorized. Then, in a fit of lunacy, she'd replaced the original white string with a red-and-white polka-dot ribbon and hung the collection in her bedroom. Seconds later she'd taken them down, deciding that was just too pathetic.

Instead she now carried them around in her purse, completely pulled in by this couple and their tradition. As if keeping them on her person was less pathetic than hanging them up in her house.

Mostly she wanted to know if anyone else was aware of the hearts . . . more, she decided, than she wanted to keep them a secret. But the letter said this was their eighth year. Did the couple send them to the Loves Park postmaster every year? Or to various places? Was the couple local? What if she knew them?

Panic washed over her. What if it was Jeremy and Lynn, his perfect little wife?

Not a chance. Jeremy was never sentimental. Besides, she knew his handwriting.

She arrived at Gigi's house—where today's Volunteers meeting was to be held—hauling the properly sorted box of letters under an arm, wondering how to ask for the previous seven years of paper hearts without sounding like she'd bought into the whole love and marriage nonsense.

She'd practically had to beg Gigi to allow her to come to the meeting at all, which she found odd. She appreciated they didn't require that she come, but having to beg for a spot at the table made her feel like her membership was on trial.

Ursula answered the door before Abigail knocked. "You're three minutes and twenty-five seconds late."

"I brought scones." Abigail held up a brown paper bag.

Ursula snatched the bag from her hand, opened it, and gave one curt nod. "You're forgiven."

The group assembled around Gigi's dining room table, a large pad of paper on an easel at one end of the room. They sat down and passed out the scones, chatting about mundane things like the weather. Finally Gigi rapped a ruler on the table and the others were instantly silent.

"This meeting has come to order."

Abigail stifled a laugh. She had no idea how seriously they took their volunteer duties. Ursula silenced her with a bushy-eyebrowed glare, and Abigail was grateful she'd made her deadline and successfully categorized the envelopes according to Gigi's instructions. It was a good thing she'd also brought back the replies she'd written to the letters that did include return addresses.

"As you know, we have much business to attend to. The Rose Ball is coming up, and then Valentine's Day only weeks later." Gigi folded her hands at her chest. "Oh, I just love this time of year."

Abigail had never in her life felt that way about Valentine's Day or any of the other made-up Loves Park holidays meant to make women swoon. Not even when she *was* dating. Though admittedly that helped a little.

"Why don't we hear your report first, Abigail?" Gigi asked. The women all turned and looked at her.

"Oh." Suddenly self-conscious, Abigail pulled the stacks of envelopes from the box and let them spill across the table. "Well, I read them."

"You read all of them?" Tess wore a look of disbelief.

"Was I not supposed to?"

"No, it's fine. It just takes a while to get through some of them. I usually end up scanning the ones without return addresses."

I have no life.

"And?" Doris leaned forward in her chair like a bird perched on a wire.

"Nothing out of the ordinary." Abigail tried to stay nonchalant. She couldn't come across like she was actually *interested* in this process.

"Nothing?" Doris looked disappointed.

"Were you hoping for someone on the ledge of Longs Peak, Doris?" Ursula rolled her eyes.

"Of course not. I just like it when there's real romance in there."

Evelyn reached over and put a hand on the older woman's arm. "It's okay, Doris. I do too." She smiled, her expression warm.

Abigail thought about some of the letters she'd tucked aside. "I guess there was romance. I didn't realize that was supposed to be part of my report, and I wasn't really looking for it."

Gigi smiled warmly. "There are no hard-and-fast rules, dear. We just wanted to get your impressions."

"I replied to this stack—the ones with return addresses—like you said."

Doris had already opened one of the replies she'd written, and Abigail cringed. She should've sealed them. She didn't like being checked up on like this. And in all honesty, her replies to some of the letters could have been more diplomatic.

Sure enough, Doris's face fell as she read through the first response.

"What's the matter, Doris?" Gigi asked.

Doris's expression changed as she glanced at Abigail. "Oh, nothing."

Ursula snatched the paper from Doris and read the note aloud. " 'While I found your letter a bit whiny and negative, I do understand the plight of a singleton. The best advice I can give is to realize you aren't a fairy-tale princess and no prince is on his way to save you.' " She snorted.

The Volunteers all turned and looked at Abigail, who shrugged. "Too much?"

"Oh, dear." Gigi swiped the stack of replies from Doris and stuffed them in a drawer. "We'll go through them all later. Is that everything you have to report? Nothing else out of the ordinary?"

"There was one letter," Abigail began. "From a

man named Monty. It was about how he missed his wife, Sylvie. She died."

The room sighed, and Abigail saw an open door.

"And another one from a couple who write love notes on paper hearts—"

A collective gasp.

"Wonderful!" Gigi stood and retrieved a small box from a nearby countertop. "I'd almost given up hope on our favorite lovebirds. They missed last year." She opened the box and pulled out stacks of neatly strung paper hearts.

Abigail's pulse quickened and she fought the urge to grab the whole pile of them and run. She wanted to read them, to learn more about this couple's story. Instead she opened the manila envelope and pulled out the string of hearts she'd so carefully studied.

"Your set makes eight in all," Gigi said. "Eight years of love letters from eight different Valentine's Days. They wanted to share their love with the world. It was as if they'd soaked up everything they could from the year and had to pass it along."

"I'd been watching for their trademark box of paper hearts to arrive. If I'd seen it, I never would've given it to you," Doris said. "No offense."

"The ones I read were stuffed in this envelope."

Gigi frowned. "That doesn't sound right. They always arrive in a beautiful decorated box."

Now Abigail frowned.

"Were they tied together?" Evelyn asked.

"Yes, with plain white string," Abigail said, noticing the frills on the strands Gigi held.

"Where'd the polka-dot ribbon come from?" Ursula snapped.

Abigail looked away. "I did that."

She could only imagine the raised eyebrows that were now turned toward her. "You did?" Gigi said, startled.

"Yes. Don't make a big thing of it, okay? I liked the story." Abigail held the hearts with an unwarranted protectiveness.

Doris patted her hand. "Maybe there is hope for you yet, Miss Pressman."

"Would you want to take the others home, dear?" Gigi asked. "Maybe you'd like to learn more about our favorite romantics."

I thought you'd never ask.

Abigail shrugged. "I suppose that's a good idea. Especially if something with the new ones seems off somehow."

"You know what seems off?" Ursula swallowed the last bite of a scone. Apparently it had been the only thing keeping her quiet. "Your plans for that doctor."

Abigail felt the heat rush to her cheeks. "What are you talking about?"

"I heard he's raising your rent."

She ran her fingers across the string of paper hearts, wondering how these women knew as much about her business as she did.

"What will you do about it?" Ursula apparently wouldn't stop until she'd successfully obtained the deed to the building and booted Jacob from town, and Abigail had the distinct impression it had nothing to do with her. Ursula was mad that Jacob had turned down her offer.

"I-I have a plan," Abigail said, stuttering like a schoolgirl giving her first speech.

Ursula raised a brow.

"I'm going to make Loves Park fall in love with me."

Ursula cackled. "Oh, kid. It's amazing you've survived this long."

Abigail frowned. Probably not the best time to admit she'd been an English major and everything she knew about business she'd learned from her father and from stocking the small business section in her own store.

"It's a good plan," Abigail defended. "If Loves Park really gets behind The Book Nook, how can he possibly kick me out? He'll look like the worst kind of person. No one wants to go to a mean doctor."

"That's all you've got?" Ursula stared.

"It's not a bad idea," Evelyn said, probably more out of pity than anything.

"It's underdeveloped." Ursula stood, walked over to the drinks Gigi had laid out on the buffet, and poured herself a cup of punch. She took a drink, poured more, and drank again. There was something distinctly masculine about this woman. And something terrifying.

"You think she needs to do more," Gigi said.

Ursula rolled her eyes. "She's trying to save her business. Yes, she needs to do more."

Abigail tried not to get any more defensive. "What do you suggest?"

Ursula paced, eyes narrowed as if she was in thought. "You need a gimmick."

" 'Sit. Read. Caffeinate.' That's my slogan."

Ursula waved her off. "No, you need to give people a reason to come in the store. Every season is tourist season around here—what can we do to turn The Book Nook into part of this town's history? Like the postmarks and the Valentine's Day celebrations."

"I know what you're saying," Tess said.

"Yes," Doris added. "You need to turn your store into even more of a Loves Park landmark than it is now. Capitalize on your status in this town."

Abigail frowned. "How is that different from what I'm already doing? Free drinks and kids' classes and—"

Ursula cut her off. "It's not enough. What these people want is romance. But you're the last single girl around."

Abigail shifted uncomfortably, figuring Ursula must have heard that she stood up Duncan at the restaurant the other night.

But Ursula didn't mention it as she plopped into the chair beside Abigail. "People who live here and visit here love that sappy garbage. They want to feel like they're experiencing a romantic dream or something. You have potential you aren't using."

"If you say so." Abigail didn't feel like arguing.

"Think about it. They hear the Loves Park legend. They come here with their sweetheart to fall more in love or to get engaged or married or whatever." Ursula stopped talking, though her thought felt incomplete.

"And if you can make The Book Nook part of the hype, they'll come to you too," Gigi said, filling in the blanks.

Tess smiled. "It's basically what you already planned, plugged into an electrical outlet."

"We don't do anything small, dear," Gigi said. "Concerts and family days are nice ideas, but they don't have the kind of lasting power you need."

"You need a gimmick," Ursula repeated.

"What do you want me to do, take out an ad in the newspaper?" Abigail said. "Give myself a tiara and a sash that claims some sort of fame I certainly don't deserve?"

Capitalizing on her family's so-called romantic legacy was a great idea in theory, but the truth was none of them—not even Ursula—seemed to know exactly how to use it to put The Book Nook on the map. Besides, Abigail had been trying to forget that blasted legacy for years. Making it part of her business felt like a complete sellout.

"Don't be discouraged, dear," Gigi said. "Just give us some time. We won't stop until we come up with something brilliant."

She pushed the box of paper hearts across the table and smiled at Abigail. "Now, you run along and catch yourself up on the paper hearts. Report back next week if you find anything of concern."

Abigail did as she was told with the appropriate amount of indifference, knowing she should feel more dejected that they hadn't figured out her business problem and likely never would. She *should* feel that way, but she didn't because the only thing she could think about was getting home, where she could read the rest of the paper hearts in peace.

Chapter 20

Seven years' worth of paper hearts meant that Abigail had a lot of love notes to read. Instead of devouring them in one sitting as she'd originally intended, she decided to bring them to work with her and find pockets of time during the day to hide herself in the office and do her civic duty.

That's what she was telling herself anyway. The others had given her a job, and what kind of volunteer would she be if she didn't see it through?

Mostly, though, she was itching with curiosity, dying to know why the first seven strands of paper hearts came all neatly tied to ribbons in beautifully decorated boxes, while the others—the ones she'd read already—were stuffed in a plain manila envelope and tied together with plain white string.

An hour or so into the morning, she stole away to her office, where she closed the door and took out the first strand of hearts. Gigi had begun numbering them after the second year's set came. Each strand appeared to be composed of several ribbons tied together, end to end.

The very first one came with a letter. She almost didn't want to open it. Somehow, this all felt so personal, so private, but if it gave her a clue as to what these people were like—these people who had the kind of love most couples only dreamed of—she'd do it.

Plus, she was far too nosy to ignore it. And she'd already seen the letter from the most recent set of hearts. She hung one of the strands around her neck to get it out of the way and started reading.

Dear Cupid,

Some couples don't make a big thing of Valentine's Day, but we always have. Even when we were dating, it was a holiday worth celebrating, so after we got married, it became an even bigger deal.

I'm not sure when it began, but one of us got the idea to spend the whole year, from Valentine's Day to Valentine's Day, looking for things we love about each other. Instead of forgetting to say them out loud, we wrote them down on paper hearts. The night before Valentine's Day, he strung his and I strung mine, and we woke up to a house filled with love. It's a little bit cheesy, but more than once throughout the year it kept us from fighting. We'd be angry about something and then he'd stop and say, "Wait, I need to go write something down."

It kept us focused on what matters, I guess. And we're planning to make a tradition of it.

You'd think we'd want to hold on to our hearts, but the truth is, we'd rather send them out into the world. Maybe someone—maybe you—will be moved to do something like this for another person. Maybe it'll make you realize that love does exist, if you're lucky enough to find it. We were . . . so we wanted to share it.

I hope it inspires you.

A couple in love

Abigail stared at the letter for a few seconds. *"Maybe it'll make you realize that love does exist."* Why was she so drawn to the words on these hearts? She carefully returned the letter to the envelope. Though many of these sentiments had shown up in the first letter she'd read, somehow they'd started to penetrate her consciousness.

And she wasn't sure she liked that.

A crash in the store drew her attention away from the hearts. She really should stop making a habit of hiding out in her office.

Abigail rushed into the store. "What's going on?" She scanned the room and saw Aaron near the back row of bookshelves, cleaning up what appeared to be a dropped tray of mugs, at least two of which had shattered.

"He's cute, but he's clumsy," Mallory said.

Abigail sighed. "Those are coming out of his paycheck."

"What are you wearing?" Mallory stared at her.

Abigail followed her eyes downward. She'd completely forgotten the strand of hearts draped around her neck. "Oh, just a project I'm working on." She took it off and set it on the counter, grabbed a broom and dustpan from the storage closet, then rushed over to help Aaron recover from the crash. She knew a little something about dropping trays and breaking dishes.

"Sorry, boss," he said.

"It's fine, Aaron."

"I can pay for them."

She held the dustpan as he swept up the shards of ceramic. "Don't worry. It was an accident."

Softy.

"I can throw this away," she said as he completed the sweeping. "You take the unbroken ones to the kitchen and get back to work."

"You sure?" Aaron stood.

She nodded and watched as he walked away, leaving her with a dustpan full of mug pieces. She loved those mugs—at The Book Nook, no two were the same.

After a quick stop at the storage closet, Abigail returned to the front of the store, where a small group had assembled around the counter.

Oh no. The hearts. She'd left the hearts on the counter.

Abigail's heart sank. She should've been more careful—those hearts deserved to be protected.

"Mallory?" Abigail pushed through the small crowd, which seemed to keep multiplying. "What's going on?"

"Oh, Abigail, is this your new idea?" Mallory asked. "I love it. It's just perfect."

"Here, look at this one." A middle-aged local named Mary held up one of the hearts. " 'In that red dress, you could stop a man's heart.' "

One long, drawn-out sigh wound around the edges of the little gaggle at the counter.

"I'm sorry, everyone," Abigail said, trying to figure out how to get the women to release the hearts without using excessive force. "These are—"

"Such a great idea, Abigail. Just what this town

needs." Smith Jenkins would know. She was one of the town's oldest residents.

"No, these aren't an idea. They're—"

"Genius," Blythe Roberts cut in. "Do you need some help putting them up? I can't wait to add my own. I'll send Michael down here on a little scavenger hunt." She moved her eyebrows up and down. "Do you have any blank hearts? I'll try to keep it G-rated."

Abigail stuttered as she searched for a reply.

"I think we left them in the back," Mallory said. "We'll go get them."

As Mallory pulled Abigail away from the squealing horde, she heard one of the ladies read another heart. " 'Never thought anyone could love me so well. Thank you for being my rock.' "

That would've been from the wife. She said things like that. He said things about the way she looked or the way she laughed. Sometimes he wrote about the way he felt, but not as often as she did. Abigail liked them already. He adored his wife, and she let him love her.

She imagined that would be difficult, to let someone really love you. To admit you needed to be loved. Especially after you'd already been hurt. The idea caught in her throat and stayed there, heavy and unmoving.

God, I don't want to think about that. I'm fine being alone. Please help me stop these ridiculous thoughts.

She glanced back at the group of ladies. Watching them pore over the hearts set something loose in Abigail's belly. Those hearts were private. They weren't meant to be shared with the town.

Or maybe she just didn't want them shared. Maybe a part of her wanted to keep them all to herself.

"This is perfect." Mallory shut the door and scrounged through the copy paper in the office, finding some that had a distinct pink tint to it. "This will do for now, and at lunch I'll run and get more."

"Why?" Abigail shook her head. "Those weren't supposed to be out there—I told you, they're a project I'm working on."

"Did you write them?"

She scoffed. "Are you kidding? I hate that stuff."

"Then what difference does it make? Those ladies love that stuff. It's just what you need. You said you wanted to put The Book Nook on the map, didn't you?"

Abigail frowned. "I guess."

Mallory pushed open the door just enough so Abigail could see the now-large crowd gathered around the paper hearts. It was like they'd formed an assembly line around the counter as they moved around it, reading the hearts as they went.

"They're eating this up," Mallory said, closing the door. "They want in on it, Abigail. It's like all your prayers have been answered."

Abigail paced, rubbing her hand over her forehead in a way that was meant to make her think. It wasn't working.

"What's wrong with you?" Mallory folded the papers and started cutting.

"Those hearts are private. They're someone's private thoughts."

Mallory stared at Abigail, accusation on her face. "Then how'd you get them?"

Abigail sighed. "That doesn't matter. I've been authorized to see them."

"You've been authorized?" Mallory shook her head. "Do you want to save your store or not?" She held up the blank hearts she'd cut.

Abigail pushed through the door with every intention of taking the strand of hearts from the others, breaking up the crowd, and telling them this had all been a big misunderstanding.

But when she emerged from the office, the chatter was infectious, the energy unlike anything she'd ever seen in The Book Nook before.

"What a darling idea." One of the old ladies held up the end of the strand so the woman next to her could read it. The other woman nodded and made that aw-how-sweet face, then showed the first woman another heart.

Abigail wondered which secrets were being shared. All those precious moments between two people in love—out on public display.

"Can I have two blank hearts to hang up here?"

A younger woman stood in front of her with a hopeful expression. "I'm thinking of leaving a message as a secret admirer. Do you think that's a dumb idea?"

The woman was mousy and a bit on the heavy side. Plain face, but kind eyes. Kind eyes full of hope.

Abigail shook her head. "Not dumb at all." But she couldn't imagine how an anonymous message hung in a bookstore could be the way to win a man's affections.

The woman smiled, hugging herself inside her winter parka. "There's someone at work. Maybe he'll see it, and he'll—" she met Abigail's eyes— "he'll think of me?" There was a question in her voice, the kind that searched for approval. Abigail smiled, reaching toward Mallory for a couple of blank hearts.

"Here," she said, handing the hearts to the woman. "It's worth a shot."

The woman smiled as if she'd just decided for the first time in her life to take a risk.

Abigail turned, amazed at the scene playing out in front of her. The women were oohing and aahing over the hearts. The story had pulled them in the same way it had her, and while she still had misgivings, it was too late now. They were texting and calling friends to come down to the store and write their own hearts. Everyone who entered the store gravitated toward the crowd, all wanting to know what the fuss was about.

And Abigail was helpless to stop it.

And why should she? Keeping the hearts to herself was no longer an option, so she might as well hang them up. She couldn't deny they brought joy to everyone who read them. Besides, hadn't the letter said this couple wanted their love to be shared? Maybe in a way this was honoring their relationship, not exploiting it.

"Oh, Abigail, all this time everyone thought your heart was cold, like a big block of ice," Smith said, a new affection on her face. "It's so good to know your family's legacy isn't completely lost on you."

Abigail begged her eyes not to roll.

"We'd just about given up on you, dear," Blythe said. "There's been talk that you're going the way of old Matthias Linden."

Abigail frowned. Matthias Linden was the crabbiest, meanest man in Loves Park—maybe even in all of Colorado. Why on earth would anyone compare her to him?

Blythe's eyes sparkled. "But maybe there's hope for you after all!"

She left before Abigail could ask about the Matthias Linden reference, one that she forced out of her mind for fear of dwelling on it and becoming legitimately upset. Her thoughts turned to the other strands of hearts—the many, many hearts she hadn't even read yet. She'd keep those to herself. At least until after she'd had a chance to look them over first.

"Here we all thought you hated Valentine's Day," another woman said. "You're a regular cupid, Abigail."

Yep. That's me. A regular cupid.

And just like that, the paper hearts took on a life of their own.

Chapter 21

Friday morning, Gigi, Doris, and Ursula made their usual trip to see Lionel Richardson, the postmaster. He gathered all of their mail and held it for them, and if Gigi didn't know better, she'd think the widower might be a little sweet on her.

At least that's what Doris said.

Gigi drove the other two downtown to the old post office, pulling her Buick into a spot right in front of the small building. The post office, like so many Old Town buildings, was built in the early days of Loves Park. Thanks to dedicated renovations, it had remained in wonderful condition. Ever since Gigi had joined the Volunteers, visiting the post office always brought such a rush of excitement.

The three ladies plodded inside, smiling at exiting customers whose faces were all familiar, though Gigi couldn't place every name. Lionel stood behind the counter, and when he saw them enter, he left his spot and rushed to the back room, where he kept their basket of mail.

By the time he returned, the three of them were standing at the counter, Doris and Gigi poised for conversation and Ursula clutching that raggedy purse like she was about to be mugged.

"Morning, ladies. Gigi." Lionel grinned.

"Lionel, do you have anything new for us today?" Gigi smiled back.

"Just so happens that I do. I imagine it's going to start picking up the closer we get to Valentine's Day, as usual." He handed the basket over the counter.

"I believe you're right about that," Gigi said. "Girls, why don't we just take a quick peek at the letters over here?"

They moved to a long counter against the wall and shuffled the envelopes around, looking for anything that stood out. It was a ritual, really, though they rarely read anything standing here in the post office.

Perhaps it was because Lionel enjoyed feeling like a part of things. Or perhaps because every time Gigi glanced behind the counter, he smiled at her like she was a princess. She returned the smile again, but Doris's excited gasp pulled her attention back to the basket.

"Doris, we're in a public place," Ursula hissed.

Neither Gigi nor Doris commented on the fact that Ursula was the last person in the world who should be reminding anyone of social graces.

"What is it, Doris?" Gigi asked, coming closer.

In her hand, Doris held a now-opened manila envelope. "More hearts."

Gigi leaned closer to inspect the hearts in the package. "These don't look like the same ones our couple has been sending."

"But they are. They just haven't been put on a string."

"Maybe they split up," Ursula said.

"Don't be so awful," Gigi said. "We should take these to Abigail. She can piece it all together."

Gigi stuffed the few hearts she'd pulled out back into the envelope while the others looked on.

"Oh, it's just like Christmas," Doris whispered.

"Yeah, on the year you find out there's no such thing as Santa Claus." Ursula picked up the basket with the rest of the letters in it, but Gigi's glare made her stop moving. "What? You can't tell me this is a good thing. Finding the hearts in this state means something is wrong with this couple, and you know it."

Gigi sighed. "I don't know anything yet. Except that we have another piece to the puzzle, and I want to get these over to Abigail right away." She waved to Lionel and pushed her way out the front door, but she couldn't ignore the worried fear that rushed through her. She didn't know what had happened with the paper heart couple, but something told her Ursula was right—whatever it was, it wasn't good. And Gigi couldn't ignore the heartbreak that accompanied that realization.

Friday morning, Jacob awoke with a new resolve. Kate took Junie to school, leaving him alone with his guilt. He'd spent the entire week working on the renovations, meeting with the electrician and the drywall guy and the plumber—yet he'd found a way to avoid Abigail every single day.

Still, regardless of his hesitation, he'd instructed Kelly to let him handle things with Abigail from this point on. She hadn't received the suggestion well.

"Really, Jacob? You're about the last person who should be handling Abigail Pressman."

Jacob reminded himself that he was in charge. This project was his. She worked for him. "I think a different approach might work better with her."

She drew in a deep breath. "A softer approach, you mean."

"Something like that, yes."

She'd eventually agreed, and thankfully Jacob didn't have to explain that their tenant had walked in on his conversation with Gwen's mother—a conversation that had scratched the surface of every raw nerve he'd tried to bury for the past two years. He'd practically been paralyzed hearing that voice on the line.

The truth was, smoothing things over with Abigail was as much about what she'd overheard as it was about the way Kelly had talked to her.

What if Abigail started digging into his past? She seemed like the curious type. He needed to make sure not to give her any more reasons to hate him—the last thing he needed was for the rumors and whispers to start up again. He'd had enough of that before they moved, and so had Junie.

So he'd do what he knew he should've done a long time ago and apologize to Abigail Pressman, but he had to do it today since his sister was requiring his attendance at her little coffee shop concert that night. He couldn't show his face in The Book Nook if Abigail still hated him.

Outside, there was a chill in the air. He trudged through the snow, thankful that in spite of the winter weather, the sun was shining. It's one of the reasons he'd stayed in Colorado instead of moving somewhere that was always warm. He wanted Junie to still be able to build snowmen and go sledding. Of course, he'd yet to do either of those things with her this year.

Some days it felt like a chore just to get dressed.

But he did. And he kept his head down and threw himself into his work. He didn't know what else to do.

On his way out to the truck, he spotted something in the distance. An animal up the hill out back, hovering around his shed. They stared at each other for a few long seconds. It looked like some sort of retriever—golden fur and those sad, hopeful eyes. The dog turned in a circle and whimpered, limping on its hind leg. Jacob squinted, trying to see any visible wounds, and while it was hard to tell from this distance, he did get a glimpse of what appeared to be dried blood on the dog's back leg.

Jacob took a few cautious steps toward the animal, careful not to startle the poor thing. The dog squared off with him as if ready to pounce.

"It's okay," Jacob coaxed. "I just want to see if you're hurt."

He moved closer, still speaking in low, gentle tones, hand stretched out, but downward because someone once told him that was how to approach unfamiliar dogs.

"Can I take a look at that leg? Looks like it hurts."

The dog bobbed its head side to side, letting out a mix between a growl and a bark.

Jacob took another step and the dog barked, turned, and hobbled off into the woods. Watching until it disappeared behind the trees, Jacob walked over to where it had been lingering near his shed. A small space had been cleared of snow next to the outbuilding—possibly a makeshift bed. The animal must have been staying there, trying to get out of the cold.

The poor dog was probably terrified. Terrified, wounded, freezing, and hungry. Not a great combination. He'd warn Junie not to go near if she saw it, but something inside him shifted—something he hadn't felt in months. The need to heal.

He'd forgotten that feeling.

In spite of the busyness of opening a new practice, he was just going through the motions. He hadn't had the desire to do what he was trained to do in a long time—not since Gwen.

He waited at the back of the shed for a few minutes in case the dog returned, but there was no sign of him.

Jacob knew he'd have to earn the animal's trust if he had any hope of fixing whatever was wrong with its leg. He made a mental note to pick up some provisions and find out if Loves Park had a vet, and he headed into town.

The Book Nook was bustling with activity, as it always seemed to be lately. He parked in the back but entered in the front to buy a quick cup of coffee before heading to the grocery store. He didn't want to abuse his position, and while he owned the building, he really had no right to come in through the bookshop's back door. Besides, he didn't want to risk upsetting Abigail any more than he already had.

It was only January, but the store seemed to be filled with Valentine's Day decorations. Or maybe there was another Sweetheart Festival Jacob didn't know about. He didn't exactly put those things on his mental calendar.

The crowd buzzed, and he scanned the store for Abigail. He found himself anxious to spot her as if seeing her face would somehow set him on the path to having a good day. He obviously had issues if seeing a woman who despised him was supposed to brighten his day. Especially after he'd been staying away from her all week.

At the counter, over to the right and as far away from the crowd as possible, he spotted her, sitting on a stool and talking to a woman with a notepad. At her side, a man with a camera. A reporter?

Uh-oh.

He inched toward the right and stood in line for coffee, but he still couldn't hear what they were saying. Abigail flashed a smile for the camera, and the photographer clicked several shots. She ran a hand through her long hair, shaking it out as if somehow she wanted to shake off discomfort.

Jacob's mind spun back to the interviews he'd been forced to undergo after Gwen's death. Rumors of foul play had followed him around for weeks. He knew a little something about uncomfortable conversations.

Abigail hardly seemed like the type to seek

out the press. The reporter stood, shook Abigail's hand, and motioned for the photographer to follow her.

"Let's just get some shots of the store and the paper hearts," she said as she passed by Jacob.

He turned, and there, dangling above the rows of bookshelves, were strands of hearts. Hearts that looked very familiar. The reporter instructed her photographer to get close-ups of at least a few different hearts. "I want people to be able to read them."

His mouth went dry. How had he not noticed them as soon as he walked in the door?

"Hi."

Abigail's voice startled him, and it only kicked his pulse up a notch. His mind spun, trying to understand how his hearts—Gwen's hearts—had ended up as decor for her store. Did Abigail know he'd written them? Sent them in every year after Valentine's Day?

Was she mocking him?

She couldn't possibly know—and yet, if she was trying to torment him, she'd found the perfect way. Now he had a new reason to shut the place down.

"Are you okay?" She stood a head shorter than he, her eyes brighter than the last time he'd been in. She looked . . . hopeful. He wrestled with his conflicting emotions for too many seconds, making her visibly uncomfortable.

Get ahold of yourself. She didn't do this to hurt you.

"Sorry. Yes, I'm fine. Just didn't expect a reporter in here." Jacob forced himself to smile.

She shifted. "Oh? Are you hiding from the police or something?"

He looked at her, saw she was smiling, and told himself again to calm down. "Just surprised is all." He forced a smile.

"Did you come in for coffee?"

He swallowed. He didn't remember why he'd come in. "Uh . . . yes."

She motioned for him to follow her. He sat at the corner of the counter, away from everyone else, and watched as the reporter interviewed a couple of shoppers, all of whom were fascinated with the paper hearts.

The pain prickled inside his chest, stinging like an electrical jolt. He wanted to tear the hearts from the ceiling strand by strand. He wanted to stuff them in a box and bury it where no one would ever be able to parade them in front of him, reminding him of his mistakes, of all he'd lost.

Abigail brought him a hot mug of coffee. "Here you go."

He hated how much he loved her coffee. Even the mugs were unique, like every detail had been perfectly planned.

She stood for a moment, and he knew he had only seconds left of her attention, but his mind had gone blank. He'd come here to apologize to her. For being a jerk. For allowing Kelly to be a jerk. For infringing on her life in such a public way.

But now, with the hearts dangling only a few feet away, he couldn't find the words.

"Do you need anything else?" She had a timidity about her that he found refreshing. As if she never wanted to impose on him. As if she could.

He met her eyes, willing away the sadness that lingered at the back of his mind. Seeing the garlands he and Gwen had created brought back too many memories.

He shook his head.

A polite smile in return. She started to walk away but turned back. "Are you sure you're all right? You have this sort of sad look on your face."

Jacob inhaled. What was it about this woman that made him want to recount his entire life's story to her? He never talked to anyone about what he and Junie had been through—he certainly couldn't start now.

He came to Loves Park so people would stop looking at him like that. And yet her look seemed to have something more than just pity inside it.

"What's with the paper hearts?" He thumbed the top of his coffee mug.

She turned toward them, seemingly pleased with the attention they drew from him. "Oh, it's the most incredible thing," she said. She handed him a sheet of paper.

At the top, a photo of two of the hearts he'd written out himself. Underneath, a brief synopsis titled "The Story of the Paper Hearts."

He skimmed the first paragraph.

Some traditions are worth carrying on, and the paper hearts is one of them—a special way to profess love. The anonymous couple who began sending their strands of paper hearts to the Loves Park postmaster several years ago were onto something. They kept their love front and center all year long by writing out what they loved about each other, saving their words on paper hearts to be strung up on garlands as Valentine's Day approached.

He resisted the urge to correct her on her facts. She'd managed to put most of it together, but the truth was, they'd waited until the night before Valentine's Day to string up the hearts, each putting their hearts together on a string meant to be read the following morning. Gwen had hung her hearts on one side of the house and he hung his on the other. They took Valentine's Day off no matter what, and they spent the day reading the hearts out loud to each other.

Gwen had been a hopeless romantic. He'd pretended to hate it sometimes, but the truth was, he'd liked watching for things he loved about her to document all year long. He liked it so much, he'd had a hard time breaking the habit.

It's why he still kept blank hearts in the desk drawer.

He read on.

Here at The Book Nook, we've decided to continue this tradition through Valentine's Day, and we invite you, our loyal friends, to join in the fun. We've provided blank paper hearts at the front counter. Write your message and place it in the box. We'll string up your message in the store, joining your paper hearts with the originals and carrying on a tradition that's bound to capture your heart.

And who knows? Maybe, in time, we'll even reveal the identity of the couple who introduced us to the paper hearts in the first place.

Jacob's mouth went dry. Were they going to launch a manhunt to find out where the hearts came from? The whole thing, including sending them to this town, had been Gwen's idea.

"We should pass them along," Gwen had said when he'd protested her idea to send the hearts away. Didn't she want to keep them so they could go back and look over the things they wrote each year? But she'd been adamant. "We should send them out into the world so we can focus on the future, not dwell on the past."

That had been her way. Always striving to look

forward, yet mired in everything behind.

Still, he wanted her to be happy, so he obliged. And he helped her box up the hearts in her typical artistic way and send them off to Loves Park, which had seemed so far away at the time.

He'd never thought about people reading them. Gwen must've known they would, but Jacob assumed they'd be tossed aside.

As much as he'd often wished he could go back and read about better times, he'd had to admit the pain of reliving those moments might be enough to pull him under. Yet here they were on the wall—moment after moment.

"Isn't it a great idea?" Abigail said, her words practically bouncing. She met his eyes, then looked away. Probably didn't like what she found there.

He couldn't respond. How long would it be before they found out he was one half of the couple they were all so intrigued by?

Walking around town had been bad enough before, but now? If everyone discovered the tragic truth, he'd have to pack up and move all over again.

Jacob cleared his throat, embarrassed by how long it had been since she'd asked her question. He swallowed his hurt and shrugged, still not capable of words.

She narrowed her eyes, an amused look on her face. "You're such a guy."

Something about the way she said it, like an accusation, made him smile—a real one—in spite of his pain. "What's that supposed to mean?"

"It's probably too romantic for someone like you." She took out her rag and wiped the counter. "Most guys won't get it."

"That right?"

She raised a brow. "You don't strike me as the romantic type."

Funny, he could say the same thing about her, though he suspected there was much more to Abigail Pressman than met the eye.

"Where'd the hearts come from, anyway?" He kept his tone casual, not wanting to let on that he was mortified and desperate to know how on earth she'd gotten ahold of his innermost thoughts.

She tucked the rag in the waistband of her apron. "You know about the Loves Park postmark and the Valentine Volunteers, right?"

He took a sip. "I think I heard something about them." *Liar.*

"We're famous as a place to send wedding invitations and love letters." She smiled. "It's actually kind of annoying living in a town that's famous for love, but it is what it is." She ran a hand over her hair. Something about the way she did it kept him from looking away. She was a walking contradiction. Quiet and shy some of the time, yet independent and direct at other times.

It added up to something strangely captivating.

"You didn't really answer my question," he said, allowing his amusement to play through. Maybe the best strategy at this point was to steer the search for the anonymous couple away from him. Be totally nonchalant.

She let out a slight laugh. "I'm one of the Volunteers who sorts through the letters. Well, sort of. I just started."

"And any of these letters run the risk of being put on display?"

She caught his glance and held it mischievously. "Only the really good ones."

He forced his eyes away from hers and took another drink. "How does one get to be a Volunteer?"

She shook her head. "Oh, that's a story for another day."

"Is it like a secret club?"

She grinned. "Something like that."

He inhaled a quick breath, reassuring himself that neither she nor anyone else knew anything about his involvement with the paper hearts. He owed her an apology now more than ever.

"Abigail, I—"

Before he could finish, the door opened and a raucous group of three familiar women entered. Their gasps and shrieks could've woken the dead.

Abigail turned toward the door with a smile.

"How about that?" Ursula stood in the doorway,

clutching a bag that would've held the entire contents of his dresser. "You did it."

"You wanted to know about the other Volunteers?" Abigail said. "There they are."

She couldn't be serious. These cackling women were responsible for sorting through the mail that came to the Loves Park postmaster?

Had they read all of the hearts too?

"Abigail, you just won't believe it," one of the ladies said, bustling her way over to the counter. Within seconds, the other two older women had joined her.

Each one of them paused at the sight of him sitting next to Abigail. The things they must be saying about him behind closed doors . . . He didn't even want to know.

That Pembrooke woman scowled at him, then shot Abigail a what's-he-doing-here? look. He resisted the urge to remind Ursula that he owned the place.

One of the other women stepped forward and smiled at him. She stuck her hand toward him. "I don't believe we've been properly introduced. I'm Gigi Monroe, and these are my friends—"

The short, plump woman shouldered her way in front of Gigi and grasped Jacob's other hand with both of hers. "I'm Doris. You're very handsome." Doris looked at Abigail, whose cheeks turned three different shades of red. "*Very* handsome."

He changed his mind. Maybe he *did* want to

know what they'd been saying about him behind closed doors.

Jacob gazed into Abigail's eyes until she looked away. He hated to admit it, but embarrassment looked cute on her.

"And I believe you've already met Ursula." Gigi's expression changed.

"Mrs. Pembrooke," Jacob said. "Good to see you again."

Ursula scowled. "Get on with this, Gigi."

Gigi turned her attention back to Abigail. "We've just been to the post office, and guess what was waiting for us?"

She shrugged. "Chocolate?"

"This is serious, Abigail," Doris said.

"We got a new package of paper hearts." Gigi pulled out a manila envelope addressed to the postmaster. The thing had been torn open, and the ladies were clamoring to pull the hearts out, spreading them over the countertop. "You won't believe what they say."

"You read them without me?" Abigail picked one up. " 'Stared at Longs Peak for a while this morning, thought about that embarrassingly loud laugh of yours. I always loved that laugh.' "

Jacob's fingers tightened around the mug. How did the women ever get their hands on these? He'd written that a couple weeks ago.

"Longs Peak?" Abigail looked at the other women. "So they are local."

"I don't know anyone this romantic, not even in Loves Park," Doris said. "Must've visited recently. There are so many cabins for rent up in the mountains."

He caught a glimpse of another one on the counter near his mug. *Thought I saw you at the grocery store today. Made me miss you.*

His mind spun back to that day, one of his first in Loves Park. He and Junie were getting used to the new grocery store, picking up the makings of their first real dinner in their new home. He rounded the cereal aisle and nearly lost his breath. In front of him stood a woman who, from the back, looked just like Gwen. Same auburn hair. Same slight build. His heart sped up and Junie must've noticed because she asked if he was okay.

He'd ignored her, moving instead toward the woman at the end of the aisle. When he reached her, of course disappointment washed over him. It wasn't Gwen. How could it be? She hadn't simply walked out of their lives. He'd put her in the ground.

His head spun. These hearts—they were the ones Kate promised to get rid of. The ones he never should've written. The ones that revealed that the great romance captivating this group of women had ended in tragedy.

What if they pointed to him somehow?

Anger bubbled at the back of his throat. How could Kate have been so careless? Now that he lived here, he couldn't have all these people in his business. He still remembered when Junie came home from her first day back at school after Gwen's death, before they'd moved here. Her head was suddenly full of confusion about what had really happened to Mommy. She'd overheard the teachers talking, and she wanted answers to questions she was too young to ask. He wanted to protect her from all of that. He wanted her to believe the best about him—about Gwen. But if she found out the truth before she was ready, how could she?

He had to protect their identity for Junie's sake. His mind spun, trying to pinpoint anything that could tag him as the author of these hearts.

"Can I keep these?" Abigail said, gathering up the hearts with more care than he'd expected. It was as if the words on the hearts meant something to her. She studied a few as she stacked them. "This set doesn't even have string." She glanced at one of the ladies, a worried look on her face.

Jacob turned away. He'd never had a reason to put them up.

"And from what I can tell, these are all written by the same person." Abigail flipped through a stack as she put them back in the envelope. "I hope nothing bad happened."

"Oh, you worry too much, dear," Gigi said. "I'm sure they're living cute and cozy. Everyone has their rough patches. But after you read through the rest, report back if there's anything we should know." She and Doris walked away, leaving only Ursula, who had turned her attention to Jacob.

"Didn't expect to find you here," she said. "You scoping out the place for when you kick Abigail out?"

"Ursula, please." Abigail's brow had turned into a thin line of worry.

"I was just leaving," Jacob said. He pulled a five-dollar bill out of his wallet and laid it on the counter, meeting Abigail's eyes. "Thanks for the coffee."

"It's on me. Anytime." She slid the bill back toward him, avoiding Ursula's steely glare.

"I insist," he said, leaving the bill where it was. "Have a great day, ladies."

As he walked away, he heard the old lady chastise Abigail. Something about remembering who he was, the person who would eventually destroy Abigail Pressman's life.

But as Jacob walked toward the door, the paper hearts caught his eye again, and it occurred to him that Abigail Pressman might inadvertently be the person to destroy his.

Chapter 22

"Kate?"

No answer. Jacob flung his keys into the little container his sister had designated as the "key caddy" and took off his coat. He'd sped home from the bookstore, mind racing with a litany of worst-case scenarios.

Someone at school could find out what happened. They could tell Junie the truth. Junie, though bright for her age, would never understand, and worse, she'd be angry with him—not only for his part in what happened to Gwen, but also because he'd lied to her about the whole thing.

She'd be permanently scarred and he'd have no choice but to move again, forcing her to leave any semblance of security they'd managed to find since moving to Loves Park.

"Kate?"

He could wring her neck. How could she have been so careless?

On second thought, how could *he* have been so careless? What in the world did he think would happen, moving to a place he was distantly connected to? Starting over was a brilliant idea, but starting over in a place he'd sent packages to for years might not have been. He supposed he wasn't quite ready to leave all of their memories behind.

Still, if he'd moved to Nevada, he'd have no idea the hearts were hanging in some woman's bookstore in Colorado.

He should've moved to Nevada.

He'd been humiliated before, but not like this. Having his life's love story plastered up in public did not sit well with someone who didn't even have a Facebook account. It didn't matter that no one knew it was his. He knew.

Personal lives were meant to be personal—end of story.

He passed through the kitchen and into his study, the room that under normal circumstances would've been the perfect place for those morning prayers he used to rely on. Maybe one day he'd feel the desire to make amends with the Lord, but today was not that day. Not by a long shot.

"Kate? You here?"

He did a quick pass through the rooms and found them all empty. When he came back into the kitchen, he saw the door that led to the back porch was slightly cracked.

A chilly breeze blew in from outside, and through the glass door he saw Kate bundled up in a blanket from the guest room bed. She sat in the white Adirondack chair that had come with the house, though she'd turned it to face out toward the mountains, giving him only a slight glimpse of her face.

Still, he could tell she'd been crying.

Grief pushed its way up to the center of his throat and lodged in the form of a painful lump that begged to be melted.

He swallowed the pain and shoved thoughts of Gwen aside. How many times had he come home and held her through her tears?

And yet, since she'd gone, he'd cried only once. One time he'd allowed himself the weakness. He needed to stay strong for Junie. And now for Kate.

But he took a step back. He couldn't do this again. Couldn't watch someone he loved vanish, all the life drained out of their eyes while he stood by, helpless to do anything for them. Couldn't fail like that another time.

His hand hovered over the door handle. Kate swiped her face dry and buried her head in her hands, shoulders shaking. He'd known something was wrong. He should've pushed her to tell him the truth when he first noticed, but now that he saw the toll it was taking on her, he wasn't sure he wanted to know more.

And he hated himself for it.

As if she'd just found her resolve, she wiped her tears and stood. Before she caught him standing there, staring, he inched his way back from the door, picked up his coat, and left the kitchen. Then he turned and walked in again as if still searching for her.

"Kate?" he called, moving loudly through the room. "You here?"

She appeared in the doorway to the porch, looking as though she'd simply been outside soaking up the mountain air. How did she do that? If he hadn't seen her, he'd never know she'd been crying.

But he did know. So now what?

"You're coming tonight, right?" Kate closed the porch door and took a seat at the freestanding island at the center of the room.

"About that," Jacob said. It might not be the best time to say anything, but he had questions for his little sister. "I stopped in at The Book Nook this morning."

Kate propped her chin up with her fist and stared at him. "Because you like Abigail?"

He frowned. "What? No. Because I was rude to Abigail. Or Kelly was, I guess, and I didn't do anything about it."

"Ugh. Kelly." Kate rolled her eyes. She'd done nothing to hide the fact that she didn't like the woman. Now that he was in business with her, Jacob wasn't sure he liked her much either, but she'd been one of Gwen's closest friends. And he'd made a commitment to open this practice with her as his business partner. Besides, whether he approved of her methods or not, she still offered a lot of solid advice about all the things he didn't want to have to think about. These days, that was worth a whole lot.

"Kelly isn't the issue here," Jacob said. He glanced at Kate, hoping she was okay, realizing the anger he'd been feeling had subsided the second he saw her crying.

"Right. The issue is you and Abigail. And how you don't want her to hate you."

"Kate. The whole store is covered with paper hearts." Jacob leaned against the counter and leveled his gaze.

She sat up straighter. "What do you mean?"

"What did you do with the hearts I asked you to throw away?"

Panic skittered across her face. "Oh, Jacob . . ." She brought a hand over her mouth.

He sighed. "Did you send the newest ones?"

She grabbed her purse and started rummaging through it. "Jacob, I'm so sorry." Finally she pulled out a few plain white hearts. "I didn't send all of them."

He'd cut these hearts himself out of some scratch paper he'd found. Nothing like the ones Gwen had cut, which were usually colorful and bright and happy. There was something pathetic about his version.

Kate slid them across the counter. "I kept the ones that mentioned Loves Park. Just in case."

Jacob didn't bother informing her that she'd missed a few.

> Had a conversation with a woman today in Old Town.
> Felt like I was cheating on you.
> Living in Loves Park seems like a betrayal sometimes. I know how much you loved it here, G. But it's the only place I can be close to you without feeling haunted. So sorry.

"I didn't read them all, I promise."

There was a third one, one where he mentioned Abigail's bookshop.

> You'd love this Book Nook, G. It's got that kind of small-town atmosphere you like so much.

And Abigail Pressman would read the others and probably piece the whole thing together in a matter of days.

Jacob pushed himself away from the counter. "I came here because no one knew all this stuff, Kate. It was my chance to start over." He raked his hands through his hair, a dull ache starting to pulse just above the bridge of his nose.

"But you're not starting over. You're standing still." She glared at him as if she'd just issued a challenge.

"I don't want to get into this with you right now. If you're going to be around for a while, I need you to do what I ask—not do what you think is best for me." Jacob kept his tone even.

"I'm sorry." She stared at her folded hands. "I tried to throw them away. I just couldn't." Her eyes filled with fresh tears. Sometimes he forgot that Gwen's death affected other people besides him and Junie. Maybe that's what this was about. Gwen had been the only sister Kate had ever had—of course she was sad.

She could probably use a sister about now. Not a brother who didn't know how to fix whatever it was that had her in tears on the back porch.

Besides, how could he be upset with her when he'd done exactly the same thing himself? This wasn't the first envelope of homeless hearts the postmaster had received. When he and Junie were moving, he'd gathered up the last strand he'd written, shoved it in a plain envelope, and sent it to Loves Park ahead of him. Somehow it seemed like the right thing to do, yet now he wished he'd simply stuck them in a box at the back of the closet.

Living here changed things. It changed everything. Had he mentioned Junie in his ramblings on those hearts he'd sent? He didn't give a lot of care to what he was writing because he never expected to see them again.

"Gwen told me she sent them to the postmaster every year," Kate continued. "When you said you were done with them, I guess it just seemed fitting. Like now you could have closure."

"I think it's going to take more than sending off

a box of hearts for me to find closure." He walked into the living room and stood in front of the windows, stared out at the mountains. The picture-perfect view seemed an incongruous backdrop to his broken life.

"Like not turning into the kind of person who destroys someone else's life just to get what he wants?" She followed him.

"Don't push me right now, Kate." He walked away, afraid of what he might say if she didn't back off. Afraid of what she might say if he didn't leave. Almost everyone who knew what had happened wore kid gloves around him, but not Kate. And while he appreciated that she challenged him, right now he'd had just about enough.

He changed into his warm-up pants, a T-shirt, and a hoodie, then slipped out through the side door, heading off into the woods for the kind of run he only took when he had too much on his mind. Fast and furious.

Within seconds he was winded, the thin air not enough at this pace. He slowed to a jog.

The air was crisp, snow still caked on the ground, though their winter had been mild so far. Of course, it was only January. The unevenness underneath his feet kept him focused on his footfalls and not on the barrage of unwanted thoughts assaulting him.

Amid the clamor in his head, Jacob heard the

same sentence repeating over and over again at the back of his mind—almost like a prayer. *Please don't let anyone find out the truth. For Junie.*

And just like that, an indescribable peace seemed to wash over him, and his fear went away, for the moment at least. Somehow he trusted that he and Junie would be okay—no matter what happened with his secret.

Chapter 23

The paper hearts had already started doing their job. It was exactly what she'd been searching for—a way to heighten interest in her store—yet Abigail never would've thought to hang them up in the store on her own. Not those hearts. Not that story. But she couldn't deny they seemed to have a power that captivated the entire town.

It had only been a couple of days, but word had spread. Tourists and locals had made their way into the store. Couples and singles alike came in, wrote on the hearts, and tucked them in the box. They shared their innermost thoughts, sometimes admitting feelings they'd been bottling for years. And each evening, Abigail and Mallory strung the newest hearts together and decorated the store with them.

Even Betsy and Romano had stopped in during

a recent visit to town. Abigail supposed they were certain that writing on those hearts would solidify their love for each other.

She had been in a meeting with a supplier when her sister dropped by.

Thankfully.

As much as she hated to admit it, she still found Betsy's engagement difficult to digest.

Abigail appreciated the attention the store was getting, especially since word had spread about the possibility of her losing the building. People wanted to rally for her, for The Book Nook. They wanted to be a part of what was happening, and she loved that.

But the envelope of hearts Gigi had set on her counter that morning had stolen most of her attention. Though it was ludicrous, she found herself worried for the fate of her couple. Another manila envelope, another pile of hearts apparently written only by the man—it didn't bode well for the lovers' future.

What if something terrible had happened? What if she'd cheated on him and left? Or worse, what if he'd simply stopped loving her and realized his mistake after it was too late to get her back?

Thoughts turned to Jeremy, to their final real conversation.

"I just don't love you anymore. I'm not sure I ever did."

She viewed every relationship through the Jeremy lens.

But not this couple. They had to be different. He loved his wife in a way Jeremy had never loved Abigail, and if she was honest, the wife loved him in a way Abigail wasn't sure she was even capable of.

She needed to believe they were okay. This couple had almost single-handedly restored her hope in romance again. She hadn't even been looking for hope in that department. Not consciously, anyway.

As she put the finishing touches on the store in preparation for her first-ever Book Nook concert later that evening, Kate walked in, looking adorable in a way Abigail never had.

Jacob's sister was trendy without trying. The kind of girl who marched to her own drummer—and didn't seem to care if the pattern in her scarf clashed with the pattern in her shirt.

Somehow it worked for her.

She carried a guitar case and a large turquoise bag. She spotted Abigail and smiled, strode toward her, and set down her things. "This is really exciting."

"For me too. Look." Abigail motioned toward the stage Jacob had set up earlier. "I've been wanting to figure out a way to do this, and I guess meeting you was just the push I needed."

Kate laughed. "I am pushy—that's a fact."

Abigail grinned. "I didn't mean it like that."

"I was kidding. I know." She laughed again—the kind of bubbly, infectious laugh that made others want to laugh too.

Abigail walked over to the little stage in the corner. She'd been handing out concert flyers all week, and with the addition of the paper hearts, she'd had more customers than usual. She could only hope for a good turnout—for Kate's sake and for hers.

"You go ahead and get set up, and I guess let me know if you need anything. I've got some paperwork to take care of in the back, but feel free to interrupt."

So that's what I'm calling the paper hearts now? Paperwork?

Kate nodded and knelt down to open her guitar case. Abigail hadn't meant to be dishonest; she simply needed to steal away—finally—just for a few minutes. To try to piece together the story of what had become of her couple.

She closed her office door and pulled out the new envelope, then collected the hearts in neat piles on her desk. Thankfully this couple wrote the date on the back of each heart, so she began by putting them in chronological order. After about a half hour, she'd nearly finished when there was a knock at her door.

Panicked, she looked for any way to hide her new obsession but came up empty. She decided to hope for the best—that the person on the other side of the door was Mallory or Aaron or someone she could boss away.

"Come in."

No such luck. Kate Willoughby stood in her office, shutting the door behind her and looking a little out of place.

Abigail stood and moved in front of her desk, wishing the hearts would magically disappear.

"Am I interrupting?" Kate asked, worried.

She shook her head. "Not at all."

Kate glanced past her. Caught. Abigail's face flushed.

"What's all that?"

Abigail swallowed around her embarrassment. "Is everything okay?"

"Yes, but Mallory sent me back here to get you." She smiled. "You've got an interesting problem out there."

She frowned. "What do you mean? Did something happen?"

"I guess you could say that."

"Do you have everything you need to play? I called a guy from my church on Tuesday—he said he'd bring over a microphone and some other portable thing."

"It's not that, Abigail," Kate said, pulling her toward the door. "Look."

Heart racing, Abigail couldn't help beating herself up for being irresponsible enough to leave the front of the store when everyone else was setting up for the evening.

All because of her obsession with those paper hearts.

As they entered the store, Abigail gasped, stumbling backward and nearly knocking Kate over.

Kate steadied Abigail with a hand on her shoulder. "It's something, isn't it?"

People. Clusters and clusters of people. They filled the store from one side to the other.

"Are you famous?" Abigail asked, not looking at Kate.

She nudged Abigail. "I don't think they're here because of me."

Her little store had never had so many people in it for as long as it had been open. She couldn't believe the chaos. All the tables were taken, and small crowds were situated around the perimeter of the floor. "Where'd they all come from?"

As if she were a genie that had been summoned, Ursula appeared beside her. "It was in the *Courier*."

"I had no idea anyone still read the newspaper," Abigail said.

"Well, it was on the Loves Park Internet too."

Abigail frowned. "You mean the Loves Park website?"

Ursula's brow became one tight, bushy line. "Everyone is on it, Abigail. The website. Even I have over one hundred friends." She hugged her bag to her chest and glared.

"Do you mean Facebook?"

For several seconds, Ursula didn't flinch. "Whatever it's called, the hearts were on it. Told you all you needed was a gimmick. This town is smitten, like schoolgirls with their first crush. You're golden. No way the doctor can kick you out now."

Abigail's eyes went wide and she cleared her throat, silently begging Ursula, for once, to take a hint. What if Kate was offended?

"It's fine," Kate said. "I don't want him to kick you out either. But you've got to cut him a little slack. He wasn't always this cranky. He's just . . ." Kate's voice trailed off as something near the door caught her eye. "He's here. Huh. Junie's hanging out with a new friend tonight. I guess he got bored."

Abigail followed Kate's gaze to the front door, where, sure enough, Dr. Jacob Willoughby had just come in. She took a moment to watch him maneuver through the crowd, admiring how he looked out of place yet perfectly comfortable at the same time. He had such an easiness about him in spite of the troubled look that always furrowed his brow.

And he sure was attractive.

But he was the enemy. He and that woman. That woman he probably had a thing for. Within seconds Abigail felt herself shrink as if everyone could read her mind, as if everyone would know how foolish she was for even thinking the doctor was handsome. He would never look twice at her.

And yet, when Abigail glanced across the swarm of people, she met his eyes.

He was still in the middle of the crowd, but his eyes had found *her*.

She told herself to focus on the fact that she'd turned the store into the talk of the town in just one week. Sure, it had been completely accidental, but he didn't need to know that. If he and that woman booted her out, or even raised her rent, the town would revolt and their doctor's office would go under before it even started.

They had to let her stay now, didn't they?

Jacob inched through the crowd until he finally reached Abigail and Kate—and Ursula, who made a point of ignoring him.

"You came?" Kate seemed genuinely surprised.

"Oh, did I have a choice?" His eyes widened.

"I was only pretending to threaten you. I would've been fine if you stayed home."

"Nah," he said with a shrug. "Couldn't miss your big night."

Something about him read sweet. A side of him Abigail hadn't seen before. She liked it.

"This is quite a turnout," he said to Abigail. "You must be some marketer."

Abigail smiled.

Gigi and Doris appeared in their circle in much the same way Ursula had—like magic. Gigi leaned closer to Jacob. "Abigail's store is a town treasure, Mr.—Dr.—Willoughby," she said. "You must know how very well loved she and The Book Nook are."

He glanced at Abigail. "That's not so hard to believe."

Abigail's heart stopped for a second. *It's not?*

"It would be a *shame* to see anything *happen* to this place, don't you think?" Gigi said, emphasizing random words as she spoke.

"Gigi, it's okay," Abigail said hurriedly. "You ladies need to put your heads together on something other than my store."

"Oh? I thought that was our top priority."

Jacob raised a brow.

"No, Gigi, the top priority is finding chairs for these people to sit in." Abigail wrung her hands. She'd never anticipated this kind of response to her coffee shop concert.

She could hear people talking about the paper hearts tradition, and the counter had run out of blank hearts twice already. It seemed the Volunteers were right—this town loved romance, and she'd captured something pretty special.

"Loves Park Presbyterian has lots of folding chairs. Pastor won't mind if we use them," Doris said.

Their little circle had Jacob looking—and

probably feeling—more awkward than Abigail had ever seen him. He shifted his weight and folded his arms, but he still looked like he'd rather be having his wisdom teeth pulled than be standing there with them.

"Are you sure?" Abigail was desperate.

" 'Course I'm sure. I'll just send him a phone note and tell him not to call the cops when you go get them." Doris riffled through her purse until she produced her ancient cell phone.

"A phone note?" Abigail frowned.

"A note over the phone."

"A text?"

Doris waved a hand in Abigail's face. "You kids and your fancy names for everything. Whatever you call it, Pastor is getting one. Now, go get your chairs. They're in the basement."

She handed Abigail a small key ring with two silver keys on it. As church organist, Doris had the run of the place, though Abigail suspected it had more to do with the fact that the woman had worked as the church secretary for years. When she retired, nobody had asked for her keys—and she had no intention of turning them over.

Abigail sighed. "Have you seen my car?"

"Jacob can get them," Kate offered.

They all turned and looked at Jacob in unison. Abigail almost felt sorry for him.

"He has a truck." Kate smiled at him, but he didn't look amused.

"Oh, Jacob, that is so nice of you to offer," Gigi said, wrapping her hands around his arm. "Perhaps I've misjudged you." Her eyes twinkled.

Jacob looked like he might let out an audible groan at any minute.

"Why don't you take Abigail with you?" Gigi said. "After all, you're new to town. You probably don't even know where the Presbyterian church is."

Jacob cleared his throat, then looked at Abigail. "Uh, no, I don't."

"I can't leave," Abigail said in protest. "Look around."

"Oh, look, Abigail," Gigi said. "I think Duncan just walked in."

Abigail spun around. "All right, I'll go with."

"We'll take care of the people—don't you worry about it. We'll make sure they're all still here when you get back." Gigi started moving toward the back door, hands still wrapped around Jacob's arm. He had no choice but to go along for the ride, and apparently neither did Abigail.

Minutes later, Abigail was pulling the shoulder strap in his truck around herself and fastening her seat belt. The truck was clean inside. Meticulous, actually. She supposed that fit his personality. Doctors seemed like clean people, what with all that hand washing.

She drew in a slow breath, mindful of the scent of cologne. Not the gaudy, disgusting kind, but the

258

kind that made you want to keep inhaling through your nose.

He stopped at the edge of the parking lot, an expectant look on his face. "Which way?"

"Oh, turn left and go to Cumberland and turn right. The church is just a few blocks away."

Silence filled the cab, and Abigail's mind spun, trying to find something—anything—to say.

"So your plan seems to be working," Jacob said, his words cutting the silence.

She preferred the silence to this topic of conversation. She'd never been very good at withholding information.

"My plan?" Even she knew she wasn't fooling anyone. Nothing about her response came across as innocent.

"Turn your store into the talk of the town? Isn't that the idea? I read the interview."

Abigail did remember saying something about that to the reporter, though she thought she'd been off the record. Didn't make much sense to tell him her plan, did it?

"I especially liked the part where you said you had a new landlord who didn't understand Loves Park culture, but you hoped he caught on quickly how important The Book Nook was to the community."

"I didn't say that," Abigail protested, her mind reeling.

He tossed her a look that said, *You wanna bet?*

"I said that?"

He nodded. "You did."

"Well, it's a fair point. Besides, if you close me down, I'm afraid people might turn on you."

Now he frowned. "Turn on me?"

"They won't want you to be their doctor."

"Is that how it works around here?"

She shrugged. "There's the church."

He turned in to the parking lot, and Abigail pulled out the keys Doris had given her.

"So you decided to take one couple's relationship and broadcast it all over your store, to get people to come in? To prove to me that I shouldn't raise your rent?"

Well, when you say it like that . . .

Jacob got out of the truck, leaving her speechless and questioning once again whether it was a good idea to pin up the paper hearts. Maybe she should've trusted her gut. Her gut told her not to let anyone else read them, but then, her gut was known to be rather confused.

Look at how many people were being encouraged by those hearts. Abigail would be the first to admit her own cynicism, but even she couldn't argue with community-wide inspiration.

Did it matter that she reaped the benefits?

While she sat contemplating, the truck door opened and Jacob held out a hand to help her down. She stared at it.

"It's a pretty big step," he said. His kindness felt like an inconsistency.

Slowly she reached out and took his hand. As she did, he looked away, eyes focused on her feet, and when they hit the ground, he let go.

As he should. Of course. This wasn't a date. It was a mission. A mission for chairs.

"Hanging the hearts wasn't my idea," she admitted as she unlocked the side door of the little church. She sounded like she was making excuses, and after seeing the way people had responded to the paper hearts, she didn't feel much like apologizing. He was just sore because now he'd be the bad guy.

Jacob didn't respond.

They walked downstairs to the basement as Doris had instructed, and Abigail opened the closet doors to find two racks of folding chairs.

"Do you think we should take them all?" she asked.

"There were a lot of people there."

"There were, weren't there?" She smiled. "I hope your sister is a good musician."

Jacob actually laughed. He had a nice smile, the kind of smile that made her want to smile in return. She wished he smiled more, but then he might seem less like a mean landlord and more like someone she wanted to get to know better. Heaven forbid.

He pulled out the first rack of chairs. "I don't

know that they're actually there to see her." He took two chairs in each hand.

"You think it's stupid, don't you?" She pulled out the other rack of chairs and tried to pick up three of them.

"Whoa, don't kill yourself. Just take two."

She squared off with him. "I can take three."

His eyes widened, but he said nothing. Instead he turned and started up the stairs. She followed but halfway up realized she absolutely could not manage all three. But there was no way she was going to let him know that.

He must've sensed her struggling because he reached the top and hollered a quick "You okay?" in her direction.

"Fine."

"Liar."

She glared at him, bracing the chairs against the stairwell wall and trying to catch her breath, but he'd already gone outside. Seconds later he returned, took all three chairs from her, and loaded them into the back of the truck.

Thankfully he didn't say any more about it. They hauled and loaded in silence and, when they'd finished, locked up the church and headed back.

"You know, people send those letters to the postmaster knowing someone is going to read them," Abigail said. She'd said it to herself several times over the last few days; might as well say it out loud.

"Sure," he said. "But do they know everyone in town is going to read them?"

She chewed the inside of her lip. "You think I should take them down."

"I didn't say that." He made the turn onto her street. "Besides, whoever wrote them will probably have no idea you're using their honored tradition to get people to shop in your store."

"You make it sound so cheap," she said. "And you never know. We think they might actually be local."

He raised a brow. "You really think locals would send anything to those women who sort the letters?"

"That's fair." She frowned. "Maybe you just don't want the whole town to fall in love with me."

He glanced at her.

Heat rushed to her face.

"I didn't mean that the way it sounded." This was why she shouldn't be allowed in close quarters alone with a man. She always made a complete idiot of herself.

He turned his attention back to the road, and Abigail let out a hot stream of embarrassed air.

She could really use a paper bag to put over her head right about now.

She slunk down in her seat and dared a cautious glance in his direction.

While she couldn't be positive, when the light from the streetlamps hit his face, she thought maybe he was smiling.

And something about that made her stomach topple over itself like clothes in a dryer.

Chapter 24

After unloading the chairs, Jacob sat in the back of Abigail's store and watched people read the paper hearts he and Gwen had written to each other in much better times. Kate sat on the small stage he'd built, strumming that guitar and singing her heart out as if she were the only person in the room.

Each folk-inspired song she sang seemed to reveal those emotions Kate typically hid so well. When she performed, it was almost as if she could finally be something other than her usual perky self. Jacob stilled as her voice filled the space, riveting the crowd in a way that surprised him. They seemed as enthralled with his sister as they were with the paper hearts.

Every once in a while, he'd catch a whispered phrase as customers combed through his personal life with reckless fervor. Pain hitched in his throat, and he ached for peace.

A middle-aged woman passed by his table. "Oh, aren't these just the neatest little things?"

Jacob nodded, but he didn't respond.

"I'm Trudy Sanderson. My husband is the principal at Loves Park Elementary." She stood beside his table, obviously expecting a response. That was the polite thing to do, wasn't it? And yet he really just wanted to be alone.

After too many seconds of silence, he reciprocated. "Jacob Willoughby." A forced, phony smile accompanied his halfhearted introduction.

The woman tilted her head as she sized him up. "Oh, my. Aren't you . . . ?"

His stomach knotted as he finished the sentence in his mind—". . . *the one who wrote the neatest little things?*"

". . . that doctor who bought this building? I read it in the paper."

A cocktail of relief and dread swirled together in his chest. "That's me."

Her eyebrows drew together. "I think it's just terrible what you're doing to poor Abigail. She's been here for years, you know. And who will take care of her if you take away her business? She doesn't have a husband."

Jacob glanced at his sister, who had just finished her set. She already owed him for the stage, but now she *really* owed him.

Another woman met his accuser beside the table, a matching glare on her face. She had obviously been eavesdropping. "Let's go, Trudy. We have nothing to say to him."

The two hurried off.

Once Kate's concert was over, customers began to filter out of the store. Before leaving, some of them made their way to Kate, who smiled graciously while they undoubtedly heaped compliments on her. Instrumental music began to play through speakers in the ceiling.

"Do you need something clse to drink?"

He looked up and saw Abigail approaching his table. Nothing about her seemed malicious, yet she was well on her way to turning the whole town against him.

"I'm good, thanks."

He expected her to move on to the next table, but she just stood there. When he made eye contact, she looked caught like she didn't realize she'd been staring.

"Thanks for helping me with the chairs," she finally said. He got the impression being nice to him took a lot out of her.

"No problem."

Never mind that Doris had already made it clear he would be responsible for taking all of the chairs back. "You just go ahead and keep those keys, Doctor," she'd said. "That way you won't forget you need to return the chairs safe and sound tonight."

He'd considered protesting, but she'd hurried

away. What he really wanted was to go get Junie from her friend's house, tuck her in, and go to sleep himself.

But here he sat, the crowd substantially smaller than it had been earlier. The old ladies had all gone. Only one family—a woman with two small children—was still seated. The others milled around the shelves, a few making last-minute purchases.

"Your sister is really good," Abigail said.

Kate moved toward them, a smile on her face.

"I asked her to come back next week," Abigail said.

"Oh?"

"I said yes," Kate said, still beaming.

The woman at the nearby table stood and put a hand on Kate's shoulder. "That was so wonderful," she said. "We're just passing through Loves Park, and we saw all the commotion over here in this darling little store."

Jacob stifled a groan.

"We're so glad we stopped in."

"Mama?" The little boy tapped on the woman's arm.

"You looked like you were having a blast up there," the woman continued, ignoring the boy. He ran back to the table.

"It was so much fun," Kate said. "Abigail, thank you for letting me play."

Abigail brushed her hair away from her face.

"No, thank you. It was a wonderful night. Much more exciting than my typical Friday." Abigail's face flushed red as if she'd embarrassed herself. A habit of hers, it seemed.

"Well, we just loved it, didn't we, kids?" The woman glanced back at the table and let out a gasp. "Avery! What's wrong?"

Jacob moved aside to get a good visual of the little girl, whose skin had a distinct bluish tone to it. Her brother stood next to her, a worried look on his face.

"Avery, what happened?" The mother took the girl by the shoulders, then looked frantically around the store. "Please, someone, help me!"

Jacob put an arm around the woman and moved her aside. "Step back, please, ma'am. Kate, call 911." He crouched beside the girl. "Avery, are you choking?"

The girl nodded, terror in her eyes. She wasn't coughing or making any sound at all, so he pulled her to her feet and quickly administered the Heimlich maneuver. Three sharp thrusts. Avery went limp.

"No! Help!" the woman screamed, growing more and more panicked.

Jacob's heart kicked into high gear, but he forced himself to remain calm. The last thing this mother needed was a doctor who let his own fear paralyze him. Still, a question nagged at the back of his mind. *What if I lose her?*

He forced the unwelcome worry away, laid the girl down on the floor, and opened her mouth. He saw something lodged in her throat, so he swept it out with his finger, then started CPR. After a few scary moments, Avery finally coughed.

He held her head, then gently raised her upright. "Avery, can you hear me?"

She grabbed her throat, then nodded, tears gathering in the corners of her eyes. She threw her arms around him, sobbing.

He hugged the girl and helped her to her feet. "You should chew your food more carefully next time."

She nodded again, still seeming disoriented, and her mother pulled her into a tight embrace.

"The paramedics should be on their way. You need to let them take her in just to be sure there was no damage done."

"Thank you so much," the woman said through tears. "You saved her life."

Around them, the remaining patrons had gathered. They'd likely gone without air themselves, waiting to see if the little girl came out alive.

"I'm glad I could help," Jacob said, wishing he could've done so without the audience.

After a few seconds, someone in the back started clapping. Before long, the entire room broke out into applause, taking their turns shaking Jacob's hand and thanking him.

The principal's wife, who'd practically smacked him with anger earlier, walked straight up to him and poked a bony finger into his shoulder. "I might've misjudged you, Doctor."

"Happens all the time," he said.

"Still. What you did for that girl was pretty wonderful. I'd be happy to bring my business your way when you get the practice off the ground."

Abigail stood only a few feet away from the conversation, and she'd obviously heard the remark. She swallowed, looked away, then disappeared into the back room. He wanted to follow but held himself back.

After the crowd dispersed, Kate appeared at his side. "Well, that was exciting."

Jacob's heart was still racing, a rush of adrenaline nearly preventing him from keeping his composure. Thankfully he'd gotten really good at faking it. "I thought I was going to lose her there for a second." These were the kind of demons he could never fully get rid of.

The paramedics walked in, and Jacob gave them the necessary information on Avery. The little girl still sat at the table, her face a bit pale but otherwise composed.

"Thanks for saving my life," she said as the paramedics began their examination.

The words hit him in just the right place, chipping away at the walls he'd carefully stacked around himself. "My pleasure, Avery."

Kate put a hand on his arm as he stepped away. "That has to feel good."

Jacob wanted to pretend it was all part of the job, but these days it wasn't, and Kate would know that. He'd been working around the clock to get the new practice going, but it had been so long since he'd actually helped someone, he'd begun to wonder if he'd ever be a real doctor again.

He missed it. The healing. The helping. He wished he could do more.

Kate slung her purse over her shoulder and picked up her guitar case. "You ready to go, hero? Looks like it's snowing pretty good out there."

"Actually, I have some chairs to return to the church," he said. "Maybe you could pick Junie up and get her to bed?"

Kate glanced up at the hearts fluttering in front of the ceiling vent. "Thanks for coming. It meant a lot to me."

He silently accepted her apology. "Wouldn't have missed it."

Kate followed the last of the patrons out the door, leaving him alone in an otherwise-empty bookstore. He began stacking the chairs against the back wall, wondering how long Abigail would hide herself away. After all the work she'd done, it had to be hard to hear one of her faithful patrons turn on her so quickly.

Just as he gathered the last of the chairs, she appeared in the doorway.

"You really don't have to help me with these. I mean, it's not your responsibility or anything," she said, unnecessarily adjusting the positions of a few of the chairs.

"I think Doris would disagree." He fished his keys from his pocket. "It was a great success," he said after a long minute.

She stopped and met his eyes. "It was, I suppose. Though it doesn't quite compete with saving someone's life."

He shrugged, looking away. It was unfortunate timing for her, he had to admit.

She glanced at the hearts above him, sadness on her face. "A part of me didn't want to share them with everyone else." She reached up and touched a pale-pink heart. "I liked being the only one who knew about them. That's so selfish of me, isn't it?"

Jacob looked away. Oh, he understood.

She pulled her coat on. "We should probably go."

"I came here earlier to apologize to you," he said.

She stopped.

"For Kelly. She shouldn't have said the things she did to you—at least not the way she said them." He looked at her, feet of emptiness between them. "So I'm sorry."

She waved him off. "You don't have to apologize. It's your building. You can do whatever you want with it, and after tonight, you won't have any trouble getting business."

Jacob took a few steps toward her. "What would you do with it?"

She raised an eyebrow. "You mean if I were a rich doctor?"

He laughed. "Let's go with that, yeah."

She shrugged, shaking her head at the same time. "No one has ever asked me that."

He studied her. He couldn't help it, he realized. She seemed unaware of her own beauty, and perhaps that was what made her so beautiful.

Guilt followed the thought that had been dropped into his mind without his permission. Still, he couldn't keep from watching her as her eyes seemed to drift away to a place locked somewhere inside her imagination.

"Show me," he said.

She looked at him. Frowned. "What do you mean?"

He jangled the keys to the other side of the building—his side. "Show me what you'd do."

"You're not serious."

He walked toward the back of the room and stood by the door to the outside until she finally followed him.

Once outdoors, Abigail hugged her coat around her. Snow blew at them with a force she hadn't expected. Jacob hurried with the keys and finally pushed open the door to the other side of the building, holding it ajar as she passed through before him.

"I didn't know it was so bad out," he said, closing the door behind them.

She laughed. "That's Loves Park for you. Sunny and perfect in the morning and a whiteout blizzard by nightfall."

"You don't think it's that bad, do you? We have chairs to return."

"Yes, I'm sure you're just dying to put all those chairs back in the church basement."

Jacob smiled, and for the briefest second the pain that usually bubbled at his surface seemed to subside. He motioned to the former mercantile. "Well?"

Abigail hesitated. "Um . . ."

Worry settled on his face. "I'm sorry. Maybe this was a bad idea."

"Of course not." She turned her back to him and inhaled deeply.

Maybe she could make him understand that this building was more than just brick walls and wood floors. This building was her future. Everything she'd been planning for and dreaming of—it was all wrapped up in one place.

But she couldn't say that. Not out loud. Not to him.

Especially not now that she'd lost any of the leverage the paper hearts, the concert, the family days had brought her. None of that mattered when she was competing with a local hero.

She saw the way they'd all reacted to him saving that little girl. They were as smitten with Jacob as they were with the paper hearts. And by morning, she was sure, it would be all over town.

Standing in the mercantile used to energize her. All the ideas that spun through her mind. Tonight, though, it only made her sad.

"I'm not really a businesswoman," she said, still facing away from him.

He took a step closer. She could feel him standing only a few feet away. "Did you spend your evening in the same place I did?"

She smiled, looked down at her feet, standing on the wide wood planks she'd always loved.

"I mean, I don't care as much about the money—" she turned to him again—"the way businesspeople do. I want to do well and be successful, but expanding my store was never about money."

He was watching her. She could feel his eyes on her, and for the first time, her nerves didn't come unraveled under his gaze.

"What's it about then?"

She dared to meet his eyes, held them for several long seconds. In those seconds, she almost felt like she had been granted a sixth sense—the ability to hear and see and smell every little thing. Time stopped.

But she couldn't do it. Couldn't talk about her father and what it had meant to her when he left her the store. Couldn't talk about how this store was her attempt to fill the void a broken heart had left. Couldn't cross the line and open up to this man who had too much power over her already.

"What's to stop you from stealing all my ideas for your clinic?"

He grinned. "Nothing, I guess."

Quietly, she ran a hand over the mercantile countertop. "I'd leave this," she said. "It was handmade by Harriet's grandfather. Her family owned the building since it was built, years ago."

"It's amazing. Kelly wants to tear it out."

Abigail bit back the words she wanted to say. She waved a hand toward the back wall. "I'd have built-in shelves installed here and fill this whole wall with the work of local artists." Abigail could see it as clearly as ever. "The center of the store would be a showcase for furniture I've restored." She gestured toward the spot she meant, hoping he was beginning to picture it too. "On the weekends, I'd host classes for the community. Some things I might teach myself."

"Like bracelet making?"

She laughed. "Yes, I do have a knack for that, don't I?"

"According to my daughter, yes," he said.

"I'd have art classes, but then I'd bring in

teachers to do workshops in all the things I wish I knew how to do. Knitting. Jewelry making. Watercolors." She could see the tables lined up in the center of the store. She could hear the women coming together, forming a unique bond with each other and with her—the kind of friendships she'd always dreamed of having.

"I'd paint the walls a creamy white. Get rid of the dark. I'd knock out the wall between the two spaces and let natural light fill the place. I love the idea of opening it up." She pivoted on the balls of her feet. How could this dream be so real and yet so far out of her grasp? "I'd sell the kind of items you couldn't find anywhere else. Antique quilts. Hand-painted signs. Vintage treasures."

"So would there be a Do Not Enter sign for men on the outside of your store?"

She laughed. "It does sound girlie, doesn't it?"

"A little bit." He leaned against the counter in a way that embodied easygoing and laid-back. How he could do that, she didn't understand. She almost never felt laid-back.

His gaze left her and she followed it outside, where the wind seemed to have kicked up even more, blowing snow feverishly.

"Did you hear anything about a winter storm?" He walked toward the window. "It's pretty nasty out there."

Just then his phone buzzed. He took it out, frowned, and answered. "Hello? Kate, slow down." Pause. "Are you okay? . . . Is she okay?" Pause. "All right, I'll get there as fast as I can."

When he hung up, he looked at Abigail, the color gone from his face. "Kate picked Junie up from a friend's, and they slid off the road and into a ditch near our house."

"Are they okay?"

"She said an ambulance took them to the hospital to check them over." He paced. "I need to get there. I'm sorry. Can we do the chairs later?"

Abigail watched as panic washed across his face. He moved toward the back door.

"I'll come with you," she said.

He stopped and looked at her like he was making up his mind if he wanted her there.

"Or not," she backtracked. "Maybe you need to go alone."

"You'd come with? Are you sure?"

Was that relief on his face? "Of course." She met him at the door, followed him into the blizzard, and pulled herself into his truck.

Inside, she shivered, the cab of the truck every bit as cold as the outside.

He started the engine but didn't pull away. Instead he sat still in the driver's seat, hands on the steering wheel, head down, eyes closed. Was he . . . praying?

Or was he simply trying to bear the weight of what Kate had said on the other line?

She reached across, put a hand on his, and said

a silent prayer of her own. His eyes opened and he took a deep breath, then let it out.

"Thanks for coming with me, Abigail," he said. "I just need them to be okay."

Something about the way he said it struck Abigail, and for the first time since the day they'd met, she wondered exactly what had happened to cause the pain behind Dr. Jacob Willoughby's mysterious eyes.

Chapter 25

The drive to the hospital would've normally taken five minutes, but in this blizzard, it was exactly thirty-seven minutes before he pulled into the parking lot of St. Andrew Memorial Hospital. Abigail chose not to fill the silence with questions, though she kept asking herself why she'd come along. Instead she prayed in her head, asking God to take care of her new friend and Jacob's daughter.

She'd been so consumed with her own troubles lately, a part of her felt good to turn her attention toward praying for someone else for a while, even if it was the man who'd been the cause of so many of her worries.

He turned off the engine and stared at the hospital, dread flooding his face.

"Jacob?"

He looked at her, startled, as if she'd interrupted his private thoughts or he'd forgotten she was there.

"You okay?"

He didn't look okay. He looked like he might throw up, but he nodded and got out of the truck.

She met him on the sidewalk in front of the building. He stood, hands in fists at his sides, staring at the front door. He seemed unable to go inside.

"Come on," she said, slipping her hand around his arm and starting toward the door.

Inside, the dazed look on his face only worsened. Sweat gathered at his hairline and on his top lip. Something was wrong. Something was terribly wrong. She wondered if he might pass out.

Abigail led him to a chair in the waiting room of the ER. "Sit here," she said. "I'll go find out where they are."

Her mind flooded with the worst kinds of scenarios. What precisely had Kate said to him on the phone? What if Junie was really hurt? What if Jacob's daughter was somewhere in this building fighting for her life?

Heart racing, she tapped on the window to get the attention of the person working the front desk, a large woman whose name tag read *Ina*. "I need some information. My friend's sister and daughter were in an accident."

"Name?"

"Willoughby. Kate and Junie Willoughby."

The woman flipped through some pages on her desk. Abigail glanced at Jacob, who sat stock-still in the exact spot where she'd left him. She wasn't sure he'd blinked or breathed since they walked in the door.

"And who are you?" She looked up at Abigail with a scowl.

"Just a friend."

"I can't give you any information if you're not a relative."

Abigail glanced at Jacob. "My friend is a relative."

"Then have him come over here and I'll give him the update."

Abigail leaned in closer. "He's having a hard time with this—can you just tell me if they're okay?"

"Rules are rules."

Of course. She walked over to Jacob, who was fixated on the emergency room doors, his expression trancelike. "Jacob?"

No response.

"I need you to come to the desk with me to find out where they are."

He shook his head, though she got the distinct feeling it happened involuntarily.

She pulled him to his feet. He cleared his throat. "I'll go. I'll be okay."

He stood a foot taller than Abigail, but she could tell by the way he looked past her that he'd set his sights on the front desk.

"Are you sure?"

He met her eyes though he didn't seem to have an ounce of resolve in his own.

But he nodded and started toward the counter. The woman behind the desk glanced up at him. "Willoughby?"

He nodded again, showing her his driver's license.

"You're the one who saved that little girl's life tonight, right? Paramedics were talking about it. Come on back."

He started toward the doors, leaving Abigail standing at the counter, unsure if she should follow or wait. She wasn't family. In truth, she had no business being here at all. They weren't even friends. But here she was. And her insecurity kicked into overdrive.

This isn't about you, Abigail.

She started toward the waiting room chairs, thinking through her options. But before she could sit down, Jacob was beside her again, grabbing her hand. "Come with me?"

Abigail stared at his hand around hers as the oversize double doors opened to reveal the woman from the desk, waiting to take them to Jacob's family.

"Of course," she said.

She expected him to let go of her hand as soon as they started down the hall, but instead he slipped his fingers through hers and squeezed a little tighter. Somehow she had the distinct impression that he was relying on her strength to walk him down the hall.

God, she prayed silently, *help me to know what he needs. And please let Kate and Junie be okay.* Even in that moment, she found it odd how overcome she was with the desire to pray for Jacob and his family. And it was about more than feeling helpless—it was about truly, truly wanting them to be okay.

They followed the woman down the hall to a large room at the back of the ER. Couldn't she have at least told them Kate and Junie were okay? Couldn't she have said, "Don't worry; they're still alive"? Anything would be better than this silence.

She stopped at the door to room 109 and held out a hand as if she were a magician's assistant. *Ta-da.*

And then she walked away.

Jacob stood still for a beat. Then two. He squeezed her hand again, though she was pretty sure he had no idea he was still holding it.

"It's okay," she whispered. "Go ahead."

He drew in a deep breath and closed his eyes.

When he opened them, Abigail saw tears gathering in the corners. This was a man who had secrets she wasn't sure she wanted to know. The kind that hurt to remember.

Then, as if he'd found a quiet resolve some-where, he pushed open the door.

The room was sterile the way all hospital rooms are, but his little girl lay in a bed that seemed to swallow her whole.

Jacob took a step back when he saw her.

Kate jumped up from a chair in the corner and rushed to him. "She's okay. She's just sleeping. Her leg is broken and she has some cuts and scrapes."

Kate's eyes landed on Jacob's hand, holding Abigail's. She glanced at Abigail, who gave her a silent shrug.

"Jacob," Kate said, forcing him to look at her, "she's going to be just fine."

"She's asleep," he finally acknowledged, letting out a huge, shaky sigh of relief. "She's going to be fine, though?"

"They gave her something because she was pretty worked up," Kate said. "When she found out she had to go to the hospital, she kind of lost it."

Jacob looked at his sister. Something silent passed between them, and Abigail felt like an intruder. "I can leave you guys. I'll go get coffee or something."

"Stay," Jacob said. He looked at her. "Can you?"

Kate's brows shot up in surprise. Abigail imagined hers did the same.

She said nothing. Instead she took off her coat and sat down in one of the chairs against the wall, out of the way.

Kate rested a hand on Jacob's arm. "They're going to set her leg now that you're here. They just need you to sign some paperwork."

Jacob's jaw tensed. "Fine."

"It's okay, Jacob," Kate said.

"It's not okay, Kate. Look at her." Jacob turned toward his daughter. "She's just lying there. She looks like—"

"She is fine," Kate reassured him.

Abigail noticed a few scrapes above Kate's eyebrow.

He sighed. "Tell me what happened."

Kate pressed her lips together, then began. "I went to pick her up like you told me to, and it was slick but I thought we would be okay. Until we hit the hill leading to your street. It wasn't plowed, and I kept sliding. I couldn't get up over the hill, and a car came from the other direction and lost control. It hit us and knocked us off the road and into a tree." Kate's eyes filled with tears. "Junie's leg was pinned in the car. They had to cut her out."

Abigail expected Jacob to take Kate in his arms, hug her, and tell her none of this was her fault, but he did none of those things. Instead he stared at the child in the bed, making Abigail wonder if he'd heard a word his sister had said.

Kate stood still for a long moment and finally

glanced at Abigail. "I'm going to go find the doctor."

She left them alone, a palpable pain filling the room.

But Abigail had the distinct impression that the pain had less to do with Junie's broken leg and more to do with something deep and buried in the past.

More than ever, she wanted to know what secrets the doctor held so close to his heart.

Jacob sat down next to his daughter, carefully taking her hand as if it were valuable and could break in pieces at any moment. Abigail couldn't help wondering what it would take to get her landlord to open up and let her in on whatever it was that brought this kind of grief to the surface.

Chapter 26

Not long after Jacob arrived, the doctors whisked in and took Kate away.

"She refused treatment until Junie had someone here with her," one of the nurses told him.

A little later, the nurses took Junie away so the doctor could set her leg. They informed Abigail that both Kate and Junie would be staying overnight for observation. An hour after that, Abigail found herself nodding off in the uncomfortable chair against the wall. Every time she woke up, she saw Jacob across the room at Junie's side, a pained look on his face.

Twice she'd tried to leave and twice he'd inexplicably asked her to stay.

Why this man—this man who was apparently intent on ruining everything she'd worked so hard to build—wanted her to stay here with him, she might never know.

But she stayed. Because that's the kind of person she was.

And because there was something so desperately heartbreaking behind his eyes.

Morning came, and Abigail awoke to the early sun pouring through the windows. Saturdays at the bookstore were busy, but the thought of going into work made her cringe. Outside, snow had blanketed all of Loves Park. Plows had been working all night, but they'd been unable to keep up with Mother Nature.

As if she believed in Mother Nature.

Why, God? Why this accident? Why these people? She closed her eyes. *Bring him peace, Lord. Your kind of peace. The kind that makes no sense.*

Kate had been admitted with a concussion doctors wanted to monitor. Jacob hadn't received the news particularly well, but at least they'd put both Kate and Junie in the same room. Now, with everyone sleeping—Jacob still in a chair beside

Junie—Abigail saw her opportunity for a clean getaway. She wasn't responsible for this man's happiness—or his sorrow. She had no reason to stay another second.

And yet . . .

Hospital coffee would probably taste like sludge, and after the night they'd all had, they could use some of the good stuff. She fished Jacob's keys from his coat pocket, but when she turned, she found Kate's eyes open and locked on her.

"Hey." Abigail made her way around Junie's bed and over to Kate's.

"What are you doing?"

"Getting some coffee. I figured we could all use some."

Kate opened her mouth, then closed it again. "My mouth is so dry."

Abigail poured her a cup of water. She drank it, then forced out a thank-you.

"Do you need anything else while I'm out?"

Kate swallowed. "My own pajamas? And Junie's teddy bear."

Abigail glanced at the little girl, still sleeping soundly. They'd likely be going home later that morning, so why did she need a stuffed animal?

"She's going to freak out when she wakes up," Kate said, answering the unspoken question. "We aren't exactly hospital people." Kate gave a

288

halfhearted smile. "Key's on the ring. You know the address?"

Abigail knew the address. The house had been on the market for almost a year before Jacob bought it. It had been the talk of the town. A beautiful place in the mountains. The kind of place everyone dreamed of buying. She nodded. "I don't feel comfortable going through anyone's things, though."

Kate's eyelids looked heavy when she blinked. "It's fine. Maybe grab him a change of clothes too."

Now she really felt awkward about this mission, but what could she say? They didn't have anyone else, and the little girl needed her teddy bear. "I'll be back."

She reached the door just as Kate said her name. Abigail turned.

Jacob's sister slowly glanced at him, dozing in the chair and looking more uncomfortable than she'd felt throughout the whole of the previous night. "He really needed you last night. Thanks for being there."

Abigail bit her lip, unsure how to respond.

"He doesn't ever let on that he needs anyone, but you just seemed to know." Kate brushed a hand over her hair. "Thanks."

Abigail gave a nod and walked away, her head spinning as she tried to make sense of her role in all of this. Surely Jacob had only latched on to her because she was there—not for any other reason. Not because he wanted anything more from her than just the typical tenant/landlord relationship.

Or maybe they could be friends.

Good friends?

Don't push it.

She rushed out to the truck and drove as carefully as she could toward Jacob's house on the edge of town. The roads were snow-packed and slick, but she'd been driving in this weather her whole life. She could read the road under the tires.

Still, she let out a sigh of relief when she pulled into the long driveway in front of the house. Out back a dog stood near an old shed, looking hungry and mangy. Jacob seemed like the kind of guy who'd have a dog, though she would've expected him to take care of it a little better.

When she got out of the truck, the dog took off into the woods behind the house. She'd look around for food and a bowl, but only after she got what she came for.

She stood on the porch and inhaled a chilly breath. "Let's get this over with."

Abigail pushed open the door. She'd always wanted to see the inside of this house. She could've walked through it so many times, but Wyatt was the listing agent, and the thought of running into him had been enough to keep her away.

She passed through the entryway and into the living room. Windows lined one wall of the living space, and at the center of the other wall was a fireplace that nearly took her breath away. Stones in various shapes and sizes framed the fireplace and its thick wooden mantel, making their way up to the peaked ceiling. Piles of chopped firewood had been stacked on the hearth. An image of Jacob out back chopping logs raced briefly through her mind, but she shoved it aside.

Remember why you're here.

Abigail thought she recognized the couch and chairs from the real estate photos online. Maybe he'd purchased the place furnished. People did that, right? The furnishings certainly didn't suit the space, in her opinion. Her mind, as it often did, began redecorating. What she could do in a room like this one. Some of her refurbished furniture would be just the thing.

As she passed through the living room into the study, she tried to remember what she'd come for. Surely it wasn't so she could snoop around the doctor's home, though that was tempting. Maybe she'd uncover more about his life—something, anything to explain why the hospital had warranted such a strong reaction.

After all, he should've been accustomed to hospitals, given his profession.

The hallway leading back to the bedrooms was long but not narrow. No photos on the walls.

Nothing personal in the house anywhere, really. But he'd only moved in a few months ago, she reminded herself as she flipped on the light in what she soon found out was Jacob's bedroom. Maybe that was why there were so many boxes piled up in the corner.

Kate had said to bring him a change of clothes. She stood outside the closet, staring into the sea of dress shirts and ties. She'd never seen him wearing any of these. Not that she'd seen him every day or anything, but they seemed out of place given what she knew of him. She ran a hand over the shirts, all pressed with that chemical dry-cleaned smell.

She hadn't wondered before, but now it occurred to her that it was strange for a doctor to up and move to another town, then buy a building that looked nothing like a clinic just to renovate it and turn it into a medical practice.

And he didn't seem to be in any hurry, otherwise he wouldn't be doing any of the work himself. Was he independently wealthy?

Obviously. He'd had enough money to buy the building in cash.

Abigail shook the thoughts away, fully aware of how ridiculous it was to speculate—and fully aware of how little she really knew about this man.

Doctor who didn't currently practice. Divorced. One kid. Nice sister. A little bit too good-looking.

Terrible business manager who could single-handedly ruin Abigail's life.

That about summed it up.

She let out a groan and moved to the dresser, where she found a pair of jeans, a T-shirt, a sweatshirt, and socks. The skinny drawer at the top likely held his—Abigail could feel herself blush.

Don't be such an eighth grade girl. It's just underwear.

And yet everything about her being here felt like an invasion of his privacy. She pulled open the drawer, grabbed a handful of whatever was on top, and shoved it in the bag she'd found at the back of the closet.

Quickly she gathered what she needed from the room where Kate slept, then moved into Junie's room. An adorable patchwork quilt covered her bed, which was made of distressed white wood and an ornate headboard. Abigail nearly gasped. It looked like something she would sell in the store of her dreams.

She wished she could paint the room a pale-pink color pulled from the sheets and blankets. Currently the walls were mostly bare with the exception of a bulletin board showcasing the little girl's art. Beside her bed, one framed photo stood next to a tiny ceramic jewelry box.

Abigail sat down on the bed and picked up the photo. Jacob, Junie, and a woman with reddish hair and eyes like almonds smiled back at her.

They'd been a family—a solid, happy family. Abigail had so many questions about Jacob's ex-wife. What kind of mother could leave her own daughter? Where was she now? Why did she leave them?

Maybe they, like Abigail's own parents, had drifted apart, leaving nothing but the realization that they'd been a wrong fit from the start.

But it wasn't her place to judge.

Abigail picked up the ratty old teddy bear sitting on Junie's pillow. She went to stuff it in the bag, but something caught her eye. Pinned to the front of the stuffed animal were two simple hearts, obviously hand-cut and decorated by a child.

Abigail gasped. Paper hearts.

When had the child been back in the store to see the tradition they'd begun? Or maybe she'd heard about it at school or in the paper.

She ran a finger over the hearts, taking in Junie's carefully printed words and the strawberry drawn on the second heart.

Come home, Mommy.

I miss the way your hair smelled.

Empathy, as it often did, formed a tight circle of emotion right in the center of Abigail's throat. She closed her eyes tightly so she wouldn't cry. This poor girl had been through so much already. Abigail knew what it felt like to be rejected. The pain never really went away; it just stayed hidden for a while, showing up about the time you got close to someone again.

And it always did just enough damage to start the process all over.

She didn't want that for Junie. She didn't want that for anyone. But this girl—this sweet, innocent, wide-eyed girl—especially didn't deserve it.

Abigail hugged the teddy bear to her chest. Of course, she herself hadn't deserved it either. She was just a kid when her father had left. And with Jeremy? Maybe it had been for the best, but it was still an open wound that failed to heal.

Was that what she wanted Junie to grow up believing? That all the people you love leave you?

Abigail drew in a deep, shaky breath and expelled it all at once. She didn't have time to experience a personal revelation sitting on a six-year-old's bed. She had to get these clothes back to the hospital.

But before she turned out the light, she stopped and gave one last look at the bedroom, imagining the tears Junie cried in the dark when she missed her mom the most.

How many times had she cried similar tears after her father left? A familiar pain returned—one she wasn't sure she could ever fully forgive.

Chapter 27

Jacob awoke twisted in an uncomfortable chair beside Junie's bed. He forced his eyes open, rubbed his face with both hands, and then realized what a stupid idea it was to fall asleep in that position. On the other side of the room, Kate lay in a bed identical to Junie's. The two people he loved most in this world, and they'd both ended up here.

And as always, he couldn't do a thing about it.

Why was it that he seemed able to save everyone else from harm, but when it came to his own family, he was always, always helpless?

Why had God allowed even more pain? Why couldn't they all heal in peace?

He stood and moved toward the windows overlooking the parking lot of the small hospital. He vaguely remembered pulling in the night before, but so much of what had happened was a blur. He was standing in his new building with Abigail when he got the call. She'd come with him. She'd gotten him here.

Where was she?

She probably bolted the second he fell asleep. What kind of woman would stick around to wade through his mess? Certainly not one whose heart he was in the process of breaking, professionally anyway.

He turned as Kate's eyes fluttered open. "Hey." Her voice was hoarse like that of a person who'd spent the night screaming at a concert for her favorite band.

"Hey, yourself."

"I guess I fell asleep."

"You must've needed the rest after what you've been through."

A thick line of worry spread deep across her forehead. "What I've been through?"

Jacob sat on the edge of her bed. "You have a concussion, Kate."

"Oh yeah, I know. The nurses kept waking me up to make sure I didn't have any other issues. One of them even made me get up and walk." Her laugh sounded nervous.

He frowned. "What did you think I was talking about?"

"Nothing. Is Abigail back yet?"

"Back? No. Where'd she go?"

"I sent her out to the house for a few of our things. Just in case we're here for the rest of the day or another night or something. I think they're waiting for Junie to wake up again before they decide. Abigail's getting her teddy bear."

Jacob stood and faced her. "You sent her to *my* house?"

Kate made a face. "Yeah. That's where our stuff is."

His mind reeled, scanning anything that might

give him away as the author of those paper hearts. When he came up empty, he said a silent, impulsive prayer. *Please don't let her find out anything. Not like this.*

He'd tell her in his own way. When it felt right. Or maybe never at all. He liked that idea better. He saw no reason Abigail or anyone else needed to know the truth about the hearts or Gwen or his past.

Besides, at the moment, nothing felt right. "I need to get some coffee."

"Abigail's bringing some back."

He walked toward the door. "Then I need to get some air."

Or something. Anything. *I need to get away. I need to get a life. I need to get some closure.*

He headed out into the hallway and started walking, his mind wandering back to the night Gwen died. They'd released her with a clean bill of health, certain she was fine. But she wasn't, and by the time he got her back to the hospital, it was too late. He couldn't save her. They couldn't save her. God couldn't save her.

Or wouldn't. He was still wrestling with that one. *Why didn't you save her? You're supposed to be the Almighty.*

He rounded a corner and saw a sign for the hospital chapel. How cliché. He'd never gone in any of the chapels before, and in truth, he wasn't the type of person who believed God could only be found within the walls of a church. In fact, more often than not, he met with God through prayer in very different places, like hiking in the mountains or in the car on the way to work.

But that was before. Lately, God had just been horribly, unaccountably *silent*.

But then, so had Jacob.

Now, though, he had questions. Why him? Was he being punished? And if he was, how could he make it right? And couldn't God take it out on him instead of on Junie and Kate?

He took a seat at the back of the chapel—first time for everything—and stared at the cross hanging on the opposite wall. He'd grown up believing that God was good and merciful and kind, but the last few years had been anything but those things. The last few years had been awful and terrible and brutal.

At the beginning, when things went wrong with Gwen, he'd prayed faithfully. He believed everything would be fine—otherwise, why would God have given them a child to take care of?

And just last week, he'd felt that overwhelming peace that God was protecting them.

"Where are you now? How do I wake the sleeping giant?" Jacob's whispered breath hung in the air.

He waited in the silence, for what, he wasn't quite sure. That feeling he used to get. The words he used to hear. The knowledge that he hadn't been forgotten.

Forgive.

It came in spite of his anger and did nothing to appease him. Jacob scoffed. Just like that? Just snap his fingers and forgive the One who took his wife away?

He understood. He had to forgive in order to be forgiven. He'd learned it all those years ago at church, yet now that he was faced with the brutal choice, it was much easier said than done. But he shouldn't have to forgive God, should he?

Every time he thought he'd made a little bit of progress, it all came rushing back, pulling him under, into the mire of quicksand that threatened to steal his last breath. Something else would always happen to make him feel caught in God's crosshairs. Would he ever recover? Would he ever be able to move past any of this?

Junie's face flooded his mind. Her screams when they set her leg. He'd held her, rocked her. He wanted to tell her it would all be okay, but she knew better. She knew from experience that "Everything is going to be okay" was an empty promise. Instead, he said nothing. Just held his baby girl and tried to be brave—and when she finally fell into an aided sleep, he escaped into the bathroom and allowed the sobs to overtake his body.

"I don't forgive you." Words he'd felt for months and never spoken escaped without warning. "I don't forgive you for destroying my life. For taking her away. For this accident. For making it clear I don't deserve to ever be happy again. I don't forgive any of it."

No, Jacob. Forgive yourself.

The unwanted thought popped into his mind without his permission. He stood, hands in angry fists at his sides, and he fought the urge to scream at that cross on the wall at the front.

Instead he stilled, a coldness racing through his veins. "Never."

When he turned to go, he had the distinct feeling that he'd finally used up his last chance with God. What kind of God would take him back now?

And why would Jacob even want him to? He was getting what he deserved. He'd made a mess of his life, so his life was a mess.

What happened to the peace he'd felt the other day? Here he was again, right where he'd started. And God wasn't doing a thing about it.

Chapter 28

Getting coffee turned out to be a lot more difficult than Abigail expected. With Jacob's bag, Kate's pajamas, and Junie's teddy bear in the passenger seat, she'd pulled into the lot behind The Book Nook, parked the truck, and taken a deep breath.

She'd considered closing the shop for the day, but with all the excitement over the hearts, it would be terrible timing. Instead she'd had Mallory call in a few part-time employees, and she was assured all would be fine.

"I'll take care of it, Abigail. You just go make that doctor fall in love with you," she'd said. Abigail didn't have the energy to correct her. Admittedly, she hadn't given much thought to her own sad situation since Jacob first got the call about the accident. It was kind of nice to worry about someone besides herself for a change.

Now, standing in her office, Abigail waited for Aaron to bring her coffee. She'd decided not to go out into the store for fear of getting sucked into the paper heart craziness, and she really just needed to get the coffee and go.

Someone knocked at the office door. Aaron? Abigail swung the door open and Gigi entered her office without ceremony, followed by Doris and Ursula.

"What happened, dear?" Gigi said, taking her hands. "Mallory said you were in an accident?"

"No, not me. Jacob's sister and daughter."

"Ohhh." The three ladies went wide-eyed.

"The doctor's sister," Doris said.

"Yes."

"We call him Jacob now," Gigi corrected.

Abigail shrank under the weight of their stares. "Or Dr. Willoughby. Whichever."

"How about 'spawn of Satan'?" Ursula har-rumphed.

Abigail pulled her hands out of Gigi's grasp. "He's not so evil."

Gigi's eyebrows shot up. "That's right. I heard he saved a little girl's life in here yesterday. The whole town is buzzing about it."

Abigail wasn't surprised.

"So he's not kicking you out anymore?" Doris clapped her hands together.

Where was Aaron with her coffee? "No, nothing's changed. He's just . . . different than I thought."

The three ladies all leaned back with a unified "Oh?"

"I can't get into it now. I told them I'd be back with Junie's teddy bear and fresh clothes."

"So you're running errands for him now?" Ursula put her hands on her hips.

If only Aaron didn't move at a turtle's pace. Abigail walked toward the door, intending to check his progress. Aaron entered before she reached it, holding three large cups of coffee in a drink carrier. Abigail took them without a thank-you and pushed past the three women, leaving them, she was sure, to speculate on this turn of events.

For Abigail Pressman's entire opinion of the good doctor had seemed to change overnight.

And if she knew the Valentine Volunteers, that meant speculation.

But she couldn't think about any of that now. Instead she drove back to the hospital, her memory replaying last night's events in a continuous loop. She didn't know what the Willoughby family had been through, but whatever it was, it wasn't good. Her heart broke for the little girl, for Jacob—even for Kate.

And as she pulled into a parking spot, she heard herself say out loud, "Maybe I could help them find whatever it is they're looking for."

She shook the ridiculous thought aside. Who did she think she was? She wasn't in the business of playing God—not for herself and certainly not for handsome doctors. She gathered the things she'd picked up at his house and headed inside.

As she made her way down the hallway, Hailey Martin popped out from behind the desk. "Abigail?"

She and Hailey had gone to school together. They both grew up here in Loves Park, and Abigail had to say she couldn't think of a better nurse for the Willoughby family.

"Hey, Hailey," Abigail said, slowing her anxious pace.

"You came in with the Willoughbys last night, right?" Hailey's brow furrowed the way a nurse's did when she had bad news to deliver.

"Has something happened?"

"Oh no, everyone is okay—they're all resting, I think." Hailey looked away like she was checking to see if anyone else was around. "I'm not supposed to say anything."

Abigail's throat went dry. "Hailey, what is it? Is it Junie?"

Hailey shook her head. "The other one."

"Kate?"

"Abigail, how well do you know her?"

Abigail shrugged. "Not that well. Why? She's just staying with Jacob for a little while, I think."

"We had to take some X-rays." Hailey pressed her lips together as if she was summoning the professional in her. "We found some concerning things."

"What kind of things?"

Hailey looked away. "I probably shouldn't say."

Abigail frowned. "Hailey, what's wrong?"

"There appears to be a history of . . . abuse."

Abigail pictured Kate in her mind's eye. She didn't know her well, but Kate generally seemed happy and laid-back. "Are you sure? She seems fine to me."

Did Jacob know about this?

"We're pretty certain. We tried to discuss it with her, but she wasn't receptive at all."

"What kind of history?" Abigail didn't have a lot of experience with battered women, but if she could help her new friend, she'd like to try.

"She's had several severe bruises consistent with being beaten. Her collarbone was broken, and from what I can tell, this isn't her first concussion."

Abigail's stomach dropped. She never would've guessed that about Kate.

"Why are you telling me this, Hailey?"

"Her brother doesn't seem to be doing very well. He was in the chapel this morning, and with his little girl's leg—I just couldn't tell him. I saw pictures of the car they were in, Abigail. They're lucky to be alive."

Abigail sighed, suddenly anxious to get back to them, to make sure everyone was okay.

Hailey smoothed her ponytail, looking nervous. "I shouldn't have told you."

Abigail was pretty sure Hailey had violated all kinds of codes and oaths in sharing this with her.

"Promise me you won't tell anyone, Abigail. I could lose my job."

Abigail let out a nervous sigh. "Then why did you say it?" Abigail certainly didn't want to be rude, but she didn't like having this information.

"Someone needed to know. Someone who cares about her."

Sadly Abigail wasn't sure she was worth confiding in. What in the world was she supposed to do now? Pretend she didn't know? Bring it up with Kate? Tell Jacob?

She slung the bag over her shoulder, hugged the teddy bear, and started down the hall. When she reached the room, the door was partially open and a familiar voice met her before she could go in.

Kelly.

The woman had set her shiny black bag on the end of Junie's bed and now stood beside Jacob's chair, rubbing his back with her perfectly French-manicured hands.

Abigail stopped short before walking through the door, thankful they hadn't seen her. Her eyes fell to her own hands, wrapped around Junie's bear. Dried paint lined her fingernails and her knuckles wore a fading coat of primer.

"I'm so sorry I wasn't here last night, Jacob. I'm sure you really needed someone to be here with you."

"Abigail was here."

She stilled at the mention of her own name.

"She was?"

"She drove over with me."

A long pause, and then finally Kelly responded. "Well, good. Do you think you'll be up to finalizing some building plans later on?"

"You're not supposed to be here on Saturdays, Kelly." Then it was Jacob's turn to pause. "But I'm glad you are. Why don't you keep things going with the renovations for a while? I think I need to be here with Junie and my sister."

"Of course," Kelly said. "That's what I'm here for. I think you're making a wise choice to keep moving forward. I'll handle everything for now. You just take care of your girls." She glanced sideways through the door and started when she saw Abigail. "Why don't I see if I can find us some coffee?"

"I think Abigail is bringing some," Jacob said as Kelly turned toward the hallway.

She kept her gaze locked on Abigail's as she headed for the door. Jacob didn't turn around, but even from his profile Abigail could tell he wasn't in good spirits. She understood why Hailey didn't want to disrupt him with any more bad news than he was already processing. Still, Abigail was more certain than ever that something else was at play here. Kids broke bones. Junie was going to be fine, yet Abigail didn't see any trace of relief on his face.

Now, standing nearly a foot shorter than high-heeled Kelly, Abigail wanted to crawl under a rock or run to the mountains and hide.

Kelly closed the door, keeping her tone even and her voice low. "I heard you spent the night here."

Abigail swallowed, stuttered, and mumbled all at the same time. "Yes."

"That's just wonderful of you to be a good neighbor like that. I'm sure Kate appreciates you for being such a good friend to her." Kelly swept her hair behind her shoulders and leveled her eyes. "As for Jacob, however, I can take it from here."

Abigail's expression must've matched her inner confusion, but she said nothing.

"Jacob is a very special man, and he needs a certain kind of woman right now. I'm sure you're wonderful in your own way, but you're young and inexperienced. He needs to be cared for, and sadly, I'm not sure you have the skills required to do that." Kelly made a superior, condescending face. The kind of face Abigail wanted to punch.

"I think there's been a misunderstanding," she said, trying to keep her tone as even as Kelly's.

"No, I don't think there has," Kelly said matter-of-factly. "You don't have to say a word. Your little crush is obvious, and it's very cute, but you should know that he's not available. Are we clear?"

Abigail nodded.

Kelly took the coffee, the bag, and the teddy bear with the two paper hearts pinned to its chest. "Wonderful. It was so nice of you to bring us coffee. I'll be sure they get these."

Abigail swallowed the lump forming in her throat, willing away that left-out feeling that plopped her right back in middle school.

Kelly put a hand on the door but quickly turned to face Abigail again. "I almost forgot. Jacob's letting me handle things for a little while, and we're moving ahead with the renovations."

"I figured as much," Abigail said, though she desperately wished against it.

"He's authorized a larger budget, so we're going to do phases one and two at the same time. No sense dragging out the construction, is there?"

"I don't understand."

"We're going to need your space vacated sooner than we originally thought."

Abigail's heart wrenched. "How much sooner?"

Kelly's lips pulled into a tight smile. "I think we can give you three more months."

Abigail's jaw went slack. "Three months?"

"That's being generous. I could have you evicted the first of next month." Kelly stood a little taller, no doubt to make herself seem even more powerful.

"Does Jacob know about this?" Abigail's voice sounded annoyingly mouse-like in her own ears.

Kelly laughed. "What do you think?" She held up the drink caddy. "Thanks again for the coffee, Abby."

Abigail watched as the wretched woman disappeared into the hospital room where she herself was apparently no longer necessary.

My name is Abigail.

Chapter 29

This week's meeting of the Valentine Volunteers had gotten off to an odd start. The women all gathered around the charts they'd created for Abigail, but nothing was clicking into place.

"We've never had this much trouble finding potential matches for someone," Doris said, worry in her tone.

"Not everyone is meant to be matched, you know," Ursula said from across the room. She sat in Gigi's armchair with a plate of cookies and a cup of tea.

"I just can't believe that," Gigi said. "Abigail is such a sweet girl. She'll make a wonderful wife. We just need to find her the right match."

Ursula crunched. "Well, it wasn't Duncan. She didn't even bother to cancel their date—she just didn't show up."

Doris made a face.

"What's that for?" Ursula asked.

"I don't blame her. That Duncan was a little strange."

Ursula cozied into her chair, a content smile on her face. "Duncan served his purpose."

"Making sure she never goes on another date again?" Evelyn sat tall like a supermodel in the armchair at the back of the room.

Tess laughed. "Good plan."

Ursula's narrowed glare shut Tess right up. "Showing Abigail what she doesn't want will make it a lot easier for her to recognize what she does."

The room stilled.

"That's almost brilliant, Ursula," Tess said, doing nothing to hide the surprise in her voice. "So you do care about Abigail finding a match."

Ursula scoffed. "Let's not get carried away. I just love a good challenge is all."

Gigi didn't like it when they got off track. She

clapped her hands together three times. "Ladies, back to the task at hand."

A collective sigh wound its way around the perimeter of the room.

"What am I going to tell Teensy?" Gigi had promised Abigail's mother results. Perhaps she'd spoken too soon. She didn't anticipate all of this professional turmoil getting in the way of Abigail's nonexistent love life. This should've been much easier than it was.

The door opened and everyone gasped. "Teensy?" Gigi whispered.

Ursula had the best vantage point to see who was there. "It's Abigail," she hissed, gathering the papers and shoving them into manila folders, sliding the charts behind the sofa.

But it was too late. Abigail stood before them, a horrified look on her face. "What's all this?"

"Abigail, it's so good to see you." Gigi attempted to steer her into the kitchen, away from the evidence, but the younger woman would have none of it.

She turned in a circle, back toward the hub of their operation. "Why do you have my picture here?" She walked over to Doris and took the top paper off the stack. Her photo was stapled in the upper left-hand corner.

"It's our selection process, of course," Tess stammered. "You know how picky we are about who joins the Valentine Volunteers."

Abigail flipped to the paper below hers in the stack. Gillian Moore's photo was next in line, but underneath her picture, Doris had written *MATCHED* in bold red letters. Gigi had always thought Doris should be more discreet.

Worried glances crisscrossed the room, and Gigi put a hand on Abigail's arm.

"What *is* all this?" she asked, pulling away.

"Abigail, we can explain," Gigi said.

"You don't have to. I think I get it. All of this wanting me as a Volunteer was just a way to find me a match. Poor, pathetic Abigail Pressman, on her way to dying alone." Abigail plopped down on the sofa, dejected.

"That's not it, dear." Gigi sat next to her. "It's true that we want to find you a match. But you have potential to be a wonderful addition to the Volunteers."

"A wonderful addition with no prospects and, soon, no business." Abigail looked as though she might cry at any moment.

"That can't be. The hearts are wonderful. I was there this morning, and there was a line out the door." Gigi patted her hands.

"I gotta hand it to you, kid. Using the hearts was genius." Another crunch from Ursula.

"I can't take credit for that. It just sort of happened." Abigail had a faraway look in her eyes as if she were remembering. "All I wanted was to find out who the couple is and what happened to them. I wonder if they know how lucky they are."

Gigi studied her for a long moment. Clearly something besides love was bothering this girl. "What is it, dear?"

"They gave me three months."

"To live?" Doris jumped to her feet. "What do you have?"

Abigail held up a hand. "No, Doris, not to live. Three months in my building."

Gigi gasped. "They can't do that."

"They can. I can't stand that Kelly. And *Jacob!* I can't believe I ever felt sorry for that man."

"I thought you were making some progress, though I suppose being a local hero has its perks. He must feel like he can move up his timeline now." Gigi sighed. "Oh, dear, I'm so sorry."

"I'm just so confused. I've worked so hard for my store. Why isn't it helping?"

"You did say you thought this was going to be a year of change," Doris reminded her.

"Yes, but I don't want that change to mean I lose everything." Abigail let out a long sigh.

"Can't you talk to Jacob?" Gigi asked. "This Kelly woman doesn't have the final say."

Abigail looked like she'd already given up. "She said he put her in charge for now."

Ursula stood. "You get on over there and tell him you're not leaving. This is business. Stop feeling sorry for yourself, Pressman, and keep your head in the game."

Abigail looked at Ursula. "I'm not like you. I don't have the fight-or-die gene."

"No, you have the idealized version of what it'll mean to run a business. But you should know by now that business is messy. You've got to fight for what you believe in. You have to fight for the things that are worth fighting for."

Abigail stared at Ursula for a few long moments as if considering what she had said. "I appreciate your help, but I don't appreciate you trying to find me a match. Obviously, this isn't a very good time for me to have a relationship. I'm too angry to care about much else."

"Oh, honey, there's never a good time for a relationship." Doris giggled. "The best ones are the ones you don't have any time for at all. Because you steal the time and all the moments matter."

Abigail wore a defeated expression. She glanced at the easel. "Right, but it looks like you've come up empty anyway."

The others looked away. At their hands. At each other. Anything to avoid meeting her eyes.

"Promise me you'll stop trying to find me a match. Let's focus on someone else for a while, okay?"

Silence fluttered through the room.

"Okay?" Abigail sat up straighter.

They all mumbled in agreement.

"Thank you. I'm sorry—I have to go. I need to think this through."

Gigi saw Abigail to the door, and when she returned, a dark cloud seemed to have filled the room.

"Don't look so sad, girls," Gigi said. "I think I know why she doesn't want us to match her."

"Because she doesn't want us to match her. There's no more reason than that." Ursula had returned to her chair. Now she polished off the last of the cookies on her plate and appeared likely to go to the kitchen for more.

"No, because she's stopped believing in love," Gigi said. "Simple as that."

Doris glanced at the easel. "Can't say I blame her."

"But deep down, she does want to be loved. We simply need to work harder."

Ursula's sigh was loud and disruptive. "You really should listen to me, Gigi. The doctor is the perfect match for our girl. But we've got to crush his business before love will blossom."

"What in the world are you talking about, Ursula?" Evelyn said, putting a voice to the expression on each of their faces.

"You can't stand the doctor," Tess added.

Ursula waggled her heavy eyebrows like a child with a secret.

Gigi crossed her arms. "Ursula. I admit the other night at the concert, the thought did cross my mind, but did you hear Abigail just now? Were you sitting in the same room we were?"

"I did, Gigi, which is why I'm shocked you didn't pick up on it. Hatred is one tick mark away from love. That girl hasn't been so passionate about anything else since the day we met her."

"She's passionate about her business," Tess said. "Not the doctor. Though I can't figure out why. He's just so good-looking."

"Tess. Focus." Gigi clapped her hands. "Despite a fleeting hope that he could be, the doctor is not her match. Besides, why would crushing his business before it even starts cause any kind of love to blossom?"

Ursula leaned back in the armchair. "That's for my benefit. I'm still mad at him for rejecting my offer. Fact is, once I crush him, Abigail can help him pick up the pieces."

"It's going to be hard to crush him now that he's gone and saved that little girl's life. Did you see he was on the front page of the paper this morning?" Doris reapplied her bright-pink lipstick. "Shame. They could've done an article about that concert in The Book Nook, but he went ahead and stole her lightning right out from under her."

Gigi sighed and turned to the others. "Girls. Let's put our heads together. Surely there's someone we've overlooked."

Doris sighed. "There isn't, Gigi. I think Ursula might actually be onto something."

Gigi shook her head. "It's out of the question."

"Do you have a better suggestion?" Ursula

stared at her, but Gigi's mind drew a blank. And not for lack of trying, which was what she'd been doing for weeks.

What if Ursula was right and their unfortunate circumstances were the only thing keeping Abigail and the doctor apart? He *had* shown a kind side of himself the other night, helping Abigail retrieve all those chairs.

"Fine. The doctor could probably use a good meal right now," Gigi said, feeling a bit like a traitor.

"And we've been known to ask our newest recruits to make those deliveries," Tess pointed out, most likely remembering the numerous house calls she herself had made in the last two years.

"Very good, then. It's settled," Gigi said. "We make dinner for the doctor, and Abigail delivers." She looked at Ursula. "And we'll see if Ursula is right about the unlikeliest of pairings."

Chapter 30

The day after the accident, both Junie and Kate were released from the hospital, and while Jacob was relieved, the effects their pain had on him lingered.

More than once Kate had asked if he was okay. More than once he'd lied and told her everything was fine.

Saving that little girl's life had reignited something inside him, but that flame had gone out the second he got Kate's call.

Junie seemed to be in a daze, content to stare at the television and try not to move.

"She'll get back to her happy self very soon," the doctor told them as they were wheeling her down to the front door of the hospital.

Jacob wanted to ask how this man knew that Junie had a happy self, but he decided to let it slide. No sense getting into a fight with the doctor —he was just trying to do his job. Still, it irritated him. Had Jacob been that kind of doctor? The kind who presumed to know more than he did? Was that why Gwen had been such a difficult case for everyone? Because he got in the way, diagnosing conditions and disorders he knew nothing about?

"But you're a doctor; you would know." That's what they'd all said to him. Like he should've known better. Should've helped her somehow.

His failure taunted him all day.

"Jacob?" Kate stood in the kitchen wearing pajamas with an oversize sweatshirt and a pair of fuzzy slippers that looked more like boots. She wore no makeup, and her hair was pulled back in a loose ponytail. The color had gone from her cheeks, and a bandage was stuck to her forehead.

"Hey, do you want some juice?" Jacob poured her a glass. "You need to go lie down."

"I know." Kate stood on the other side of the

island as if she had more to say. "The doctor came and talked to me. He's concerned."

"Why? Did they find something more wrong with you?"

"Not with me. With you."

Jacob rolled his eyes. "He's concerned about *me*."

"He said your reaction to the accident was worrisome."

"Kate, after everything we've been through—"

"That's what I told him. I said you just had to process it all because of some personal trauma."

Jacob turned away. Now the doctors were evaluating him. He couldn't even grieve in a way that made sense. Couldn't shed a tear without someone making it a cause of concern.

"You aren't responsible for what happened to us, Jacob. It was just an accident."

Her words danced around his head, but he refused to let them in. She stood in front of him, making him look her in the face.

"You aren't responsible for what happened to Gwen either." Kate's eyes filled with tears.

He shook his head. "You don't know that."

"I do too. I was there. I saw the way you loved her, the way you always took care of her. You did everything right, Jacob."

"And it still wasn't enough." Jacob hated the thick ball of pain at the back of his throat. All these months he'd been pushing it down, and it always found a way to return.

Kate reached over and put a hand on his arm. "Everyone's okay. You need to get that. You have to stop trying to be everybody's hero all the time." She took her juice, poured another glass for Junie, and went back into the living room, leaving him there alone.

He stood in the kitchen staring at the wall, trying to consider Kate's words rationally, when his sister called out to him.

"You need to get in here," she said.

He rushed toward the living room, heart racing. "Is everyone okay?"

Junie had fallen asleep and Kate sat in front of the television, watching the news.

"Look."

Kelly stood in front of his building, wind blowing her hair, alongside a reporter holding a microphone in front of her face. "We have huge plans for this building—you know, it's something of a landmark for Loves Park. We wanted to celebrate that."

"When you say 'we,' of course, you mean you and the building's owner, Dr. Jacob Willoughby," the reporter followed up.

"Yes. Jacob is the most incredible family practice doctor. In fact, he saved a little girl's life in this very building just last night. His new practice will be unlike anything you'll find in the sterile walls of a hospital. We've got so many amazing ideas in store."

"Television? Is there a television station in Loves Park?" Jacob stared at the screen in disbelief.

The reporter flipped the mike back at herself. "Can you share any with us?"

"Well." Kelly tossed her hair over her shoulder. "I can tell you that we're going to transform this building and create a welcoming, homey environment where we can diagnose your ailments and find the very best way to get you on track for a speedy recovery. You won't even feel like you're in a doctor's office at all."

Kate groaned.

"And what are the plans for Abigail Pressman's Book Nook? Will she be a part of this redesign?"

Kelly glanced at Abigail's store behind her. "We expect our remodel to include the entire building, but we certainly wish Miss Pressman the very best of luck with her little store."

The camera returned to the reporter, who smiled, thanked Kelly, and said something about bringing more news on this story as it developed, leaving Jacob with a sour taste in his mouth.

Kate was staring at him. No, make that a glare. Kate was glaring at him.

He groaned. "Don't even say it."

"What were you thinking, getting into business with that woman?" Kate hissed the words so as not to wake Junie.

"I guess I wasn't thinking."

"Jacob, you have to fix this."

Great. Something else that needed fixing. As if his daughter's leg, his sister's head, and his entire life weren't enough. "What is a television station doing covering the news in Loves Park anyway?"

"Loves Park is a tourist town, Jacob. What did you expect? Abigail's store is well-known. I saw it in one of the travel journals as a 'must-stop.' They have a little station with round-the-clock Loves Park coverage. Helps visitors figure out what to do when they're here." Kate clicked the television off.

Jacob paced. "Maybe it's better this way. Let Kelly figure out the business side of things and let me get on with my life. Isn't that what you said I should do?"

Kate stood. "Are you crazy? This is not getting on with your life. This is destroying someone else's."

Jacob remembered something he'd meant to ask her. "Kate, what happened to Abigail this morning?"

Kate shook her head. "I don't know. I guess she came back to the hospital—Kelly brought in the coffee and that stuff from the house, but Abigail must have given them to her."

"Why wouldn't she just bring them herself?"

"Jacob, there's no way she wouldn't have come back in to check on all of us, unless . . ."

He let out a long breath. "Unless Kelly said something to her."

Kate put her hands on her hips. "You're really sending Abigail some mixed messages, you know."

"What do you mean?"

"Holding her hand at the hospital. Asking her to stay with you there. Kicking her out of her building."

"My building."

"Whatever. You're being a jerk. Do you even know how she got home, Jacob? She rode to the hospital with you. How did she get home?"

Jacob sighed. He didn't need this right now.

He grabbed his coat and the car keys, but before he reached the door, Kate stopped him.

"She even brought Junie's teddy bear to the hospital."

Jacob turned. "I know, Kate. Remember how happy I was you told her to do that?"

Kate picked up the stuffed animal from the couch and held it in front of him. "Look at it."

The two paper hearts had been pinned to its chest with delicate care. He knew because he'd pinned them there months ago. Sometimes he found hearts in Junie's bedroom, tucked under her pillow or used as bookmarks for whatever picture book she fell asleep reading.

They always said the same basic thing. *I miss you, Mommy.* Or *Come back home.*

In her six-year-old mind, Junie still didn't understand what it meant for someone to die. Jacob thought she'd decided her mom had just left home for a really long time. He couldn't bring himself to correct her.

"You think she knows?" His stomach dropped. If Abigail knew he'd written the original hearts, it wouldn't be long before everyone knew. Then the questions would begin. The truth would come out. And suddenly Junie's absent mom would be replaced in her mind by a skeleton or some other horrifying image, and Jacob's medical practice would be over before it started.

What kind of person would want someone like him for a doctor, anyway?

Kate just shrugged and walked away, leaving Jacob standing in the kitchen with his coat on, keys in hand and no desire to go anywhere.

Still, he opened the front door and was surprised to find Abigail standing there, arms loaded with what appeared to be a box of dishes.

She wore a miserable expression and possibly a scowl, both reserved for him, he was sure.

"Gigi made me bring this over," she said, annoyance in her voice.

"She made you?"

A shrug.

"Come in."

She hesitated but finally relented, and when she walked past him, he inhaled a deep breath, wanting to memorize the scent of her, wondering if this could be one of the last times he ever spoke with Abigail Pressman.

Chapter 31

Abigail was still in disbelief. Why had she gone along with this?

"Let me get that." Jacob took the box from her hands, leaving Abigail with only the couple of items she'd brought for Junie and Kate.

"I just have a few books and things for Junie, and I brought some of that coffee Kate likes so much." She began pulling things from the bag on her shoulder, but he stopped her.

"Come in. You can give it to them yourself."

When Gigi had arrived at The Book Nook with a box of food for the Willoughbys, Abigail practically slammed her office door in the old woman's face.

"There is no way I am taking this to that man. He can eat dog food for all I care." She plopped in her chair. "Actually, he can't do that. The man is so heartless he doesn't even feed the dog."

Gigi looked puzzled but ignored her. "This is part of your duty, Miss Pressman. We take care of the sick and wounded whether we want to or not."

"And what about the psychopathic and deranged?"

"You were so sympathetic to him yesterday, dear. What's changed? He's still a human being, one of God's creatures. He deserves our care."

Abigail didn't want to take care of Jacob or anyone else. She wanted every distraction to go away so she could figure out what in the world to do about Kelly's ultimatum. Three months. She couldn't find a decent apartment in that time, let alone a new space for The Book Nook.

Worse, Abigail had finished reading the most recent paper hearts earlier today, and while she couldn't be positive, she had the distinct impression that her couple had split up.

The fact that it was affecting her mood tonight was beyond ridiculous, but there it was. Not that she'd tell Gigi any of that.

In the end, she'd been guilted and bribed into delivering a casserole, a pot of homemade soup, two different desserts, and an assortment of side dishes to one Dr. Jacob Willoughby.

Now she stood in his entryway wishing she could disappear.

She followed him into the kitchen, reminding herself that despite his charm and good looks, he was even more her enemy now than on the day she first met him.

Never mind that a part of her actually liked him. Never mind that today she'd relived the way her hand had felt wrapped inside his more times than she would ever admit. Never mind that she sometimes accidentally thought about what it would be like to kiss him and she always, always ended up with a racing heart and flushed cheeks.

This man is ruining your life.

And he didn't even have the courage to do it himself. He had a *business manager* to do his dirty work for him.

He set the box down on the counter and started unpacking its contents. "This is a lot of food."

She shifted. "Gigi is very serious about her cooking."

"You mean you didn't make all this?" He shot her a sideways glance.

"Most nights my dinner consists of a can of soup and a piece of toast," she said. "I promise I didn't make any of that." She didn't even care what he thought of her lack of cooking skills. She was done caring about this man's view of her.

He smiled. It was a nice smile, as always. Figured.

"You should stay for dinner."

"Me? Oh no, I can't." Abigail looked away.

"I insist. There's a ton of food here, and we can't eat it all." He caught her gaze. "Besides, I owe you a thank-you."

The seconds ticked by before she could respond. "You don't owe me anything."

He took a step closer. Close enough to set her heart racing but not close enough to make her palms sweat. Yet.

"Thank you for coming with me to the hospital. I-I know I . . ."

"It's okay."

"No. It's not. I'm sorry. I just don't know what I'd do if anything happened to them."

Abigail saw that same tortured look on his face, and she thought about the things Hailey had told her about Kate. How did she break the news to Jacob that the doctors thought his sister had been beaten? Repeatedly? Maybe it wasn't her business. Maybe she could justify keeping that to herself. Hailey shouldn't have told her in the first place. Maybe it would be enough if she just told Kate she knew and offered her a shoulder to cry on. Or whatever a battered woman might need. A punching bag? A box of chocolates? A new identity?

Her mind spun. She didn't want to be privy to anyone's secrets.

Except maybe Jacob's. She still found herself wondering what it was he kept hidden.

Jacob reached out and took her hand. "I know you probably really hate me right now, but I . . ."

He seemed incapable of finishing his thought. Instead he brushed a strand of her hair behind her ear, letting his hand linger on her cheek.

What in the world?

She swallowed, her throat dry. Her lips—dry. Oh. No. Her lips were dry. What if he tried to kiss her and her lips were like sandpaper? What if their lips stuck together from all her dryness, or worse, what if she wet her lips and it all went sloppy, not unlike her first kiss with Ryan Brooks in the ninth grade?

Now her palms were sweating.

"I'm really glad you were there," he said, hand still hanging out on her cheek.

She didn't reply. What could she say? Her mind had turned to oatmeal, and all she could think about was the current moisture status of her lips.

When Kate walked in, Jacob practically tore his hand away from her face. The calm demeanor she'd grown accustomed to disappeared as he buried his head in the box of food.

Kate watched him, then gave Abigail a questioning look.

"I brought food," Abigail said.

Kate's smile started behind her eyes and traveled to her lips. A smile from someone who knew exactly what she'd walked in on but had decided to pretend otherwise.

"I was going to go lie down for a little bit before dinner. Is that still okay?"

"Of course," Jacob said. "Is Junie sleeping?"

"I moved her into her room." Kate started toward the door. "So you guys will have the place all to yourselves for a little while." She looked amused. "You know, in case you need some privacy."

"Kate." Jacob's tone sounded like a warning shot.

She held up her hands and backed out of the room.

"Sorry," he said, meeting Abigail's eyes.

"I should probably go."

"Because you're mad at me."

She looked away. *Yes. Because I'm mad at you. And because I've already started obsessing about the smell of your aftershave.*

"I don't know what Kelly said to you . . ." Jacob paused as if waiting for her to tell him, but she couldn't. She couldn't repeat the humiliating words out loud. Maybe he hadn't asked Kelly to tell her to stay away from him, but he certainly would've authorized her new three-month deadline. And here he stood, pretending to be unaware of all of it?

"I heard she was on the news."

Jacob looked away. "I didn't know about that either."

"Sounds like your employee is out of control," Abigail said.

For a brief moment, he looked like he might smile. "You *are* mad at me."

Her pulse quickened. "That store is my life."

"And you don't think you could have a life without that store?" He watched her, waiting for an answer to a question she'd asked herself a thousand times. He couldn't understand that without it, she had nothing. Less than nothing.

She'd fade off into oblivion and disappear forever. Prove to herself that she really was a hopeless cause.

"I don't really want to find out." She chewed the inside of her lip, working up the courage to say what she really wanted to say. "I just wish you'd told me yourself instead of having Kelly do it." But she knew he didn't owe her that. They weren't even friends—not by any definition Abigail had ever known. The problem was, this thing with him felt so impersonal and so personal at the same time.

"Abigail, I can explain—"

"And the way you went on and on about how stupid the paper hearts were, but your own daughter has them pinned to her teddy bear." The hypocrisy of that needled her. She'd recently concluded that, most likely, this little girl had discovered the tradition of the hearts because her father had introduced them to her. The real question was why. Why did he come home after disapproving of Abigail for hanging them, then coax Junie into writing her own? Did he actually see the value in putting feelings on paper?

And if so, why didn't he say so? Couldn't he at least give Abigail credit for that? At least admit that something she'd done had been worthwhile— not just for the community, but for his family?

Not that it mattered. Now that Kelly had the reins, Abigail didn't stand a chance.

He started to speak but quickly went quiet. Finally he said, "She misses her mom."

"And the hearts are a great way for her to

express what she's feeling." Abigail crossed her arms. "My store is bringing that safety, that inspiration, to the rest of the community—don't you see? It's not just about money or books or coffee for me." She thought of stocking the shelves with her father when she was young. Of all the conversations she'd had in that store with customers over the years. Of all the dreams she'd had of finally making it her own. Anger wound itself in a tight ball in her belly. "You're taking that all away."

He closed his eyes and let out a sigh. "I'm sorry."

"No. If you were really sorry, you'd stop doing this. You'd call off your attack dog and let me stay in my store." Apparently anger fueled her courage.

"I will find a way to make it up to you; I promise."

Tears sprang to her eyes and she closed them, turning away so he wouldn't have the satisfaction of seeing her cry. "I have to go."

"Abigail, please." He grabbed her arm, but she couldn't make eye contact. She couldn't stand the disappointment of what he was doing to her.

"I think if things were different, we could've actually been friends," she said. "Maybe that's what's saddest of all."

She pulled her arm from his grasp and slipped out the door, holding back tears even when the sharp wind struck her face on the way to the car. But as soon as she pulled away, her pain spilled out onto her cheeks like a stream of heat she had no hope of containing.

Chapter 32

"Abigail, we are all just sick over what's happening to your store. How are you doing?"

Celeste Dixon was an old high school classmate, and Abigail was surprised to hear from her. She hadn't even seen the woman in over a year. But Celeste worked for the local cable channel, so Abigail didn't have to stretch too far to imagine what she was calling about.

"I'm fine, Celeste," she lied.

"Did you see the story on the news tonight? It's all anyone was talking about at work."

"I heard about it." And heard about it. And heard about it. It seemed everyone in town was intent on talking about how Kelly the barracuda and Jacob the puppet master were throwing her out. Clearly there was not much actual news happening these days.

"I was just wondering what you thought of the whole situation."

"I think it stinks, Celeste," Abigail said, unable, for once, to resist a listening ear. "It stinks that just because someone has money, they can come in here and buy up our buildings and turn them into whatever they want. And it stinks that people who've lived here their whole lives end up paying the price."

"It does seem unfair."

"The worst part is the doctor sends that woman to do all his dirty work. He doesn't even have the decency to fight his battles himself. Sure, he can save lives and everything, but all I've seen is him ruining mine."

She closed her eyes and the image of Jacob standing in front of her, brushing her hair behind her ear, popped into her head. Why did he think it was okay to send such mixed signals? Was he dense or just cruel?

Celeste was quiet for a moment, and then Abigail heard a click.

"Celeste?"

"Yes, sorry, Abigail. I just want you to know that I'm really hoping this works out for you. I would hate to see your store go out of business."

It wasn't until the next day's five o'clock evening news on Loves Park's tiny television station that Abigail realized the click she'd heard was Celeste turning off whatever recording device she had on. Abigail watched in horror as her angry words played on the television over B-roll of Jacob walking into the mercantile as Kelly stood outside, waving her arms toward the building as if deciding on signage or some other nonsense. They were painting Jacob as the good guy and Abigail as the angry, bitter one.

"She recorded me?" Abigail threw her pillow at the TV. It had been obvious to her that their conversation was off the record. Or so she thought.

The wicked witch's theme rang out from her cell phone. Abigail picked it up. "Not now, Mom."

Before she hung up, she heard Teensy say something about letting that wretched business go once and for all, but she silenced her and turned the phone off for the night. She awoke the next morning to several voice messages and a congratulatory "phone note," as Doris would say, from Ursula.

Way to fight, Pressman. Proud of you.

Another text, this one from Betsy, simply read, You okay?

Abigail stared at the text. She suddenly missed her sister. She wanted to pick up the phone and call her, but she knew Betsy didn't have time for Abigail's drama—not when her wedding approached so quickly.

Abigail texted back a quick I'm okay. You? And left it alone.

She had half a mind to call Celeste and demand the woman apologize to her for recording her without her knowledge, but what good would that do? She should've assumed something was up.

Why else would Celeste call her? Certainly not out of concern for Abigail.

She sighed. She was tired. Worrying about the store had worn her out. Worrying about her life had worn her out. By Sunday afternoon, she'd had about all the self-pity she could handle. Her favorite flea market was located ten miles out of town, and she'd made up her mind that regardless of the fact that she had no reason to acquire vintage furniture for her store, she did still love a good find. She was going whether she felt like it or not.

This Colorado winter day was surprisingly mild, and she didn't need anything more than the hoodie over her skinny jeans and boots. She pulled her hair up into a loose bun, dabbed on some lip gloss, and called it done. She never saw anyone she knew at these things anyway.

As she drove, the mountains in front of her, her mind spun with the countless ways her life was falling apart. She'd racked her brain trying to figure out what she'd do next, now that losing the store was, in fact, a reality. Worse, she couldn't stop replaying the harsh tone of her voice when she talked about Jacob and Kelly in that recording. She'd been so hateful. So much for taking the high road.

"I'm so sorry." Her whispered prayer cut the silence in her car. She'd acted badly and she regretted it, no matter how angry she was at Jacob.

"I don't want to be angry and bitter, even though everything feels so unfair right now."

The truth was, the idea of losing her store terrified her. She'd have to finally answer the question she avoided every time she considered her future.

What do you really want, Abigail?

The question had appeared off and on over the past couple of years like a relentless mosquito intent on eating its fill. She shooed it away, but it continued to nag her.

What did she really want? What should she really want?

Before she could answer, the sign for the flea market appeared up ahead. Thankful for the distraction, she pulled into a makeshift parking space, slung her bag across her chest, and tugged on a pair of gloves.

It wasn't cold enough for a heavy coat, but the crisp air still bit her bare skin.

She walked toward the entrance, paid her admission fee, and started browsing. She usually came to the flea market with some sort of plan, but not today. Today, the only thing on her agenda was getting lost and forgetting her woes.

Abigail stopped by the small café at the center of the market first and ordered the largest cup of coffee they had. She doctored it up with the necessary amounts of cream and sweetener, stirred, and decided even this oversize cup likely wouldn't be enough to sustain her. Not today.

Back outside, the market had just started to get busy. People had already begun haggling for the best prices on antique furniture—chipped wood and naturally distressed, just the way she liked it. Furniture renovations allowed her to turn her brain off for a few hours and create something beautiful. She could use a new project about now.

Mel Dandy's booth was tucked away in the corner, which made it something of a lost treasure, one that no one seemed to notice. But Abigail always made a point of going to Mel's first. The man was a bit too talkative, but he had the best stuff.

She made a beeline for the booth, but when she arrived, she found herself face-to-face with the last people she wanted—or expected—to see here. Kelly and Jacob. Together. If she didn't know better, she'd have assumed they were a couple.

But then, maybe she didn't know better. And what difference did it make anyway? They'd set out to ruin her life and they'd succeeded. But the fact that they were at *her* flea market made her blood boil. At least Jacob had the decency to look as shocked as she felt.

"Abigail," Kelly said. She motioned to an old buffet. "Tell Jacob he has to get this for the practice. It's a great find, don't you think?"

Abigail frowned. Was she serious? Wasn't she the same person who'd told Abigail to stay away from Jacob? "It's, uh, nice," she muttered, wishing she'd never gotten out of bed that morning.

Mel stood, hiking up his overalls as he did. "Nice?" He gave her a once-over. "It's better than nice, Pressman. This is quality. They don't make 'em like this anymore. Seven hundred is a steal and you know it. Tell her."

Abigail studied Mel, who was in full salesman mode. He wouldn't bother trying anything on Abigail because she'd see straight through his spiel, but who was she to stand in the way of him working one over on Kelly? Maybe the woman would nickel-and-dime Jacob out of the rest of his money and he'd fire her.

"Only seven hundred?" Abigail widened her eyes, then looked at Kelly. "That is quite a steal. Actually, I might want it for myself."

Kelly tossed her hair over her shoulder like she always did. How annoying.

"Oh? Did you find a new space for your store already?"

Abigail liked this woman less and less.

"What's wrong with the place you're in now?" Mel obviously didn't watch the news.

Abigail glanced at Jacob, who dropped his eyes. Had he replayed that fleeting moment in his kitchen as many times as she had? Had he wondered what would've happened if Kate hadn't interrupted them? She shoved the thoughts aside.

"Didn't you hear? Dr. Willoughby here is opening up a new medical practice and he needs the whole building, including the space where my *little* store is."

Mel frowned, turning to Jacob. "So you're kicking her out?"

Kelly ignored him. "Jacob, I think we need to get this. We'll put it along the side wall when patients first walk in. That's where the receptionist will be, and we want to make it homey. Once we get rid of that dreadful counter." She touched his arm. "You said you didn't want it to look or feel like a hospital or clinic. This will really help. I think it's perfect for a display of all your literature."

Abigail forced herself not to stare at Kelly's hand on Jacob's bicep.

"Seems like an awfully big expense for something to set business cards on," Jacob said, moving away from Kelly's wandering hands.

Kelly laughed, looked at Mel, and nodded. "We'll take it."

Jacob glanced at Abigail, who decided he was miserable. He looked away.

Kelly paid Mel, who gave her a ticket with instructions on how and when to pick up her new piece—a piece that could desperately use Abigail's touch if she did say so herself. He marked the buffet with a red Sold tag and thanked Kelly for her patronage.

Kelly tucked the receipt in her purse and breezed past Abigail, linked her arm through Jacob's, and tossed a thoughtless good-bye over her shoulder.

Jacob shoved his hands into his pockets and followed his so-called business manager to the next booth, leaving Abigail alone with her devastation.

"Thanks for backing me up there, Abs," Mel said.

She smiled. He was about the only person in the world she'd allow to call her that. "You know I wouldn't have paid a dime over three hundred for that."

He winked at her. "Like I said. Thanks."

While Abigail didn't feel at all like shopping anymore, she plodded on, and by late afternoon, she'd purchased a small table and two old pieces of artwork she'd likely hang in her guest room. Not surprisingly, her retail therapy had done little to soothe her weary mind.

Back in the café, she ordered a sandwich and sat down with her journal, content to let her mind wander while she refueled before heading to the other side of the market. There were only a few more booths worth seeing, but she couldn't bring herself to leave without at least perusing the goods.

She'd assumed Jacob and Kelly had grown tired of the flea market scene by now, so when he walked in and got in line at the counter, Abigail was surprised. She took a moment to study him. He looked like he might've been an athlete. Not a football player, maybe a swimmer. Or a baseball player. Or a golfer. Didn't all doctors play golf?

He stood in the line, studying the menu board. She considered telling him to avoid the tuna fish but decided to let Kelly worry about his food selections. No sense butting in.

Still, in spite of everything, she couldn't shake the image of the man she'd seen at the hospital. So desperate and worried. She had the distinct impression that a part of Jacob had gone on autopilot and there was much about his life right now that wasn't his own.

How was it possible for her to feel so sorry for a person and so angry with him at the same time?

He must've felt her watching him from a distance like the creeper she was, because he turned and caught her eyes just before the woman in front of him moved, making way for him to order. The eye lock took her so off guard that she held on to it for far too many seconds. By the time she tore her gaze from his, it was too late. He ordered, paid, and walked straight toward her.

Abigail shifted things around on the table, avoiding his eyes. Maybe if she stayed busy, he'd keep walking.

No such luck.

"Mind if I join you?"

Did she look lonely? She needed to work on her

I'm-eating-alone-and-I'm-fine face. She glanced up and shrugged, suddenly feeling guilty she'd let him fork over seven hundred dollars for that buffet.

"I'm surprised you're still here," she said. "This doesn't seem like your scene."

He set his tented plastic number in the center of the table and folded his hands. "It's not, but Kelly's my ride. She's insisting on decorating the office in this weird old style."

"Vintage."

"Something like that."

The waiter set his food down.

"You didn't get tuna fish, did you?"

He laughed. "No, pulled pork."

"Oh, that's good." She bit into her sandwich. "Where's Kelly?" She refrained from calling her the dragon lady, but that didn't stop her from thinking it.

Jacob waved his hand. "Over there somewhere." He took a bite. "I can only take so much."

"Of Kelly?"

He laughed, covering his mouth with his napkin. "Of shopping, but maybe her too."

Her face flushed and she sipped her soda. "I do some vintage decorating myself, you know."

It burned her a little that Kelly probably had gotten her vintage ideas from Abigail's store in the first place. Nothing about The Book Nook was fancy or modern, and it just so happened that

Abigail had a knack for breathing life into the old pieces everyone else had decided to cast off. She was still pleasantly surprised by how happy it made her to take castoffs and give them a second chance.

Jacob crunched a couple of potato chips. "Really? So what would you think of it in the office?"

Abigail cringed. Did he really expect her to tell him what she thought of his decorating plans for the office that would put her out of business?

She liked the idea of a doctor's office that felt comfortable. She liked the idea of the buffet holding literature about chicken pox and vaccinations. She liked the idea of the waiting area being filled with pretty things that instantly calmed people. She liked all of that and hated herself for it.

"Sounds fine." She bit carelessly into her sandwich.

"I thought maybe you had some ideas for the space."

Abigail frowned, remembering the night he'd asked her what she would do with the building. Kate's car accident had prevented her from telling him much of anything, but maybe that was for the best. "Yeah, when I thought it was going to be mine."

"Sorry," he said, then looked away. "Never mind. That was insensitive of me."

At least they agreed on that.

"I'm just out of my depth here. I'm kind of tired of Kelly calling all the shots. Not usually my style."

She searched his gaze for a deeper meaning but came up empty. He had no intention of revealing his secrets. In spite of that, she felt close to him all over again.

"I heard you on the news last night," he said, brow raised.

She could tell by the heat in her cheeks that her whole face had turned crimson. "I'm really sorry about that. I had no idea Celeste was recording me."

He sat back in his chair. "I believe you."

"I mean, I meant what I said. I just shouldn't have said it like that." *Stop talking, Abigail.*

"I want you to know I've never sent Kelly to say anything to you," Jacob said, holding her gaze. "That's not my style either. I let her take over the renovations for now, but just until things are okay with Kate and Junie again."

Now Abigail leaned back. "I actually believe you too."

"Good."

They sat in silence for a long moment, each of them finishing their lunches. Abigail searched for something else to say, wondering how awkward it would be to ask him why he'd grabbed her hand in his kitchen.

"You can't let her take out the old mercantile counter," she said when her search came up empty.

"You really love that counter, don't you?" He laughed and took a sip of his drink.

"It's too beautiful to just toss away." She thought so anyway.

Jacob folded his hands. "It is a shame when people toss away beautiful things."

She cleared her throat. "I'd carve out a reception area right where people walk in. And make sure to hire somebody local as the receptionist."

He popped a chip in his mouth. "Agreed."

"I have a few pieces that might look really nice in there, actually." What was she saying? She wasn't going to actually *help* him make the clinic less clinical, was she?

He seemed taken aback too.

"I like to refinish furniture in my spare time." She looked away. "Selling it was supposed to be part of my expansion."

He cleared his throat, but before he could respond, something behind Abigail caught his attention. She couldn't be sure, but she thought she heard him groan.

"There you are." Kelly was not within appropriate distance to be talking to him yet, which meant she practically yelled across the café. Abigail tried not to roll her eyes.

She failed.

"I've been looking for you. I'm starv—" Kelly paused beside the table as if she'd just that second noticed Abigail sitting across from him. "Oh."

"Abigail and I were talking about the clinic," Jacob said. "She has some great ideas about the decorating."

"I see."

"I'll come look at those pieces we talked about, Abigail," he said. "And I'd love to get your input on the rest of the project."

"Jacob," Kelly said, "won't that be a conflict of interest?"

"What, do you think I'm going to make it ugly out of spite?" Abigail laughed. "Actually, that's not a bad idea."

She caught Jacob stifling a smile.

"We'll pay you for your time, of course," he said. "If there's anyone who knows how to capture the feel we're going for, it's you."

He stood and picked up his tray.

"Thanks," Abigail said, unsure of Jacob's angle.

He met her eyes. "Maybe we can still be friends after all."

After he walked away, Kelly stood there for a long moment, befuddled. "I don't know what you're up to, but don't think this changes anything."

Abigail didn't respond, but when she glanced at the door, she found Jacob standing there, watching her, a slight smile playing at the corners of his mouth. She let her eyes settle on his for a few seconds that felt like very long minutes, and she stayed that way until he pushed open the door and disappeared.

Chapter 33

Monday morning, Jacob had begun to rethink his kindness toward Abigail Pressman. The sidewalk had filled with a small crowd of good old-fashioned picketers, and it seemed his tenant was keeping them well caffeinated.

"I was being generous giving book girl three months," Kelly said, slamming her notebook on the counter. "I can't wait until she's gone and we can knock this whole wall out. I guess your superhero status was short-lived."

"Perhaps you just underestimated her."

"Don't be ridiculous. This woman is no match for me." Kelly had taken the demonstration as a personal insult, and knowing her, she'd likely have a rebuttal tactic worked up before lunch.

He knew helping Avery on Friday night had won him some loyal followers; however, Abigail still had pull in this town. It was almost as if a line had been drawn and people felt they had to choose sides.

He looked around the future clinic space. He'd been working whenever he had a free moment, and it felt good to throw himself into the project. Every time he started to feel guilty about needing Abigail's space, he remembered Junie—his main priority.

Why the main things he wanted seemed to be in direct conflict with everything else he wanted, he didn't understand.

Two of the workers they'd hired strolled in through the back door. Kelly spun around. "You're late."

The men looked at each other. "It's just now eight," one of them said.

"Didn't anyone ever teach you five minutes early is on time? On time is late."

Both men stood frozen.

"Well? Get to work! You're wasting our money!" Kelly huffed and turned her attention back to her notebook. The men glanced at Jacob, who gave them a slight head shake before they disappeared into the back room.

"Was that necessary?" Jacob asked, forcing himself to be patient.

Kelly waved him off. "Don't question the way I do things, Jacob. They need to know they can't get away with that."

Jacob drew in a deep breath. The fresh-start idea had sounded so good, but the price he was paying to work with Kelly was starting to wear on his nerves. "They were on time. I don't want to hear you talking to them like that again."

She looked up, eyes narrowed. "If it weren't for you trying to make Abigail Pressman your *friend,* none of this would be happening in the first place. How do you expect to open a practice with picketers on the sidewalk?" She pointed toward the crowd that had gathered outside The Book Nook. They carried signs with slogans like *Reading Is the Best Medicine* and *Save Our Book Nook.*

"I think maybe we should've thought about that before we made an appearance on the news," Jacob said.

She scoffed. "I am trying to build your business for you. That's what you hired me to do."

He glanced back at the crowd. "The way I see it, making nice with Abigail Pressman is the only thing we can do."

Kelly rolled her eyes. "You've certainly been doing your share of that, haven't you?" She clicked a button on her phone and started sliding things around on the screen.

"I'm sorry if I don't see the point in picking fights with innocent people."

She motioned to the sidewalk again. "You call *that* innocent?" Kelly set her phone down and took a few steps toward him. "She wants you to feel sorry for her, so now she's being nice— maybe even trying to get you to like her. What else is she supposed to do?"

Kelly had no idea what she was talking about.

"Why else would she pretend to offer her help decorating this place?" Her gaze traveled beyond him, over to The Book Nook, where now even more people had gathered. Thankfully his door was locked, though he wondered how long until the picket signs became more hostile.

"She's pretending to be all sweet and innocent to your face, but how much do you want to bet she called these people and asked them to come down here? She probably painted all the signs herself. Don't forget the things she said on the news. She's not as nice as you think she is." Kelly turned her back to the mess of picketers outside.

Was Kelly right? Was this just some ploy his seemingly kind neighbor had cooked up in an effort to save her store?

No. That would be a complete contradiction to the Abigail he knew and respected.

The Abigail he couldn't stop thinking about.

"Jacob, focus on what's in front of you and get your head out of that cloud. That woman is not your concern. You have every right to take over this building that *you* own and do whatever you want with it. For your own family."

She knew how to push his buttons. "It's going to be awfully hard to launch this practice if all of these people hate me."

She softened. "It'll blow over. You know it will. This crowd would be a lot bigger if you hadn't saved that girl the other night. As soon as one of them has a sick baby or a head cold, you're going to see that they'll buy in to your idea of what a doctor's office should offer." Kelly seemed so confident, he almost believed her.

"I hope you're right."

She smiled, easing the tension in the room. "Of course I am. This is what I do." She stared at him for a few seconds and reached up to touch his cheek. "I've been wondering . . ."

His stomach lurched. No. He couldn't go down this road. "I do appreciate your help, Kelly. You're great with numbers, but I—"

"I'm not asking about business, Jacob." Her hand found his and she inched closer. "You can't tell me you don't feel what's going on between us."

Jacob started to respond, but before he could say a word, her body was pressed up against him, her mouth covering his. He held still for too many seconds before pulling away, her eyes still intent on his.

"I've been wanting to do that for a very long time."

He heard himself mumble something, but he couldn't even decipher it. Had he kissed her back?

"You're so cute when you're flustered." She smiled.

A crash at the back of the store pulled their attention, and Jacob's mouth went dry. The horrified look on Abigail's face told him she'd seen it all.

"Oh, look," Kelly said. "Book girl brought you coffee."

Abigail's scorched face pulsed with embarrassment. Of all the times to trip over a metal paint tray, this was certainly the worst.

Jacob pulled himself from Kelly's clutches, looking mortified.

But why? He didn't need to explain himself to her. Clearly she'd misinterpreted his relationship with Kelly, but what did it matter? He and Abigail were the furthest thing from a couple.

"Abigail."

"I'm so sorry. I never knock loud enough." She held up the pathetic cup of coffee in her hand. "It's a peace offering."

Kelly's heels clicked as she walked toward the counter and picked up her purse. "Really, Abby, you have the worst timing." She whisked back toward Jacob, letting her hand drape across his shoulders as she whispered something to him about "finishing this later." Then she strode toward Abigail, eyes fully on her face as she passed through the door.

Jacob drew in a deep breath and let it out over the course of the next several seconds. "I'm really sorry you had to see that."

Abigail shook her head a little too feverishly.

"Not at all. Perfectly normal. Two consenting adults and everything."

Stop talking.

"I always thought maybe you two were together," she said to her own horror.

A smile skittered across his face. "You thought about that, did you?"

Beet-red cheeks all over again, before she'd even had a chance to get them back to their normal pale pink.

He looked at her then—the kind of look that prompted her to turn away—and yet she couldn't.

"We're not," he said.

"What?"

"A couple." He still held her with his eyes.

She laughed, not because anything was funny but out of sheer nervousness. "It's really none of my business, Jacob. You can kiss whoever you want."

He smiled. "I wish that were true."

For a split second, the air left her lungs and she thought she might have a panic attack over the possible implications of that comment, but she quickly reminded herself not to read anything into it.

He was not her friend, let alone her kissing buddy.

Just the idea of it sent her mind spinning. She cleared her throat, begging herself to keep it together. "I wanted to tell you I've asked them to leave twice now, but they're quite persistent."

Abigail motioned toward the sidewalk. She'd purposely skulked over through the back door, hoping no one would see her, though her secrecy had only landed her smack in front of something much worse than overenthusiastic supporters.

Would she ever get the image of the dragon lady kissing Jacob out of her head?

She appreciated everyone coming out to rally behind her, but she hated some of the things she saw on the signs in front of her store. *We support LOCAL.* As if to say no one else was welcome here. That wasn't the feeling she wanted to convey.

She truly didn't want to destroy Jacob when she thought about it—she simply wanted to save her own store.

"I thought I saw you handing out cups of coffee earlier," he said, his tone teasing.

Some of the heat left her cheeks. "You were watching me?"

He started to respond but snapped his jaw shut, though she could tell he was trying not to smile. He took a drink of the coffee.

"Anyway," she said. "I'm sorry, I guess. That's really all I wanted to say."

Jacob set the coffee down on the counter and leaned against it. He looked relaxed in his jeans and hooded sweatshirt. Her mind turned to the rows of dress clothes she'd seen in his closet. The ties. The nice shoes.

The man in front of her certainly didn't look like

a doctor. Sometimes she wondered if he did that on purpose.

"I think between the two of us, I'm the one who needs to apologize. I don't even know how you got home from the hospital the other day." Jacob ran a hand over his whiskered chin.

Was that regret she saw behind his eyes?

She looked away. "Mallory came and got me. It was fine." *It was terrible.*

He paused. "I was hoping I could come by your place tonight and look at the furniture," he said. "If the offer still stands."

She nodded. "Of course. I'll be done at the store around six."

"I'll meet you then. Follow you home?"

This is business. "Sounds good." She started toward the door.

"Abigail?"

She turned to face him, trying not to memorize the way he said her name.

"Do you think we could maybe call a truce?"

She glanced outside. Ursula would tell her she'd gotten to him. Her plan was working. He needed to stay in her good graces if he had any hope of launching a successful practice.

And yet, looking at him, his eyes intent and unnerving and filled with something she could only describe as sorrow, she didn't want to believe any of that.

She wanted to think that maybe he'd come to

his senses and changed his mind about the three months. About the one year. About kicking her out at all.

But she knew better. She didn't have a leg to stand on and she was well aware of it.

He extended a hand in her direction. "Truce?"

And even though it made no logical sense, she reached out, shook his hand, and hoped for the best, telling herself if he really wanted to get on her good side, there was only one way she'd let him do it—if he promised not to close down her store.

Chapter 34

"You've got a lot of nerve showing your face here."

Jacob could've met Abigail out back in the parking lot, but in a rare moment of insanity, he decided to come in through the front door five minutes before she closed.

Now, standing face-to-face with the three older ladies, he regretted it. The picketers had left just after lunchtime, but he'd gotten more than his fair share of dirty looks since he'd walked in the door.

On the other hand, some locals had come over to shake his hand and thank him for saving the young girl on Friday night. The town, it seemed, was torn, and he imagined that didn't sit well with anyone in Abigail's camp.

What was he thinking? They'd called a truce. No more camps. She seemed to have finally accepted the fate of her store, and it shouldn't take much longer for the rest of the town to follow suit.

"Ladies." He moved past them to a seat at the counter but quickly realized he'd given them the perfect opportunity to back him into a corner.

The paper hearts seemed to have multiplied. Abigail had certainly turned a simple tradition into something of an epidemic. If he hadn't been the original author of the hearts, he might've actually found it charming.

He opened his newspaper and spotted Abigail over on the other side of the store, talking with a customer. She hadn't seen him come in, and he would have enjoyed watching her for a minute if these three women weren't glaring at him.

One of them walked to his other side while the remaining two parked themselves in chairs beside him. Ursula, unfortunately, was one of these two.

Not a single one of them said a word. Just stared at him.

"Can I help you ladies?" He closed his newspaper—not that he was reading it anyway—and returned their stares.

"This is all your fault. Kicking our girl out onto the street. She's practically given up over there." Doris wore a pout.

Jacob's thoughts turned to the loud chants of the picketers he'd endured for the entire morning. They'd forgotten none of this was comfortable for him either.

"Doris, stop." Sensible-looking Gigi put a hand on her friend's arm. "The man has a right to renovate the space however he sees fit." She huffed, then narrowed her eyes at Jacob. "But you know she won't find anyplace that captures the spirit of The Book Nook in three months."

"And she'll never forgive you," Doris said. "Especially not now, what with all the kissing and everything."

Jacob started to respond but thought better of it. He clearly had no secrets in this town.

Doris and Gigi walked away, leaving Ursula sitting next to him, staring. "You've really gone and messed this one up, haven't you?" she accused.

"Mrs. Pembrooke, please. I'm just trying to earn a living."

She sucked in air. "Seems to me you've got plenty to live on, Doc." She gave him a deadly stare, then got up and left.

What was she implying? Did she know about the lawsuit? About his past?

Jacob opened the newspaper again, trying to shove aside the unwanted worry that conversation had produced. Those women had spoken aloud the fears he'd been mulling over for days.

Weeks, even. Ever since the day he bought the building. He knew he'd stomped on Abigail's dreams like a child running through a pristine garden, trampling perfectly healthy flowers underfoot.

But they'd called a truce, and even if she'd done so out of some ulterior motive, it gave him a chance to at least try to make amends.

On the counter beside him, he spotted a stack of blank paper hearts and a jar of pens. He looked around to make sure the older women weren't watching him. When he was sure he was in the clear, he slipped a couple of hearts off the stack and quickly scribbled on them, then stuffed them in the box. Someone would find them, read them, and hang them up later.

And as much as it terrified him, he hoped that someone was Abigail.

He caught her glance from across the room. She shifted and quickly averted her eyes, but he swore he saw a smile on her face before she did.

Doris was wrong. Abigail might be angry and she might blame him for crushing her business, but he had to believe she might actually forgive him. Someday.

If he played his cards right.

A few seconds and several dirty looks from the older women later, Abigail tucked her bar rag into her apron and made her way over to the counter where he sat. As she did, people around the bookstore took notice, making him feel like he was onstage. Were his hands shaking? And if they were—and he wasn't saying they were— was it because all eyes were on him or because of the woman walking toward him?

"I have to give you credit for coming in here," she said when she reached the counter. "After the picketers and the chanting and the public outrage, I thought you'd meet me in the parking lot out back."

A quick glance around the store told him she was correct. The ones who supported his heroism were nowhere to be found.

"It wasn't the best idea I've ever had."

A soft smile found its way to her lips. Today her hair was loose and wavy around her face. He wanted to run his hands through it. She always downplayed her looks, but right now something about her ivory skin seemed to glow. She was beautiful.

"I had some ideas to show you." She pulled a crumpled piece of paper out of her apron pocket and unfolded it. She set it on the counter and slid it toward him, keeping her hand on top of it, then looked in the direction of the table of older ladies, who were all staring at them.

She leaned in closer to him.

"Now who's the brave one?" He watched her tuck her hair behind her ears, drawn in by the familiar gesture.

"Despite what you might think, I actually don't like conflict," she said. "Besides, what good is a truce if it doesn't change anything?"

He regarded her for a few long seconds, surprised by her words, then turned his attention to the sketch underneath her fingers. "Are you going to let me see it?"

Shyness took over and she suddenly felt unable to show him what was on the page. "It's a very rough sketch."

He smiled. "I can't wait."

Slowly she removed her hands—long, elegant fingers that he noticed were stained a bit with charcoal from the sketch. She wore a simple silver band on her right hand. Nothing on her left. He knew she wasn't taken, yet the reminder still made him smile.

"It's awful, isn't it?" She'd covered the sketch back up before he'd even had a chance to see it. Somehow her insecurity made her even more . . . adorable. It was the word Kate had used to describe her, and he was beginning to see why. It seemed to suit her perfectly. He quickly grabbed the paper and pulled it from under her grasp.

Before she could steal it back, he held it up so he had the best view possible.

"You drew this?" He couldn't believe the image she'd sketched. His clinic, complete with the open wall that led to the space they currently sat in—her space—all outlined on the paper. The look she'd captured, full of thoughtful touches and vintage furniture, even made him want to pull up a chair and stay awhile.

She picked at the edges of her fingernails.

"You're an artist."

She shook her head. "No. It's nothing."

Jacob looked back at the sketch. He decided any more attention to her talent would make her uncomfortable. The more he got to know her, the more she seemed unlike anyone else he'd ever met, and something about that made her very appealing.

But regardless of what she said, the sketch he held in his hand was a work of art, especially considering that the subject matter was the place she'd once dreamed of owning herself. You'd never know it, looking at the precision of her drawing. She'd captured the light and the shadows of what had to be that perfect afternoon sun. Had it been difficult for her to set aside her own dreams to focus for a moment on his?

Her kindness shamed him. He certainly didn't deserve it.

"Is this a logo?" He looked at the page more closely, squinting to see faint marks that read *Willoughby Medical*.

"Oh yeah. It was just an idea. I have an old sign we could repaint. It would be kind of cool."

Her excitement buzzed in his direction, but he must've had a concerned look on his face because her expression went blank and she said, "What's wrong?"

He shook his head as if that would bring him out of his daydream. "You said 'we.' "

Color raced to her cheeks. "Sorry. I meant 'you.' Of course."

"No, I like it." He glanced back at the sketch. "With Kelly it's always 'I.' "

She stilled. Why did he bring up Kelly's name? *Idiot!*

"Well, you guys can do whatever you want with that. We should probably get going." She scribbled something on a little notepad she pulled from her apron. "My address. Just in case I drive too fast for you." She smiled, but something had changed as soon as he mentioned Kelly. What he wouldn't give for a rewind button.

He folded the sketch and handed it back to her. "Have you eaten?"

She laughed. "Soup and toast on the couch when I get home, remember?"

"I'll stop and pick up dinner. It's the least I can do." *Plus it'll give me more time to convince you I'm not the villain you think I am. And more time to push the image of Kelly kissing me out of your mind.*

She swallowed, her once-red cheeks now as white as Casper's. "You don't have to do that."

"I know," he said, standing before she had a chance to change her mind. "But I want to."

As he walked away, he was well aware of the stares that followed him all the way to the door. But instead of being angry, he found himself wondering if Abigail was staring too.

Chapter 35

"What was that?" Ursula practically accosted Abigail the second the door closed behind Jacob.

"Oh, relax," Abigail said. "I'm tired of hating him."

The hearts must've made her soft. She hadn't figured out exactly what had happened between her couple, but she was more certain than ever that it wasn't good. The most recent hearts still sat in an envelope in her desk drawer. She couldn't bear to put them up—not when they were full of one-sided sadness and sorrow. How had such a beautiful love story ended so badly?

If she was smart, she would learn from the couple. Because if their seemingly ideal love story had ended in tragedy, what hope did the rest of them have? Still, something she'd read on one of these hearts gave her pause, made her think twice about hating anybody.

So many years I spent taking you for granted. Taking us for granted. Now that you're gone, I realize I had my priorities out of order. I should've put us first. I'm so sorry.

She'd read the words on the anonymous couple's hearts every day since the last envelope had come to her. They'd convicted her. She'd spent so many years consumed with this store, with making something of herself in spite of her persistent singleness, that she'd been guilty of pushing people away.

Not that she needed to put a ton of effort into her relationship with her landlord, but she wanted to treat people differently. Worry less about her own difficulties and focus on what she could do to love others. She hated to admit it, but she needed to start with her own family. Sure, Teensy and Betsy both presented unique challenges, but they were family.

That had to mean something. Especially now. She'd done what she could to save the store— more programs, more interest, the paper hearts. But the fact was, she didn't own the building. And while the prospect of losing everything still made her heart hurt, it had turned her attention back to what was really important.

Maybe she'd had it all wrong. Maybe it really was time to stop trying to control everything and finally trust God with her future.

"That's good, Abigail," Gigi said, joining them at the counter. "Hate is never the answer."

"No, but neither is rolling over. What happened

to fight or die, Miss Pressman?" Ursula looked like she might swallow Abigail whole if she answered wrong.

Abigail began pulling today's collection of hearts from the box on the counter, laying them out next to a long strand of ribbon. She'd get these hung and then go home.

Where Dr. Jacob Willoughby would meet her. With dinner.

"I'm not like you, Ursula. Maybe you were right. Maybe I'm not cut out for business." Abigail smoothed the hearts. Just twenty or so.

Gigi and Doris gasped. "You told her that?"

"I never said that." Ursula's brow furrowed. "That's not what I said."

"Well, he called a truce. And I agreed. No more picketing or name-calling."

Ursula slapped her hand down on the counter. "Are you really this hopeless? Of course he called a truce. Like I always said, how's he going to open a business in a town that hates him? He gets you on his side and he's golden."

Gigi slowly shook her head. "I don't know about this, Abigail."

"It's fine," Abigail said. "If God wants me to keep The Book Nook, then he'll make a way. Right?" As she said the words, she said a silent prayer, begging God to make a way.

Their collective jaws snapped shut and they all nodded in unison.

After all, who could argue with that?

Abigail quickly attached the hearts to the ribbon.

"All right, but this isn't how I'd do it," Ursula said, yanking her purse off the counter and stomping toward the door.

"It's just fine, Abigail," Gigi said. "You do what you need to do."

Once they'd gone, Abigail glanced at the strand of ribbon she'd been working with when she realized one of the hearts was facedown. As she pulled it off and began to reattach it, she read the words: *You make me want to live again.*

She did a double take and read the words again. The handwriting—was that . . . ?

She hurried back to the office and tugged the envelope of hearts from her desk. She pulled out one of the hearts and set it next to the one in her hand.

Abigail compared the handwriting letter by letter. Some similarities. Some differences. Not a perfect match—but was it possible?

What if the person who'd written the hearts in the first place had been in the store? She ran through a mental Rolodex of people who'd taken a particular interest in the hearts—people she saw often but might've overlooked.

So many people were enamored with the paper hearts. It could be anybody. Her mind spun. This appeared to be the man's handwriting, and if her couple had split, it would be someone recently divorced. She closed her eyes and remembered one lonely Loves Park native who'd been in the store nearly every single day since she'd first hung the hearts. Rob Dubois had even been quoted by the newspaper and had come out as one of her biggest supporters. In fact, it turned out he'd been the one to organize the picketers in the first place.

Rob's wife, Dana, had left him just a few months ago, so it was certainly plausible. Were they the type of couple to carry on this kind of tradition? Did he hope that Dana would find out about this citywide obsession and come running back to him?

And if not, who had he written this heart for? *You make me want to live again.*

Had Rob met someone else? Abigail's mind spun back to the last conversation she'd had with him. He'd gone out of his way to find her after the picketers were set up.

"Thought we'd get down here and show you our support, Abigail," he'd said. "We're all pulling for you. I don't know what I'd do if I couldn't come down here and get my coffee from you every day."

"Thanks, Rob," she'd said. "I appreciate that. You really don't need to organize picketers, though. I doubt it'll change my landlord's mind."

Rob scoffed. "That guy doesn't have a clue.

We'll make sure he knows how valuable you are to Loves Park."

Abigail gasped, closing her fist around the heart. *Did Rob write this to me?*

She shoved the heart in her pocket and shook the silly idea away. She was looking for connections where there weren't any. Rob wasn't the one who wrote the hearts, and he certainly hadn't written a love note for *her*. How ludicrous.

Yet, as she drove home, her mind still reeled at the notion that she might've discovered the original author of the hearts.

Somehow, having a face to go with all the words would be disappointing. Rob and Dana weren't the couple she'd imagined in her mind.

They had never been the picture of romance.

But then, that was the point, wasn't it? Why look for something that doesn't exist?

It wasn't until she rounded the corner of her neighborhood and saw Jacob's truck in her driveway that panic set in. She'd been so consumed with the hearts she'd failed to properly fret over the evening in front of her.

She parked alongside his truck, realizing she was twenty minutes late. Had he been waiting that whole time? From inside her car, she could see him on the porch swing at the front of her little bungalow, the house she wouldn't be able to afford if she didn't find another way to make money once he put her out on the street.

Stop thinking like that. He called a truce.

Ursula's words rushed back at her as she turned off the engine and glanced at her house, where Jacob now stood at the top of the stairs, a bag of takeout in one hand.

What was she thinking, having dinner with this man?

He lifted his free hand and waved, kindness in his smile.

"Here goes nothing," Abigail said, her mind spinning. She got out of the car and walked toward the house. "Sorry I'm late. I got sidetracked."

He waved her off. "No problem. I hope you like Italian."

"It sure beats soup." Abigail unlocked her front door and walked inside, throwing her keys onto the front table in the entryway.

"You've got a really nice house," he said as he closed the door behind him.

"Thanks. I like it." She loved the wide-planked wood floors and the thick crown molding—it reminded her a lot of her store, in fact. She loved the charm, the character, the built-in shelves in the living room and the stone fireplace. She loved the painted-white cabinets in the kitchen and the screened-in porch off the back of the house.

They walked into the kitchen, and as she set her purse down, she turned to find Jacob admiring the built-in bench in the breakfast nook. "It's really beautiful."

"I've done a lot of work in the house over the years. When I moved in, it was pretty rough."

He met her eyes. "You really do like this sort of work."

She shrugged. "I love it, actually." Thoughts turned to the displays she'd already assembled in her mind for what was now Jacob's half of the building—displays that would've been a perfect complement to The Book Nook half but still completely unique. People would drive for hours to pick through her store. Part of her was more excited about that idea than about anything in The Book Nook.

But she'd never admit that. Not out loud. And especially not to Jacob.

"Do you want something to drink?" She opened the refrigerator.

"Water's fine," he said, leaning against the counter on the other side of the freestanding island in the kitchen. She handed him a bottle and grabbed one for herself.

"Should we eat first, or would you rather look at the furniture?"

Jacob took a long drink. "Are we in a hurry?"

She must've given him a puzzled look. After all, his question puzzled her.

"You seem like you might need a minute to decompress."

Did she? She drew in a deep breath. Maybe she did.

"Kate's with Junie, so I'm not in a hurry. I mean, I won't overstay my welcome, but don't rush around on my account. You just walked in the door."

What would it be like to always have someone here to remind her to go easy on herself? Something about the idea nicked a hidden wound she'd buried a long time ago, and an inexplicable lump formed in her throat.

She turned aside and began digging in her purse. For what, she wasn't sure, but she knew she didn't want Jacob to be able to read anything in her expression at that moment.

Abigail took the opportunity to remind herself of a few facts. She didn't need anyone else to watch out for her. She would take care of herself. She knew how relationships ended—there was no point pining away for a man.

"I'm fine," she said before she faced him. "I've got that sketch here somewhere." She fumbled with her purse again before remembering she'd stuffed it in her pocket. When she pulled it out, the heart with the suspicious handwriting came out too. Both landed on the island in front of her, in plain sight.

Jacob's eyebrows shot up. "What's that?"

"Nothing," she said, covering the heart with her hand.

"Bringing your work home with you?" He smiled, his tone light.

The whole town was obsessed with these hearts, but no one as much as her. She knew how ridiculous that made her seem, especially since she'd sworn off love a long time ago. "It's stupid."

He took another drink. "Why? I thought you loved the way the hearts brought people together."

She looked at him. "I can't tell if you're making fun of me."

"I'm not. I promise. Just trying to get to know you better."

She chewed the inside of her cheek, and after several seconds, she set the heart back on the island. "I found this in the box today."

Jacob picked it up and read it out loud. " 'You make me want to live again.' " He looked up, a question on his face. "Sounds kind of desperate."

She snatched the heart back. "Never mind. Let's go look at the furniture." Abigail started for the door, but he moved in front of it, blocking her way.

"Sorry. I'll try to be less of a guy about this. What's so special about this heart?"

Abigail tried not to let the nearness of him affect her, but she wasn't having much success. She took a step back. "Nothing. It's just . . ."

He said nothing, but he smiled gently as if to encourage her to continue.

"The handwriting. It's really similar to the original hearts."

Jacob leaned on the counter again, giving her

the space she needed to see straight again. "And that's bad?"

"Not bad, but if it's the same handwriting, then the couple must live here. They could even be locals. I could've seen them every day for the last ten years and not even known it."

"I suppose it would make sense for someone local to start a tradition like this, right? I mean, the town was founded because of some great love story."

"Don't remind me."

"Oh, that's right," he said, smiling. "You're part of the Loves Park royal family."

She stuffed the heart back in her pocket. "Forget I said anything."

"Why do you want to know who it is?" he asked. "Wouldn't that ruin it for you? You know this couple won't live up to your expectations."

She didn't respond. Instead she wrestled with that idea for a long moment because she knew he was right. And when she was faced with reality, any shred of hope that had been restored would be dashed all over again.

Especially if it did turn out to be Rob and Dana. What a disappointment.

But what did she think would happen? Disappointment was inevitable.

"Sorry, I didn't mean to make you mad," he said.

"No, you're right. Finding out the truth probably would be a letdown." She forced a smile, thankful he'd brought her back to reality. She was not the head-in-the-clouds type, especially when it came to love and romance. Why start now?

"Hungry?" He pulled the foil-covered containers from the bag and smiled.

"I'm starving."

"Good. Let's eat."

Chapter 36

Jacob had nearly stopped breathing when he saw the paper heart he'd written on Abigail's counter, but he forced himself to play it cool. He couldn't let on that the handwriting in question was his. The last thing he needed was for Abigail to find out he was one half of the unfortunate couple she'd taken such an interest in. Like she said, finding out the truth would be a huge disappointment. No one knew that better than he.

He'd tell her, but not yet. And not like that.

And he certainly couldn't let on that he'd written this new heart . . . because he'd written it for her.

Why, he still didn't know. What a careless thing to do. He was just grateful she hadn't put all the clues together. Now he needed to find a way to direct her attention away from the paper hearts and onto something else.

Abigail gathered plates and silverware, and Jacob cracked open the containers of pasta, meatballs, and French bread he'd picked up at one of the little hole-in-the-wall restaurants he'd been meaning to try. They filled their plates and he followed Abigail to the dining room.

Abigail bowed her head for a brief moment as if to offer silent thanks, then put a napkin in her lap. When she looked up, he realized he'd been staring at her, so he quickly looked away, searching his mind for something to talk about.

He came up empty.

"This is a great choice. How'd you know Joe's is the best Italian in town?" she asked.

He shrugged. "The small, local places are always the best."

She stopped midbite, and he realized his remark conjured thoughts of The Book Nook.

"I agree," she said. "You should try to capture that in your clinic."

"Good idea." He took a bite. Wow. It was good.

"You've been working awfully hard to get this thing open as fast as you can." She sipped her water.

He swallowed. "It'll be good to return to work."

"It seems like more than that."

"How?"

"You're very focused, I guess. It's good you have Kelly. She can clear away all the distractions for you."

He looked away. "I'm doing this for my daughter. It's our best option."

And that's all he'd tell her. Nothing more. But when he looked up, he saw a question behind her eyes.

"So it's your dream?"

He set his fork down. "I guess so, yeah. My dream is to take care of Junie. To give her a quiet, normal life."

"She didn't have that before?"

His throat felt dry and his face flushed.

"I guess that would explain a few things," she went on. "Why it's so important. Why you can't seem to entertain any idea other than getting the practice open as quickly as possible."

He silently completed the sentence for her. *No matter who you hurt in the process.*

"Didn't we have a truce?" he asked.

She held her hands up in surrender. "I'm not picking a fight, just making sense of it all."

Seconds ticked by.

He took another bite. Chewed. Swallowed. "Out of curiosity, what would you have done if you were me?"

She cleared her throat. "I'm not sure."

He leaned back. "I have this kid. This awesome, funny, silly kid, and my choices have impacted her in ways I will always regret."

Abigail stilled.

"Kelly convinced me to move here. To start over

and make a new life for us. Me and Junie. That's why I'm so focused."

"I'm sorry for whatever you've been through," Abigail said, her voice quiet.

He shook his head. "You don't need to apologize. We're fine. It's just—I never meant for anyone—" he looked at her—"to get caught in the cross fire."

She folded her hands and put them in her lap, studying them as if she'd never seen them before. "It is too bad, isn't it?"

When their eyes met, he nodded, watching her chew on the inside of her lip and fidget with her napkin. Each of her habits made him smile inwardly.

He could love this girl.

Oh. The realization left him stunned. *I could love this girl.*

"Maybe I'm just meant to do something new," she said. "Even though that scares me to death." She let out a nervous laugh.

He wouldn't tell her so, but he could understand that fear.

An excitement washed over her face. "I can hardly sit still when I think about expanding my store. It was going to be a place where everything I love would come together under one roof."

"And that's different from what you have now."

She nodded. "Now I have coffee and books."

"Both good things."

"Right, and I love them. But what I'm really excited about is what I create with my own two hands. I've just never had the guts to do anything with it before."

Jacob watched her for several seconds until finally she stood.

"I'll show you. Follow me."

He did as he was told, abandoning his meal and following her through the side door and into her garage. She flipped on the lights to reveal a space that looked more like a workshop than a garage. No way she could pull a car in here.

"These are the pieces I wanted to show you." She walked over to an armoire. "I stripped and sanded it and then repainted it. I think it could look really nice here." She pulled the sketch from her pocket and pointed to a spot against the wall in his hand-drawn office. "And that buffet from the flea market—" she pointed to another part of the drawing—"just needs some love. It really could be great for holding all that boring literature you always find in the doctor's office."

He laughed. "Dress up the boring stuff; is that what you're saying?"

"If it helps." She smiled.

He walked past the piece she'd just shown him and found a row of other projects in various stages of progress. "When do you have time to do this?"

"I've always done it. It helps me relax. I used to go to flea markets with my dad, when he ran the bookstore. He called it treasure hunting. He taught me to never take anything at face value—some-times things that look unappealing at first are really buried treasures. So now whenever I'm at a flea market, I feel like somehow I'm finding the treasures everyone else has forgotten or thrown away. I'm giving these things another opportunity to be beautiful."

"Buried treasures, huh?"

She shifted as though suddenly aware of his gaze. "Silly, right?"

"Not at all. I think you should do this. You've obviously got a lot of passion for it."

She ran a hand over the armoire. "I do. I mean, you probably feel the same way about medicine."

"I did once." Not anymore. Not since the day Gwen died. Now throwing himself into work had less to do with passion and more to do with the need to forget.

He was stealing Abigail's dream in an effort to cling to the only thing that might help him feel normal again. But all the searching in the world wouldn't take away his guilt.

Abigail stood just out of his reach. She was beautiful. And broken, thanks to him. Or maybe she'd been broken for a while and he was only making it worse. She seemed resigned to the fact that her dreams wouldn't come true, and yet he sensed she was developing this inexplicable peace about it.

The silence turned awkward, and she shifted. "I've sold quite a few pieces just from word of mouth. I guess that's where I got the idea to expand the store in the first place. Obviously I didn't think it all through. Maybe it's better this way. Maybe it's God's way of saving me from my own mistakes."

Her excitement seemed to dissipate like air from a tiny hole in a balloon.

Jacob looked away. "I am sorry, Abigail. Some days I wish I'd never bought the building in the first place." Guilt, that familiar demon, wound its way further into his soul and squeezed.

"Doesn't make any sense to dwell on it," she said. "It's done. Maybe something good can still come of it."

"How do you do that?"

She looked caught. "Do what?"

"See the good in the worst possible situations?"

She ran a hand through her hair. "I force myself to sound like that. It's not really the way I feel."

He let his eyes travel to her lips. They were full and soft. He wanted to kiss her. "How do you really feel?"

"Embarrassed. Like a failure." She closed her eyes. "That store defines me. Who is Abigail Pressman without The Book Nook?" She opened her eyes again. Her question hung between them, begging to be answered, but he didn't know what to say. He didn't know who she was without the store—but he knew he wanted to find out.

"You're not a failure," he said. "Trust me. If I hadn't come along, you'd still be living your life exactly the way you always were."

She looked at him and gave a slight shrug. "Maybe that's not such a good thing either."

He searched her face, trying to remind himself of what he knew to be true: Abigail Pressman saw him as an obstacle to reaching her goals. Kelly's warnings sounded in his head, but he took a step toward Abigail anyway. "Maybe not."

She stood so close to him now. He inhaled the scent of her—vanilla. He inched closer and slowly reached over to touch her face. As he did, his thumb just barely grazed her lips. He took her face in his hands and held it until finally she met his eyes, fully aware that she could smack him and order him to leave. He had no business touching her, but he couldn't help himself.

"What are you doing?" she whispered. "You're supposed to be my enemy."

He shook his head. "I don't want to be your enemy, Abigail."

She looked away. He didn't want to have to convince her. He wanted her to respond without any coaxing, so he stayed silent while the seconds ticked by. Finally, after what felt like an eternity, she glanced at him, *that* look in her eyes at last.

He brushed her hair back and leaned toward her, first kissing one cheek, then the other cheek and her forehead, waiting for the moment when she finally turned her face up toward his and he drew her even closer and truly kissed her. He reminded himself to go slow, to be tender, when what he really wanted to do was lose himself and kiss her through all the pain and the fear and the doubt and the guilt that always, always got in the way.

He wanted to silence all the voices that told him what a mistake it was, so he pushed them aside and moved her toward the old counter at the back of the garage. She wrapped her hands around his neck as he lifted her up onto the counter, leveling their eyes.

She stared at him and her words rushed back. She was sorry for what he'd been through, but she really had no idea. He hadn't allowed her to know, and for the first time in years, he wanted to share the pain of it with someone else.

As if she could make it all go away.

"What are you thinking about?" he asked, cupping a hand behind her head, giving himself a second to catch his breath.

"That this is all wrong," she said, eyes still intent on his.

His heart sank. It was, wasn't it? Wrong to give

in to his selfish desires when she had every right to hate him. Was he manipulating her? Did he have ulterior motives without even realizing it? Or did he simply love the way she smelled? Love the way her hair fell out of her loose ponytail? Love the way her lips tasted?

Couldn't that be enough? Why did they have to make sense of it?

"I'm sorry, Abigail. I didn't mean—" He started to move away from her, to give her space and hold on to whatever ounce of dignity he might have left.

But she didn't loosen her grip around his neck. Instead she moved her hands down to his shoulders and brought him closer. "I don't want to care about any of that right now."

He looked at her. "Are you sure?"

As soon as she nodded, he kissed her the way he'd wanted to kiss her—without inhibitions or reservations. And she kissed him back, clinging to him as if she'd just had the same revelation he had.

It didn't matter if it made any sense. In that moment, the only thing that mattered was the two of them. He drew her in closer and deepened his kiss, inhaling every bit of her. The way she smelled, the way she moved, the way she tasted. He marked each detail in his mind, all the while hoping this wouldn't be the last time he got to kiss her.

She pulled away and looked at him, an expression he couldn't place in her eyes.

"Uh-oh," he said, taking a step back. "You look upset."

She slid off the counter. "I-I don't know."

He closed his eyes, running his hands through his hair. "I'm so sorry, Abigail. I thought . . ." What? He thought what? That he'd kiss her and their relationship would magically change? He wouldn't be the man ruining her life?

She stood unmoving, as if trying to process her conflicting feelings.

"I should go."

"Jacob—" She moved in front of the door, blocking his path. Frustrated or humiliated or full of regret, he didn't know, but the mix of emotions tumbled around inside him like pinballs.

Her eyes filled with concern for him. "Don't go like this."

"I don't want to hurt you any more than I already have, Abigail." He was careful not to look away—not now, when it mattered most. "I never wanted to hurt you."

He kissed her forehead one more time, then slid around her and out the door, trying to pretend he didn't notice the tears on her cheeks as he did.

Chapter 37

Jacob drove home, replaying every moment of his time with Abigail. He'd memorized the way her soft skin felt under his fingers. He could easily recall the way her lips had moved against his. He could still smell her warm vanilla scent, but he knew everything about this fantasy was wrong.

What if he'd mistaken his feelings for her? Had he taken advantage of her?

How could he have been so careless?

And yet, how could he not? The only thing he wanted was the chance to kiss her again. He wasn't lying when he wrote those words on the paper heart. She did make him want to live again, in a way that he hadn't since months before Gwen died. But admitting that, remembering that, made him feel like a jerk. What kind of man tires of taking care of the woman he loves?

Jacob pulled into the driveway, mad at himself for buying that stupid building in the first place. He could've been up and running if he'd just settled on the space in the new mall on Dover Parkway. And he wouldn't be distracted by this Abigail Pressman business.

Before he turned his lights off, he caught movement up by the old shed.

The dog. Back again.

For over a week now, he'd been putting out fresh food and water for the injured animal, but Jacob had a feeling it needed more than nourishment if it had any hope of healing.

If he could get close enough, he might be able to help.

And yet, why should he care? This wasn't his dog. It wasn't his problem the same way Abigail's not having a space for her store wasn't his problem.

Trouble was, he did care. No matter how hard he tried not to, he did—about the dog *and* about the girl. It was how he was raised. It was how he was trained.

He got out of the truck and shut the door, leaving the lights on so he could see where the animal had gone. As he walked up the hill toward the old shed, he saw it burrowing near the back corner of the outbuilding, whimpering softly.

"It's worse, isn't it?" Jacob squatted just a few yards from where the dog had lain down. "Get over here and let me see if I can help you."

The dog inched a little closer, then quickly moved away. Stupid thing had no idea what to do.

Jacob moved in. When the dog stayed put, he dared another small step in its direction. "Can I help you? I've been feeding you—that's got to count for something, doesn't it?" He kept his tone low even though he knew the animal had no idea what he was saying.

When he came within arm's length, the dog recoiled a bit but didn't run away. Jacob moved slowly until he could finally reach it. He stroked its head, shushing it and telling it he was there to help.

After several minutes of coaxing, he figured out a way to slip his arms underneath the dog and carry it toward the house. He went up the back steps, laying the animal on the rug in the middle of the screened-in porch. As he did, Kate opened the door.

"What happened?"

Jacob took off his jacket and turned on the light. "Can you bring another lamp out here and get me some towels?"

Kate jumped into action, bringing him what he asked for. He pressed the towels onto the dog's leg wound but not so hard as to cause pain.

"I'm going to need some scissors to cut her fur back. Can you grab my kit? It's in the front closet."

Kate did as she was asked, returning seconds later with the kit.

"I don't have what I need to clean this wound." He bent over the dog, trying to get a good look at what must've been a bite or scratch from another animal. "Did the coyotes get you?"

The dog lay still, maybe too still, as he cleaned and irrigated the wound with warm water and a bulb syringe. Kate served as his nurse while he did what he could for the animal.

"I think she might need stitches," he said. Then, to the dog, "If you'd let me help you a week ago, you might not be so bad. I'm going to wait till morning when I can get a better look."

The dog whined.

"No collar. No tags," Kate said. "But she doesn't seem wild. She's a retriever."

"Probably lost." He rubbed her head. "We'll take care of you." He glanced at Kate. "You actually seem to know a little bit about what you're doing with this injury."

She shrugged. "Dogs aren't that different from horses, I guess."

He supposed training horses was about more than getting thrown off over and over again. He hadn't thought about that before.

"Do you miss it?" Jacob tended to the animal's wound, aware of Kate's watchful eyes.

"Sometimes," she finally said.

The dog whined, and Kate rested her hand on its head, whispering quietly in calming tones. Once its back leg was sufficiently cleaned, Jacob worked on bandaging it, thankful the animal wasn't putting up too much of a fight.

"Why don't we make her a bed out here for tonight?" Jacob said, standing. "I'll check on her every few hours." He glanced at Kate, who was staring at him, a lopsided smile on her face. "What?"

"Welcome back, Dr. Willoughby." She pushed the door open and disappeared inside, leaving him alone with his patient.

He did care. Even about this stupid mutt. It's what had always made him a good doctor, and yet somehow he'd shut that part of himself off. He'd lost himself in the barrage of guilt and self-hate. Even after he'd helped Avery that night, he'd told himself not to care. He couldn't get attached to healing anymore—and yet . . .

Forgive.

That word again. An instruction he couldn't seem to wrap his head around. Jacob rubbed his temples, willing away the dull ache that had settled there. How could he forgive himself for letting Gwen die? How had he ever pretended to be someone who could heal when he'd stood there and watched his own wife slip away?

"Jacob?"

He spun around, expecting Kate, but found Abigail instead.

"Your sister let me in."

Oh, man, how long had she been there? He'd been on the verge of a meltdown over a dog.

"Are you okay? Kate told me about the dog." She knelt down and petted the wounded animal. "She seems to be doing okay."

"She'll be fine, I think." He crossed his arms. Why was she here?

Thank God she's here.

She stood. "After you left, I tried to stop thinking about what happened, but I couldn't."

He hesitated. "Me neither."

"Mostly, I don't want you to feel bad about it. The truth is—" she looked away—"I wanted you to kiss me."

"I thought so, but . . ." He faced her. She wore workout pants and tennis shoes with a pullover hoodie and her hair in a mess on top of her head. And he'd never seen her look more beautiful.

She smiled. "I really liked kissing you."

He returned her smile. "You did."

"Very much." She drew in a deep breath. "I was thinking about that paper heart—the one I brought home."

His stomach dropped. *I'm such a fraud.* She'd figured the whole thing out. Now she'd find out the truth about Gwen. His failures would be plastered all over town.

"What about it?" He reminded himself to stay calm.

"What it said—'You make me want to live again.' "

He remembered.

She stared at something in the distance, then back at him. "That's exactly how I feel about you."

He didn't—or couldn't—respond.

"I know I should be really mad at you—and I still am—but there's this part of me that just wants to thank you."

"To thank me?" Was this a joke?

She took a few steps away from him. "I mean, I'm sad about the store, of course, but I realized something, Jacob. I hide behind The Book Nook. I always have. That's not living, is it? Being scared of everything. Refusing to get close to anyone because you know you're going to get hurt?"

"I know a little something about that," he said quietly.

"If you hadn't come in and shaken everything up, I'd be doing the same thing I've always done. Coasting along, telling myself that one day I'd finally find the courage to do more. You forced me to ask myself the one question I've been avoiding: What do I really want?"

He stilled. "So what *do* you really want?"

She smiled. "I'm still working that out. But for the first time, I feel like maybe it's all going to be okay. Even if there's no more Book Nook."

"Maybe there's buried treasure inside you somewhere after all."

"I hope so."

"Does this mean I get to kiss you again?" He took a step toward her. "Because I really liked kissing you too."

She hid her smile with her hand, but he didn't miss her nod. He pulled her into his arms and brought his lips to hers, drawing her closer and wishing he could freeze this perfect moment forever.

Chapter 38

Going to Jacob's house had been impulsive, especially since it had gotten late and she had no idea if he'd even be awake. Now, over an hour later, she had to leave him, and she didn't want to.

And a part of her hated herself for that. How susceptible was she that she'd gone weak-kneed at the doctor's kiss?

They stood at the front door, and it seemed like he didn't want to say good-bye any more than she did. Wrapped in his arms, she thought over everything she knew about falling in love, and she wondered if maybe none of those things really mattered after all.

"Jacob, can I ask you one thing?"

He kissed her forehead. She loved the way his lips felt on her skin. "Anything."

"Does this have anything to do with the building?"

He frowned and took a step back. "What do you mean?"

"You probably can't afford the bad press. I wondered if you were being nice to me so I'd stop fighting for my store." Ursula's words had done more than scratch the surface unfortunately—they'd burrowed their way in good and tight.

"Abigail, no. Of course not," he said, eyes intent on hers. "I would never do that to you. To be honest, this—you and me—is kind of a surprise. I didn't think I'd ever feel like this again."

She smiled. "Feel like what?"

He looked away, a shyness coming over him. "Like this." He put his arms around her and held her there for a long moment.

"Good enough," she said. "I'm glad we called this truce."

He laughed. "Just don't go calling a truce with anyone else, okay?"

It struck her then how very much she liked him. More than she ever expected. More than she wanted to.

"I should go."

"Do you have to?"

"If I want to get up on time, yes. Some of us work, you know—at least for a few more months."

He reached out and touched her cheek. "I hope you get everything you want, Abigail."

She touched his hand. "I kind of hope so too."

One more kiss and then he opened the door for her. When she walked outside, she inhaled the night air, thankful for the surprise of Dr. Jacob Willoughby.

She started toward the steps when movement off to the side caught her eye. Her heart jumped and she spun around in time to see Kate sitting on one of the porch chairs.

"Sorry. I didn't mean to scare you," she said. "I wanted to give you guys some privacy."

Abigail looked away, certain her cheeks had turned hot pink. "Thanks for that."

"You're good for him, you know," Kate said. "I haven't seen him happy in a really long time."

Abigail wanted to know why. She wanted to understand this man who'd stolen her heart, but somehow, she wanted him to be the one to explain things to her.

She really needed to get home, but standing out here with Kate, she couldn't ignore the possibility that this was the open door she'd been praying for. "Mind if I sit for a minute?"

Kate hugged her afghan around her. "Of course not."

"I've been wanting to talk to you for a long time about something, but I wasn't sure how to bring it up. I thought about telling Jacob, but that didn't feel right either."

Kate frowned. "What is it? Are you okay?"

Abigail fished her gloves out of her pocket, wishing the open door she'd received had been in a heated room. "I am. It's actually you I'm concerned about."

"Me?"

Abigail sighed. "I don't even know how to say this."

Kate sat up. "You're kind of freaking me out."

"I know. That night at the hospital, they did a bunch of X-rays on you."

Kate nodded.

"They found . . ." Abigail looked away. "They found evidence of broken bones and severe bruising." She met Kate's eyes.

"They mentioned something about that." Kate looked away.

"Kate, if you were abused, you might need—"

"That's what you think?" Kate ran a hand through her hair.

"That's what the nurse thought."

Kate shook her head. "Who is this nurse? I'm pretty sure she broke all kinds of laws telling you about my X-rays."

"Please, Kate. I don't want to get anyone in trouble. I was just concerned. I wanted you to know if you need to talk, you can come to me. I won't say a word."

"Right. You're not going to run to my brother and tell him all of this."

"I'm not. I won't." Abigail never should have said anything. She should've minded her own business. She hated it when she misinterpreted people's signs. "I'm sorry. It's not my place to say anything. I just really like you, and I wanted to make sure you were okay."

Kate pulled her knees up and hugged them. "I'm fine."

After several awkward seconds of silence,

Abigail finally stood. "I'm sorry I said anything."

When Kate didn't respond, Abigail started to leave.

"Wait." Kate didn't move. Instead, she stared out across the blackness of the yard as if remembering something painful.

"Kate, it's fine. I shouldn't have pushed you. I mean, it's not like we know each other all that well or anything." Abigail felt caught between the escape of her car and Kate's lingering sadness.

"I don't like to talk about it," Kate said, her voice quiet. "And I really don't want Jacob to know."

Abigail moved toward Kate and sat in the chair next to her. "I won't say anything, but don't feel like you have to tell me. I just wanted you to know you're not alone."

Kate sat unmoving, still hugging her knees. "You don't understand."

Abigail was sure that was true. She'd never been in an abusive relationship before. Besides Jeremy, she'd never been in any serious relationship before. She was the last person in the world Kate should be talking to about this.

"And Jacob would kill me if he found out."

"I doubt that's true. He seems like a pretty understanding guy," Abigail said as if she had authority to speak on the subject of Kate's brother.

"He is, about most things. But not with this. I mean, you saw him at the hospital." She looked away. "He hates it when he can't fix everything.

He just doesn't understand that some things weren't meant to be fixed."

Abigail drew in a breath of cool night air. "Maybe he'll surprise you?"

She shook her head. "You have no idea what he's been through."

Abigail's gaze fell to her hands in her lap. "You're right."

"I can't burden him with my problems when he's finally getting his life back together." Kate reached out through the blanket and swiped what Abigail assumed was a tear. She wished Kate would elaborate. What exactly had Jacob been through? Had his divorce completely destroyed him? She wouldn't presume to understand the feelings one had to sort through in that situation. Maybe it was that devastating.

"So who was he?" Abigail felt unequipped for this conversation.

Kate stilled. "Titus."

"Did you love him?"

Kate wiped her cheeks again. "Very much."

Abigail sat back in her chair. "Is he still in the picture?"

"Sadly, no. They made sure of that."

Abigail frowned. "I don't understand."

"It's not what you think. Titus is a horse. I used to ride. Years ago. I had a few pretty scary injuries, and after the last one, Jacob made me promise to quit." Kate dried another tear. "I've always been something of an adrenaline junkie. Jacob hates it. But when I discovered horses . . ." She pulled her knees closer to her chest. "I don't know. It was about so much more than adrenaline."

"I had no idea."

"I was in the hospital with a broken collarbone and Jacob was dealing with a lot. I didn't mean to lie to him when he told me to promise I was done. It caught me off guard. After my bones healed, I realized I couldn't just walk away."

"So you ride horses." Abigail started to piece it together. Kate wasn't in an abusive relationship— she was in a dangerous sport. Her mind spun back to the hospital, to Jacob's reaction to the car accident. For whatever reason, something made Kate keep this from him.

"I guess a part of me always knew he wasn't mine. I didn't own him, but they put him in my care. I loved that horse. I spent two years with him, and while they said I nursed him back to health, the truth was, he gave me a reason to get up in the morning. Taking care of that horse made me feel like I had a purpose."

Abigail remained quiet through a long pause.

"Stupid, right?" Kate let out a nervous laugh.

"Oh, not at all," Abigail said. She knew a little something about letting her work define her.

Kate continued. "He got hurt. He injured his hoof in a race and the owners decided I wasn't a good fit for him anymore."

Abigail didn't even have a cat, so people's attachment to animals always baffled her a little. Still, she could see Kate's pain was very real. Losing Titus had been like losing a family member.

"They honestly thought he could still race. I told them it was a terrible idea—he wasn't ready—and they told me to pack my bags. Those men only cared about getting everything they could out of him. It didn't matter if it destroyed him."

"Kate, I'm so sorry."

"The worst part is, I know he won't perform the way they want him to, and when he stops winning, they won't put him in a stable somewhere. They'll put him down."

Kate's pain encompassed them both, tugging on Abigail's emotions.

"The broken bones, the bruises—those were from Titus. Working with him was never easy." Kate put on a halfhearted smile. "They say nothing worthwhile ever is."

Abigail watched as sadness washed over her, and she realized she really knew nothing about this family at all. "So that's why you're here."

"I had nowhere else to go." She nodded, then buried her head in her knees. "Without Titus—without training . . . well, I'm just not sure who I am anymore."

A sentiment Abigail understood more than she cared to let on. And while a part of her had started to accept she would soon be starting over—

finding a new dream to chase—another part of her would die the day her store officially turned into half of Jacob's medical practice.

"I can't explain it," Kate said. "Titus and I were a team. I was supposed to go wherever he went. I sold out to that dream, but I failed. How do you ever accept that your dream is just dead?"

Abigail looked away, visions of her store fluttering through her mind. She thought she'd made her peace—how else could she ever have a relationship with Jacob?—but now, listening to Kate, she wondered if she'd just been caught up in her emotions. Did she really want to give up if she still had a chance to fight for it? Maybe a part of her was falling for Jacob in the hopes that he wouldn't make her leave.

But then nothing would change. She'd be stuck in the same holding pattern she'd been in before, waiting for something to open up, waiting for phase two of her big dream.

"Maybe there's another horse? Maybe you can begin again?" Abigail didn't know anything about riding. Or horses. Or even about love.

"It would hurt too much," Kate said. "Losing Titus was heartbreaking."

Loss she understood.

"I keep asking myself, is it better to hide myself away, bury my head in something totally different, just so I don't get hurt again?" Kate shrugged.

"I suppose you could be missing out on another

great horse, one that you could train. You could find the perfect fit and it would make all of this pain a distant memory."

"Kind of like love, huh?"

Abigail paused. "I suppose it is."

"It's really pathetic that in my scenario, we're talking about a horse."

"I'm sorry, Kate. I'm so sorry you lost your friend."

Kate let out a staggered breath. "Thanks for that." She stared out into the darkness again. "Jacob is going to be furious with me. He'll never understand why I would continue to put myself in danger. He's too blinded by his own situation to get it."

Abigail started to finally ask what happened when the door popped open and Jacob walked out, wearing sweats and a T-shirt. "You're still here?"

Abigail smiled. "I was talking to your sister."

Jacob looked at Kate. "Is everything okay?"

Kate glanced at him, then at Abigail, then back to him. "Everything is great. I'm going to go to bed. Night, Abs."

Jacob winced but said nothing till Kate closed the door behind her. "I'll tell her not to call you that."

Abigail couldn't believe he remembered. "Actually, it's okay," she said. "I kind of like it. Makes me feel like we're friends."

"Well, good. Now go home, would ya? Some people have to work, you know."

Chapter 39

Jacob spent most of the night half-asleep, stumbling out to the porch to check on the injured dog. How he'd become nursemaid to an animal, he had no idea.

"She looks better," Kate said from the doorway behind him.

"I think she's going to be okay."

The dog whimpered and sniffed his hand. He'd actually helped her. With Junie's injury, he was mostly relegated to serving her whatever food and drink she wanted as well as putting in a new DVD when necessary, but the dog didn't have other doctors to help her. Only him.

"I bet it feels good," Kate said. "To fix her."

Jacob laughed. "I do like to fix things, don't I?"

Kate stood at his side, a steaming drink in her hand. "Jacob, I need to tell you something."

He stood and faced her.

"Remember that I'm an adult before you say anything."

"Why do I get the feeling I'm not going to like this?"

Kate sat on the porch chair and told him about training a horse named Titus. A wild and dangerous horse who threw her off more than once. She told him about Titus's hoof and the callous owners who wouldn't let him retire.

When she finished, she wiped her cheeks dry. "I know you hate it when anything happens to one of us, and after what happened with Gwen, it was even worse for you. How could I tell you I was putting myself in danger every single day?"

Jacob inhaled and sat down next to her. "You know, Kate, you really shouldn't have to put your life on hold just because you're worried how your big brother is going to react."

"But I know how hard it's been for you."

He put an arm around her. "For all of us."

She nodded, then sniffed.

"Maybe I've been too careful," he said. "Maybe it's time we start living again."

She pulled out of his grasp. "Really?"

He shrugged.

"Because Abigail said something about maybe training a new horse and I haven't been able to stop thinking about it since. I mean, I loved Titus and I think a part of me will always miss him, but I shouldn't stop training because of it, right?"

Jacob shook his head. "No. You shouldn't."

Brightness enveloped her then as her whole face lit with a genuine smile.

"It's good to see you happy again," he laughed.

"Feels good to finally tell you the truth." She hugged him. "I hate keeping secrets from you."

Something about her words made his body tense.

"Jacob?"

He looked away, his laughter gone.

"What's wrong?"

He shook his head. "Nothing. I've got to go take a shower."

He went through the motions of getting himself ready for the day, but all he could think about were the secrets he was keeping from Abigail. About the paper hearts. About Gwen. It wasn't fair, and a part of him was completely closed off because of it.

If he told her now, she would know he was both a liar and a failure, but the alternative—how did he live with that? What chance did they have if he was always worried about her discovering the truth?

He needed to tell her. Today.

Jacob finished getting dressed, then drove into town, anxious to see Abigail again before he lost his nerve.

His stomach wrenched at the thought.

He walked around the building and went inside The Book Nook, inhaling the aroma of Abigail's special coffee. She stood behind the counter, talking to a middle-aged couple, unaware he'd come in.

He watched her for a few seconds before she turned toward him. A smile washed across her face, pulling the attention of the couple next to her.

They'd probably have a few choice words for the man who distracted her, but he didn't care. It was worth it to start his day talking to Abigail.

He sat down on a barstool and she placed a fresh cup of coffee in front of him before he had the chance to say a word.

"This one won't buy into any of it," she said to the couple. "He thinks the paper hearts are a stupid idea."

Uh-oh. What had he just walked into? "I never said that."

The couple turned to him. "I'm telling you, they were exactly what we needed," the husband insisted.

Jacob took a drink and glanced at Abigail, whose I-told-you-so expression was not to be missed.

"Is that right?" he asked. Polite, not overly interested.

The woman linked her arm through the man's. "It was the sweetest thing. Jimmy is not romantic, but he must've realized we needed to spice things up, if you know what I mean."

Jacob noticed a goofy smile forming on Abigail's face. She was either smitten or gloating —he couldn't tell which.

The woman went on. "Well, he left me clues on paper hearts throughout the house, but I had to come here to find the actual messages. He'd marked them with a gold star so I could find them. It took a while, but I finally did it." She grinned. "The best one—" she looked at Jimmy—"was the one where he asked me to get away with him for the weekend, and when I turned around, he was standing in the doorway with our suitcases. We hopped in the car and drove over to the hot springs for the whole weekend. He'd arranged for the kids to go to my parents' and everything."

Jimmy shrugged, looking a little like his manhood was being called into question. "Gotta keep the spark alive, brother."

Jacob patted him on the back. "Good work." He turned to Abigail. "Do you have a minute?"

She smiled. "Sure. Mallory, can you cover for me?"

"No problem." Mallory grinned like she was in on their secret, only he didn't know if what they had was actually a secret or not.

He followed Abigail into the office and closed the door behind him.

"I told you the hearts were a good idea," she said. "See how they're making people's relationships better?"

He sat on the edge of her desk and pulled her closer, wrapping his arms around her waist. "I don't really want to talk about the hearts anymore."

Her eyes sparkled, studying his as a soft smile crossed her lips.

He held her face, brushing his thumb across her lips. "You look beautiful this morning."

Color rushed to her cheeks as she whispered a thank-you.

When he kissed her, all the doubt and worry, all the unknowns fell by the wayside. As if there were nothing else in the world that mattered, because in that moment, there wasn't. He wanted to stay here with her, to figure out a way to tell her everything he'd been up all night thinking about.

To come clean about Gwen. To tell her the truth about why he'd moved here in the first place. But it embarrassed him how scared he was of losing Abigail. He'd never expected to be happy again. She'd been one of the best surprises of his life.

He didn't want to lose her. Not yet.

She pulled back and looked at him. "You seem deep in thought."

He forced a smile. "No, I'm not. I have a meeting with my contractor soon."

"Ah. Lots on your mind." She stepped away from him, but he stood and grabbed her hand before she could go very far.

"Are you okay?"

She studied his shoulder for a few long seconds before looking up. "I really am, I think."

But he didn't miss the sadness lingering behind her brown eyes. Probably not a good time to come clean about everything he'd yet to tell her.

"I should go. Do you want to do dinner tonight?"

She rose on her tiptoes and kissed him. "I'd love to."

And he loved how natural it felt for her to do that.

Tonight would be a better time to tell her. After dinner.

She saw him out the back door, and he resisted the urge to kiss her one more time, just in case anyone was watching. He didn't need to answer questions right now, and he doubted Abigail did either. After all, few people would understand how she could forgive him for putting her out of business.

He walked behind the building toward his back entrance, taking a minute to stop and inhale the fresh Colorado air. For the briefest moment, he almost felt happy. Content in a way he hadn't since before Gwen had died and, if he was honest, since long before that. He wondered if there would ever be a day he could move past it.

I'm sorry, Gwen.

The words washed over him in the stillness. *I'm sorry.* He remained quiet for a moment, praying that somehow she could forgive him. Maybe then he could forgive himself.

"What are you doing out here?" Kelly stood in the doorway. How long had she been there? "We have a situation. You need to get in here."

Jacob drew in one last breath of fresh air and

ducked into the building, following Kelly to the main space.

"Where is everyone?"

"I fired them," Kelly said.

"You did what?"

Kelly sighed. "I came in here this morning, and Ralph was talking about redoing the entire floor plan. Keeping this awful counter and installing built-ins along the back wall. He'd actually spent time drawing them up." She rolled her eyes. "What a waste."

Jacob inhaled a deep breath, hoping it would calm him down. "Kelly, how many bridges do you plan to burn before we open this place?"

Her eyes widened. "What are you talking about? I'm doing my job."

"No, you're ticking everyone off." His mind spun to his conversation with Ralph. He'd faxed the contractor Abigail's sketch and Ralph must've gotten right to work. *He* had done his job.

She stood taller, almost eye level with him. "I'm trying to save you money."

"Not everything is about money, Kelly. This isn't Denver. If you fire someone, he's going to tell people, and in a small town, that will come back to hurt us."

She took a few steps away from him, casting her gaze out the window. "What's this really about, Jacob?" She shot him a look.

"This is about my practice." He faced her. "Ralph was doing what I asked."

She narrowed her eyes. "You told Ralph to redo the plans?"

He responded with silence.

"I know what's really going on here." Kelly shook her head, an incredulous look on her face. "Unbelievable. You are so naive."

He held her glare.

"She's using you. You know that, right?"

Jacob's thoughts turned to the kiss he'd just stolen from Abigail. She might be using him, but she'd have to be a really good actress if she were. "She gave me a plan for this space that included knocking out the wall and renovating her space too."

Kelly's mouth snapped shut. "That doesn't mean anything. She's got to have a reason for that, Jacob. Are you so blinded by her big brown eyes that you can't see that?"

"You don't know what you're talking about."

"I do. I know women. And sweet and innocent only works for so long. You'll see her true colors soon enough."

"Kelly, I think you should go back to Denver. Today."

Her jaw went slack. "What are you talking about?"

"You should go. I think this whole thing was a mistake."

She put her hands on her hips. "You're firing me?"

"I am."

She scoffed, then walked over to the counter and picked up her bag and phone. "How long do you think you can keep your secrets about Gwen? How long until this whole town finds out what really happened?"

"Kelly, don't threaten me."

"Oh, *I'm* not going to tell them." She stood close—too close. "But the truth always has a way of coming out, doesn't it?"

He didn't move, and he didn't respond.

"I sure hope your little secret stays safe, Jacob. Otherwise this whole town will discover that you're the reason Gwen's dead." She hitched her purse up on her shoulder, but before she turned, Jacob saw the regret on her face. No matter how angry she was in that moment, Gwen had meant something to Kelly.

And everyone grieves differently, he supposed.

After she'd gone, Jacob stood in the empty space, dust particles catching the light as it streamed in the windows.

Kelly's words hung in a thick cloud overhead, prodding him, begging him to give them the attention they wanted. He wished he could swat them away like annoying insects, but in the deep places of his mind, he believed them.

If Abigail learned his part in Gwen's death,

she would see he had no business practicing medicine. Worse, she'd see he had no business attempting to have a relationship with her.

Still, she deserved to know the truth. All of it. And if that meant losing her, then so be it.

He was tired of living in the shadows.

Chapter 40

Abigail stood behind the counter at The Book Nook but kept one eye on Rob, who sat at a table in the back. If he did intend that heart for her, he certainly wasn't showing it. With the exception of a polite thank-you when she brought him his drink, he hadn't so much as glanced in her direction. Part of her was thankful. She hadn't wanted to believe Rob and Dana were behind the paper hearts anyway.

But who could it be?

The bells on the door jangled, drawing Abigail's attention away from her only suspect. Betsy walked in, brushing snow from her hair. She met Abigail's eyes, then looked like she might bolt back into the cold.

After a few long seconds, Betsy approached the counter and sat down, setting her purse on the stool next to her. A quiet apology passed between Abigail and her sister. They'd both been in the wrong, and if Abigail could take it all back, she would. Besides, she knew now that Betsy was right. Abigail had always only wanted one thing —to be loved. She just couldn't admit it before.

"Hey, Abs." The nickname, one she usually despised, felt cozy and familiar coming from Betsy.

"Hey, Bets."

Her sister looked away. "I'm sorry for the things I said."

Abigail wiped the counter, then started Betsy a white chocolate mocha, her favorite. "No, I'm the one who's sorry. I didn't mean to ruin your happy news. I should've been ecstatic for you." She looked at her sister. "I guess you were right. I measure love on a weighted scale. I'd stopped believing it was real a long time ago, but I'm sorry I let that get in the way of us." She clapped a hand over Betsy's. "I *am* very happy for you. And I'd love to be in your wedding if you'll still have me."

Betsy's eyes filled with tears. "No, Abigail. You were right."

Abigail set the coffee down. "What do you mean? About what?"

"About all of it. About love. It's not real. We had it right all those years ago. I just lost my way for a minute. I guess I was caught up in Romano's eyes or something ridiculous like that." Betsy quietly wiped a stray tear that had escaped. Abigail handed her a napkin. "I can't believe I thought he really loved me. From now on, I'm done with men. I'm going to be smart like you and throw myself into work."

Abigail said nothing, just stared at her.

"What is it?" Betsy crumpled the napkin in her fist and sniffed.

"*I* was wrong, Bets." She looked at her sister through her own clouded vision.

Betsy's eyes widened—clearly she was processing what Abigail wasn't saying. Her shoulders dropped as the realization washed over her. "Who is he?"

Conflicting emotions tumbled around in Abigail's mind. "Let's not talk about it, Betsy. Let's talk about you. What happened with Romano?"

"You're in love."

She shook her head. "That's not the reason I— maybe I was a little too cynical. Too quick to write it off because of everything I thought I knew."

"No, you weren't. You were right. You've always been right. That stupid fairy tale about our great-great-grandparents is the only thing that's wrong. No one can live up to that, so why even try? That's what you said."

Abigail sighed. "I know what I said, Betsy."

"You can't tell me now that you think you were wrong."

Abigail stood unmoving. "I . . . hope I was wrong."

Betsy closed her eyes and turned her head away. "I thought you'd understand. If anyone in the world was going to understand, I thought it would be you."

Abigail did understand. She knew all about broken hearts, but she wanted to believe something different. Jacob made her want to believe something different.

"You told me I was going to end up old and alone if I kept on the way I was."

Betsy looked at her. "I said I was sorry."

"No. You were right. I've been so closed off I didn't even let myself believe I wanted a different life." She drew in a breath. "I've been hiding, Betsy. Behind this store. Behind business. Behind my own cynicism. But I've been fooling myself. I think maybe I really do want someone to love me. You made me realize that."

Betsy shook her head, visibly attempting to hold back tears.

Abigail took her hands. "Betsy, what if God is just closing this door because Romano isn't the right person for you? What if Jeremy leaving me was God doing me a favor because he's got something better for me?" What if that something better was Jacob? Had God been saving her for him all along? Or was it possible God never intended her to be married at all? Could she learn to trust him in spite of her disappointment?

Betsy gave a halfhearted shrug.

"I know you don't want to hear it right now, but maybe this is a good thing."

She sniffed. "Well, it sure doesn't feel like it."

"I know." Losing the store certainly didn't feel like a good thing either, but somewhere in the back of her mind, Abigail almost felt excited to see how God would take this and turn it into something good. She had to believe he hadn't forgotten her.

Because if he had, everything she believed would be wrong.

The door opened and an unfamiliar older woman walked in. She moved toward the empty counter.

"I'll be right back, Betsy." Abigail reached the other end of the counter and smiled as the woman approached. "Good morning. What can I get you?"

The woman hugged her purse to her chest and put on what seemed like a forced smile. "I'm not sure you can help me," she said, looking around, eyes landing on the paper hearts. "Are you Abigail Pressman?"

"I am." Probably a vendor. Maybe she could pass this woman off to Mallory.

"I heard about the paper hearts."

Abigail smiled. "Yes, aren't they wonderful?" She handed the woman one of the flyers outlining what she knew of the story.

"Yes, they are." The woman glanced at the flyer. "When I discovered Jacob owned the building, it gave me hope."

Abigail frowned. "What do you mean?"

"That maybe he'd found the closure he needed." The woman opened her bag and fished out a large envelope. "Is that why he let you hang them?"

"Um . . . I'm not sure I understand."

"Do you know if he'll be in today? Jacob? I don't want to disturb him. I know he wants me to keep my distance."

Abigail's mouth went dry as she tried to swallow, not sure who this woman was, but quite certain she was about to flip Abigail's world on its ear. "I-I'm not sure."

"Would you mind getting these to him? They're the rest of Gwen's hearts." She held a large envelope in Abigail's direction.

Abigail took the envelope. It was open, so she peeked inside. She pulled out a small paper heart. *I wish you all the happiness in the world. No matter what.* The writing was familiar. Too familiar. Abigail forced herself to take a breath. "I'm sorry; who did you say you were?"

"Oh." The woman's laugh was nervous. "I apologize. I'm Cecily Gregson. Jacob's mother-in-law."

"And what are these?" Abigail held up the envelope.

Cecily's eyes lingered on the package in Abigail's hands. "Gwen's hearts. I found them after the funeral. Jacob was in no condition to pack up Gwen's things, so I took care of it for him."

"I'm sorry. Gwen—Jacob's ex-wife—she

passed away?" The air seemed thinner as Abigail attempted to inhale, panic constricting her heart.

Cecily met her eyes. "He didn't tell you."

"No."

"I assumed if he told you about the hearts, he'd tell you about Gwen." Cecily moved her purse to her shoulder. "I'm so angry with him for refusing to talk about her anymore. How on earth will we preserve her memory? I was so happy when I heard about the hearts. Do you believe there was a story about it in the newspaper in Denver?"

Abigail assumed the question was rhetorical.

"I thought maybe he'd changed his mind, told someone—you—about this beautiful tradition he and Gwen shared."

What was she saying, that Jacob and his wife were the ones who started the tradition? That Jacob and Gwen were *her* couple? That couldn't be. It wasn't possible. Abigail's mind whirled, trying to make sense of what Cecily had said.

Her thoughts spun back. Jacob had been against hanging up the hearts in the first place. Junie's teddy bear—those hearts weren't the result of a visit to her store. They were there before Abigail ever hung a single strand.

Was he angry that she'd put something so private on display? If she'd known, she never would've allowed anyone to see those hearts. But he hadn't explained. He hadn't said a word. What else was he hiding from her?

"He didn't tell me," Abigail said, her voice barely audible.

Cecily's face fell. "I guess I should've known. I'm sorry. I shouldn't have bothered you." She put her hand out as if to take the paper hearts back.

"No, it's fine." Abigail looked at the envelope. Inside, the rest of the story. The answers to all the questions she'd been pondering. How could she just give them back? "Do you want me to hang them up?"

Cecily's eyes filled with fresh tears. How many tears had she cried over her daughter's death? She nodded. "Yes. I suppose it does seem like the right thing to do."

Abigail hugged the package to her chest. "Yes. I suppose it does."

"Gwen always said it was pointless to keep all the good things in life for ourselves." Cecily smiled, dabbing her eyes with a napkin. "She was always thinking about other people that way. I think she'd want you to share the rest of the story. Her story." She glanced across the room at the other hearts, combined with the hundreds they'd added in recent days. "Thank you for keeping her memory alive. It seems you're the only one who is."

Abigail nodded. "I'm so sorry for your loss, Mrs. Gregson."

She squeezed Abigail's hand. "Me too, dear." She turned and walked away, and it occurred to

Abigail how quickly her own life had changed.

Abigail stood motionless, holding the paper hearts—the last sentiments Jacob's wife had shared with him before she died—and suddenly she felt a wave of nausea come over her.

"Abigail?" Betsy walked around the counter to her sister. "What's wrong?"

Pain welled up inside her. A familiar pain, and with it the memory of why she'd buried her head in this business for so many years. She'd been protecting herself from a very real threat.

It was the memory of Jeremy, of her father, of the lies and the pretending all rolled into one big emotional assault. She should've seen this coming.

"What I said before, Betsy," Abigail said, choking on her own sorrow. "I was wrong. Love really is nothing more than a fairy tale, and I don't know anyone with any sense who actually believes in fairy tales."

Chapter 41

Abigail sat in her office, staring at the envelope filled with Gwen's paper hearts. How could she open it now, knowing who'd written them? Suddenly it all seemed like a terrible invasion of privacy.

The knock at the door startled her, and when

Jacob's face appeared in the doorway, she nearly lost her breath.

"Hey, do you have a minute?"

She looked away.

"What's wrong?" He sat in the chair across from her desk but leaned forward and covered her hands with his own. "You look upset."

She slid the envelope toward him. "This is for you."

He frowned. "Someone delivered my mail to you?" He picked it up. "It's already open."

"It came like that." She pressed her lips together in an effort to keep from crying. She thought she'd been heartbroken over the loss of her store, but that pain didn't even compare to what she was trying to process now. In a matter of weeks, she had fallen—hard—for the man who had single-handedly turned her world upside down.

It embarrassed her how much it hurt to know he'd let her prattle on and on about the hearts, pretending they were a silly idea, when all along he'd been the one who started the tradition in the first place.

He reached inside and pulled out a small handful of paper hearts. He stared at the hearts in his hand, carefully reading one, then two, then three of them. "Where did you get these?" He glanced up, horror and pain on his face.

"From your mother-in-law."

"Abigail." Jacob closed his eyes and leaned

back in the chair. "This is what I was coming to talk to you about. It's why I came by this morning."

"But you didn't tell me. Not a word about this or about the fact that your wife didn't leave you, Jacob. She died. Why would you keep that from me?"

He stood and took a few steps toward the back of the office, staring out the window. Was he trying to formulate an acceptable response?

She stood. "You had plenty of chances to tell me the truth."

He shook his head. "You don't want to know the truth, Abigail." He looked at her. Now she was beginning to understand the sorrow behind his eyes.

"Don't you want me to know?" She nearly choked on her own question. It embarrassed her that she wanted him to know everything about her. Why didn't he feel the same?

He let out a stream of air. "I don't want to lose you."

Abigail's mind kept spinning. In front of her stood a broken man, someone with more pain than she could probably imagine, yet he'd found a way to keep it all from her. The same way Jeremy had led her on for months when he'd actually stopped loving her long before he said so.

"What happened, Jacob?" She braced herself for whatever his answer was. Whether he trusted her or not, what he had to say would certainly change things.

He stood still for a long moment, and then his eyes went blank as if he was replaying some awful memory. He dropped into the chair and let his head fall into his hands. She sat down across from him. As mad as she was that he'd lied to her, she found his pain overwhelming. She didn't wish that on anyone.

"Gwen died on a Thursday." He stared at the floor as he spoke, his tone low and even. "We buried her on a Saturday. That was the end of a long road of pain." He looked up. "And I'm the reason she's dead."

Abigail tried to steady her shaky breath. "What do you mean? You . . . killed her?"

"Gwen was depressed. Horribly depressed. She always struggled with it, and when she was good, she was great. But when she was bad . . ." He covered his mouth with his hand. "Sometimes she'd lie in bed for weeks. After Junie was born, I didn't know if I'd ever get my wife back again. Then she just snapped out of it."

Abigail searched for an appropriate response, thankful when Jacob continued.

"She did really well for the better part of three years and then, at one point, the lights just went off again." He stopped, his memories choking him. "I tried to be there for her and for Junie. I hired a nanny. I did what I could, but I was working long hours and she didn't like when I was away."

He blinked hard several times in a row, visibly upset at having to recount these memories.

"Jacob, stop. You don't have to tell me anything." She felt like a bully for bringing it up at all.

But he ignored her and continued. "One day I came home and she had gotten bad—really bad. I took her to the hospital and they talked to her, examined her. She'd stopped eating, and they were concerned, so they admitted her. She was angry with me for letting them do that. She didn't understand why her husband, who was a doctor, couldn't take care of her."

"I'm so sorry."

He drew in a deep breath. "After a week, they released her to my care. Gave me instructions on what to do for her. They said she'd be okay—that she would start getting better now."

"But she didn't?"

"The next morning, I woke up and found her in the bathtub." His chin quivered at the memory. "She killed herself. While she was in my care." He met her eyes. "It was my fault."

"No, Jacob, she was sick. There was nothing you could've done."

"Abigail." Anger flashed across his expression. "A part of me was relieved. I couldn't take away her pain. I couldn't fix it. All my education was useless—I wasn't enough to save my own wife."

"You can't beat yourself up for that. No one could possibly blame you for not wanting her to suffer."

"No." He shook his head. "I was relieved because of how she made *me* feel."

Abigail stilled at his admission.

"Helpless. Worthless. Like a total failure." He pushed at the bridge of his nose. "I was never going to be enough for her, and it tortured me."

She watched as he forced himself through the pain of sharing this with her, and a part of her wished they could go back a couple of hours. Had it been only that morning she'd welcomed his kiss?

"I wasn't right for a long time, and I needed someone to blame. I even sued the hospital I worked at for negligence. If they hadn't released her, my lawyer argued, she'd still be alive." He stared at the floor. "They settled to avoid going to trial. Feels like blood money now."

She swallowed, wishing she had words to ease his pain. But none came.

"So now you understand why I will never be enough for you either," he said, voice thick with regret. He stood. "Now that the word is out, everything will change. People will start looking at me the way you're looking at me now."

She quickly changed the expression on her face. "No, I'm not looking—"

He held up a hand to interrupt her. He was quiet for several seconds, then quietly reached over and touched her face. "You really did make me want to live again."

The breath caught in her throat as she remembered the words on the heart she'd found only yesterday. He'd written that. For her.

He placed a soft kiss on her forehead. "I'm so sorry, Abigail."

She watched as he headed for the door. "Jacob, wait."

He turned toward her, looking like a boxer who'd just been dragged out of the ring after a fight. She picked up the envelope and handed it to him. "This belongs to you."

Disappointment filled his eyes. "Right." He took it and left.

When the door closed behind him, she collapsed in her chair, rested her head on the desk, and cried. For Jacob. For Gwen. For Junie.

For herself.

How would she ever recover?

Another knock on the door prompted Abigail to quickly wipe her cheeks dry, check her mascara in the mirror on her wall, and blow her cherry-red nose. She opened the door to find Ursula, Gigi, and Doris standing outside the office.

"It's not really a good time."

Gigi smiled. "It's always a good time to save your business."

Abigail opened the door a little wider and sat back down behind her desk. "I've made my peace with the fact that it's time for me to start over. It might even be a good thing."

Ursula and Gigi sat across from her. Doris stood off to the side, admiring the knickknacks on Abigail's shelf. She picked up a picture frame, then replaced it. No way around it—they were here to stay.

"What's wrong with you?" Ursula snapped. "You've given up."

"We're just worried about you," Gigi said.

Abigail leaned back in the chair. "Why? Because I actually fell for the one person who set out to ruin my life?"

Doris let out a quiet gasp.

Gigi's brows drew together in a tight line. "What are you talking about?"

"I told you she fell for that doctor." Ursula squinted at her. "Fell hard too, from the looks of it. You really should invest in some waterproof mascara."

"It was a mistake," Abigail said, dabbing at her tears with a tissue. "I was so wrong about him." She swallowed. "He and his wife were the ones who wrote the paper hearts."

Another gasp from Doris, this one not so quiet.

"You're kidding." Gigi shook her head.

"The dead wife?" Ursula's words came out cold. They all looked at her.

"You knew she died?" Abigail felt like a fool. How had she not seen it?

Ursula shrugged. " 'Course. I do my research."

"What else do you know?"

The old woman opened her mouth to say something, then snapped it shut as if she'd thought better of it.

"What aren't you telling me?" Abigail balled up the tissue in her hand.

"Let's get your business back." Ursula slapped her hand on the desk. "Fight or die."

Abigail rolled her eyes. "I'm not in the mood, Ursula."

"What else have you got? You roll over on your business and you're left with nothing."

"Thanks for the reminder."

Ursula harrumphed. "Someone needs to be straight with you. That man isn't worth your time. If he was, he would've told you his wife died and he wrote the hearts. Time to move on and save yourself. If you ruin him in the process, so be it."

"You knew about the paper hearts too." Abigail felt numb.

"That was just a hunch."

"Ursula, why didn't you say anything?" Gigi asked.

"You never believe me anyway," she said.

Abigail sighed. Her thoughts turned to her dinner with Jacob at her house, the night he first kissed her. He'd told her this was their fresh start, and now she understood why. But losing someone you love wasn't something you just got over. She knew that better than anybody.

"What's the plan?" Abigail sat forward in her chair as Gigi pulled out a stack of papers. Now that everything had changed, maybe it wasn't time to make her peace quite yet.

"This is your lease."

Abigail nodded. "I know. I've read it."

"Yes, but you didn't read this." She flipped through a few pages, then pointed to a highlighted portion. "I finally got in touch with Harriet. She's in Indonesia or somewhere, but she wrote me back."

"And?"

"She told me in addition to your lease, there's also a signed agreement between her and your father."

"I didn't see any agreement," Abigail said. "I thought they shook hands and called it good."

Ursula scoffed. "Give your dad a little credit, Pressman."

"The agreement is all about what happens to you if someone else buys the building," Doris said.

Abigail took the stack of papers from Gigi. On the top, a letter that had been signed by both Harriet and Abigail's father. "They had it notarized," she said, noticing the stamp. "Where was this?"

"I had to dig through Harriet's desk," Gigi said.

"But she pointed me to the right spot and here we are."

Abigail stared at the paper, unable to believe what she held in her hands.

"I guess Harriet was looking out for you after all," Gigi said.

"I wish she'd told me that in the beginning," Abigail said, scanning the document. "This says that I'm entitled to stay throughout the duration of my lease. That's another five years." Abigail read it again.

Doris leaned in. "Isn't it wonderful?"

Abigail's stomach flipped over. "I don't have to close the business."

Ursula sat back, a satisfied look on her face. "That's one way to stick it to the doctor." She gave a satisfied nod as if that was the only proper way to punctuate her sentence.

In her haste, Abigail hadn't even questioned that Kelly had the right to kick her out on Jacob's behalf, but of course Harriet had made sure that couldn't happen. She'd been looking out for Abigail since day one; it was wrong of Abigail to assume she'd have stopped.

"Want me to take this over to the doctor right now?" Ursula asked. "You know I'll give it to him along with a piece of my mind."

"No, Ursula. I'll do it." Abigail looked at the legal document in her hand, and sorrow threaded its way through the fabric of her being. This was the answer to her prayers. She should be celebrating, but stealing Jacob's second chance had never been her intention. Especially not now, given what she knew.

Doris and Ursula left her office, jabbering about being victorious or some such nonsense, but Gigi didn't move.

Abigail looked at her across the desk.

"Are you sure this is really what you want?" Gigi's face was kind and void of judgment. "I'm only asking because I want you to know that just because a solution seems to present itself doesn't mean you have to take it."

Abigail's mouth had gone dry. "Doesn't it? He lied to me, Gigi. About everything. He probably doesn't even have feelings for me at all."

But even as she said the words, Abigail doubted them. The way he looked at her—like she was the only person in the world who mattered—didn't feel phony to her.

Gigi nodded in silence, but Abigail could see by the look on her face she had something else to say.

"Oh, come on, out with it."

Gigi held her hands up. "I don't want to overstep."

The look Abigail shot her told the older woman she wasn't buying it.

"I suppose I feel a bit responsible for your backward view on love and marriage." Gigi shifted in her chair. "All you ever heard from us was the good."

Abigail waved her off. "My parents showed me plenty of the bad, believe me."

Gigi pressed her pink lips together. "I suppose that's true. I do know how Teensy likes to pretend."

It struck Abigail then how sad it was that everyone knew this about her mother, though Teensy thought she had them all fooled.

"But I'm talking about your great-great-grandparents."

Abigail sighed. Not this again. "I know the story, Gigi. Epic love story. Modern-day fairy tale. The stuff of legend."

"Yes, that's what they say, isn't it?" Gigi's eyebrows held an expectancy in them.

"What are you saying?"

"That no love story is really that perfect, dear, and that's why you've always been so disappointed."

Abigail nodded. "But that's what I've been saying all along."

"No, you're misunderstanding. It was an epic love story. A wonderfully romantic tale, but it wasn't perfect. The story implies that John and Elsie abandoned everyone they knew and loved to set off together and go on a grand adventure."

"Right. They defied everything to strike out on their own and do something wild and rebellious, but their love held them together. Even through sickness and drought and every bad thing that could've happened."

Gigi paused.

"What is it, Gigi? What aren't you telling me?"

"Somewhere along the way, people have forgotten that Elsie left your great-great-grandfather for a time."

"What?" Abigail had never heard anything but tales of romance concerning her great-great-grandparents.

Gigi nodded. "Teensy may not even know the whole story, but I do. My own great-grandmother was there. She was Elsie's very best friend in the world. And she left a journal behind when she died."

"Saying what?"

"That Elsie was homesick. So very homesick. And when John decided to settle here, he didn't consult with his wife. He'd planned to settle a town all along, but he never said a word to his wife until after they were married."

"He just made the decision for her?"

Gigi gave a slight shrug. "In those days, that's the way it was. But Elsie wasn't the typical wife. She was stubborn and set in her ways and she wanted to go home."

Abigail could imagine. That stubborn streak seemed to run in her family.

"So what happened?"

"She started traveling east but somewhere along

the way discovered she was pregnant. That is the only reason she came back. She knew her parents would disown her if she tried to raise her baby without a father."

Abigail sank into the chair. "She didn't choose Loves Park?"

Gigi shook her head. "No, dear, Loves Park chose her."

"I can't believe it. That isn't at all how the story goes. The story is that they were adventurers. They set out to build something together. Something amazing. Not that they were trapped by an unplanned pregnancy."

"Don't misunderstand, Abigail. They had a wonderful love story, but that's because they chose to forgive. John forgave her for leaving. Elsie eventually forgave him for dragging her out here into the middle of the mountains to colonize a town. They became the very best of friends, and in the end, their story *was* like a fairy tale. But the very best love stories are the ones that are flawed and full of forgiveness and pain and joy and challenges and happiness. All these things make up a love story. What would've happened if Elsie had continued back home? What if she hadn't forgiven John?"

Abigail understood the implications.

Gigi stood. "The choice is yours, dear. But perhaps it's best to find out the whole story before you make any rash decisions. I'd hate for you to be walking away from your own epic love story just because you can't find a way to forgive."

Abigail's gaze fell to her hands on the desk. Gigi had spoken the truth to her, but that didn't mean she wanted to hear it.

It was easy to say she needed to forgive Jacob. Actually doing it was far more difficult.

Besides, how could she argue with the fact that God had answered her prayer and provided a way out of this mess? Nothing had to change. Everything could go back to the way it was. As she read the agreement between Harriet and her father one more time, though, she couldn't ignore the nagging feeling in her gut that maybe, just maybe, that would be the biggest mistake of all. And that maybe the answer to her prayer would come in a different form entirely.

Chapter 42

Jacob left the building after his conversation with Abigail, his chest tight like it had been on the day he buried Gwen. How had this happened? He should've told Abigail everything from the start. He'd let her believe Gwen had simply walked out of their lives, something she could relate to. He'd stood in her store how many times, in the midst of those paper hearts, and never confessed to writing a single one. Maybe he hadn't lied, but he'd left out a big part of the truth.

Now that she knew, she would never forgive him—and why should she?

He still hadn't forgiven himself.

He went home and changed into his running gear, checked on Junie and Kate, quickly examined the dog, who was still recovering on the back porch, and took off behind the house. The trails were the only thing that could distract him from what a mess he'd made of everything.

Junie's face flashed through his mind. He hated that he had let her down again. How would he ever break the news to her if they ended up having to move? And what now? It was only a matter of time before the rest of the town found out everything about Gwen—and then what?

He ran higher and farther, pushing himself, pulse racing. *Nothing about this is fair. I thought you were going to protect us. I thought you were going to make sure my secret was safe.* He sprinted to the top of a hill as every nerve in his body screamed for him to stop. He didn't. He just pushed forward. *Why can't one single thing go the way it's supposed to? Why have you forgotten me?*

The lake came into view as the realization of what was really bothering him bubbled to the surface, then sat there, thick and murky like oil floating in water. He collapsed to his knees at the edge of the lake, the earth cold and damp underneath his hands. Anger rushed through his veins, unwanted but unstoppable.

Forgotten. That's really how he felt, wasn't it? Everything that had happened made him question the foundations of his beliefs.

His whole world was falling apart all over again —for what?

He'd let his daughter down. Again. His only reason for moving in the first place, and he couldn't even live up to his end of the bargain.

He'd seen the horror in Abigail's eyes when he told her the truth. That he'd been *relieved* when Gwen died. Words he'd never spoken aloud until then. Words that tormented him in the darkest nights when he tossed and turned, when sleep eluded him.

Are you happy? I told her the truth. My secret is out, and everything is ruined. "I was relieved!" His words echoed back to him over the stillness of the lake below him. "I'm so sorry, Gwen. I am so, so sorry." The sobs came over him fast and furious, all the anger, the pain, the disappointment, the sorrow and regret rushing at him like gale-force winds. Tears he'd refused to cry because he needed to be strong for Junie. Tears he'd bottled up because he didn't deserve the relief of releasing his pain.

"I failed you, Gwen," he whispered, covering his face with his hands. "Forgive me."

Familiar guilt surrounded him, but for the first time, he felt an almost-tangible peace follow right behind.

Maybe I was never supposed to be the one to save Gwen. The thought popped into his head without his permission. It contradicted everything he'd believed since the day he married her. He was her protector. He was supposed to save her.

He couldn't have stopped her from making her own choices, though, could he?

His conflicted feelings about her death had haunted him for two years now, and he'd clung to his anger like a child tightly gripping a new toy.

But being mad at himself had gotten him nowhere. If he ever wanted to be the kind of father Junie needed—if he had any hope of ever being happy again—he had to let it go. He had to move on. He had to forgive himself, to let God forgive him.

It was time to live again. Behind him, he heard a rustling in the woods. He turned with a start, expecting to encounter a wild animal, but instead he saw the injured retriever limping toward him.

"What are you doing?" Adrenaline still raced through him as the dog slowly approached. She came right up to him, panting from the long trek uphill. She sniffed his face, her wet nose cold on his skin.

Jacob wiped his face dry with the sleeve of his sweatshirt and examined the dog's bandages just to be sure she hadn't done more damage following him up here. She barked, then sat beside him, seeming plenty strong.

"You're a fighter, aren't you, dog?"

She barked again but remained at his side as if she didn't want to leave him. As if she knew he needed a friend right now.

He petted her head, staring out over the lake, wondering when everything had gone so wrong. Why had he thought keeping his secret would ever be an option anyway? He closed his eyes and saw the image of Abigail's smile. Her brown eyes. Her perfect skin.

In that moment, he realized he didn't want to keep anything from her. He wanted her to know everything about him—the good and the bad.

Somehow, shining a light on that wretched secret, the ugliest part of him, set something inside him free and brought with it that peace he couldn't explain. Abigail knew the whole truth. God hadn't prevented her from finding out. Maybe there was a reason for that.

Jacob stood. "All right, dog. Let's go home."

The dog stood and followed him back toward the trail.

He jogged slowly, checking on her as they ran. She seemed intent on keeping his pace. As he watched her, he marveled at the way she moved, carefully but still forward. Always forward.

She made it look easy. But it wasn't. Kate was

right—he'd been filling his days with busywork, but he'd been standing still.

When the house came into view, he saw Kate and Junie sitting on the back porch, waving at him.

"We wondered where she went," Kate said. "After you left, she got really agitated, so I let her out, but she took off. I guess she missed you."

Jacob petted the dog. "I guess so."

"Can we bring her inside, Daddy?"

Jacob glanced at Kate, who wore the same expression as his daughter. The dog barked. "We can only bring her in if we figure out what to call her." He looked at Junie. "Do you want to do the honors?"

Junie grinned. "I already know what to call her."

"You've been thinking about this, have you?"

She nodded. "I want to name her Daisy. Because those are the happiest flowers."

Jacob rubbed Daisy between the ears. "It's a good thing you're a girl dog, Daisy."

Junie laughed.

Later that night, Jacob stood on the deck turning his phone over in his hand, clicking on Abigail's name and then clearing it.

He wanted to talk to her, but what would he say?

Kate opened the door and joined him, pulling her sweater around her. "It's freezing tonight."

He hadn't noticed.

"Why don't you go talk to her?"

Jacob leaned his elbows on the railing of the deck and looked out across the lake. "And say what? She never wants to see me again."

"I bet you're wrong about that."

He wished he were wrong about that.

"What are you going to do?"

Jacob shrugged. "Haven't figured that out yet. Maybe move?"

Kate shook her head. "This is not unfixable. You just need to give her a chance to understand."

Jacob didn't respond. What could he possibly say? That he was too chicken to see that look in Abigail's eyes again? That he couldn't stand the thought that he'd not only successfully run her out of business, but now he was ruining her personal life too?

He did a quick online search on his phone and found the number for the one person who might be able to help him make this right.

He dialed, and when the woman answered, he nearly hung up. "Mrs. Pembrooke?"

"Who's this?" Practically a growl.

"This is Dr. Jacob Willoughby. Are you still interested in buying my building?"

Chapter 43

Abigail hadn't gone in to work for three straight days. She lay on the couch watching reruns of *Gilmore Girls* and wishing her phone would stop buzzing. Between Mallory, Betsy, and her mother, the thing hadn't stopped for hours.

She didn't want to talk to them. She didn't want to be a business owner right now. Or a sister. Or a daughter. She just wanted to be sad. She knew it was pathetic, but for once, she decided not to care.

The knock on her door just after lunchtime startled her. Who would dare come over in the middle of the day? She was still in pajamas, no makeup, hair in a ponytail. By all accounts, she looked like a disaster. And so did her house.

"I know you're in there, Pressman."

Abigail groaned and pulled the afghan over her face. "I don't want to see anybody right now, Ursula. Please?"

Ursula jiggled the doorknob, and Abigail said a silent prayer of thanks that she'd had the foresight to lock it.

It was a short-lived bout of gratitude. The door popped open and Ursula nearly fell onto the floor.

Abigail shot upright from her spot on the couch. "How did you do that?"

Ursula held up a hairpin. "Frankie taught me everything."

She decided she'd rather not know any more than that. She plopped back down on the couch and tucked the blanket up to her neck.

Ursula surveyed the room, then surveyed Abigail. "You're a wreck."

"What's your point?"

Ursula started digging through her purse. "We have more letters for you to reply to."

She could not be serious.

The woman pulled a stack of papers from her purse and set them on the table. "Just a few."

"I don't want to read any more stupid letters," Abigail said. "Just kick me out of the Valentine Volunteers, okay?"

Ursula waved her off and moved toward the kitchen. "You got anything to eat around here?"

Abigail didn't even know the answer to that question. She could hear Ursula rummaging through the cabinets. Eventually the woman returned to the living room with a plate of fruit and cheese and what looked like half a package of Oreos.

She plopped down in the chair across from Abigail. "So you're going to *wallow,* is that it?"

Abigail groaned and covered her nose and mouth with a throw pillow. "Yes. Will you let me wallow in peace?"

Ursula crunched a cookie, dropping crumbs

down the front of her shirt. "I didn't just come here to dump work on your plate. I came because your doctor called me the other day."

Abigail sat up. "Jacob called *you?*"

Ursula glared at her. "Don't look so surprised, Pressman. The man finally came to his senses. Asked if my offer to buy the building was still good." Her eyebrows shot up as if to say, *"So there."*

Abigail's heart dropped. "Did you tell him about the agreement Harriet made with my dad?"

"I did."

"And?"

"He said that's great, but he wants to sell the building so you can have the whole thing."

Abigail straightened and pulled her legs underneath her, sitting cross-legged on the couch. "But he's already so far into the renovations. The plans are perfect."

Ursula crunched another cookie. "This is what you wanted, right? Now you can move on with your original plan. Looks like everything is working out."

If everything was working out, why did she feel so terrible? It *was* what she wanted, but now that she'd entertained the idea of her own fresh start, something about going back felt wrong. And besides, how did she steal Jacob's chance at a new life—a life he and Junie needed?

"Did he say where he's going to go?"

She shrugged. "Said something about moving out East."

The air thinned and Abigail struggled to get a good breath.

"What's wrong, Pressman? Your dreams are all coming true, right?"

Abigail met Ursula's eyes.

The woman sat forward in her chair, elbows on her knees. "Right?"

Abigail shook her head. "I don't know."

"What do you mean you don't know?"

Why did she get the feeling Ursula was pushing her toward something?

"I'm mad at him, but I don't want to ruin him," Abigail said. "He's been through so much, Ursula. More than any person should ever have to go through." She glanced up. "I know you think I'm soft."

Ursula sat back and ate a slice of cheese. "Actually, I called this from the beginning."

"Called what?"

"You and the doctor. I told Gigi he was your perfect match, but she wouldn't listen."

Abigail frowned. "You're not making any sense. You've been trying to destroy Jacob from the start."

"Right." She nodded as if that were sufficient explanation.

"I hardly think you of all people would consider him a good match for anybody. You always point out all the reasons I should be angry with him."

Ursula stood. "Do you have anything to drink?"

Abigail watched as the woman disappeared into the kitchen and returned with a glass of iced tea. *Help yourself.*

She sat back down and continued eating.

"Ursula?"

"Hm?" She looked up. "Oh yes. I did do that," she said, pointing her cookie at Abigail as she spoke.

Why did she feel like a character in an episode of *The Twilight Zone*?

"But only to get you to figure out you had feelings for him."

Now she'd heard everything. "You tried to get us fighting so I'd figure out I had feelings for him?"

"Are you going to repeat everything I say?" Ursula looked at her. "Because I don't like that."

"Sorry."

"Frankie and I met in a restaurant. He was a customer and I was a waitress."

Abigail chose not to comment on the picture that painted.

"You can imagine I wasn't the kind of waitress who just took orders from people, and I didn't appreciate it when Frankie snapped his fingers at me and called me 'waitress.' Especially since he wasn't even sitting at my table. So I told him so."

Abigail felt her eyebrows rise. "Did he get mad?"

"Oh yeah. We had a knock-down, drag-out right there in the restaurant. I almost lost my job. Found out later Frankie went in and told the manager he'd stop eating there if he fired me. Said he'd only come back in when I was working."

"I don't understand."

"That man loved fighting with me. I loved fighting with him. Passion is passion. I just thought you two could use a little, is all." She twisted open an Oreo and ate one of the wafers. "And I was right too."

"I don't think so, Ursula. I think maybe you were wrong to think I had a perfect match at all."

Ursula ate the rest of the cookie, then wiped her hands on her pants. "Then I'll buy the building."

Abigail didn't respond, but something inside her shouted, *No!*

"You good with that?" Her expression seemed to accuse. "You'll get your store back and nothing will change. You'll go on living the same life you've been living. Just like you wanted." She nodded. "The doctor moves away and we all carry on as if none of this ever happened."

Abigail couldn't bear the thought of Jacob moving away. She could be a part of his fresh start, couldn't she? Would he allow her to be? Could they, like John and Elsie, forgive and move on?

"I don't want that anymore, Ursula." Abigail swallowed, her throat dry. "I want Jacob to stay."

She expected Ursula to mock her or at least make a snide remark, but instead the old woman leaned forward and took Abigail's hand. "Congratulations, young lady. You've officially learned what real love is."

Chapter 44

Ursula Pembrooke had said she would consider Jacob's offer and get back to him, but she sure was taking her time. A week after their initial phone call, she finally called to set up a meeting to discuss the terms.

"I spoke to Pressman. She's grateful and all that. Meet me at the building at lunchtime and we'll discuss the particulars then."

"Fine."

"Don't think you're gonna bleed me dry, Doc. Remember, I know what you paid for that building."

Jacob remembered. He ended the call and walked into the living room, where Kate and Junie were playing a game.

"I've got to go to the building," Jacob said. "I have a meeting."

Kate perked up. "Can we come? We've been stuck inside almost all weekend. Moon-Face needs some fresh air."

It was true—they'd been treating Junie as though she were on bed rest, but she was learning to maneuver on crutches. "Can you keep her occupied during my meeting?"

Junie nodded. "I'll bring my notebook. I want to be an artist." She held up a large pad of paper. On it, Junie had drawn what looked like a road with large red hearts on the lampposts.

"I made this heart for you, Daddy." She pointed to one at the center. He picked up the paper and inspected the words more carefully.

Thanks for the new home, Daddy. Love, JMW.

"JMW," she said proudly. "That's me, Junie Moon Willoughby. See?"

Words formed at the back of his throat, but emotion kept them locked there. Instead he kissed his little girl on the top of the head. It would break her heart to leave this place, and he knew it, but what other choice did he have?

He had to protect her. She didn't need to know the truth about the way Gwen died. If he could keep that reality from her forever, he would.

The last thing he wanted was for someone to slip and tell her before he was good and ready—the same way Cecily had broken the news about the paper hearts to Abigail. What a disaster that turned out to be.

"Stay here, Daisy," Jacob said.

The dog whimpered but did as she was told,

plopping down in the center of the porch as if to guard the house. He shut and locked the screen door.

"All right, let's go." He led them to the truck, Junie moving tentatively on her crutches.

He drove in silence while Kate and Junie belted out a haphazard rendition of the Beatles' "Ob-La-Di, Ob-La-Da."

When they reached the end, Kate turned to him from the passenger seat. "Who is this meeting with?"

He glanced back at Junie. She flipped through a book, humming happily to herself. Jacob looked at his sister. "Someone who offered to buy the building," he said, his voice just above a whisper.

"What? Why?"

He made the turn onto the main highway leading into town. "It's a long story."

He could feel Kate glaring at him. "Is this about Abigail?"

"No." He tapped his thumb on the steering wheel. "Not exactly."

"What did you do? More mixed signals?"

He sighed. "No, my signals were very clear. And then she found out about the paper hearts. And about Gwen. And about why we moved here in the first place."

Kate stared at him. "So?"

"What do you mean, so?"

She shrugged. "What is the big deal? This really

tragic thing happened to you. Big deal if people look at you weird for a little while."

Jacob held up a hand as if that could make her stop talking.

"I'm just saying, Jacob, you're so hard on yourself all the time. Give her a chance." Kate pulled her legs under her and glanced out the window. Six horses grazed in the foothills near a big ranch, and she strained her neck looking at them.

"Why don't you give yourself a chance and stop worrying about me?"

She frowned. "What's that supposed to mean?"

"Go to that ranch and get yourself a job. And if not that ranch, another one. Do what you love already."

A grin slowly spread across her face. "You mean it?"

He turned onto Wilson and headed toward Main Street. "If there's one thing I've learned, Katie, it's that if you're actually passionate about something, you've got to run with it. It's worth the risk."

The grin seemed permanently stuck on her face now. "That's good advice. You should listen to yourself once in a while."

Thanks to Avery, the little girl he'd saved after Kate's coffee shop concert, and surprisingly, Daisy, he'd rediscovered his passion for healing—but he'd have to explore that somewhere else. Staying in Loves Park would be about the worst thing he could do.

He turned down the alley behind the building, but there was nowhere to park. Every spot was filled.

"Maybe Abigail is having a going-out-of-business sale." Kate did nothing to hide her disappointment.

He hated that he didn't know what she was doing with her business. Hated that he didn't have the right to know. "I don't think she's going to be out of business."

"You think the buyer will let her stay?" Kate half mouthed the words, glancing at Junie in the rearview mirror.

Jacob responded with a nod as he parked down the alley and out of the way. They walked slowly, accommodating Junie's boot, and Jacob couldn't help but look in Abigail's window as they passed by. Even catching one glimpse of her might help ease this dull ache that seemed to follow him. He missed her. He missed talking to her and making her smile.

If he were a real man, he'd pick up the phone and call her, but that would probably be unwelcome. He'd horrified even himself with his admission about Gwen. How would she ever forget that?

No. Enough. He'd resolved to stop beating himself up over that. For Junie's sake. *I'm forgiven.* He said the words daily, and while he didn't believe them yet, he had hope that one day he would.

He noticed the door had been propped open. Ursula Pembrooke wasn't kidding. She did have connections. Someone had let her in the building already.

He pulled the door wider but was met with the sound of voices.

"What in the world?" Jacob moved into the back room of what would've been his future clinic, which looked completely different than it had before. Plastic sheets were hung from the ceiling, and as the door closed behind them, the sound of a table saw rang out in the main room. He'd told Ursula he'd sell, but the deal was hardly done. Who did she think she was, starting work before the papers were signed?

He pushed aside the plastic sheet and moved into the open space. The mercantile counter had been moved, the floors were covered with tarps, and people bustled through the room. At least twenty-five people worked at what appeared to be their assigned tasks.

Where had they all come from?

Across the room, Jacob spotted Ralph, but before he could get his attention, a woman rushed over to them. " 'Bout time you got here. Better put this on." She held up a hard hat, then hurried to a box on the counter. She returned with a pink, child-size hard hat. On it, the words *Junie Moon*. She knelt down. "Abigail said you like pink."

Junie smiled at the woman as she put the hat on the little girl's head, then handed a hard hat to Kate.

"We want to be sure you're all safe. Do you like it in here so far?"

Jacob frowned. He probably deserved her insensitivity. "It's looking good."

She pulled Jacob away from the others. "I have to tell you, when I read the article, my heart just leaped. Those paper hearts stole *everyone's* hearts. The whole town is cheering for you now, Dr. Willoughby." She squeezed his arm. "To think I thought you were the worst kind of person kicking Abigail out. Turns out you're the most loving one of all."

Jacob's mouth went dry, and he attempted a response, but the woman saw someone else come in and off she went.

Kate took a few steps toward him. "What is going on?"

"I have no idea."

"Ralph, you're a genius. I love the way you jazzed up the entryway."

Jacob turned and saw Abigail standing near the front door, wearing her own hard hat and leaning over what looked like blueprints.

His heart ached for her. He wanted to walk straight over to her, pull her into his arms, and never let go.

Instead he turned away. She'd already begun

renovating, and worse—she was using his contractor and his workers.

Maybe Kelly was right. She did have a cold side.

"Who are you meeting with?" Kate folded her arms. "And what's happening to your building?"

"Renovations. What's it look like?" Ursula Pembrooke had appeared beside them, closing the door that led to the basement.

Inspecting the pipes again?

"Don't you think you should've consulted with the owner first?" Kate hadn't had a run-in with Ursula yet. She was itching for a fight.

Jacob put a hand on her arm. "It's fine, Kate. Why don't you take Junie over there?" He pointed to a corner that looked unoccupied—and hopefully harmless.

"Can we get this over with?" Jacob glanced back at Abigail, who looked cute in that construction getup. This was good. Making her dream happen was good. She looked happier than he'd seen her before. It was a relief not to be the one standing in the way of her dreams anymore.

"Don't you want to talk to Abigail first?" Ursula's eyebrows drew together as she zeroed in on him.

"Probably better to just sign the papers and go."

Ursula gave one sharp nod. "Right." She took a step toward the front of the space. "Pressman!" she yelled. "Visitor!"

Abigail turned and met his eyes. So much for a clean getaway.

Ursula clapped a hand on his back. "You can thank me later." She walked away.

Abigail rolled up the blueprints she'd been discussing with the traitor Ralph and took a few steps to meet him at the center of the room.

"Hey." She smiled at him from underneath that too-big-for-her-head hard hat.

Before he could respond, a man approached him. "Doc, I've got this pain in my stomach every night after I eat. Feels like I'm dying. Is that the kind of thing you can diagnose?"

Jacob glanced at Abigail, who appeared to be stifling a grin.

"I could, sure," Jacob said. "Why don't I come find you before I leave?"

The man shook his hand. "Good to have a real doctor right here in Loves Park. I'll be over there. My job's clearing away refuse." He pronounced the words very carefully as if someone had given him an order.

The man walked away.

"That was Ned," Abigail said. "I'd imagine he's got really bad gas, but I'm no doctor."

Jacob raised an eyebrow. "What would lead you to this diagnosis?"

She shrugged. "He always smells like he's got really bad gas."

Despite his confusion, Jacob laughed, then

glanced around his building. "You didn't waste any time," he said as he felt his smile fade.

"Well, it was just sitting here, begging to be repaired. You got so much done so quickly."

"And you have to redo all that, I imagine?" Most of the work he and Ralph had done appeared to still be intact. In fact, none of it had been redone, only added to.

"Why would we do that? You did great work."

He looked at her. "I didn't think my plans for the clinic were conducive to your plans for the new store."

"Jacob, this isn't my store." Abigail took a step back, and he noticed she had the room's attention. Then, like an announcer on a stage, she said, "You're standing in the center of Willoughby Medical."

A cheer went up around the room, the workers now focused on him and Abigail, center stage. Once their applause subsided, Abigail continued.

"These people aren't here for me. They're here for you."

Jacob's eyes darted around the room. "I-I don't understand."

One by one, the workers approached him, shaking his hand or patting him on the back, thanking him for choosing Loves Park. Last week people held picket signs outside the building in protest, and today he was welcomed with open arms. How had this happened?

Abigail. Somehow she'd done this. She wanted him to stay?

"This town needs you. A doctor who is knowledgeable, but also someone who's caring and loving and knit into the fabric of Loves Park. They've decided they want you." Abigail smiled as the workers returned to their tasks. "Want me to show you what we've done?"

Jacob didn't have words. He just smiled and followed her to the front of the store. She opened the door and led him outside, hugging a clipboard to her chest. "I want you to get the full effect." She pulled out her sketch—the sketch she'd drawn just for him—and pushed open the door.

With the sketch held up, she began to explain the plan for the clinic. "I think we've captured a warm, welcoming environment without sacrificing any of your professionalism." She waved her hand toward the reception area, then turned his attention to the waiting room, which would have a separate section for contagious patients "because there's nothing worse than going in for an ingrown toenail and coming out with the flu."

Jacob laughed. He followed her through the entire space, then outside and into The Book Nook. When they walked through the back door and into the store, he could tell she'd already closed up shop. The space had an emptiness about it even though most of her inventory appeared to be intact.

"Abigail." He turned to face her, but she quickly interrupted.

"It'll look completely different once this wall is gone. Can you imagine how open it'll be?" She referenced her sketch, pointing out how the two spaces would become one.

She practically buzzed as she described it all, filled with a kind of infectious excitement, and by the time her tour ended, Jacob could hardly wait to open the doors.

"And that concludes your personal tour." They stood in The Book Nook, the noise of next door a world away. "What do you think?"

Her eyes were full of hope like a child giving a parent a handmade present.

"Abigail . . ." Jacob searched for an appropriate response but came up empty. "I wanted you to have the space."

"No." She took a step closer. "This is your second chance. You might not think you deserve it, but you do."

He didn't believe her. Not yet. But he wanted to. He wanted to see himself the way she apparently saw him. "Thank you."

"I had to do some damage control," she said, turning her clipboard over to reveal a newspaper article with a photo of the paper hearts.

He read the headline aloud. " 'From Evil Landlord to Hopeless Romantic: Dr. Jacob Willoughby Penned Loves Park Paper Hearts.' " He looked at her.

"I thought the best way to make the town fall in love with you was to tell them the truth about who you are. I hope that's okay." She hesitated. "And it's taken the focus off how your wife *died* and put the focus on how she *lived*. The response has been overwhelming. People have been coming down every day to help get your clinic off the—"

Before she could finish, he closed the gap between them and covered her mouth with his. He held on to her tightly, willing away a lump that had formed in his throat and thanking God for bringing him this second chance—for bringing him a woman who knew exactly what he needed when he didn't even know himself.

He pulled back and let his forehead rest on hers. "I think you might've saved me, Abigail." He stepped away so he could see her eyes. "You could've had everything you wanted."

She wrapped her arms around him and kissed his chin. "No. I realized what I really wanted was you." A shyness came over her.

"Why? After everything I kept from you?"

"Because I love you, Jacob. And love isn't perfect. If it were, we wouldn't need God to get in the middle of it."

"God, huh?"

She scrunched her nose. "He had a lot to do with all this, I think."

He drew her closer, letting an idea pass through him. All along, God had been for him. Even the painful parts of his life had led him here, to this part of his story. So how could he hold that against a God he used to treasure so much . . . and was learning to treasure again? "I think you might be right, Abs."

She grinned. "It's Abigail."

He kissed her again. "Yes. It most certainly is."

Chapter 45

Valentine's Day morning, Abigail awoke early to the sound of her phone buzzing on the nightstand beside her. She picked it up and saw a text from Ursula.

Need your assistance. Come to this location.

It was followed by an address Abigail didn't recognize. She frowned.

The phone buzzed in her hand again.

Hurry up.

Abigail rushed to get herself ready, not sure how to dress for an emergency call from Ursula Pembrooke. She pulled on a pair of jeans and a warm argyle sweater, then typed the address into her phone's GPS. When she realized she was going to an empty spot on the edge of Old Town, Abigail racked her brain. There was nothing there. Old Town ended and the ski resorts began. What was Ursula doing in the middle of the dead space between the two?

As she drove, she attempted to call the woman, but Ursula didn't pick up. She drove past Jacob's clinic, slowing to admire the progress they'd made. Willoughby Medical would be open in just a few short months, and she loved that she had played a part in that. When she'd called in a favor with the local cable channel, they had agreed to air the story about Dr. Jacob Willoughby, and Abigail had been happy to go on the air to discuss why she thought Loves Park should get behind his new medical practice.

People had come out in droves to assist with renovations in both halves of the building. They were smitten with the paper hearts and anxious to help the one who'd started such a tradition in the first place. She knew her town would embrace him once she explained the truth. Sure, she got the occasional question about how she felt losing her store, and she always answered with the truth. "It's sad anytime one chapter ends, but mostly I'm looking forward to what the next one brings."

"And what will that be?"

Abigail allowed herself a moment to dream when the question arose. She hadn't given up on her idea of turning her love of furniture restoration into a business—it just had an unknown backdrop for now. Maybe she'd start selling pieces out of her garage until she built up enough money for an actual space.

Maybe she'd take a business class. Or an art

class. Or become a crazy librarian. The point was, she'd decided to trust God to get her to the next season and to take care of her once she was there.

Gigi and the rest of the Volunteers had shown up that first day beaming with pride. "I just knew you and the doctor would be perfect together," she said.

Ursula shot her old friend a look. "Shut your yap, Gigi. I'm taking credit for this one."

Doris sighed. "These two. They hardly remember it was my suggestion in the first place."

"He sure is handsome," Tess said.

Evelyn pulled Abigail into a gentle hug. "You seem so happy. You deserve it."

Abigail hugged the other woman. She'd heard rumblings about the truth behind Evelyn's seemingly perfect marriage, and while she didn't want to put too much stock in town gossip, she had to assume everything wasn't perfect for her.

But her well-wishings were genuine. Despite her own troubles, Evelyn wanted the best for Abigail, and that realization made her thankful she'd somehow found new friends in the unlikeliest of places.

Abigail responded by handing each one a task and putting them to work for a change. "It's your civic duty," she'd said.

She'd never been more nervous than the day they agreed to reveal the plan to Jacob.

The memory of his kiss lingered. She could replay that moment, the startled look on his face, over and over again. She'd never seen such tangible evidence of the healing power of unconditional love.

God had made clear to her exactly what he needed, and it had changed him.

Her love had changed him.

He said she'd saved him, but she knew better. It was the other way around. She hadn't even known she needed to be rescued from her monotony, from her hiding place. He'd seen that in her.

"Your destination is on the left," the robotic GPS voice told her, interrupting her musings.

Abigail looked around. There must be some mistake. The GPS had led her to Matthias Linden's old, abandoned white barn set back from the road. She turned left toward the barn and stopped the car to double-check the address. Ahead, she noticed the door to the barn stood open.

And the address was correct.

What were these crazy women up to now?

Abigail drove toward the building, admiring the distressed paint on its sides. She'd always loved that old barn. It had been in the Linden family for years. Matthias had turned into a mean old man and was something of a legend in Loves Park. He'd chased teenagers from his property with a shotgun on more than one occasion. What would he do if he caught her out here, roaming around his empty barn? With no witnesses, he could get away with murder.

She shuddered at the thought but quickly dismissed it. Matthias might be ornery, but he was no killer.

Abigail parked her car in front of the barn and shut off the engine. She got out and took in the postcard-perfect picture in front of her. What a great piece of land. Matthias was smart to hold on to this stretch. Why he needed it, she'd never understand, but if it were hers, she wouldn't part with it either.

She walked toward the barn and peered around the partly open door. "Ursula?"

No answer.

The barn door let in a little light, but the space was mostly dark, maybe even creepy. Abigail pulled her phone from her back pocket and started to dial the old woman's number when she heard a click. The entire interior of the barn filled with white light from overhead.

Abigail gasped as she saw the strands and strands of white lights draped from the rustic wooden beams, illuminating the open space of the old barn. A breeze washed in from outside, and above her something fluttered in the wind. She reached up and inspected what she discovered was a strand of paper hearts.

Another light drew her attention to the back of the barn's interior, where she saw a long, wide counter and a hand-painted sign that read, *The Paper Heart.*

What was this?

"Ursula?"

"She's not here yet."

Abigail watched a figure appear from the shadows. Jacob.

She expelled the breath she only then realized she'd been holding. "What's going on?"

"What's it look like?" Ursula came up behind her, Doris and Gigi following closely. And from the other direction, Betsy and Teensy appeared.

Betsy beamed. "It's your new store."

"But not till after tonight," Gigi said.

Abigail shook her head. "What's tonight?"

"The Paper Heart Ball, of course."

She frowned. "I don't understand."

Ursula glared at Jacob. "Didn't you tell her anything?"

He hadn't taken his eyes off Abigail since he emerged from the darkness. "You all kind of interrupted me."

The ladies looked at each other. "You want us to leave?" Ursula shot him a look.

"How about we just go over there?" Gigi said, pointing to the opposite corner of the building. "You'll never know we're here."

Not likely.

They moved away, but Teensy stood still, staring at the two of them.

"Mom?"

"This is better than I ever imagined." Teensy

took Abigail's hands in her own. "I knew you just needed a little push."

Abigail glanced at the Volunteers and back to her mom. "You put them up to the matchmaking, didn't you?"

Teensy shrugged, then reached over and squeezed Jacob's hand. "Mother really does know best, dear Daughter."

"Teensy!" Ursula hissed, motioning for Abigail's mother to join them. She did, leaving Abigail beside Jacob, questions spinning around her too quickly to process.

"Well, what do you think?" he asked.

"I'm not sure what to think. I'm not sure what's going on."

"I didn't feel right putting you out of business," he said, looking away. "But I knew you weren't going to let me talk you out of it." He smiled. "You're pretty stubborn."

"I feel really good about everything, Jacob," she said. "I don't hold anything against you. I think this was supposed to happen all along."

He took her hand and pulled her in a few steps farther, toward the back of the building. "I think so too."

"Is this . . . ?" She ran a hand over the long counter she'd only glanced at before.

"The mercantile counter."

"How did you get it here?" She took a step back and admired it. It looked perfect in the old barn, a makeshift wall behind it decorated with paper hearts in all different colors and sizes.

"I have—" he looked at the ladies in the corner—"connections."

"It's beautiful."

"You said your plans for the shop were your big dream, the one that scared you." Jacob leaned against the counter.

"Yes. Very much."

A warm smile crossed his face. "I think maybe it's time to go for the big dream, Abigail."

She swallowed. "What do you mean?"

"Maybe you lost a good thing so you could find a great thing?" His casual nonchalance had returned, but the pain behind his eyes seemed to have disappeared. He looked genuinely joyful. "You did something incredible and selfless for me, so I wanted to return the favor. I wanted to help you see that you can go after the thing you want most—right here."

"In this barn?"

"Yes. Your barn."

"My barn?" She turned and looked toward the front of the room, where light streamed in through the open door. "Matthias Linden owns this barn."

"Everyone has a price, Pressman," Ursula called from the shadows in the corner.

Tears sprang to her eyes.

"Can you see it?" Jacob stood behind her, his breath on her cheek as he whispered near her ear.

"Filled with all the things you love? All the things you've created?"

She nodded but said nothing, her imagination already running ahead of her like a child who refused to slow down. She could almost hear the women of the town coming together right here in this barn to create and learn and help each other. She'd loved The Book Nook, but this space was full of hidden treasure.

And she had to believe her father would love it too.

"How did you do this?" She turned toward him, wrapping her arms around his waist.

He glanced over her shoulder. "Like I said, I had some help."

Ursula plodded toward them. "I own the place, Pressman. I'm your landlord now."

Jacob smiled. "I didn't think I wanted that gig again."

She grinned back. "I'm a difficult tenant, aren't I?"

"The worst."

She looked at Ursula. "How did you get Matthias to sell?"

Ursula stood a few feet away now, hands on her hips. "That man has always been sweet on me."

Gigi and Doris exchanged a knowing glance. "Is that right?" Gigi asked.

Ursula spun around. "Don't go getting any crazy ideas, Gigi. I'm way too old and set in my ways to ever think about anything as ridiculous as love again." She looked at Jacob, then at Abigail. "I mean, you two go for it and everything, but it's not for me."

"Ursula." Abigail took a step forward. "How can I ever repay you?"

Her eyes narrowed. "One month at a time," she said.

Gigi smacked her on the shoulder. "Tell her the rest."

"What rest?" Ursula barked.

"The part where you prove you're not as mean as everyone thinks you are."

"Oh. That." Ursula took off her glasses, cleaned them with squinted eyes, and put them back on. "All your rent payments go toward the purchase of the barn."

Abigail nearly gasped.

Doris let out a squeal. "Isn't that wonderful? We didn't even have to twist her arm, Abigail—she volunteered."

Abigail moved toward Ursula, who stepped back. "Don't hug me or anything."

Abigail grinned, then extended a hand in Ursula's direction. Ursula looked at it for a moment as though it might carry a contagious disease, but finally she shook it.

"Thank you, Ursula."

The old woman looked at Jacob. "Thank your doctor. It was all his idea."

Teensy rushed closer. "He hung the lights and the paper hearts and everything."

"He's a keeper," Betsy whispered loudly enough for everyone to hear. "The real thing, Abigail."

Jacob stood off to the side, an embarrassed look on his face.

"We have to go to town for supplies," Gigi said, bustling the other ladies away. "We'll leave you two. The crew arrives in an hour. We're going to transform this barn for our first annual Paper Heart Ball."

After they'd gone, Abigail ran a hand over the counter, then over the sign that had been affixed above it. "The Paper Heart?"

Jacob kicked at an imaginary something on the ground. "You don't have to use the name. I just sort of liked it."

"I love it." She moved toward him. "I love everything about it."

He removed his hands from his pockets and carefully tucked a piece of hair behind her ear, his eyes searching hers. Then he leaned down and kissed her. "I hope all of your dreams come true, Abigail."

She breathed in the scent of him, loving the way his lips felt on hers. His kisses breathed something new into her—hope. Hope that while she knew love would never be easy, if it was right, it was worth it.

"I thank God for you, Jacob Willoughby," she said, pulling him closer. "You are my dream come true."

A Note from the Author

Paper Hearts is a version of a story I've been wanting to tell for a long time, but I didn't have all the pieces to make it complete. I needed to live through some things to learn what this book is really about—allowing God to take your broken dreams and turn them into something new. I've been broken and felt forgotten. I've experienced loss and disappointment. I've wanted to raise a fist to the heavens and ask God why he didn't keep things from spiraling out of control.

I've lost my own version of The Book Nook. And through that loss, I've discovered long-forgotten dreams buried in places I had never planned to revisit. I've seen God take my brokenness and turn it into something better than I ever imagined.

Was it painful? Yes. Was it necessary? Absolutely.

See, sometimes we feel the darkness closing in. We feel abandoned or forgotten or disappointed. Like maybe God forgot to do what he said he would do. But even in those moments, my prayer is that you cling to the hope of his promises. My hope is that you know deep down he hasn't left you or forsaken you. He wants what's best for you, and above all else . . . *you are loved.*

Thank you, dear reader, for taking the time to get to know these characters who've become my friends. I know your time is precious, and it means so much to me that you've chosen to spend some of it with Abigail and Jacob. Maybe you'll be inspired to write your own string of paper hearts for someone you love.

I love hearing from my readers and invite you to visit my website:

www.courtneywalshwrites.com,
or drop me an e-mail at
courtneyrwalsh@gmail.com.

Courtney

Acknowledgments

It takes a village, right? I couldn't do any of it without my people. They know who they are, but I'm going to remind them anyway. My heart is full of gratitude for the ways they inspire, encourage, and help me. Even when I'm convinced I can do it on my own.

God. I know it sounds cliché, but man, I wouldn't know what to do without you. Thank you for not giving up on me even though I'm stubborn and hardheaded. Your grace is undeserved, but I am so thankful for it.

My parents, Bob and Cindy Fassler. Pretty sure it's your prayers that keep me from imploding. Thank you for believing in me and reminding me of God's promises. You are my inspiration.

Sophia. My favorite bookworm and my most honest reader. I pray you continue to dream big as you grow into your purpose. You have my heart.

Ethan and Sam. Thank you for reminding me to stop and laugh once in a while. Your giggles make me so happy.

My sister, Carrie Erikson. Your courage and bravery coupled with your wisdom and love for the Lord inspire and challenge me in the very best ways. Thank you for pointing my eyes upward in my meltdown moments.

Natalie Emenecker. I will never forget our Panera moment and all the moments since. Thank you for speaking truth to me and for your precious friendship. I will cherish it for as long as I live.

Deborah Raney. There really are no words except thank you. For being my mentor and my friend.

Sandra Bishop. We've been through so many changes together and you've always been right by my side. Thank you for helping me breathe new life into this story and for continuing to believe in me.

Stephanie Broene, Danika King, and the entire Tyndale team. Dream. Come. True. You guys are an answer to my prayers. Thank you for making my work better and for being such an amazing team. I'm still pinching myself.

And above all, Adam. My very best friend. There aren't enough words to tell you all the ways you make my dreams possible . . . so I'll simply say thank you. You make me better.

About the Author

Courtney Walsh is a novelist, artist, theater director, and playwright. Her debut novel, *A Sweethaven Summer*, hit the *New York Times* and *USA Today* e-book bestseller lists and was a Carol Award finalist in the debut author category. She has written two more books in the Sweethaven Summer series, as well as two craft books and several full-length musicals. Courtney lives in Illinois with her husband and three children.

Visit her online at
www.courtneywalshwrites.com.

Center Point Large Print
600 Brooks Road / PO Box 1
Thorndike, ME 04986-0001 USA

(207) 568-3717

US & Canada:
1 800 929-9108
www.centerpointlargeprint.com